All Her Bones Were Silver

Sarah Hunter Carson

Published by New Generation Publishing in 2012

Copyright © Sarah Hunter Carson 2012

First Edition

The author asserts the moral right under the Copyright, Designs and Patents Act 1988 to be identified as the author of this work.

All Rights reserved. No part of this publication may be reproduced, stored in a retrieval system or transmitted, in any form or by any means without the prior consent of the author, nor be otherwise circulated in any form of binding or cover other than that which it is published and without a similar condition being imposed on the subsequent purchaser.

www.newgeneration-publishing.com

New Generation Publishing

Sarah Hunter Carson

Sarah Hunter Carson took her first degree in Law at the University of Nottingham and subsequently a Master's in Criminology at Hull University. She has worked as a legal representative at a criminal legal practice, and as a freelance legal assistant, primarily dealing with Crown Court trials. *All Her Bones Were Silver* is her first novel, drawing on her legal and sociological training and hands-on experience. The novel was shortlisted for the 2010 Luke Bitmead Bursary.

Chapter One - Coming Home

His heart thudded like a brick in his chest. His mouth was dry, like a desert, he thought deliriously, like a fucking great desert. He felt his eyes scan the courtroom as though looking for water. Panic-stricken, he tried to take control of his thoughts. It's not water you need, mate, it's a bloody miracle.

He stood up when shoved by the warders, but obstinately refused to look at the little figure up there on the bench in front of him, like a broken doll in his death-black robes. I hate you, he muttered between his teeth, but could feel no emotion to match the words. He stared down at his hands, studying a broken nail as if it had come to be the whole world. The judge's voice was quiet, with an edge of an Irish accent. For some reason this accent struck him as funny, and he suddenly gave a feverish laugh, half-choked in his throat, then stopped as the warder, a small, burly pugnacious man with borstal tattoos on his fingers, frowned and glared at him. With an effort, he forced himself to listen to the judge's words.

'I have heard what your counsel has so ably said on your behalf. I take into account your difficult personal circumstances, as set out in the pre-sentence report. I give you credit for your early plea of guilty. But this', he paused. Melodramatic bastard. I could tell him now what he's planning to say. '...Offences of this type are rightly condemned by all law-abiding people. Such people need to see that the law deals with offenders such as you severely. Communities will not tolerate behaviour such as yours. Therefore, in all the circumstances, the least sentence I can impose is one of forty two months imprisonment.'

Forty-two months. Three and a half years. Could have been worse. Could have been a lot bloody better.

He raised his head abruptly. The judge, a little disconcerted, reddened, looked down and shuffled his papers. He's new. Probably thinks I'm going to have him killed or something. Not a bad idea.

He turned away, suddenly bored, and held out his wrist to be cuffed. He caught the gaze of the probation officer as he did so, a slight, bent figure with prematurely greying hair and a pale, bloated face. The same one who had done his report. Fucking backstabbing bastard. The man dropped his gaze and, bundling together a mess of untidy papers, hurried out of the courtroom with an obsequious nod to the bench. They're all scared of me, he thought, with a kind of lonely amusement. No one dares to look at me.

**

It was dark by the time Mervyn Walkinshaw finished his list. He hated the dark, resented it. He tried not to look overhead at the gathering inky clouds as he hastened into the car park, bundling his bags onto the back seat of his Range Rover. He got into the driver's seat and sat still for a few moments, breathing hard. Well, it had gone all right, even the drugs one, the one he had been dreading. It had gone all right. There had been no scene, no shouting. He did not really know what he had been expecting, but somehow he had been expecting something. He couldn't understand how it could be so easy; you just pronounce sentence, not even bothering to stand up, and the man in the dock has to serve the sentence. It's magic, he murmured to himself, remembering a phrase from one of the more avant-garde of the law lecturers in his student days, all law is magic. Sleight of hand. But like all magicians, you need steady nerves. And that's my weak spot, thought Walkinshaw, suddenly queasy despite his missed lunch.

I'm nervy. That's what Father always said, why he didn't want me to follow him into the army. He must have been an idiot if he thought law was any easier. It's probably worse. He thought suddenly and incongruously of a prison cell, cramped and neon-lit, and tried, and failed, to imagine it as home, the place he lived. His imagination just couldn't reach it. He shook his head a little to break his train of thought. There's no reason why I should be able to imagine it, he thought, just because I send people there. What prisons are actually like is none of my business. It's nothing to do with me. Sometimes I just wish I did something pleasanter with my life, that's all. But that image of the tiny cell pulled at the corners of his mind as he slowly drove away under the lowering sky.

He was used to the drive, often rather enjoyed it, but tonight he wished desperately that he were already home, safely in his warm, brightly-lit house. But then he realised that Isobel would be home by the time he got in. His dream of a little peace shattered, then. All this work, he thought bitterly, all this study and training and hours and weeks and years of work, long tiring days, all eating up the sum of his life, and he still couldn't have any peace at home. All his money couldn't buy him that, couldn't buy him that wonderful peace of mind that he so longed for. People must envy me, he sometimes thought, and his bitterness surprised even himself. He hated to see admiration and awe in the eyes of law students and junior barristers, despised them for their lack of insight, their inability to see beyond his status. I am a senior barrister and a recorder. Anything else that I might be is insignificant beside that. They hang on my every word at legal receptions, send me painfully earnest C.V.s, and in their desperate efforts to impress don't seem to realise how used I feel, how utterly insignificant as a person beneath the suffocating weight of my rank. Listen to me, he thought, smiling to himself, anyone would think I was the Prince of Wales. But the feeling of bitterness persisted, spreading like a sense of physical unease through his body; he could feel it like a deep itch. I'm a lucky man, he told himself, it fell right for me. I've been successful. He shivered.

As he neared home his mind turned to the evening ahead, and he flinched from it.
    Maybe I will go to that party after all, he thought to himself.

**

Daniel Powers stared blankly at the tiny darkened window in the prison van. It was impossible to see out of it, but by looking at it he could get some sense of the outside, a sense that they were moving through the real world, passing through it, but not part of it. A race apart. Dangerous men. Dangerous populations, that had to be monitored and controlled, like deadly viruses. Perhaps they could inoculate people against us, he thought grimly. I'm going mad. I can't think straight. He sat up sharply on the tiny wooden bench, gripping it with both hands as the van rounded a corner. I hate this, he thought. I just want to get back...home? It's not home. Well, it's your home for the next little while, mate, get used to it. That's just what I've never been able to do.
    He half-closed his eyes to quell a rising tide of travel sickness as the van skidded on the icy roads. This idiot driver's trying to make me throw up. He breathed in deeply, and there rose before his eyes again the little lonely figure of the judge. Why did those robes make him think of funerals, a lonely hearse with a wreath of

lilies glimpsed through the window? I need to get myself to the doctor, he thought, I'm losing it. But still he saw the figure on the bench, awkward and somehow in pain, and he felt a strange sort of pity for him. What a bastard life is, he thought, what a fucking bastard. There's no such thing as happiness, not really. No one's happy. He tried to remember when he had been happy, but only a jumble of half-formed images came into his mind, all muddled up as in a dream, and he abandoned the attempt. No use in thinking of happier times, anyway, you'll drive yourself mad like that, well, madder than you already are. He found himself wondering again about the judge; there had been a sort of quaver, a question almost, in his voice. As though he wanted me to forgive him or something. Yes, he was new all right. Quite a few of them started out like that. Stage fright or something. He stretched out his arm, palm upward, and examined the dull blue veins carefully, conscious of a trembling that seemed to come from deep inside his chest, somewhere behind his heart.

**

It was dark when Walkinshaw arrived at the party. All the way there, he had been trying to justify to himself his decision to go; it would be good for chambers, the clerks would be annoyed if he didn't look in, he need only stay for one drink. But as he parked his car and walked, shivering slightly, up to the restaurant, he felt suddenly sick and nervous, and found himself wishing he had gone straight home.

A burst of laughter greeted him as he pushed open the door, and he had to fight the feeling that they were laughing at him. The room was packed with people, few of whom he recognized, standing around in little groups, drinks in hands, animated, flushed faces bursting out in inappropriately loud laughter, or stretched in anxious, polite smiles. Middle-aged men in cheap suits huddled together at the bar, seeing the free bar as an opportunity for a night of serious drinking. Young girls, heavily made up and covered in fake tan, wearing glittering strapless cocktail dresses, stood around fidgeting and looking hopefully at the younger barristers. Funny, thought Walkinshaw, they should be pretty, and somehow they aren't. One of them looked round and caught his eye as he came in. She held his gaze boldly and evenly for a moment, then, without smiling, turned back to her group.

He felt a hand on his shoulder. 'Look who it is! Rob said you weren't coming. Here he is! Tell it not in Gath, Walky's missus has let him out for the night. I say, tell it not in Gath...'

Alexander Gregory. Walkinshaw winced inside as the booming voice continued. 'Hear you got that bloke Powers' sentence. What did you give him?'

Walkinshaw felt his body tense at the name. He did not like to think of it, he had come out in the hope of forgetting. 'Three and a half.'

'Light. Light. I would have thought five was nearer the mark. Going soft in your old age. What are you drinking?'

Gregory's red face beamed falsely above his, as in a nightmare. 'I don't know,' muttered Walkinshaw feebly, fighting a tide of panic.

'Don't know? Don't know? A man who doesn't know what he's drinking? You'll give chambers a bad name, old chap. We've got a reputation to keep up!'

A large, bald, florid man shuffled up to them; red-faced and sweating, his mouth hanging open slightly, his pale eyes already dull, moist and a little unfocused. Walkinshaw found himself staring at his sparse, blunt eyelashes. 'Mervyn Walkinshaw! How the devil are you?'

'Oh, fine,' he muttered, desperately trying to remember his name, or even which firm he worked for.

'Been a while since Watkins, hasn't it? That was a funny one. We had some fun in the old days, didn't we? Better than all these bloody junkies. I had one the other day, told you about it, didn't I, Alex?'

'You did,' said Gregory, stiffening with distaste at the familiarity; Walkinshaw remembered with amusement that he hated to be called Alex. 'You did tell me about it', he continued with an effort. 'Still, it pays the bills.'

'I tell you what', continued the florid man, with no sign of having heard, 'I'd hang the fucking lot of them. Line them up against the wall and shoot them. You see, in my day, there were honest villains. You know what I mean, Alex? Honest villains. You knew where you were. They knew the rules. If a copper gave 'em a good beating they'd not go whimpering off for compensation. Compensation culture. It's ruining this country. I saw a piece in the Mail about one of these,' he lowered his voice conspiratorially, 'one of these Muslims, those women with the things on.' He gestured towards his head. Well, some fellow in the office called her tent-head, you know, a joke and that, and she goes and sues and gets a hundred thousand pounds. A hundred thousand! I said to Mike, you could call me fucking tent-head for the rest of my life for that sort of money!'

Walkinshaw groaned inwardly. He found himself wondering why he had come to this party, what he had hoped to achieve. It would only delay the moment of going home for an hour or two, but it would be no less difficult for that. He felt a surge of hatred for the florid man, whose name he still could not remember, who was still talking away, regardless of the restlessness of his audience.

'Well, you're a part-timer now, aren't you? Must be good banging up them bastards, eh? I tell you what,' he continued, as Walkinshaw opened his mouth to respond, 'if I could just get my hands on some of them lowlifes they'd not do it again, I'm bloody telling you straight. No bloody excuses. My dad beat me, my mum's an alcoholic, well, my heart's bloody breaking. When I was a kid my dad was off on the ships. It was no bloody excuse for anything. I was the man of the house, wasn't I? Had to bloody grow up fast. And I tell you something else,' he jabbed a crimson, swollen forefinger into Walkinshaw's chest, 'I've never owed a penny to anyone. Never taken a penny of anyone else's money. None of these credit cards. The wife and me, we've got our bungalow paid for. Oh,' he went on, 'I heard a good one the other day. Wait for this one, Alex, you'll love it. What was it again?' He looked furtively at his mobile phone. 'Here it is. They were going to film a new series of CSI on the Crosskeys estate. Only they had to cancel it, because nobody had any dental records and they all had the same DNA!' He finished with a triumphant crescendo, his small red eyes darting from one to the other for approval.

Walkinshaw glanced at Gregory, who was very ostentatiously fumbling for his mobile phone and muttering 'I have to take this, sorry.' He disappeared into the corridor, leaving Walkinshaw stranded, scanning the room for anyone who might rescue him. This is what it has come to, he thought, here I am, listening to this stupid bastard, a man too stupid to know that he is stupid, too stupid to have any sense of inferiority, too stupid to know that he should never, never open his mouth in front of anyone with half an education. He is a mindless dim-witted idiot, thought Walkinshaw savagely, and yet he'll go home tonight all pleased with himself, probably tell his wife he chatted to me, go to bed, get up in the morning, and get on with his smug, self-satisfied, self-righteous, ignorant life. He felt a sort of hatred rise up in his throat, half-choking him; he felt that he had witnessed some sort of terrible indecency.

'I must go,' he said, and stumbled towards the door, leaving his companion with his mouth still open. He did not stop until he was outside in the cooling air, and his heart began to slow down again. He straightened up, still breathing hard, and he knew despite the nausea and the panic that he was going to be all right, this time, at any rate. I must stop doing this, he thought, I won't get away with it over and over again. People will start noticing, and saying things about me. I'm getting strange.

Slowly he walked back inside, planning his excuses. I thought I'd left my car unlocked, what with it getting stolen last year, you know. Anyway, as I have such an early start tomorrow, I think I'd better say goodnight. My God, he thought ruefully, it's like a script. We ad-lib a little from time to time, but basically we stick to the script. We know our parts, we rehearse them every day, until we become consummate actors, actors who don't know they're acting, don't realise that they are only characters in a play. When the final curtain comes they cease to exist, they just vanish into nothingness, along with all their words, all their little phrases and politeness, their swearwords and their in-jokes. All just gone, dead. And suddenly his mind was back in the little cell that had haunted him earlier in the day. What must it mean to be in that cell, really to be in it, so that there was no getting out of it? And why was he so preoccupied with it? It's a basic enough idea, he thought to himself, a five year old could tell you that bad men get locked up in prison. So why was his mind wrestling with it as an alien concept? Why had he suddenly lost the ability to take it all for granted?

A voice broke in on his thoughts. 'Mr. Wa... Your- your honour?'

He raised his head with a degree of irritation; he had felt just at that moment that he was close to realising something important, but, infuriatingly, he had no idea what, and no clue to follow if he searched for it again. It was already melting away like a dream.

'Yes?' he said, much more abruptly than he had meant to. Gosh, he thought, I'm being horrible to people tonight.

'You- you- you-'

God, thought Walkinshaw, why the hell do people with stammers go to the bar? And, more to the point, why do we keep giving them pupillages?

'Y-you may remember me from my m-mini-pupillage', gasped the young man desperately, finishing with a rush, his pale eyes seeming to burst from his flushed face. 'I was with Mr. Entwhistle. I- I'm very interested in the law of trusts. In fact, I did a civil m-moot in my final year in front of Mr. Justice Eady. Breach of fiduciary duty. It fascinates me. I love it.'

'I'm sure you know much more about it than I do, Mr....'

'Tombs. Norman Tombs. Surely you will have seen my C.V.?'

'Yes. Oh, yes.' A tide of weariness swept over Walkinshaw; he couldn't recollect seeing any C.V., but he was finding Mr. Tombs' earnest horn-rimmed gaze intimidating.

'It's good to see you again,' he said, hastily, 'but I'd better be off. You see-'

'Off?' Tombs' rabbit-like eyes protruded still further. 'B-but you've just come back in. I've wanted to speak to you all evening. In fact,' he flushed a little, 'I came here hoping to get the ch-chance of a word. I-I ... well, I was wondering if the committee has come to any sort of decision.'

'Decision?'

'About my pupillage. Oh, I know I shouldn't ask, but... well, I- I've been offered a year with the L-Law Commission.'

'Congratulations,' said Walkinshaw, more dryly than he meant to.

Tombs flushed again, and Walkinshaw felt a little guilty. 'You've done very well,' he said, trying to make his tone friendly.

Tombs gave a nervous titter. 'Well, I think they l-liked my article on floating easements. It- it- it's quite an honour to be pr-pr- in print alongside names such as Professor Popplewell and Dr. Simpkins. I was qu-quite overwhelmed.'

'Yes,' said Walkinshaw. There seemed nothing else to say.

'But I have to think long-term. About my career. I have to get it right. A false step at this stage could ruin everything.' Tombs' face was resolute, and his stammer seemed to have disappeared. Walkinshaw found himself wondering idly if it was an affectation. Of course not! Why would he pretend to have a stammer? He suddenly wanted to get away from the ambitious Tombs, and cut in briskly.

'The man to talk to is Geoffrey Bennett. He's not here tonight, but drop him a line and I'm sure he'll give you a phone call and let you know how the land lies.'

Tombs' mouth set petulantly. 'All right. Only... I have to let the Law Commission people know by the end of next week. Still,' he added quickly, as Walkinshaw shifted his weight from one leg to the other, 'I'll give Mr. Bennett a call on Monday.'

'Excellent.'

A strained silence fell; Tombs turned his glass round and round in his bony fingers, awkwardly. 'Well, thank you for your help, th-thank you very much.'

Walkinshaw smiled, a little grimly. 'I've not been any help, Mr. Tombs. But I wish you all the best. I'm sure you'll end up a Chancery law lord one of these days.'

Tombs' face flushed with pleasure. 'Oh, I don't think so. They have some first-class brains there. I've got a way to go.'

I've made his night, thought Walkinshaw, looking at his crimson, beaming face. Oh, well. Somebody might as well be happy, on this dark, rainy November night. And once again his mind flicked back to that little cell, and once again he forced his thoughts away, with an effort.

The crush of guests was thinning now. The professional drinkers, mostly solicitors' clerks, were still thronging around the bar, their laughter getting louder and their faces redder as pint followed pint. A couple of youngish, pinstriped barristers hovered on the edges of their groups, their distaste evident, but their need to network paramount. Their sycophantic laughter could be heard above the others, just out of time, just a beat too late to be spontaneous. This is ghastly, the whole thing is ghastly, thought Walkinshaw, but still he felt disinclined to leave. I can't put off the inevitable, he thought, and no matter how late I come back there's no chance she'll have gone to bed. These days Isobel never went to bed much before two o'clock in the morning, despite the fact she was always up by seven at the very latest. No, he couldn't avoid things just by hanging on at this awful party. He went up to Gregory's group and said his goodbyes, watching with a sort of amused detachment as they went through the usual mendacious regrets at his departure, and then went unwillingly to the door.

The drive seemed to go very quickly; the roads were clear. He found himself reflecting that he should have been enjoying it, a thought which made him feel oddly guilty, as though by failing to do so he was somehow letting himself down; he had some vague idea that he was being ungrateful, and would accordingly be punished. Pushing such thoughts to the back of his mind, he ran over again the day's events, appraisingly, and came to the conclusion that he had not done at all badly, all things considered. Not a bad start, no one could say that. He must just learn to be less nervous about it, not let things play on his mind. It would be no good if everyone he sentenced haunted his thoughts like that man Powers had done. He would turn into a nervous wreck before the end of the first month. It's a job, like any other, he told himself firmly. You're protecting society, a very worthwhile and important thing to do. And unconsciously he sat up straighter, tightened his jaw firmly, until he realised what he was doing and relaxed, smiling at himself.

As he had expected, the lights were still on as he pulled into the drive. He got out reluctantly, feeling for his house keys, strangely nervous at the prospect of going in. As he opened the door he called out 'Isobel! Isobel!', conscious of an anxious imperative to break the silence of the house first, before she could.

There was no answer. He glanced at the clock; it was only a quarter past ten, early by their standards. She must be working upstairs. He went into the kitchen. As usual it was strewn with papers; on the table, on the chairs, even a few bundles on the floor. It must be this Local Authority job she's got on, he thought. How on earth does she do it? He felt a certain reluctant admiration for Isobel sometimes, despite all the troubles and the distance of the past few years. He was proud of her, at least in public, he liked people to know that he was married to Isobel Thornton, who was well-placed to become the youngest woman Q.C. on the Northern circuit. In private, however, he was developing a strange nervousness around her. Sometimes he felt almost shocked at the intimacy of living with her, as though he were committing some sort of unpardonable invasion into her life; at such times he would feel frightened by the sense of distance that these feelings brought, and he would try desperately to shake them off. 'She's my wife, for God's sake!' But the feelings persisted, usually catching him out when he was least expecting them, and they gave him an uncomfortable anxiety that he was losing his mind, or close to a nervous breakdown.

He turned round to see her standing behind him.

'Did you have a good time?'

Hard to gauge her tone, he thought; mind you, it was never easy. Isobel was a little frightening even when she was being pleasant.

'Well, it was like these things always are, you know.'

'I do. Who was there, then? Did old Chester put in an appearance?'

'No.'

Isobel nodded, rather grimly. 'No. I thought he wouldn't. That bears out what they're saying about the Parkinson's.'

She turned toward the pile of papers on the table. 'Index... index... I'm sure I put it in this pile...'

'It says index here,' said Walkinshaw, eagerly proffering a bundle that he had picked up from near his foot, feeling pathetically hopeful that he might be able to please her.

She gave it a scornful glance. 'There are fifty

indices, Mervyn. It's a long time since you did civil, isn't it?'

He said nothing, feeling crushed. She continued to leaf through the papers, muttering to herself. 'Ah. Here it is. Well, I'll be getting back to it.'

'Won't you stop for a coffee with me? I've not seen you all day.'

She glanced up, gave a preoccupied smile. 'Mervyn. It's the hearing tomorrow. I simply haven't time. God knows how I'll get it all done as it is. We can have dinner tomorrow if you like.'

'All right.' As she moved towards the door he said 'Aren't you going to ask me how it went?'

'What?'

'My first day. As a recorder.'

She looked at him absent-mindedly. 'I did ask you.'

'You didn't.'

'I did. When you came in.'

'You asked about the party.'

'Well, I meant to ask about your day as a whole.'

She rubbed her eyes, emphasising her tiredness, and he said hastily, 'Well, it was all right. I'll tell you about it over dinner tomorrow.'

'Yes, do. Goodnight.'

'Goodnight.'

**

Walkinshaw lifted his bags up on to the robing room table with an effort, then turned to hang his coat up.

'Mervyn, old chap. What brings you here? Not prosecuting Gibson, are you?' Bloody Reggie Dakers. Wonderful, thought Walkinshaw, rubbing his aching temples. Dakers was tall, lean and rangy, with a supercilious stare that Walkinshaw suspected was acquired by dint of earnest practice; likewise his drawling patrician tones that had somehow developed from an unremarkable middle-class background.

'No. Defending today. A girl named Casey.'

'Then you're my co-d. Bloody hell, keep up, Walky. Big night last night, was it?'

'No.'

'Don't suppose you get a lot of big nights, married to the lovely Isobel.'

'What?' Walkinshaw turned round sharply, but Dakers just smiled blandly back at him. 'I mean with her workload. Have you seen the bit about her in this month's Lawyer?'

'No. No, I haven't. What did it say?'

Oh, the usual.' Dakers made a show of reading his brief, leaning as far back in his chair as he safely could and putting his feet on the table, like an overgrown public schoolboy. Walkinshaw took the intended hint that the conversation was over and wandered out of the room, though with no clear destination in mind. Why, he wondered to himself, do I still have no feeling of belonging here, why am I still awkward, even around the likes of Reggie Dakers, a man whose career is still where it was ten years ago? I've done better than he has, and yet I still feel as though all this really belongs to him, and I am just masquerading.

He wandered around aimlessly for a few minutes, wondering if he could be bothered to go to the canteen for a coffee. He decided against it, and went back into the robing room and sat down, pretending to read his brief, although he couldn't concentrate properly. His heart seemed to him to be beating rather too fast, and he had no idea why. After a few minutes he gave up with his brief and grabbed one of the dog-eared celebrity magazines lying on the table, with the exaggerated contempt that it was the unspoken rule to adopt in regard to them. 'Let's see what Amy's up to,' he said, to no one in particular. He was engrossed in his horoscope when he heard a voice behind him.

'Mr. Walkinshaw! Are you ready to go into battle on behalf of the scumbags of this fair city?'

He looked up and, to his horror, saw the florid man who had so enraged him at the party the week before.

'Oh. Yes, yes, I am.' He managed a smile. 'Miss Casey, isn't it? I was just having a look at things.' He waved his hand vaguely in the direction of his papers. 'I was wondering, actually, do you have a copy of the antecedents? They seem to be missing from my brief.'

What on earth is this man's name? I won't get away with it all morning. I know I've worked with him before. Who is he? He felt a sort of irritation at the florid man's failure to introduce himself. Who does he think he is, a film star who needs no introduction to his adoring public? Walkinshaw smiled a little despite himself.

The florid man ignored all reference to the antecedents. 'Yeah... another one of our town's finest specimens. Of course, when I was a bobby I knew her dad. I remember her granddad and all. I sound like a right old codger, don't I?' He rambled on, pausing every now and then to break into a discordant laugh, which seemed to shred Walkinshaw's nerves. He hoped that his distaste was not evident upon his face, but then reassured himself that his companion wouldn't notice in any event.

'Shall we go and see her, then?' he broke in at last, feeling that any more of this and his nerves would snap.

'Why not, old fella?' Walkinshaw seethed at the familiarity.

'She's in custody, isn't she, Mr.... Do you know, your name has slipped my mind,' he burst out, rather desperately. He would have to know this awful man's name sooner or later.

The florid man looked startled, then said, rather huffily, 'Ratchett, John Ratchett. Bloody rubbish memory you've got.'

They went down the dingy stairs together in silence. Walkinshaw never visited the cells without feeling a sort of awed dread, which he couldn't account for. The stale smell that wafted up the stairs always made his stomach turn over with nervous tension, even after years of cell and prison visits. He never left without a sense of relief, of luck even, at being able to walk out, never left without a strange apprehension, somewhere at the back of his mind, that they wouldn't let him go, that he would be locked up down there forever, screaming to be let out.

He pressed the buzzer and stood abstractedly, thinking, as he always did, of any infractions of the criminal law he might have committed over the years that might possibly cause him to end up down here. That last tax return... perhaps it had been a bit slapdash...

There were footsteps, and a jingling of keys, and the barred door slowly swung open. An enormous burly man with an unintelligent face said roughly 'Who are you here for?'

'We said,' said Ratchett. 'Hannah Casey. Don't tell me she's not here yet.'

'She's here,' said the burly man, grimly. 'We have the pleasure of the company of the lovely Miss Casey. Come inside, gentlemen. Don't forget to sign the book.'

A few moments later Walkinshaw and Ratchett were sitting on the same side of the table in a tiny, fluorescent-lit, windowless cell, all painted in heavy, flaking cream, oppressed by an overheated radiator, on chairs bolted to the cheaply carpeted floor. Walkinshaw cleared his throat, feeling the nerves that always overcame him when he waited to meet a lay client for the first time. Unusually for a barrister, he always took more pains with the client than the clerk, and thus was generally more popular in prisons than in solicitors' offices, where he was regarded as somewhat aloof. 'He could put himself out a bit more,' was a common complaint.

There was movement in the corridor outside, and a girl looked timidly into the room. 'Come in, love,' said Ratchett gruffly.

She came in and sat down, nervously smoothing her hair. Walkinshaw looked at her, immediately interested. She was very slim, thin even, with pale blonde hair twisted back onto the nape of her neck. Her face was thin too, and small, with large hazel eyes that Walkinshaw found immediately appealing. She was pale, with chapped lips, and her small hands played constantly with the frayed cuffs of her over-large sweatshirt. Walkinshaw decided that he liked her, and felt irritated at a society that had caused her to end up in prison.

She was looking at him, shyly, and he realised to his mortification that he must have been staring. He hastily forced himself into his professional mode.

'Miss Casey. I'm Mervyn Walkinshaw, your barrister. I'm the brief holder in your case, so with luck I'll be doing your trial, if it comes to trial. Not a lot will be happening today, just-'

She interrupted him. 'Will I get bail today - oh, sorry. I thought you'd finished.' She grinned at him, unexpectedly, and Walkinshaw smiled back, feeling suddenly happier than he had in a long time.

'No, not today. What we'll do is make a judge in chambers bail application next week. Can you make a note, Mr. Ratchett?' Ratchett grudgingly bit the top off his biro and scrawled something on the cover of his grubby notebook.

'Where could you go to live?' Walkinshaw asked her, enjoying a strange sense of intimacy that seemed to have sprung up between them.

She hesitated, her face clouding. 'I could go to my dad's.'

'Where's that, then?' cut in Ratchett, his pen poised. Walkinshaw felt vexed at the interruption.

'264 Wesley Way.' She looked down at her hands.

'On the Crosskeys?'

'Yes.'

'Near the underpass.' Ratchett scribbled again in his notebook. His writing was crude and childish, thought Walkinshaw with a sort of disgust. He felt a sort of jealous irritation at Ratchett's taking over the discussion, unjust though he knew it to be.

'He'd have you then, would he?' asked Ratchett. 'I thought he kicked you out before.'

'That was... ' again she looked down at her hands. 'That was when I was with Danny. He's all right with me now.' She did not look up.

'Right,' said Walkinshaw. 'Well, we'll get on with that next week. Your record isn't too bad. This previous boyfriend of yours was at the root of most of the trouble, and hopefully the judge we get will understand that. Now, we need to talk about today. What we must-'

Ratchett interrupted him. 'I've told Hannah about today, when I went to see her at Greenlands, didn't I, love? It's not guilty and off.'

'Quite so,' said Walkinshaw, wearily. He had a strange sense of being out of his depth, despite the fact that he had successfully handled far more difficult conferences countless times before. 'We'll enter a not guilty plea today, then I'll come and see you' - his throat tightened a little - 'I'll come and see you-'

'With me,' interposed Ratchett.

'Yes, Mr. Ratchett will come as well, and we'll have a proper chat about things.' She suddenly looked up at him and smiled. Then she turned to Ratchett. 'When will Danny get out?' Her eyes were troubled, but she spoke quite cheerfully.

'He got three and a half, didn't he?'

'Yeah, but he'd done a while on remand.'

'This is your former boyfriend, Daniel Reynolds?' asked Walkinshaw, anxious not to be left out.

'Yes,' she said, glancing quickly at him, meeting his eyes, and in embarrassment looking back at Ratchett, who was leaning back awkwardly in his plastic chair, enjoying this opportunity of vaunting his knowledge in front of them both.

'I should think he'll be out in about seven months, or thereabouts, given he did the best part of a year on remand. He'll not get a tag with his record. Well, he might, the prisons are that full. Well, we'll see you upstairs, Hannah,' said Ratchett, lumbering heavily to his feet, and looking inquisitively at Walkinshaw, who hastily got up and fumbled his papers into a pile, his heart pounding.

The girl got up too, nodded her goodbyes to Ratchett, and then, to Walkinshaw's surprise, she turned to him, holding out her hand.

'I'm glad I've got you,' she said.

**

Hannah Casey sat on the edge of her narrow bed, her knees drawn up to her chin, rocking slightly as she thought hard. She needed to think, and it was so hard to think properly in this awful place, where there was no real privacy, where everything was a commodity, where even friendship had to be bought and sold. Sometimes she wondered if she would ever be the same again, whether she could ever go back to the old way of being, of thinking, and that reflection made her anxious, gave her a feeling that she had to hold onto herself, that she must not relax her grip on her own thoughts, that she must keep impressing herself, her real self, on to her mind so as not to lose it. Thoughts whirled in her mind nearly all the time in here, even in her sleep she felt as though she were thinking, but her thoughts seemed to her to be incoherent. She felt that all she needed was to be free, and in that freedom would come the ability to think clearly again, to make sense of everything that had happened to her. Since she had come back from court that morning her mind had been racing until her head ached. She felt that something important had happened to her, but she couldn't identify it to herself. She thought of her new barrister, kept picturing him as he sat across the table from her, looking at her with kind eyes. That kindness seemed to warm her heart as she sat in her cell, still rocking back and forth, and she smiled a little to herself. She felt a little more hopeful. She had mentioned his name to one of the other girls, a little shyly, and had been told that he was some sort of part-time judge, information which had encouraged her even more. He must be high up, he must know what he's doing, she thought. And I'm sure he liked me.

Her life up until this point had been like a sort of dream, she decided, sometimes a good dream, sometimes a nightmare, but not really real, not the life that she was meant to have. She felt trapped in someone else's life. When she heard her name read out in court she felt faint, unable to take in that it was her, that she was really living this life, that she was in prison. It could not really be happening to her. She didn't feel she had done anything very bad. Nothing anyone said could convince her of that. Danny had told her to keep the stuff and she had kept it for him. There was nothing more to it than that. And now she was in this place. It didn't seem fair, and yet in a way it was nice to be away from Danny, and also nice to be away from her dad. She wondered if she would get her bail next week, and felt suddenly uncertain about it. Did she want to go back home? It would be nice to be out, but then Danny's mates could get to her. She half rose from the bed, with the idea of writing to her solicitor to say that she didn't want bail, but then sat back down again, discouraged and uncertain. If only there were somewhere else to go! If only someone else would have her! She smiled a little to herself again as she thought of her new barrister. He had been wearing a wedding ring. I wonder what his wife's like, she thought, nothing like me, I bet. She looked down at her hands, noticing with a frown her chipped nail varnish. I should have done my nails last night, she thought to herself. And again she smiled a little.

**

Walkinshaw went outside to his car, breathing hard, the cold air harsh but comforting. He had gone outside on the pretext of collecting a notebook which was actually in his bag; he had felt a desperate need to be outside, under the sky, able to think clearly and peacefully, something which he felt he couldn't do in the stuffy confines of the court building. He felt agitated, and yet clean inside, as though something had come and smoothed down his soul. He was shaking slightly, and yet he was conscious of a new contentment, which he was unable to explain. Unusually for him, who loved to analyse his every feeling, this did not bother him. He generally would weigh up carefully every feeling that he had, in an attempt to map it in his head; this is unpleasant, I must learn to avoid it, this is good, I must remember my way back to it. This time he felt that he would never find his way back, not really, this feeling was something that could happen only today, only ever today, and yet the thought did not upset him. He knew he had to go back inside, and steadied himself for a moment, breathing deeply. He thought he would wait until his heart calmed down, and that slight pain in his chest subsided, but then he realised they would be waiting for him.

Back upstairs Ratchett called to him as he passed one of the conference rooms. 'All right? You went a bit quiet earlier. I take it you'll send an advice this week on the Casey thing? We need to get weaving.'

Walkinshaw's tension came back in a rush; Ratchett's voice was like a bucket of cold water in his face. He put his hands in his pockets in case they were trembling visibly and said, trying to control his voice, 'Yes, of course. One or two things we need to tidy up in case it gets to trial. I think it might crack, though. We might get offered simple possession. She said in her proof she'd plead to that.' As he spoke he suddenly felt unreal, as though he were in a dream, and dug his nails into his palm to jerk himself back into reality.

'She'll have it, definitely,' said Ratchett. 'We talked about it at the con,' and Walkinshaw's heart was suddenly tugged with violent jealousy. 'We wrote to the CPS last week offering it, no reply.'

'Well, Marlowe was standing firm today,' said Walkinshaw. 'Still, as we both know, it's a different matter on the morning of trial.' He stretched a little, and yawned. 'Half-past four! The lists here are a nightmare, aren't they?'

'Aren't they bloody just,' growled Ratchett. 'As if I haven't got better things to do with my time than sit on my bloody arse here all day. I should have been in the nick this afternoon.'

'I expect Miss Casey is already back at Greenlands by now,' said Walkinshaw, suddenly, feeling himself colouring. Why did I say that? He was furious with himself, and felt frozen with embarrassment, sure that Ratchett would read his thoughts, and laugh at him.

'Yeah, probably. We get a fucking longer day than the scumbags. She'll be cosy in her cell right now, bless her heart.'

He had got away with it. He mustn't push his luck any more. Yet somehow he couldn't resist asking 'Have you known her long?'

'Who?'

'Hannah Casey,' said Walkinshaw bravely, feeling that the name would stick in his throat. It seemed unpronounceable.

'Well, like I say, I knew her dad. Right bugger, he is. Not known her long, not much form. She seems a nice kid, in a way. Poor lass, with a dad like that. He's a right bastard.'

Stop talking in circles, thought Walkinshaw angrily. This man was infuriating.

'What sort of a bastard?'

'Oh, a bad lad, you know. Up to all sorts.' Ratchett was exploring his ear with his little finger. 'Not met the girl before Christmas time, it would be, when she was turning tricks up near the Embankment.'

Turning tricks! Didn't that mean prostitution? Walkinshaw didn't dare ask, but he went hot with horror. His imagination could not reach it, and yet the idea held him tightly, in a dark, fascinating grip. Could 'turning tricks' have another meaning he was unaware of?

'You mean she was—?' It didn't sound like his voice.

'Yeah. Sad, isn't it? I sort of like her. She's cute, in a scummy way.' Ratchett leaned back, smirking. 'I'd give her one. Then again, maybe not.'

Walkinshaw looked at his sweaty face, his sandy eyelashes, his bull neck bulging over a grubby collar, and felt almost violated. He loathed this man, he decided. He hated him, and wished he would die. Ratchett seemed to sense this, and stirred uncomfortably. There was a tense silence, which was suddenly and mercifully broken by the court tannoy announcing Walkinshaw's last hearing of the day.

He was still shaking with tension and excitement when he got home. He had turned the radio up loud all the way home to drown out his thoughts and give his mind a break from it all, but the images of the day were still imprinted vividly there. He tried to remember how he had felt leaving home that morning, and failed utterly. The morning seemed like another, paler time, a ghost of a life. He had raced all the way back, feeling an urge to get home, but now as usual his spirits sank as he neared the house, and that special unease that only afflicted him at home began to form knots in his stomach. It would be better once he got in, he decided. Going home to Isobel was like jumping into an ice-cold swimming pool. The first bit was the worst, then you got used to it. As long as your heart didn't give way first. Thus speaks the devoted husband, he thought, and smiled resignedly.

Isobel's car was outside. He expected her to be home, but still he got a slight shock, he didn't know why, to see it there. He felt almost as though it were an extension of her, watching him, and he fluttered with nerves again.

She was sitting at her desk, as usual, when he got in. As he entered the room she looked up sharply, her face creased, and he felt suddenly sorry for her.

'How are you today? You look tired.'

'I am tired. Got two hours' sleep last night.'

'Yes, I didn't hear you come to bed.'

She chuckled, rather sourly. 'That's because I didn't.'

'You must give yourself a rest every now and then,' he said, genuinely concerned. She looked exhausted, and older. 'You need some time to yourself.'

'You don't get silk by taking time to yourself.'

Walkinshaw sighed, and bit his lip. 'You know what I mean, Isobel. You're only human, you know. If you don't get silk this year it's not the end of the world.'

Her mouth tightened. 'Well, I want it this year. I want to show them all.'

'Show who?'

'All those patronising bastards. Penningdale and the others.'

'So you're going to work yourself to death just to score off Penningdale?'

'No!' she burst out in frustration. 'I'm doing it for me as well. And for us. We could get that place in Provence if it all goes right.'

He felt an anxious fondness for her, remembering the days when he had first known her. Miss Thornton, new in chambers. How attractive she had been then, only twenty-five, and full of energy, an energy which had seemed to draw him to her like a magnet. He had felt that he would be safe with her, that her vitality would be enough for both of them. He remembered her eager, intelligent face, across the dinner table from him, in those years that now seemed an age away. It was only fifteen years since they had met. He felt a kind of remorse now, as he looked at her, her good looks marred with worry and lack of sleep, small veins pitted around her eyes, and a new hardness showing itself around the mouth. He should not have let this happen. He should have taken better care of things.

'Yes, that would be good.' He tried to smile. His heart was so heavy he felt he couldn't move.

She smiled back at him. 'You look nice today, Mervyn. Did you get your hair cut?'

'No. No, I was going to, but I didn't finish at court until quarter to five. I'm pretty tired myself, actually.'

But her attention had already wandered back to the papers in front of her. He hated them suddenly, longed to throw them all out of the window, into the bin, and see what was the worst that could happen. He longed to tell her all about the day, even about Hannah Casey and his attraction towards her. He wanted to confide it all and be forgiven. But she was immersed in her work again, and he knew he had to go out quietly and close the door.

**

The next morning brought a letter for Hannah Casey. She took it and fingered the envelope with a mixture of excitement and dread, wanting to open it and yet not daring to. She turned it over and over in her hands, as though its contents would somehow transmit themselves to her through the envelope, without the need for her to face the letter itself. She remembered how in the past she would take letters like this to her mother. 'Tell me what it says,' knowing that the harshness of any shock it might contain would be softened and made palatable, and then she would feel such comfort from that companionship that she would find the courage to read the letter herself. But her mother was dead now, and she was all on her own, not even a friend whom she could beg 'tell me what it says'. Anyway, she knew that really this wasn't a letter she could show anyone, she wouldn't even have shown mam if she'd been alive. She had to open this letter herself. A shadow of pain crossed her heart as she tore at the envelope. Why did this have to be her life? Slowly she pulled out the dirty, lined paper, folded into eight, so that it lurked at the bottom corner of the envelope. Lying in wait for me, she thought, and shook her head, impatient with herself. She opened it out and went straight to the end of the letter to check the signature, although she knew perfectly well that the letter was from Danny. Then she began to read it, slowly at first, then racing through it as fast as she could, in an instinct to know the worst.

Dear Hannah,
I heard you got picked up from Steve. You know I can't say anything in this about it all, but I've enough to say to you when I get out of here. I wish I could talk to you properly.

It's fucking hell in here, isn't it? Now you know how I feel. Now you know why I said I couldn't do it again. Now you know I wasn't making it up. Are you going for bail? Lisa was in court when you and Burnsy were up, she says you are. When you get out, and I reckon you will, you come and see me. I know you won't not come. I know you won't let me down. We've been through too much, haven't we, babe? I know you wouldn't want to hurt me. You'd never want to hurt me. You know what it's like when I get hurt. Everyone in my whole bloody life lets me down, but not you, Hannah, cos you're gold, darling, you always were.

You know I got three and a half from that cunt in Sheffield, wasn't worth half of that. I wanted to kill him. I was going to get married to you if all that shit hadn't happened. You come and see me, all right? Because I'm going mad in here, I can't stop crying, I tell you, I can't go on like this, I'm a broken man, I need you, Hannah. You don't let me down, all right?

Who's your brief now? I got this fucking idiot from Manchester, couldn't hardly talk, what he said for me in court was a load of rubbish, I just wrote to Dennis, I said to him, give me a wanker like that again and I'm walking. It's disrespect.

When you see Mick again you tell him from me that I haven't forgotten. I'm not making any threats, I just haven't forgotten. I've always had a good memory. You know what I mean.

You write back to me right now. And if you get out, I reckon you will, I'll send you a V.O. I'm fucking desperate to see you, babe. I need you. I really need you.

Danny xxxx

She put the letter down on the bed, trembling. The letter was so Danny, so much his voice, with its wheedling menaces, that she felt that he was in the room with her. She felt that if she went to see him she would die, her skin crawled at the thought, but she also knew that she would go. She would not escape him now.

She got up abruptly and went to the window, feeling a sudden claustrophobia. She wanted to open the window, and even felt for the handle, knowing all the time that none of the windows in this place opened. She felt suddenly angry, and felt hot tears running down her face, which she wiped away roughly with her sleeve, furious with herself for crying. This is all your fault, she said to herself. This is all your fault, you stupid, stupid, stupid, fucking bitch. She repeated it to herself over and over again, like a refrain, like a lullaby, although she knew well that by this time there was no need to work herself into a frenzy to do what she had to do.

**

Walkinshaw sat in his room, pretending to work. He hated being in chambers, preferred working from home, but felt obliged to put in an appearance every now and then. He found it impossible to concentrate; his naturally secretive nature made a shared room a torment, and even besides that there were constant interruptions. Today, moreover, he was particularly distracted; today was the day of Hannah Casey's bail application. He knew that he ought not to care, really, one way or the other, and certainly he must not be seen to care. But he did care. The thought of her free, back out on the streets, walking around the same city as he did made him feel faint. He imagined himself running across her somewhere in the city centre, at lunchtime, perhaps, as he went to Marks and Spencers for his sandwich. What would he say to her? What would she say to him? The excitement of such a meeting made his hands tremble. She'll have forgotten you, you sad old idiot, he said to himself. You'll be just another boring middle-aged man in a suit. But somehow or other he did not really believe himself, and he felt so overwhelmed with a sort of thrilled apprehension that he almost wished she would stay in prison.

He looked at his watch. Quarter to twelve. Judge in chambers bail applications were usually first on the list, it would most likely be over by now. Dare he phone Ratchett's office on some pretext, and then ask, as a by-the-way, just wondering, what happened with that JC this morning? He rehearsed it to himself in his head, and each time it sounded thinner and less plausible.

'All right in there, my old china plate?' Alexander Gregory loomed in the doorway. Walkinshaw's nerves were so on edge that for once he was not sorry to see him; he felt in desperate need of distraction.

'Oh, well,' he muttered, 'same as usual. Nothing much going on.'

'Not in court today?'

'No.'

Gregory paused; there was a sound of bottles from the plastic bag in his hand. He looked embarrassed. 'Present from a grateful punter.'

'Lucky you.'

'Mind you're at that meeting on Friday, old boy. No excuses. Got to sort out this pupillage thing once and for all. Hoped to be able to rubber stamp it, but you lot, you just can't make up your bloody minds, can you?'

'I thought that fellow Tombs was the front runner,' said Walkinshaw, stretching.

'He was, but... well, Entwhistle says there's something a bit creepy about him. Besides, he's got something lined up at the Law Society or wherever it is. He doesn't need it.'

'He is a bit creepy, certainly.' Walkinshaw remembered that meeting with him at the party, and felt a sudden foreboding, almost a fear. 'I wouldn't go with him, if I were you.'

'Not your call, sweetheart. You missed the interviews, remember?'

'Anyway, I don't think Tombs is the man, for what it's worth,' said Walkinshaw, feeling an odd anxiety at the prospect of having him in chambers. 'I can't see him fitting in.'

'I can't see any of them fitting in. Wish we didn't need a pupil. Funny, they seem to get worse and worse each year, despite all this competition. Competition should drive standards up, not down. I don't get it. I mean, Tombs must be bright, he's won all those awards and everything, but he's like a bloody machine. No personality.'

'Or an unpleasant one, at any rate,' said

Walkinshaw, remembering the naked ambition that had glinted behind Tombs' glasses.

Gregory gave him a shrewd glance. 'He must have rattled your cage. What did he say to you?'

'Nothing,' said Walkinshaw, flushing. 'I just don't like feeling used.'

Gregory laughed bitterly. 'Wait until you get to be head of chambers, then. Well, catch you later. Better get on with things. Mind you're there on Friday. If we speed it up we should have time for a curry afterwards.'

Walkinshaw felt a strange sort of solitude after he had gone, a sort of pleasant sadness. He strolled over to the window and gazed into the street below, hearing snatches of conversations from the people going by. The air seemed still and fresh, and he felt a joyous anticipation, though for what he could not have said. He felt satisfied, like a king surveying his subjects, and for a moment he felt that he liked people, that he liked the world and his life and he would be sorry to lose it. Then he stepped back from his thoughts, and pain had him by the throat again. He could feel it moving inside him, and he wondered if it were an enemy or a friend. Sometimes he felt as though it were a friend, a dark, secret, mysterious friend whose presence hurt, but also marked him out; he could wear it like a secret badge only the initiated could recognise, or could detect its existence in the seams of anxiety around his mouth, or the hollowness of his eyes.

He was disturbed from his thoughts by the telephone ringing. He rushed over to it, his heart pounding.

'It's John Ratchett for you from Caldwell's.'

'Put him through,' said Walkinshaw breathlessly.

There was a pause and a click, and then Ratchett's bullying voice. 'Mr. Walkinshaw? We need to get moving on that con with Vinson. Can you do one pm this Friday? We need to talk some sense into the little shit, pardon my French.'

'Certainly,' said Walkinshaw, his heart still thumping, hardly knowing what he was saying. 'I'll get Rob to put it in the diary. Anything else... anything happen on the other thing?'

'What other thing?'

'Casey. The girl. Did she get her bail?' I have to know, thought Walkinshaw; to hell with what he thinks of me.

'She did, yeah. Let's see if she shows up for her trial now. All fun and games, isn't it?'

**

Hannah Casey sat on the train, staring blindly out of the smeary window. Her mind was pleasantly pillowed with diazepam, and she felt unreal, but comfortably so. She wished idly that her wrists were not so sore, so that she could have a sleep, but they chafed painfully against their bandages and kept her awake. Better not sleep anyway, don't want to miss my stop. She was self-conscious about her bin liner of belongings, wondered if the other passengers knew what it meant. Maybe they'll just think my bag broke, she thought, and I had to find something else. She knew this didn't make a lot of sense, but she was too sleepy to think it through and work out what was wrong with it.

She looked vaguely at her own reflection, partially glimpsed in darkness as the train went through a short tunnel, and felt pleased that it was her, that that face was hers. It gave her a sort of comfort, that face is mine, no one else's. She stared hard into her own eyes. 'What's going to happen to you, Hannah? What are you going to do with yourself, girl?' But her eyes held no answer at all, and she turned away, a slight smile on her face.

The tablets were wearing off a little now. They had given her some to take after she had cut herself, but she had saved them up and then taken the lot that morning. She was glad she had, it made the journey a lot pleasanter, to be mildly off your face. She grinned at her own face in the window. What a pretty girl you are, my love. That's what her grandma used to say to her, all those years ago. What a pretty girl you are. She closed her eyes.

She woke up, as if by instinct, as the train slowed down as it approached the station. She stretched, enjoying that lovely peaceful lethargy that only benzodiazepines ever brought her, and took hold of her bin liner, feeling ashamed of it again. No one would be there to meet her, it didn't matter. No one cares. Suddenly she had the idea that she might meet her barrister here at the station, he might have come to see someone off or something, and there she would be with her wrists bandaged, clutching her life in a bin liner. She went hot at the idea. What would he think of her? What did he think of her? Had he thought of her at all? For a moment she imagined herself studying law, becoming one of those lawyers herself, in a dark suit, talking to him about whatever they did talk about, and decided it would be boring. But the image of herself in the suit pleased her, and she decided she would get herself some new clothes for the day of her trial.

She walked along the platform slowly, still a little cloudy-minded, but enjoying the early spring sunshine on her face. She liked the feeling of being alone in a city, alone with all these people walking by. She hugged her solitude to herself. She felt a sort of significance; she was a private person again, no one could lock her up, the future was hers again. I can do anything, she thought, anything at all, I am me, no one can read my thoughts, they belong to me, I belong to myself. She treasured this feeling as she walked through the city, heading for her favourite place, the park. She loved it, it seemed to soothe her soul. She had loved it for years, had come to think of it as hers; it was the thing she had missed the most in prison. Even the fact that Danny went there to deal at night had never spoiled it for her; it seemed to be inviolable, no matter how many sordid things went on there it was never soiled for her. It seemed to be above all that. It understood her and she understood it; and because of that it shared its secrets with her.

It has been waiting for me, she thought, it knew I would come back. She stopped and knelt on the grass, overcome, tears pricking her eyes, suddenly overwhelmed with love, though for what or for whom she didn't know. She was conscious of a new capacity within herself for something, something important, she didn't know what, but she knew that she must hold on to it, that it might prove to be her salvation, even in the midst of all her troubles. This feeling gave her a kind of solemn joy, and she felt almost serene as she sat there on the grass, gazing out across the small lake.

**

Walkinshaw sat at his desk, chewing his pen, until it had grown dark outside his window and the street below hummed with rush-hour traffic. He listened to the sounds of the early evening as they filtered up to his window, and felt a disinclination to join them, a desire to stay up there in his room, all alone, for the whole night, until the dawn broke. He had developed a dislike of the night, of the darkness, it almost seemed dirty to him. As the sun set his spirits sank with it. He put this down to the stress of overwork, and yet he was also uncomfortably aware that he was doing less and less work. Papers were piling up on his desk, and he could feel nothing but indifference towards them. He knew they were important, but somehow he didn't care, they seemed ephemeral to him, and he had no urge to reason himself out of it. He felt as though for the first time in his life he was obeying his instincts, and it gave him a feeling of secret pride, like a naughty schoolboy. He had taken to winging it in court, and enjoying the feeling that at any moment he might be caught out. So far his experience and skill had averted any mishaps, but he knew that he wouldn't get away with it for ever, and yet he had no inclination to take more care.

Isobel would not be home for another few hours. He was not going to do any more work tonight. He felt that this was an opportunity to do something, what he didn't quite know, although an idea was forming at the back of his mind. He got up suddenly, went over to the corner of his room and rummaged through a pile of papers, until he found the brief in the case of R. v Burns and Casey.

**

Hannah knew she had to go home. She couldn't sit in the park all night, though she wanted to. She knew her father would be expecting her, might even, if he were in one of his good moods, have got tea ready. She felt that she couldn't eat anything, but she knew that she must go and face things, however bad they were. The prospect of arriving home loomed in her mind threateningly, and she knew that she would feel better once it was done and over with. So she made her way slowly to the bus stop, dragging her bin liner behind her, and stood shivering slightly, waiting for the white lights of the number 17. She hated buses, especially after dark when they were all lit up, like skeletons, she thought incongruously, like white ships made out of bone, all searingly filled with fluorescent light, so that there was nowhere to hide.

She watched the lights of the city, swirling and opaque, and closed her eyes with a shudder, wondering why she had wanted so much to get out of prison. The bus jerked its way through the city centre, and then lurched through the estate where her father lived. She felt her stomach knot in fear, and yet she wanted so badly to get off the bus. She found herself watching the streets pass anxiously, watching for her stop. My stop, she thought. It isn't mine. None of this is mine, I shouldn't be living here. She leant forward, stretching out her arms between her knees, trying to avoid the eyes of some teenage boys sitting opposite her. She thought she knew one of them, but she would not look up. The bus shuddered to a halt by the old bridge, two stops early for Hannah, but she scrambled off, dragging her now torn bag behind her, wanting to get away from the boys, who were now openly staring at her. Without looking back she walked as quickly as she could towards Wesley Way.

'Look who it is. Her ladyship returns.' Her father stood grimly in the doorway of the tiny terraced house. He seemed far too large for it, and Hannah's mind reeled suddenly in disorientation. 'Are you going to give your dad a kiss? Are you going to say thanks, dad, for saving my arse?'

'Yes, thanks,' she mumbled, trying vainly to get past him into the house. He still stood there, like an enormous ugly statue, and she could smell his sweat and the beer on his breath. She could hardly look him in the face. He looked older; though she had only been away for six weeks he seemed to have changed. He seemed much uglier, much more crudely drawn. His face seemed larger, redder, and in some obscure way angry, and something inside her shrank in fear. She could not look into his eyes. 'Thanks, Dad. Let me past.'

'Let me past! Let me past! Whose house is this, sweetheart? Listen to her, Lisa,' he called over his shoulder, and Hannah realised with a flood of relief that he was not alone in the house. Behind her father's bare shoulder a woman's face appeared, lined and merry, with a sort of meretricious glamour. She laughed, and her laughter seemed mocking to Hannah, who felt a sudden urge to slap her.

'Come inside, love,' she said, her voice not more than a husky croak. 'Is it nice to be home, then?' Hannah looked at her; she seemed incapable of recognising people tonight, people she had known for years seemed to be terrifying caricatures. For one mad moment she wasn't sure if she knew Lisa in reality, or had only dreamt her, and now here was her dream come hideously to life. She looked into Lisa's bright, cold blue eyes, and felt herself sway vertiginously. This could not be real. Her father stood aside at last, yielding to Lisa, his bulky figure seeming to block out all the light, almost as though he absorbed it. Hannah dared to glance at him, his heavy, bull-like face, and noticed that he had a purplish bruise spreading outwards from his left eye. She did not dare to say anything, though, and as his eye caught hers and he saw that she had noticed, she flinched away, busying herself with taking off her coat.

'Your lovely fella did this,' he said abruptly, with a kind of savage triumph.

'Danny's in prison,' she said, trembling.

'I know fucking Danny's in fucking prison, you stupid little bitch!' he shouted, the dam of his fury bursting. 'It was that mate of his, that -'

'Leave her alone, for God's sake, Mick,' came Lisa's croak from the kitchen. 'Hannah's finished with him now, she's a good girl, your Hannah, don't take it out on her.' She emerged from the kitchen, wiping her hands down her front. 'Anyhow, you got him back. He smashed his windscreen,' she went on, turning to Hannah, 'smashed it with a great big fucking hammer, and he was shouting, 'Do you want me to do your head and all?'' She gave a conspiratorial wink, her face shining with admiration. Hannah looked at her with revulsion, feeling that she hated Lisa, and that the last thing she wanted on earth was to have to feel grateful to her.

'She's got nothing to do with Danny now, have you, darling?' Lisa pressed on, oblivious. 'She's told him, haven't you, love? See, Mick? She's told him.'

Her father grunted. 'You'd better have.' He swung his livid face round suddenly on hers. 'You'd better have, you little cow. If I find out you're still seeing him, I'll fucking cut your head off.'

Hannah shuddered; involuntarily she put her hand up to her neck. She felt the old unreality sweep over her again, and this time she did not fight against it. She looked straight ahead like a sleepwalker, knowing that there was nothing she could say that would not make him angrier. Tears started to her eyes, they rolled down her cheeks, but she didn't even brush them away; she felt so numb that they didn't seem to belong to her. She tried to recall her afternoon in the park, but it seemed disconnected from her, as though it had happened to someone else, some other girl, not her. This was her life. She turned and ran away from him, out of the door and down the path, her father still shouting at her as she vanished into the night.

**

Walkinshaw shivered at the wheel of his car, his hands clutching it to stop them from shaking. He hardly knew what he was doing; he felt impelled by some primitive impulse of excitement with which there was no reasoning. He knew what he was doing might be viewed as reckless; he knew it would be viewed as reckless by those around him, or worse, ridiculous. He wondered suddenly what Isobel would say if she found out, and the unpleasant idea struck him that she would be amused rather than anything else. He had no power to make her jealous, he knew that; she would be concerned only that he should not make a fool of himself, and thus of her. He felt a bitterness as he thought of this, and drove on with a new anger, through the familiar streets, and then on into ones that were not so familiar. He felt a sort of angry excitement as he went on. The changes in the surroundings were at first gradual, then sharp; he felt a little nervous as he passed boarded-up shops, derelict terraces, but his nerves were of anticipation rather than fear. He imagined himself living there, and felt a sort of freedom at the prospect. A couple of very lightly-dressed girls fluttered past his headlights; as he sped past he felt them staring at him, and he wanted to turn back and talk to them, be friendly, but he knew that would be madness. This is my city, he thought, and I hardly know it.

He was nearing the underpass to which Ratchett had referred, and as he saw it his stomach seemed to turn over. What had he been thinking, coming out here? He must have been mad. The odious words 'mid-life crisis' hovered at the back of his mind, and he resented their glib dismissal of what were for him very real feelings and impulses. Other men might make fools of themselves with flash cars and so on, but I am on a journey of self-discovery, he said to himself, smiling. He felt a guilty exhilaration, as though he were breaking the law. What would he say if anyone saw him here? Alexander Gregory, for example? But then, he reasoned, Gregory would be equally constrained to explain his own presence in this area. A mutual silence would be most expedient.

The sign for Wesley Way was upon him almost before he realised it; the name in black and white gave him a shock, almost as though he had not really believed it existed. It seemed to be a depressing cul-de-sac of grey, box-like council houses, lit up with yellow, unforgiving street lights, and his spirits sank despite himself. This awful place could not be where she lived. It seemed to emphasize the gulf between them, a gulf which he felt was far more painful for him than it could ever be for her. She could never know the awful alienation that he felt at that moment. Rationally, he knew that such an idea was nonsense, but yet somehow the sight of Wesley Way awakened in him a sort of oblique self-pity.

He had pulled over, but he knew that it was not safe to remain there for long. His car would attract attention soon. He tried vaguely to think of a reason for his being there, but nothing occurred to him. He felt a little disappointed, as though he had expected more to happen. This night was a night for something important, he knew that, but he had no idea beyond that. He felt a sort of unformed romantic impulse to do something dramatic, something irrevocable.

Then he saw her. She ran across the road, right in front of his car, and on into the night. He felt that he could not believe his eyes, but he knew at the same time that he was not mistaken. She had just run out in front of him, unseeing, her face had been different, he thought, perhaps she had been crying, she saw nothing, just ran over the road and away, away for ever, from him, from that house and from Wesley Way. He felt bewildered, and yet he also felt a strange new admiration for her. Vague classical allusions swam around in his mind; she was a nymph, she was Leda, with the swan bearing down upon her; she was Syrinx, running in an unheeding pelt from lecherous Pan. She was no goddess, she was a mortal, always a mortal, woundedness written on that pale face, as she ran, with her hair loose, past the car of her middle-aged potential protector. He thought of turning the car round, of trying to find her, but he knew there was no finding her. She had hidden herself in the darkness of that great grave city, and there would be no finding her until she chose to be found. Very slowly, his heart in his mouth, aching with a sort of awed solemnity, he drove away.

Chapter Two – A Taste of Blood

Walkinshaw sat uncomfortably in the large committee room, generally the only room in chambers that he liked. It was large and generous, with high ceilings, a fireplace and a genuinely good oak table. As a rule, though, he was only ever in it for meetings, which he dreaded. This meeting he was dreading more than usual. He hated meetings of the pupillage committee even more than he hated ordinary chambers' meetings, mainly because there was no way of avoiding making a decision which he knew would cause disappointment to a lot of young hopefuls, even if it brought elation to one. He had a strange squeamishness about ending the hopes of strangers in this way, even though he told himself that they were well out of it, and that he wished he'd been refused a pupillage in his time, then he might actually have enjoyed his life.

'Right. Let's make a start.' Gregory, at the head of the table, fumbled awkwardly with his papers. 'We pretty much narrowed it down to three last time, didn't we? James Wilson, Amina Hussein and Norman Tombs. He did a mini pupillage with you, didn't he, Entwhistle?'

'He did.' Entwhistle was a thin, reedy man with a thin, reedy voice; he blinked behind his large, unfashionable glasses and cleared his throat nervously. Walkinshaw looked at him curiously. He quite liked Entwhistle, was perhaps fonder of him than he was of most of his colleagues, but nevertheless would go out of his way to avoid him, as he was possibly the most boring man he had ever met in his life.

'He did, and I found him very able.'

'Able?' interposed Gregory, with a touch of scorn in his voice for the lawyerly, cautious word, so typical of

Entwhistle.

'Well, he has very impressive legal ability, there's no two ways about that. He knew more about one or two aspects of recent caselaw that I did!' Entwhistle gave a simpering laugh, to make it clear that this was of course a joke, but no one laughed with him and his voice trailed off in embarrassment.

'Wasn't sure about his interview, though.' This was Helena Gough, leaning forcefully across the table. Walkinshaw winced a little. She was chambers' most senior woman, like himself, recently made a recorder. Unlike himself, she was fiercely ambitious, a terrifying woman, he thought, tall, statuesque, but rather strident. Famously, once, a court reporter, seeing her from the back in wig and gown, and hearing her deep and resonant voice, had mistaken her for a man. She was an expert on criminal procedure, and appeared occasionally on Channel 4 News and Newsnight. Between her and Isobel there existed a deep and implacable hatred.

'We do need well-rounded individuals in chambers.' Walkinshaw groaned inside at the well-worn cliché. Against his better judgement he decided to chip in.

'So just because he doesn't play squash, or go hill walking at weekends-'

'Oh, don't be stupid, Mervyn,' she turned on him with sudden venom, 'you know quite well that's not what I mean. I felt that he was lacking in...'

'Social skills?' prompted Entwhistle. The words were so astonishing coming from him that Walkinshaw was momentarily struck dumb.

'Exactly, David.' Helena Gough favoured him with one of her icy smiles. 'We must remember that our new pupil will be an ambassador for chambers.'

'Yes,' said Entwhistle, pleased but nervous at this sudden approbation, 'an ambassador for chambers. I can't help feeling that dear Mr. Tombs is... well... perhaps a touch... well... odd.'

'Pots and kettles,' thought Walkinshaw to himself, smiling.

'Odd is the word.' Helena Gough and Entwhistle seemed to have formed a strong alliance. Walkinshaw felt piqued, though he had no idea at all why he should.

After all, he had no desire to have Tombs in chambers, and he could hardly disagree that he was an odd and uncomfortable person. Despite that, though, he found himself feeling a little sorry for him.

'Anyway,' went on Helena, 'doesn't he have something lined up at the Law Commission? I thought he might have pulled out of the running by now, actually.'

'No, the Law Commission thing fell through.' This was Geoffrey Bennett, a man so unobtrusive and unremarkable that Walkinshaw had hardly noticed that he was in the room. 'He told me so when I ran into him that time.'

'Fell through?' Helena was frowning. 'These things don't fall through. Either he never had it in the first place, or he blotted his copybook in some way. Another mark against him, in my book,' she went on, with relish.

Walkinshaw felt a little sickened. 'So you have no idea what went on, or why it fell through, yet you're still going to take it as a point against him? So much for the instinctive fairness of the legal mind!'

He knew he had gone too far. Helena Gough turned a furious scarlet face to his, her eyes seeming to scorch his skin. 'How dare you,' she was beginning, but Alexander Gregory hastily interposed.

'Come on, come on, this isn't getting us anywhere. No point in falling out about it. Now what about this girl, Amina Hussein? Must say she made a good

50

impression on me.'

Walkinshaw leaned back in his chair, secretly rather pleased with himself. He was already impatient to tell Isobel what he had said to Helena Gough, imagining her approval of his worsting of her enemy.

The meeting dragged on. He watched it grow dark outside the window. Still it went on, with Helena Gough a passionate advocate for Amina Hussein, and Geoffrey Bennett arguing for James Wilson. Entwhistle seemed to favour Wilson too, but, faced with the prospect of losing Helena Gough's approval, capitulated and voted for Amina Hussein. Gregory, clearly anxious to get the meeting over with as soon as possible, also chose Miss Hussein, and so the matter was decided with no need for Walkinshaw to open his mouth again.

He savoured the solitude of the drive home, having been forced to go out for a curry with Gregory and Bennett. He had sat, anxious, impatient and with little appetite, while they talked inconsequentially and, it seemed to him, foolishly; several times he had to make a conscious effort to hold his tongue and not break out in irritation. Gregory had drunk far too much and the other two had had to help him to a taxi, Walkinshaw looking with disgust and pity at his filmy eyes, the spittle running feebly down his reddened chin. He could hardly speak, his furred tongue seemed too large for his mouth. Yet he would be up and on his feet in the morning, his abilities restored as though by a miracle, a rather depressing miracle, thought Walkinshaw, and one that occurred with monotonous regularity, until one day it would not happen at all.

It was nearly midnight as he pulled up outside the house. Isobel's car was nowhere to be seen, and this alarmed him. She was never out this late. It occurred to him that her car might have broken down, and that she might have had to get a taxi home. That had happened a couple of times before. He unlocked the door, feeling a strange sense of foreboding, suddenly afraid.

He went all around the house, calling her name. She was not in. He felt a little panicky, unsteady, despite not having drunk anything at the curry house. His heart was beating fast as he roamed uselessly from room to room, as though she might mysteriously manifest herself any moment in a room which had been empty seconds before.

He tried her mobile phone. It was turned off, and he swore as it went straight to her formal voicemail message. The third time he rang it he left a short message, 'For God's sake, Isobel, it's midnight, where on earth are you?' But he knew his voice sounded needy, and that leaving a message on a phone that was switched off was futile anyway. He tried vainly to remember whether she had said anything about her plans for that day. He was sure she had said nothing about going out in the evening. Where on earth could she be? It made no sense, and he began to feel really frightened. He walked up and down the hall, twice going to the phone with an idea of calling the police, then pulling back. He wondered wildly whether she had left him, whether she had gone away for good. But there was no note, no nothing. And he began to panic again. He felt afraid of the loneliness, of the silence of the house, its very largeness and comfort seemed to oppress him, and he began to imagine that he would find Isobel's body in a cupboard or in the bath. A shadow across the door nearly made him scream.

As the hands of the clock stood at a quarter to one he began to rack his brains for people he could call. He tried to think of Isobel's friends, but she didn't really have any; lots of acquaintances, but no one whom she would visit at this hour. Her father was dead, and her mother lived in France. Her only sister was in America. He tried her mobile again. There was still no answer. At last, in a kind of wild desperation, hardly knowing what he was doing, he phoned Alexander Gregory. The phone rang for a long time, then he heard Gregory's voice in a hoarse, angry whisper.

'What the hell is it, Mervyn? Margaret's asleep.'

'Sorry, sorry. I'm sorry. Isobel's gone, that's all,' said Walkinshaw, close to tears.

'What do you mean, she's gone?'

'She's not at home. I got back and she'd gone.'

'Oh, for God's sake,' said Gregory, not unkindly. 'Is that all? She'll have gone out with some friends or something. It's not even one o'clock.'

'She never goes out. Not without telling me,' he said obstinately. 'She must have had an accident.'

'Oh, Mervyn,' said Gregory wearily, and Walkinshaw found himself wondering how he came to sound so sober. 'You've got to learn to live and let live.'

'What?'

'Live and let live. Don't be so melodramatic, old boy. She'll be back in the morning.'

He is drunk, thought Walkinshaw. 'How are you feeling now?' he asked, feeling he should, out of politeness.

'All right. All right. Puked in the taxi, but now I feel fine. Seriously, let it go, Mervyn. Call me if she's not back in the morning. But she will be.'

'But-' said Walkinshaw. The line had already gone dead. Slowly he walked back into the hall. He felt more troubled than ever, with an oblique sense of betrayal. He opened the front door, wanting to feel the cold air on his face. The house seemed suddenly to be oppressively warm. He realized that he was still dressed, and he wondered whether to go and have a bath and go to bed, or whether to stay up and wait for her. He felt he didn't want to be in his pyjamas when she came home, he wanted her to know how anxious he had been. Gregory had reassured him slightly, and he even began to feel a little angry with her, and to plan what he would say to make her feel guilty when she did come in.

He sat down, put the television on, and tried to concentrate, but couldn't. He sat there, huddled with tension and panic, and overwhelmed with a feeling of his own powerlessness.

Suddenly, just as he felt he had given up all hope, there were lights in the road outside, and he heard a key in the lock. He sprang to his feet. 'Isobel! Isobel!'

She came into the room, remote in her best blue cashmere coat, and he stared at her as though she had come back from the dead.

'Where on earth have you been? I've been so worried about you, I thought-'

'Out. I've been out, Mervyn. Is that good enough for you, or do you want an affidavit?'

He was dumbfounded, horrified. She was staring back at him, her face hard, as hard as flint, he thought, the word coming to him in the welter of his thoughts and feelings. They stood there like duellists, the air tight with pain and anger. He thought he would cry and willed himself not to. He longed to know what she was thinking, longed for a sign of weakness, of guilt, of unhappiness, but there was nothing. She looked tired, but also somehow elated. There was a light in her eyes which made him afraid. It was as though she were someone else, as though other, new eyes were looking at him from inside hers. For a moment he had the insane idea that it was not her, that someone was impersonating her.

He tried to hold on to his thoughts. 'Isobel, I've been worried about you,' he said, trying to keep his voice level. 'I don't think it's unreasonable to ask where you've been.'

'Unreasonable!' she said, mocking his tone. 'No, no, it's not unreasonable. It's not unreasonable at all.'

He could not gauge her mood, or divine her meaning. She was a stranger to him, and inwardly he was terrified, and in desperation took a conciliatory tone, hoping in some way to bring back his familiar Isobel.

'I just thought you'd be in, that's all. I got a shock coming home and finding the house empty. You can't blame me for that.'

Her glance was still cold and even. There was a pause for a moment, and then she said, with a sigh, 'I worked late at chambers. I got involved in what I was doing and didn't realize how late it was, then when I did set off home the traffic was awful.'

'The traffic was awful? At midnight?'

'If you refuse to believe me I don't know what more I can say.'

Walkinshaw did not believe her, but he did not say so. There was a brief silence, and then she said, a little more gently, 'I'm not going to stand here talking about it all night. I'm going to bed. Early start in the morning. Who did you pick for the pupillage?'

Without looking up, he said 'Amina Hussein got it.'

'So Miss Gough got her way, then.'

He thought of how he had wanted to tell her about the meeting and what he had said, and for a moment he thought he would, to restore the normality between them. He began to say 'You should have heard her...' but he found he couldn't, and his voice trailed off.

Isobel had moved to the door. 'Bed calls. May see you in the morning.' The door banged behind her, and

55

still he sat there, uncomprehending, staring sightlessly at the television.

**

Hannah Casey sat at the kitchen table, turning the spoon in her bowl of cereal round and round, her head lowered, trying to avoid the eyes of her father, who sat opposite, heavy and menacing in his stained vest. She found her eyes wandering to the faded blue tattoos that ran up his arms, and she winced with a sudden tightness in her chest. He had noticed her glance.

'Remember me getting this one, do you, love? Remember mam giving me grief about it? You were only little.' His eyes were misty with sentiment, and Hannah felt hot and sticky. This was his dangerous mood.

'Remember it, do you, sweetheart?' He was not going to let it go. She mumbled something unintelligible without looking up, and he gave a heavy, self-pitying sigh.

'Still mardy about the other night, are we, princess?'

'No.'

'I was narky because of this.' He indicated his eye. 'But it wasn't your doing, was it, love? You'd never want to hurt your old man.'

She said nothing, staring intently at a mark on the table, concentrating on it as though it could reveal all the mysteries of the world. Her dad went on.

'You know this is your home, don't you, Hannah?' She flinched at his use of her name. 'You know I don't want you going back there. When's your trial?'

'In about a month.' She felt a reluctance to tell him the actual date; she had a horror of him turning up at court, and – she felt pale inside at the thought – coming face to face with her barrister, maybe even having a go at him for some perceived failing. The thought made her faint, and she knew she must at all costs keep her father away from court. She would prevent him meeting Mr. Walkinshaw if she went to prison for ten years for it.

'When?'

'I can't remember.'

He grunted. 'Oh, get little Miss Casual. 'I can't remember'', he mimicked. 'I can easy find out, it'll be in all that stuff they gave me about your bail conditions. Got to be there when my dear little girl gets life in solitary, haven't I?'

He stood up, stretching, and Hannah shrank back despite herself, then straightened up, hoping he had not noticed. He had.

'What's the matter with you, girl? Don't you want to give your poor old dad a kiss?'

'No,' said Hannah, with courage that surprised herself. 'I don't want to.'

She expected him to hit her, but he only stared at her for a moment and then grinned, slowly, his chin bluish in the morning light that filtered into the tiny kitchen.

'Where's Lisa?' said Hannah thickly, filled with a sudden panic.

'Out.'

'I have to go, dad. I'll miss my bus.' Her hand was already on the door, she was fumbling for the handle.

'Off you go, then, Hannah. Don't forget your curfew.' He still stood there by the table, grinning. His voice seemed to be both in her ear and far away at the same time. She stood frozen in the doorway, then with an effort she picked up her bag and ran out of the door and down the path. Out of the corner of her eye she could still see her father, still standing there by the table, still with that grin on his face. For some reason she had the impression that she could taste blood in her mouth.

**

Norman Tombs stared blankly at the letter in his hand. He had already read it three times, and yet he found himself reading it again, as though by doing so he could change its contents. His eyes narrowed, and he put a hand to his mouth as he felt the nausea of disappointment and anger sweep across the pit of his stomach. He felt a bewildered incomprehension.

'Norman! Norman! Is it the letter? What does it say?'

He breathed deeply, and stuffed the letter back into the envelope, noticing with fury that his hands were shaking.

'What does it say, Norman? Goodness, why doesn't the boy answer me? You like keeping your old mother in suspense, don't you?'

He turned and looked at her, her old face harsh with eagerness in the morning light. For a moment he felt something like disgust, but with the discipline born of years of practice he smothered it quickly. Poor Mother. She will be so disappointed.

He realized that with that unsettling quickness of hers she had realized that there was something wrong. The eagerness of a moment ago was turning into the old hardness he knew so well. 'Mother...'

'I don't believe it,' she said, slowly, and the words seemed to drop like rain in the tiny room. Tombs abstractedly noticed tiny specks of dust swirling around in the bold sunlight. He did not dare to look at his mother, but he was aware that she was getting up from her chair and coming over to him. With a sigh, supporting her bulk with one hand on the kitchen table, she snatched the letter from him. He winced. 'I don't believe it,' she said again, and hatred stirred in Tombs' pale heart. He bit his lip. 'It's there in black and white, mother,' he said, his voice high and unnatural.

'Quiet. I'm reading it.'

Don't tell me to be quiet, he wanted to shout, don't ever tell me to be quiet again, I won't be quiet, I'll never be quiet again. But he was quiet, standing there beside her as she turned the letter over in her gnarled hands, breathing heavily and infuriatingly, and he felt as though he were dying, he felt as though she were about to kill him. She read the letter slowly, spelling out the words as she read, like a child, and he felt a sort of angry irritated pity. Don't lose your temper, he said to himself. Don't say something you'll regret later.

She turned over the page as though there might be something else written on the back, then put the letter on the table and scrutinized the envelope.

'I don't believe it,' she said for the third time. 'Did you tell them about that prize you won?'

'Yes,' said Tombs, his voice almost a whisper.

'What? What? Stop mumbling. Did you mumble like that in your interview?'

'No.' He tried to make his mind a blank, counting the seconds until it was over, and he could run upstairs and nurse his grief in his little bedroom.

'Well, what can have happened? What did you do?'

'I didn't do anything. I did it – I did it all right, like they tell you to do. I don't know what happened.' He paused, dizzy, tears of anger forming in his eyes. 'Maybe it's like they said in the letter, a lot of other strong candidates.' Unbelievable, he thought, she's got me defending them.

'You said you were the strongest candidate. You said that, when you met the others that time.' She was remorseless.

'Oh, mum, don't be angry,' he blurted out, despising

himself. 'I'm sorry.'

'Sorry isn't going to put it right.' She gave a heavy sigh. 'Your father would be so disappointed.'

'These things happen, mum. Pupillages are hard to find, I did say that all along.'

She ignored him. 'And all that money! How much do you owe the bank? Your father wouldn't have understood it. He had this place paid for when he was your age. He was doing a proper job when he was fourteen. He'd not have understood all this carry-on. What are you going to do now?'

Tombs felt a fresh wave of nausea; the tiny kitchen seemed unbearably stuffy. 'Keep on looking, I suppose.'

'Well, if you're not good enough for this lot, why should anyone else have you? You need to buck your ideas up. I suppose you're going to stay living here? That bedsit is off the agenda?'

'You need me here, mum. You know you can't keep it going on your own. It'll be better when you've had your hip done.' He felt a relief in talking about anything else, anything other than the crushing, world-ending loss contained in that now-crumpled letter lying on the kitchen table.

She snorted. 'Nurse says I've got to lose two stone first. Cheeky so-and-so. They get a kick out of seeing you in pain.'

There was a leaden silence. Tombs looked at the dishes piled up in the sink, and at a sticky patch on the floor; he had better get the cloth out and clean it up, otherwise mother might slip on it.

'Who was that one you met at that party?' she burst out suddenly. 'I always said you shouldn't have gone to that party. Pushing yourself forward.'

'It was you told me to go,' he said, stung by the injustice.

'Shut up. I'm thinking. Who was it you met? The one you said wasn't nice to you?'

'He wasn't not nice to me. I just thought he was a bit standoffish.'

'He'll be the one has queered the pitch, you mark my words. What was his name? Winchester or something.'

'Walkinshaw.'

'That's it. I'll write to him.'

'Oh, no, mother, you can't!' he burst out in horror.

'I will. We can't just do nothing about this. He's the one who put the spanner in the works, I'll bet. You said he didn't like you.'

'It was just a feeling, that's all.'

'It must be him,' she persisted. 'You said that Mr. Entwhistle as good as promised you it. He thought you were the bee's knees, that Mr. Entwhistle.'

I tell her far too much, thought Tombs. Then again, I've no one else to tell.

'And what happened to that Law whatnot thing in London? Oh, you were going to live in London, you were going to be the Lord Chancellor and I don't know what else. All come to nothing, hasn't it? Just like this has all come to nothing. There's a common denominator here, and the common denominator is you, Norman Tombs!' She sat back in her chair, breathless, and closed her eyes. 'All this has made me come over funny. You'd better get me one of my tablets.'

He went obediently over to the cupboard like an automaton, and found the packet.

'And a glass of water!' As he put it down on the table she muttered under her breath, 'Honestly,' and he felt like striking her.

'I'm going out,' he said desperately, fumbling under the chair for his anorak.

'Out? Where? You've not done the dishes.'

'I'll do them when I get back.'

'Well, mind you're not long. I don't want the place a sight when Doreen comes round.'

'She'll not be round before tea, mum. I'll be back by then.'

He put his coat on, and turned to the door. From behind him he heard her make a strangled sound. He turned round and saw her shoulders heave. 'Oh, mum, it's not so bad. Mum, don't cry.'

She had buried her face in her hands. He looked with a nightmarish feeling at the thin grey scalp, her fat hands with the rings embedded in them. Ought to get those rings made bigger, he found himself thinking, they can't be good for her circulation.

'It'll be all right, mum.' He put a hand on her shoulder awkwardly, inwardly recoiling.

'I went to the shops yesterday while you were out,' she said through her sobs. 'I got that cherry cake you like, I thought we could have a celebration.'

'Oh, mum, I'm sorry. We can have it anyway.' He took his coat off. There was no use his going out now.

**

Hannah lay back against her seat and closed her eyes. She felt vaguely that she should use this bus journey to conserve her energy, that she ought to try to sleep, but she was far too excited and nervous. Her heart pounded with dread and yet she longed to be there, the bus seemed to her to be going absurdly slowly. She kept imagining that she had left her bag behind, and every few minutes she would reach down and feel for it, then sit up again, reassured.

She wondered if her dad suspected anything. He hadn't seemed to. When she told him she was going shopping in Leeds he hadn't said much, hadn't even asked the expected question about how she came to have any money to go shopping with. He had just looked hard at her for a moment, then smiled, that new smile of his that she had come to hate. She had smuggled her bag out of the house, not wanting him to notice that it contained a change of clothes. She had no idea why she wanted to look her best for Danny. She felt that she hated him, and yet somehow she wanted to look good for him, she didn't want to look like a victim. She had taken her best dress and shoes and tried to stuff them into the top of her handbag, but it was too small, so she had borrowed one of Lisa's bags and put them in that. She couldn't bear the thought of her father seeing her in that dress. She loved it like a friend. It was short, tight and cream, with batwing sleeves. It was by Morgan and she had got it for twenty pounds in the sale, just before she got arrested. She smiled at the thought of it, and once again felt under the seat to make sure it was still there.

It seemed to her as thought the journey would never end, and yet when eventually the bus shook its way into the depot she felt a strange reluctance to get off. As she climbed down she felt as though she were waking from a dangerous dream. She would need to keep her wits about her. Still, she made her way to the toilets and changed into the dress, looking at herself in the mirror with that odd sense of disorientation that came over her so often now when she looked into her own eyes. She applied her eyeliner carefully, artistically, her hand steady, her whole body a study in concentration. She knew she must get this right, she felt obliquely that this might be an opportunity. She stood back from the mirror at last, and felt pleased with herself. She felt a regret that Walkinshaw was not going to see her today, and she wondered if it would be all right to wear the dress to court.

She sat at the table, suddenly so nervous that her mind was a blank, she felt unreal, detached, as though she were floating. She gripped her wrist tightly to stop her head swimming. She wanted to get up and run out, run out now, before he came in the room and saw her. She felt as though she would be sick, or faint. She felt as though the sight of him would kill her stone dead, and she wondered who on earth that dreamy girl putting on her best cream dress in the toilets could possibly have been. She looked down at her hands, which were leaving damp marks on the sticky black surface of the table. She breathed deeply, and made up her mind that she would go, she would run out of here, she could not possibly go through with it. She stumbled to her feet, breathless, and looked up to find Danny standing in front of her.

He was thinner. Most people put on weight in prison, but Danny never did; he just got leaner, stronger, more defined, more dangerous. She felt faint with fear, and yet there was a relief in getting the first shock of seeing him out of the way. She hastily sat back down again, hoping he would not have realized that she had been about to leave.

'Where were you off to?'

She made an attempt at a smile. 'Felt a bit faint. Thought I could get some air.' Her voice seemed to be detached from her, she seemed to have no control over her words, and she felt a surprise that they came out in her voice.

He was frowning at her. 'What? What's up with you? This is a fucking prison, you don't go out for air.'

She was disconcerted and alarmed. The tone of his letters had led her to expect him to be affectionate and grateful, at least superficially. She had not expected this, and her instincts rose up in fear.

He looked at her sulkily. 'Well, hello, darling. Lovely to see you again. So nice of you to come and see me. Aren't you going to give me a kiss?'

She leant timidly across the table, and as her lips brushed his she felt the old familiar rush of excitement and revulsion, and she closed her eyes. She felt as though she were on board a pitching ship.

A silence fell between them. She did not want to look at him, but felt her eyes drawn inexorably towards his face. He was still good-looking, she thought, with his high cheekbones and gunmetal eyes, but now there was something new, something frightening, formidable about him, and the set of his mouth made her draw back in fear. She had always been afraid of him, she realized, but before it had been an excited fear, a fear that lost itself in desire. Now it was just fear, and she felt that she could see a new hardness in him, a new brutality. Or possibly it was not new, but she was only now able to see it. The panic, which she thought she had overcome, welled up in her again, and she willed herself to stay in her chair and see it through.

'You're bloody quiet,' he said at last. Then, with a pleading note in his voice, 'I've been waiting to see you for fucking ages. I meant what I said, you know.'

'What?'

'About us getting married. I am going to marry you.'

Hannah's stomach turned over. She could not meet his eyes. Desperate for something to say, she said, 'My dad would kill me. He'd kill me if he knew I was here now, let alone–'

'You're scared of your dad?' His tone was derisive. 'I told you, the minute I get out of this shithole, your dad is going to get it. Don't worry about your precious dad. I'm going to sort him.'

'What will you do to him?' Hannah found herself

imagining how she would feel if Danny killed her father; the idea of her father's death seemed both wonderful and terrifying. Then there would be no one to keep Danny at bay. And now that Danny was inside, there was no one to keep her father at bay.

He ignored her. 'Do you think I'd let that little fucker stop me marrying you? The bastard's lucky he's not in here, and he'd get fucking done if he was.' He looked hard at her. She looked down at the table. She felt that her heart was on fire. He went on mercilessly, 'He's lucky I took you on. A lot of blokes wouldn't.'

She looked up suddenly, her eyes blazing. 'Don't – talk about that. Ever. Ever.' She was almost choking with anger, and despite herself a heavy tear rolled down each cheek.

'All right,' he said pacifically, watching her shrewdly. 'I won't talk about it. But you're the one who started talking about him. How's living back there? Worse than prison?'

'I'm coping with it.' She felt a sudden urge to tell him all about everything, to let him take care of everything, like in the old days. But those days had gone, and they wouldn't come back. Her heart suddenly ached for the days when she had loved him, when he had made her happy. She owed him something for that.

'I've got something to tell you,' he said, leaning across the table, and lowering his voice. She knew immediately that he was going to talk about business, and felt an immense relief that the conversation had taken a turn away from the topic of marriage. In her gratitude she leant eagerly towards him, and he noticed this and misinterpreted it.

'Good old Hannah,' he said affectionately, 'I knew I could count on you. Thing is, darling, I've got a present for you.'

**

Walkinshaw drew up alongside a black Audi in the court car park. 9 RJD. Wonderful, Reggie Dakers is here, along with his never-exhausted supply of sarcasm, usually at my expense. I wonder why he dislikes me so much, he wondered vaguely, as he manoeuvred into place. He would dearly have loved to scratch Dakers' beloved paintwork, but it would be more trouble than it was worth. He glanced at the girl sitting beside him. They had driven the sixty miles in near silence, a silence which he found oppressive and irritating, but was disinclined to break. She was impossible to talk to. He looked at her clear, aloof profile, her black glossy hair, and the pearl earrings pale and cool against her dark skin. She's a pretty girl, he thought, she's the sort I ought to want to have an affair with. He found himself making the contrast with Hannah Casey's pale skin, her shabby, cheap finery, and her air of timid lostness, and felt ashamed of himself. He looked at Amina Hussein with something like anger.

'Journey's end,' he said rather curtly, and she scrambled out, banging the door behind her rather harder than he liked.

'I don't want to do crime,' she said, conversationally, as they stood in the lift together, 'but I thought I'd better do this bit of work experience before my mini-pupillage gets underway. I'm really pleased you picked me. Don't you want to do something other than crime? Don't you find it... well... a little bit sordid? Don't you want to have a good shower when you get home at night?'

Walkinshaw, who had had this conversation a hundred times before, groaned inwardly. 'Miss Hussein-'

'Don't you think you'd better call me Amina, since

we're going to be colleagues?'

The lift juddered to a halt and he got out quickly, pulling his suitcase behind him, whilst Amina casually gathered up the rest of the paperwork.

'I hope I haven't offended you,' she said, trotting behind him, her arms full of papers, 'I just wonder how you can defend someone you know did it. I mean, don't you think some of these people belong in prison?'

For a moment Walkinshaw had a horrible feeling that he simply could not get through the day. The feeling was so intense that his head swam for a moment, and he wondered if he could ring chambers and say that he had been taken ill. He felt a deep, unbearable unease, like an itch he could never reach, and the queasy pain in his stomach was back again. He longed to be somewhere else, anywhere else. He forced himself to speak, trying to make his tone pleasant.

'Would you mind if we discussed this another time? I'm a bit preoccupied with the practical side of things at the moment.'

'Yes, of course. We could go out at lunch. I'd like to have a good chat about things. It's all so exciting!'

He hoped that the fates would have mercy on him, and keep Reggie Dakers out of his way. Not to be, he thought grimly, as he emerged from the toilets, where he had been taking Gaviscon, to see Reggie sitting in his usual chair in the robing room, engaging Amina in a bantering conversation.

'What a waste, a lovely girl like you stuck with a boring old bastard like Walkinshaw,' he was saying, then turned round in mock surprise. 'Walky, old boy! Just admiring your excellent taste in pupils.'

Amina Hussein, Walkinshaw noted with disgust, was blushing and giggling. 'Mr. Dakers-'

'Call me Reggie.'

'Reggie', she blushed again, 'Reggie has been telling me he feels the same way I do about criminal practice. You have to do it, obviously, but civil is so much more satisfying both morally and intellectually.'

'I'd be astonished if Reggie managed a sentence like that,' said Walkinshaw, as coolly as he could, but Dakers just smirked and leant across the table to Amina.

'He's jealous, that's all. Mind you, civil is time consuming. Poor Mervyn hardly ever sees his wife, do you, old chap? She works every hour of the day... and night.'

'Is she in your chambers?' asked Amina.

'Yes, she keeps us all in line.' He yawned. Walkinshaw suddenly had a strange sensation, like déjà vu or a half-remembered dream, but the instant he turned his mind to it it was gone.

'You do see life when you do crime, though,' went on Dakers. 'I had one the other day, little prostitute, I kept her out and she went, 'Oh Mr. Dakers, come round any time and I'll do you for free!' I thought, ' Not likely, sweetheart!'

Amina Hussein was staring at him, open-mouthed. 'No! That's disgusting! What disgusting people there are!'

'And did I tell you about the girl who sold her baby – for heroin, of course. They're like animals.' Dakers was well away. Walkinshaw decided he could stand no more, and slipped out of the room. Amina Hussein, wide-eyed and rapt, did not give him a glance.

He thought a hot drink might help to settle his stomach, so he went upstairs to the little, claustrophobic canteen on the third floor. There was no one else there. He winced under the fluorescent lights, and went over to the self-service drinks machine. A very fat middle-aged woman in a greasy overall watched him suspiciously.

'A hot chocolate, please,' he said, nervous under her stare. 'Do I get it myself?'

'Hot chocolate's out,' she said, unsmiling, still staring at him.

'A cappuccino, then.'

'The froth thing isn't working. Is it all right without froth?'

'I think I'll just have a plain coffee.'

'An Americano?'

'Whatever you call it,' said Walkinshaw desperately, fumbling in his pocket. She looked at him hard, her eyes narrowing. 'Are you being funny? We don't serve abusive customers, you know.' She indicated a sign on the wall with a flabby hand.

'I'm not being abusive,' said Walkinshaw, feeling that he was going mad. 'I just want a drink.'

She turned away, and poured grey looking coffee from a jug into a paper cup. She set it down in front of him with force, so that a little of it jumped over the rim. 'One large Americano. That'll be two pound ten.'

Walkinshaw's mouth fell open, but he caught her eye, and decided he didn't have the nerve to complain.

He sat nursing his coffee, noticing with slight nausea the bubbles of grease that floated round and round on the top, when the door behind him opened, and a boy of about nineteen, pale and haggard, wearing a baseball cap, came in. Walkinshaw knew his face instantly, but could not think in what connection. He felt that it was something important, and while the boy was over at the canteen he racked his brains to place him. In some way the boy's face was associated with an emotion, an emotion that he must have been feeling at the time when he met him, or saw him, for he had a feeling that he had only seen the boy before, not spoken to him. He tried hard to recall that emotion, and could only feel a confused sort of nervous excitement. He must remember who this boy was, before he took his unappealing cup of tea down the stairs with him and the chance was gone.

It seemed that the boy also recognized Walkinshaw. He turned round to look at him twice while buying his tea, and then, on his way over to the door, he suddenly stopped by Walkinshaw's table and said,

'You're Hannah's lawyer, aren't you?'

Of course! How could he be so stupid? It was Jonathan Burns, Hannah's co-defendant, the boy at whose flat she had been staying when she'd been arrested.

'I am, yes,' he said eagerly. 'How is she?'

Burns looked surprised, but pleased, at his friendliness. 'She's all right, I think, but she has to live with her dad, because of her bail, but her dad's a twat,' he said in a rush. 'That's why she came to live with me.'

'What does her dad do to her?' asked Walkinshaw, but Burns was away again, his narrative pouring out, as though he had been bottling it up for years. 'And Danny's been a prick, I said to him, I mean everyone's scared of Danny, but I've known him for years, I knew him when he was running for Barker, you know, old Barker, and he was shit scared of him, so I'm not going to be scared of Danny, am I? I said to Danny, you and me'll take care of it, you don't need to get her mixed up in it, you know?'

'We shouldn't really be discussing the case, you know,' said Walkinshaw, feeling almost faint in his keenness to hear everything Burns could tell him.

'I wasn't!' said Burns, with the habitual quickness of one who is well accustomed to refuting accusations. 'I was telling you about Hannah. I said to my barrister,

I'll go guilty to the – the – being – what is it again?'

'Being concerned.'

'Being concerned. I'll go guilty to the being concerned if they drop it against Hannah, but they're not going to, he says, so we're both going not guilty.'

'Sometimes the prosecution accept offers like that on the morning of trial. We'll probably have to wait until then.' Walkinshaw knew he ought not to be discussing any of this with Burns, but he was so anxious to glean what he could about Hannah that he didn't care. 'So is she all right, living with her dad?'

Burns seemed not in least surprised by his interest. 'I think so. He's a bastard, though. I fucking hate him. He thinks he's hard, he thinks we're all scared of him, we know he's a fucking nonce. Danny's going to kill him when he gets out,' he continued with relish.

'Does he-' began Walkinshaw, but was interrupted by the court tannoy. 'Jonathan Burns to Court Number Four. Jonathan Burns.'

'That's me,' said Burns, setting down his cup of tea on Walkinshaw's table. 'I wish you were my barrister. Hannah really likes you, she goes on and on about you, it's funny. Mine's a fella called Dakers, I liked him at first but now I think he's a wanker. Can you do my trial instead?'

'I can't represent you and Hannah,' said Walkinshaw, his heart singing within him, 'but I'll be happy to represent you for anything else you have outstanding, or if you get into any more trouble. Just mention my name to your solicitor.'

Burns grinned. 'All right. See you then.' And he was off through the door, leaving Walkinshaw staring into space with a wide smile of pure happiness on his face. She really likes me! She goes on and on about me! It's funny! All the rest of that day he floated about, wreathed in joy, and even Amina Hussein's endless questions about Reggie Dakers' marital status and personal life on the journey home could not disturb his ease of mind.

Chapter Three – From A Great Height

Norman Tombs looked around him with distaste at the shabby little waiting room, with its peeling wallpaper, chipboard table and dirty green carpet, a nauseous green, he thought. I hate this place. His mouth tightened with a tension that was becoming more and more habitual to him, and he made a slight movement as though to get up, but then sat back down in his chair resignedly. He looked down at his suit, a dusty navy in need of a good iron, and his dark grey shirt and tie, and wondered if he should have made more of an effort. But he had not felt able to wear his best suit, the lovely black pinstripe he had worn at the chambers interview. That suit was waiting for his luck to change. It would not cheapen itself by appearing here.

There was a movement in the outer office, the sound of voices, and the door swung stiffly open.

A fat, middle-aged man, his bald head ringed with ginger-grey hair and wearing a suit even more disreputable than Tombs' lumbered into the room, looking about him belligerently. Tombs divined at once that he was in a bad mood, and felt a fresh wave of anger and humiliation at finding himself in this awful place.

'You must be Norman,' said the fat man, gruffly, holding out a red, damp hand. 'Welcome to Caldwell's. You don't have to be mad to work here, but it helps. John Ratchett's the name, we spoke on the phone. Let's wend our way up to my office and we'll have a chat.'

Tombs followed him nervously out of the waiting room and through the typing pool, a room just as dismal as the waiting area, with a couple of listless girls sitting with headsets on, typing in a desultory way. Nothing seemed to be urgent at Caldwell's. A large, militant woman with very short bleached hair stood frowning at them, leaning against a gaping filing cabinet.

'This is Linda, our office manager,' said Ratchett. 'She's the real power round these parts, forget Dennis Caldwell. Even he's scared of our Linda.'

The large woman smiled, clearly pleased. Tombs noticed her very tight cardigan, and the silver eyeshadow caked onto her crepey eyelids, and felt a sort of creeping sensation. He wished desperately he had never had to come to this place, and the anger swept over him again.

'This'll be the brainy one you've been telling us about,' she said, still smiling. 'About time someone around here actually knew what they were doing, eh, John?'

Ratchett snorted. 'Round here it's about knowing your arse from your elbow, forget all that fancy law. He's new to it all, Linda, he'll learn. Won't you, mate? He'll learn. I heard a good one today,' he went on, 'just give us a minute, what was it? Oh yes,' having refreshed his memory with a quick glance at his mobile phone, 'my uncle was a rubbish ventriloquist. He used to put his finger up my bum and tell me not to say anything.'

Tombs looked at the floor in blank horror, aware that his face was scarlet. Linda screamed with laughter until she almost choked, clutching at the desk for support. 'John, you are awful! That's disgusting!'

Ratchett smirked back, pleased by her response, his oily face sweating under the harsh fluorescent light. 'It's good, isn't it? What do you think, Norman? Jesus, Linda, look at his face! Blotted my copybook, have I?'

'Bless him,' said Linda indulgently. 'You can tell he's new around here, John,' and she dissolved into laughter again.

'Come on, lad,' said Ratchett. 'Let's get on. I've got to be at the nick in half an hour.'

As they went out Tombs caught the eye of one of the typist girls as she passed in front of him, chewing, and managed a nervous smile, but she merely gave him a hard stare. As the door closed behind him he could hear them giggling, and he knew with twenty-two years' worth of bitter experience that they were giggling at him.

He sat down opposite Ratchett, his nerves now replaced by a sort of frustrated resignation. He had to put up with this now, but this was short-term, it was not forever, he would get his due one day, and then people would respect him, and tarty, stupid girls everywhere would know better than to laugh at him. Still he was unnerved, and he watched the clock anxiously as it ticked its clammy way against the dirty ochre of the walls, waiting for the time when Ratchett had to go to the police station, as a child waits for the end of school and home time.

'So you didn't get the pupillage then?' said Ratchett. 'Well, you'll just have to do your best to put up with it here. It's a friendly enough place when you learn how to fit in. We just don't like stuck up types. Horse sense stands you in better stead than all these degrees when you're down the cells with a raving nutter at two o'clock in the morning. We might seem rough and ready, but we've got to be. Some of these educated types – no offence – they haven't got the sense they were born with. Know all about philosophy and what have you, not got the sense to come in when it rains. I might not have letters after my name, but I know how many beans make five.'

Tombs had already stopped listening. He stared over Ratchett's shoulder to the window at the far side of the room. It had begun to rain, and rivulets were forming, running slowly down the frosted glass. Tombs stared hard at them, and bit his lip to hold back the tears that were stinging at the back of his eyes.

**

Walkinshaw sat in the kitchen in the pale early morning light, staring blankly at the cup of coffee on the table in front of him. His stomach was knotted with nerves, but he was so used to that by now that he only noticed it vaguely, at the back of his mind. What was making today different from all the other days, days just like this one, days in which even anxiety was just part of the routine, was the wild excitement hammering at his brain, an excitement so intense that his head span slightly, and there was a smile in his eyes as he lifted his cup with trembling hands.

'Aren't you having any breakfast, Mervyn?' Isobel came in calmly, immaculate in her best black suit. She already had her shoes on, dramatic four-inch heels that had cost three hundred pounds from some designer place in Leeds. Walkinshaw wondered idly if it was some sort of special occasion.

'What have you got on today?' he ventured, then faltered a little, wondering if he ought to know. 'Is it that arbitration?'

She looked at him scornfully. 'Mervyn! The arbitration is Friday. I'm having lunch with Penningdale and Gilbert today. It could be important. If I can get old Gilbert to back my application it could make all the difference.'

'Hence the heels.'
'Hence the heels.'
'How are you going to drive in them?'
'I'm not. I'm going to chambers first, Reggie is

picking me up. He'll be here in a minute, actually.'

'Has the car packed up again? You didn't say.'

'No, the car is fine. I just felt like a break from driving, that's all.'

He was a little taken aback. 'But you don't like Reggie. You said he was an arrogant, sexist, intellectual inadequate. Don't you remember? You were saying he has that awful sleazy way with women, that thing he does where he looks them up and down, you were saying he made you uncomfortable. I can't think why you'd want a lift with him.'

'Did I say all that?' Isobel laughed. 'What a drama queen I am. Reggie's all right really. Anyway, I know how to handle him. You ought to eat something, Mervyn. I know you get that nervous stomach thing, but when the nerves wear off you're going to be starving. What are you up to today, anyway? Staying local?'

'Yes. PCMH and two sentences this morning.'

'Oh,' she said, already turning away, but he had to tell her, he had to tell someone.

'Then I've got a lunchtime conference.'

'Anything interesting?'

'Being concerned. May go to trial, I don't know yet.' He felt as though his face was on fire, but he also felt a pressing need to tell her about it. He felt a strange desire to have her worm it all out of him.

'God, I'm glad I'm out of crime these days. It's depressing just hearing you talk about it. Have you seen my phone anywhere? I could have sworn I left it here.'

'No.' There was a pause, while Isobel rifled through her bag. 'Here all along,' she said with a sigh of satisfaction. 'I think that was Reggie's car. Better dash.'

'She's a very pretty girl,' he said, desperately, with a sort of suicidal impulse.

'Who?'

'My lunchtime conference. The being concerned.'

'That's nice. Oh, that is Reggie,' as a car horn sounded in the road outside. 'See you tonight, maybe. Have a good day.'

The door banged behind her, and for a moment Walkinshaw felt a sort of panic at being alone. The house seemed frighteningly empty, and he imagined himself running out into the road and pleading with her not to go. He felt he could see the scorn and amusement on Dakers' face, and the embarrassment on Isobel's, and he felt almost as disturbed and humiliated as though it had really happened.

Then he remembered the conference, and excitement flooded through him again. He looked at the clock. Only ten past eight! Surely one pm would never come. Slowly, forcing himself not to rush, he made his way upstairs and set about the business of choosing a tie.

**

Less than ten miles away, in her father's tiny house on Wesley Way, Hannah Casey was also preoccupied with what she should wear. She had been in a state of nervous confusion ever since the previous morning, when she had got a call from John Ratchett asking her to come to the Crown court the following day for a conference with her barrister. She had felt faint, unreal, joyful. 'Will it definitely be him?' she had dared to ask, and Ratchett, who had been in a hurry to get off the phone, had snapped, 'Well, that is the general idea of having a conference with your barrister, love,' and had banged the phone down. She had felt a pressing happiness over her heart, almost suffocating her, and she felt that she would die for lack of a confidant. She immediately began to think about what she would wear, and with a strange pang she remembered the day when she had come home on the train and she had imagined herself in a black suit, like one of those girl lawyers. But that wouldn't do, she mustn't overreach herself. Her mind turned inevitably to the cream dress, but she had an idea that she should save that for the trial itself. She felt instinctively that it would be a mistake to wear her best outfit first, and condemn herself to be a disappointment from then on. She thought about it until her head ached, and still she couldn't decide what to do. She considered for a moment going out and trying to shoplift something, but her shoplifting days were over, and, anyway, it would be a stupid risk to take.

She tried to think of what Danny had liked, but that was no good. Her barrister was sure to have much better taste than Danny had ever had. In fact, he would probably hate what Danny had liked, and vice versa. Then it suddenly hit her that, in the welter of her thoughts about clothes, she had not really taken in that she was actually going to meet him again, and for a minute or two she was floored with nerves, and actually wanted to phone Ratchett and tell him to cancel the conference, to find her another barrister, one she could look in the eyes. Twice she went over to the phone, and twice she put it back in the cradle without dialing.

Still in her dressing gown she went slowly downstairs. She could hear her father's voice calling her from the front room, and she wanted badly to ignore it, but she knew she couldn't. She went into the small, smoke-filled room, her heart throbbing inside her, and sat as casually as she could on the arm of the sofa.

'What's this?' he said thickly, his face forming into the familiar creases which she knew so well preceded an outburst of anger. She looked at him with hatred; his face, both lined and puffy, his skin, which was a horrible livid colour somewhere between red and grey, all these things, in juxtaposition with her fantasies of Walkinshaw, seemed to her to be a sort of personal insult. Since meeting Walkinshaw her anger towards her father seemed to be new and more defined, as though she were beginning to understand in some oblique way how great was the stain that he had made on her life. She felt a new shame, and anger burned sourly inside her stomach.

'What's what?' she said curtly, not looking at him.

'This.' He threw a letter at her, with force, but it fluttered harmlessly to the floor at her feet. She bent to pick it up. She knew immediately it was from Danny. She recognized the prison envelope, and anyway, no one else ever wrote to her.

'Who's it from, then?' said her father sarcastically, but she ignored him, anxiously checking that he hadn't opened it.

'I haven't been reading it, don't worry. I don't want to know what that scumbag's got to say for himself. But I'll tell you this, Hannah,' with an effort he raised his bulk in his chair, and stared at her balefully, 'I'll tell you this. If you've had anything to do with him while you've been here, you're fucking out of here. You're not staying under my roof.'

Hannah had heard this so many times that she hardly listened. She clutched the letter to her chest, as though to protect it from her father.

'Don't you hear me, you bitch? Haven't you got anything to say to your father?'

'No.' She still would not look at him.

'No. That's nice. Well, don't say I didn't warn you.' He settled himself back into his chair, and closed his eyes. She got up to leave, as quietly as she could.

'Where are you going?'

'Upstairs.'

'No, I mean where are you going today?'

'What do you mean?' she asked, colouring.

'You're going to meet him, aren't you?' His eyes, small, bloodshot and angry, seemed to bore into hers. She felt as though she were going to faint.

'What?' she stammered, still clutching the letter as though it could protect her.

'Don't lie to me, I know when you're off to meet him. You little bitch. You lying little bitch,' he said, almost with admiration in his tone.

Suddenly Hannah penetrated his meaning, and she nearly laughed with relief.

'I'm not going to meet Danny,' she said, contemptuously. He wasn't as clever as he thought he was, the stupid old bastard.

'Don't you lie –'

'I've got a conference with my barrister at one o'clock. Ring Mr. Ratchett if you don't believe me.'

He stared at her, ugly in his incomprehension, as she turned away.

'But...' he began, and then his voice trailed away.

'But what?' She ran out of the room and up the stairs, leaving him staring after her in bewilderment.

**

Walkinshaw drove to court slowly, carefully, as though he had to balance something fragile on the roof of his car. He had no idea why he felt this need to be careful, but something in him urged a sort of anxious caution. He felt, without having any idea why, as though there was some great danger to be avoided, and his skin prickled with excitement and fear. He wondered why he should feel like this, what the point of it was, and worried that it signified some sort of emotional immaturity. Surely he shouldn't feel like this at his age, surely he should realize by now the ultimate shallowness of this sort of giddy feeling? Surely he should, by now, have learned that love is gravity, solemnity, patience, even sorrow? This wasn't love, it was absurd to imagine that it could be, and if it wasn't, well, what sort of man did that make him? Isobel is the woman I love, he told himself, except that his love for her simply did not seem to soak in, to absorb, it was like trying to varnish metal, it would not seep in, it just ran off the hard surfaces and collected in a puddle on the floor. So that his love, which should be part of her now, which should be absorbed into her being, was returned to him, unused, available. What a bizarre idea, he thought, perhaps I should be a poet. Nevertheless the idea persisted, and gave him a little thrill of unease as he parked up in the too-familiar court car park, and went inside, through the automatic glass doors, through the metal detector, and upstairs to the robing room, towards a day which he felt must be either wonderful or disastrous, anything but ordinary.

He had expected to find himself unable to concentrate on anything but his lunchtime conference, and had resigned himself to a morning of jittery nerves and incessant clock-watching, but one of the two sentences he was defending had become suddenly and unexpectedly complicated, as the defendant had decided, on that very morning, as the reality of a possible prison sentence bit, that he wanted to change his plea to not guilty and have a trial. Walkinshaw, like all criminal barristers, was not unused to this; it was a reasonably common occurrence, and he did his best, with his practiced blend of reassurance and firmness, to explain to Davidson, a large, sweating former trawlerman, who filled the tiny room with the unmistakeable scent of fear, that the evidence against him was overwhelming, and that a trial would only add to the length of any custodial sentence. Besides, there was no guarantee that the judge would let him vacate his plea in any event. Eventually his explanations, along with murmurs of assent from the solicitor, a grave middle aged man who was not best pleased at being summoned away from the office, caused Davidson to capitulate and sign with a large, red, trembling hand a hastily prepared statement accepting his guilt and his willingness to abide by his earlier plea. Looking at his name on the paper, in shaky, pitiful capitals, Walkinshaw felt a pang of sudden guilt, as though he had been complicit in something shameful, and as the large man made his way out of the room, suddenly enfeebled, trailing defeat behind him like a cloud, he could not look him in the eyes.

'I feel sorry for him,' he ventured to the solicitor, a Mr. Greer, who was noting up the case in a precise hand, radiating disapproval.

Greer raised his head in surprise, his cold blue gaze pitiless. 'Sorry for him? I think we should feel sorry for the taxpayer. Over fifty thousand pounds in false claims? Don't waste your sympathy, Mr. Walkinshaw,' and he gave a light, sarcastic laugh which gave Walkinshaw a shock of anger.

'He genuinely injured his back,' he said, stubbornly.

'And then milked it for all it was worth. Why work, when you can get paid for doing nothing? I hope we get on soon, I've got auditors back at the office who won't be rejoicing at my absence.'

I would, in their place, thought Walkinshaw mutinously.

Greer went on, calmly, 'He's a coward. The big day dawns, and the cold sweats begin. Shades of the prison house. I think he'll go down, I'm told Judge Robertson has been in a foul mood all week. And he particularly hates benefit cheats. Is there anywhere here I could charge up my phone?'

The wait seemed interminable. He sat in the small, comfortless conference room, watching the clock, which seemed to him to be counting one minute for every two. He felt as though he had caught Davidson's fear like a virus; it seemed to be eating into him. When at last it was called over the tannoy he leapt to his feet, breathless, with a horrible attack of stage fright. As he went into court in his wig and gown and saw Davidson's face grey in the dock he felt a sudden terror, as though he were about to see a man fall to his death from a great height, and his head swam. What is wrong with me? he asked himself, as he had so many times recently. Just do your job, the best you can. No one can ask for more than that. He made a point of raising his head and looking the judge, an obese, bearded man who specialized in false bonhomie, straight in the eyes. He did his best for ten anxious minutes, his confidence growing at the sound of his voice, and as he sat down he felt a rush of hope. The judge smiled pleasantly at him, after he had given Davidson twelve months, and as he rose from the bench mouthed at Walkinshaw 'Good job. Well done.'

It was nearing one o'clock. He felt unreal as he changed into a collar and tie, standing in front of the mirror in the robing room. He looked at himself, at his own face looking back at him, and wondered what he really looked like, whether he was good-looking or not. He felt that he genuinely had no idea. He decided his hair needed brushing, and not for the first time cursed his wig for making his hair stand upright. I look ridiculous, he muttered to himself as he tried to flatten it down. Then, suddenly, out of nowhere, he felt a great wave of depression and sadness, so intense that it gave him the feeling he must sit down for a moment. He waited numbly for it to pass, and as it lessened, gradually, ebbing away, he began to feel really afraid. Something really is wrong with me, he thought, I'm losing my way, I'm losing control. What have I got to be so sad about? He thought of Hannah Casey, presumably now sitting out there in the waiting room, and of Isobel, at her all-important lunch with Penningdale and Gilbert, and the sadness of it all seemed to eat into him like acid. He felt a new and frightening consciousness of the aloneness of everyone, of that strange spiritual isolation that, he thought, most people school themselves to ignore, to pretend does not exist, because to look at it, to think about it, is to go nearly mad with loneliness and fear.

He raised his eyes to his own in the mirror again, all his excitement gone. His heart was still throbbing, but now with terror, and he felt the only thing he wanted in life was to go home and go to bed.

He felt something close to horror as he saw John Ratchett approaching him from behind in the mirror. Hastily he arranged his face into a presentable expression, and hoped desperately that tears were not standing in his eyes.

'Aye aye.' Ratchett clapped him on the shoulder in his customary gesture, and Walkinshaw felt that he would die in the effort required not to flinch away.

They walked together through the concourse in near silence, Walkinshaw trying to compose himself, and mentally running through the details of the case, which seemed alarmingly to have disappeared from his memory. The building seemed to have gone to sleep; he was familiar with this strange lull that affects courtrooms at lunchtime, as though the building itself, exhausted with all the effort and emotion of the morning, has to lie down and have a nap. No one seemed to be about, except a pale, overweight young barrister with a bad complexion who hurried past them with a bag of fish and chips. The smell made Walkinshaw's stomach turn over, despite the gnawing emptiness he was beginning to feel, having had nothing but a coffee since breakfast.

'I've put her in a room,' said Ratchett, 'left her reading the deps. It's a bugger the Pros not taking simple possession. She doesn't want to be pleading to this.'

'I know,' murmured Walkinshaw, wondering why Ratchett seemed to feel the need to explain things to him as though he were a novice. 'I put all that in my advice.'

They were outside the room now, and he tightened his grip on his bundle of papers. He felt as though he were in a dream, or a badly-scripted play. Ratchett opened the door and there she was, sitting in the corner, looking, he thought, pale and a little over-dressed. Her face was tight with nerves, and she seemed somehow diminished. He felt a sudden and unavoidable lurch of disappointment, which strangely seemed to boost his professional confidence.

'Now, then,' he began, catching her eye and giving his best reassuring smile, 'we've got a lot to get through. Mr. Ratchett's given you the statements to look over, I see.'

'Yes.' She kept her eyes on the table. He felt that she had read his disappointment with her, and he felt a tug of remorse. Why was everything going so wrong today? It was turning into a disaster.

'Well,' he began with a feigned brightness, 'let's just go over the basic facts to begin with. Your former boyfriend, Daniel Reynolds –'

'You're not with him still, are you, love?' cut in Ratchett, eyeing her with a friendly suspicion.

She was silent for a moment or two. 'No, I'm not with him,' she said eventually, with a dignity that gave Walkinshaw an uncomfortable feeling that they, the two men, were transgressing, intruding into places where they should not go.

'Your former boyfriend, Daniel, owned the flat in question-'

'He only rented it,' broke in Ratchett.

'He rented it.' Walkinshaw began to feel he would never get a sentence finished; he was conscious of an unpleasant clammy feeling down his back.

'He was then arrested as part of Operation Cleaver, a police initiative designed to crack down on local drug dealers. They searched the premises and found...' He paused and fumbled through his papers for a moment, his brain numb. 'They found a considerable quantity of heroin; they're saying there was five hundred and eighty pounds worth.' Hannah winced, almost imperceptibly, but he noticed, and looked up.

'I didn't know how much there was,' she said, then stopped abruptly, and took a deep breath. She began again, more calmly. 'Danny and Burnsy – Jonathan – were using, so there were drugs around. I had nothing to do with any of it....where it was kept, all that, I didn't know. I was only there for two weeks.' Her voice was rising, and there were tears in her eyes. Walkinshaw looked at her in a sort of confusion. He felt horrified, ashamed of himself, he felt as though he should not be there, that she should not be there, that she should not be telling him any of these things, and that he should not be asking her to. He felt as though things between them were being soiled, that with every word spoken in this squalid little room was another rub of dust from a butterfly's wings. He felt so anguished he half rose to leave, before recollecting himself and sitting down again.

'You were only there for a couple of weeks, weren't you, flower, because your dad chucked you out?' For once Walkinshaw was glad of Ratchett's interruptions.

'Yes. My dad said he wouldn't have me any more, so I went to stay with Danny. It was only meant to be 'til things calmed down at home.' She addressed herself to Ratchett as though it were just the two of them, not looking at Walkinshaw. He saw this, and it made his heart hurt. He had lost her trust and must win it back.

'Well, we'll put it to the jury you had nothing to do with it, simple as, won't we, Mr. Walkinshaw? You were just a guest in the house, you didn't know what them lads were up to.'

Her eyes were troubled. 'I don't want to get Burnsy into trouble. He's been a friend to me.'

'You don't have to. You just say you don't know a thing about it, full stop, end of story. Isn't that right?' he pressed, turning to Walkinshaw.

'Yes,' said Walkinshaw slowly, 'but-'

'You think they won't believe me.'

She was looking straight at him, defiantly, and he went hot with shame. He tried to smile at her, as frankly as he could.

'That's the risk you run with jury trials.'

She continued to look straight into his eyes. 'Do you think they'll believe me?'

Flustered, he began to make a weighing motion with his hands, but felt that it was stupid and futile, and let his hands drop, foolishly. 'It's impossible to predict what a jury will do,' he said at last, painfully conscious of the weakness of his words. Through his own whirling thoughts he saw fear spread itself across her face, and he rushed to find words of reassurance. 'I really think we've got a good run, though. I really do,' and he found himself looking at Ratchett for support, who nodded sententiously, chewing the end of his pen.

'We have, love, we have. Especially when the jury hears about your Daniel's previous. They'll know you weren't a mover and shaker in all this.'

She looked alarmed. 'Will they talk about Danny much? What will they say?'

'Oh, just that he pleaded to it all. Good news for us, because, you see, the jury won't feel like no one's been punished.' He gave a knowing wink.

'He won't come and give evidence, will he?' Her face was a mask of fright; in her fear she sought Walkinshaw's face, which gave him a rush of satisfaction.

'No, no,' he said, as soothingly as he could, 'there's no statement from him. He'll have nothing to do with the trial.'

'Police evidence only,' said Ratchett, picking his teeth. 'We're listed for two days, but it'll probably only be one and half, be finished by Tuesday lunchtime, I should think.'

'If we get a good start,' said Walkinshaw, mechanically. He felt an overwhelming urge to stare at Hannah, suddenly the attraction was back, fierce, now that she had looked straight into his eyes, now that her fear and her anger had broken through all the constraints, and flooded the little room with her realness. He felt a tight, choking excitement in his chest, and began to play nervously with the pink ribbon tied around his brief.

'Well, see you in a week, then, Hannah.' Ratchett was getting to his feet, filled with the false camaraderie that so often came over people in pre-trial conferences, thought Walkinshaw. You might imagine the three of us as life-long friends.

She was getting up now, fumbling under the table for her bag. He waited for a few nervous seconds, then as she was in the doorway and face to face with him he said, on an irresistible impulse, 'It'll be all right, you know,' and then cursed himself for giving a reassurance he had no right to give. But he was rewarded with a smile as she disappeared down the corridor, herded along by Ratchett. And then she was gone, and he stood dizzily in the tiny room, unable to comprehend any of it.

All the way home he was nagged by a sense of something left undone, something forgotten, and he played the conference over and over in his head like a tape, trying to find the thing that he should have said or done. He was ten minutes away from home when suddenly he remembered. He had entirely forgotten to visit Davidson down in the cells.

Chapter Four – A Stream of Gold

She ran out of the building and down the steps in a sort of light panic, hardly noticing the cars that shot past the front of the building, oblivious to the angry stares of passersby into whose paths she ran. She wanted to run the confusion and the resentment out of her heart, the strange disappointment, betrayal even, which she had felt welling up inside her in that terrible greying little room, a dirty room, she thought, and she found herself breathing deeply as though to rid her lungs of its air. She stopped at last, panting, and she knew at once that the pain would still be there, that the hurt inside her would not run itself away, however she tried. She had read that glance, that glance of his at the moment he came into the room, and she had known then everything was spoiled and tainted, she had ruined things. She looked down with a sort of disgust at the blue faux-sheepskin jacket, with its furry collar blowing extravagantly in the wind, and she knew in a moment that it was cheap, and that he had recognised it as such. She went hot with shame that she had worn it, a fifteen pound bargain from a market stall, in a conference with him. She was astonished at her own audacity. Then she remembered his smile, his eyes, and she felt her heart melt a little even in the midst of her embarrassment. Had he understood? Could he understand? Her mind whirled with excitement and hope; she realised that she was breathing hard and shallowly, through her mouth, and that people walking past were looking at her strangely. She put a hand to her mouth, still breathless, and tried to make her legs, which were now shaking and weak, carry her on through the streets.

All through the morning she had felt Danny's letter

there in her bag; it had seemed to be burning a hole there, like acid, and she felt almost surprised that neither of the two men had divined its presence, she felt as though it must be written on her face. Danny's letter seemed in some strange way to be an extension of himself; knowing it was there in her bag she had felt somehow inhibited, as though it were listening to everything she said and would report back to him. She smiled to herself. Even Danny's not that clever, she thought, even he can't plant listening devices in pieces of prison paper. Still she had a sensation of being watched as she made her way slowly along the canal path. She must not, she dare not, disobey Danny.

The sky was clouding over rapidly; the sunshine of the morning was replaced with banks of lowering grey-black cloud which Hannah felt were pressing down on her head, suffocatingly. Several times she passed her hand over her head and then looked up with narrowed eyes at the heavy sky. She began to walk more quickly. A fat raindrop landed heavily on the sleeve of her coat, followed quickly by several more. She began to feel unaccountably afraid, and kept looking over her shoulder to make sure that no one was following her. But she was now inside the perimeter fence of the disused factory, and there was no one around. As the rusty gate swung behind her she went hot with fear, and had to fight an impulse to turn and run. But she remembered the letter, and she knew what she had to do. The old factory loomed up in front of her; the dirty brick façade, that she knew so well, seemed different, threatening, unfamiliar, and she walked past it hastily, with head bowed, fear hammering at her heart. She felt that something terrible was about to happen, and with a sort of fatalism she felt she wanted it to happen at once, that the greatest torture was waiting, powerless. The black, broken windows seemed to look down on her like evil eyes, and she wanted to scream. At one of them she fancied she saw a man's face, watching her coldly, and at that she broke into a frantic run again, the rain lashing her face as she pounded along, panic boiling inside her. At last she was through the gates on the other side, and with a sigh of relief she knelt on the pavement for a moment to catch her breath. She straightened up slowly, and looked around her. Ransome Drive. She had always thought it was a pretty name, but it was not a pretty street. It seemed short, somehow broken or truncated, as though in some way its growth had been stunted. Ten small, box-like, grey houses stood, back-to-back, as though they had quarrelled, on broken concrete through which the weeds could hardly break. Even weeds did not care to live in Ransome Drive. Hannah felt as though the fear in her heart would kill her. She took the letter out of her bag as though to draw strength from it, as though some of Danny's spirit would transmit itself to her. Danny was never afraid of anything, it was what she had loved about him, before she was old enough to know better.

The street seemed deserted. A pram stood outside one of the houses, a beaten-up car outside another, but the street itself was quiet, and she suddenly wished for some noise, some company. It was too quiet, and she suddenly felt conscious of something sinister, here in this street where she had lived, even, perhaps, been happy.

The house where she had lived was boarded up. She got a shock when she saw it, like seeing a person she knew well blinded. She felt a curious pain when she saw the window of her bedroom, the room she had shared with Danny, the light blocked out of it with heavy wood, and she felt a spurt of anger as she looked at it. Everything is taken away from me, all of it, she thought, even this horrible, ugly house, surely I could have been allowed this at least. It might be ugly, but it was mine. And Danny's. Her mind suddenly lurched into memory, and she felt something of the old desire for him, something of what she had called love, once. Danny wouldn't have let this happen. Then she realised that it had all happened because of Danny, that in a way it was all his fault. But it was no use thinking in terms of fault with Danny, it was the way he was, it was his nature, like a wild animal. He did the things he did because of that spirit of his, that spirit that no policeman, no judge, no prison sentence could break. Danny was an outlaw, a rebel, he took his chances, and when his luck ran out he took that too. She felt desire for him crawling inside her stomach, and for a moment she wondered if she could go back to him, if that old life would ever make sense again. She remembered long afternoons up in that sightless bedroom, and shuddered inside at the terrible strangeness of it all, and felt herself, despite everything, to have been lucky to have been there, to have had this life.

Of course they had changed the locks. The doors were heavily chained, front and back, and she walked round a couple of times before she decided she would have to get in through the kitchen window, the only one they hadn't bothered to board up, she presumed because it was at the back of the house. Still, it seemed to her to be an odd stroke of luck, and it was with a sense of uneasiness, as though she was walking into a trap, that she carefully prised open the window and climbed inside.

It was strange to be inside again, in that familiar and yet alien little kitchen, in which she had been so many times, sometimes trying to make dinner, in a vague attempt at imposing some sort of domesticity on their lives, sometimes – often – at the washing machine, trying to get the blood out of Danny's trousers and shoes. The washing machine had gone. She didn't know if the police had taken it, or if it had been stolen, and she didn't care.

The only thing that mattered to her was in the cupboard under the stairs, and she made her way there, breathless, terrified. The house was stifling her, and she felt the fear rise again like a tide inside her throat. She felt sure that someone was watching her, that the house was not empty, that at any moment a policeman would emerge from the shadows and arrest her. She felt that if that happened it would almost be a sort of relief. The silence in the house was oppressive; it seemed to be real, like a person, somehow more real than herself. She had a sense that the house would consume her, that she would be obliterated by it. She hardly dared breathe its air as she fumbled with shaking hands in the cupboard. It did not seem to be there, and yet it must be there, surely even the police would not take a vacuum cleaner. Then it occurred to her that they might well have done, perhaps, she thought confusedly, to examine it for particles of drugs, and she half rose from her knees, feeling that she had an excuse, that she could tell Danny truthfully that she had looked, but that the police had already got it. But then she felt her fingers close around the long stem of the hoover pipe, and her heart rose into her mouth. Gently she pulled it out, and twisted it away from the body of the vacuum cleaner. She already knew that it was there, she could feel its presence, she felt a kind of awed shame. Slowly she stretched out the palm of her left hand, like a supplicant, and into it flashed a stream of gold.

**

Walkinshaw stretched himself out luxuriously in the bed, enjoying the clean linen against his skin, and the contrast between the pleasant physical sensation and the whirling thoughts besieging his brain. He felt obliquely that he had done wrong, that somehow he had betrayed himself, and her, in that conference, that somehow he had failed to show that understanding which he felt instinctively that he did possess. If he didn't, at least he should have shown that he badly wanted to understand, that he wanted her to help him understand. Instead, all he had managed was a standard pre-trial conference, in which he contrived to be both ineffectual and patronizing, the two things he couldn't bear to be. He had always prided himself on being good in conference. That one must have been my worst in years, he decided. Everything had been wrong, the whole day had been wrong, it was wrong from the moment he had been there in the kitchen, and Isobel had come in, looking radiant, more attractive than she had in some time. Isobel. Something pulled again at the corner of his memory, like a half-remembered face seen across a street, the same sensation he had experienced in the robing room when Reggie had mentioned her working all night. That was an exaggeration, of course, but – he put his hand to his mouth, slowly. He had a feeling that he was sliding between two worlds, and one was a frightening place, filled with secrets that he would rather never have known.

Isobel. He thought of her with a sudden fear. What was happening to him? What was happening to them? He had known for some time, of course, that the marriage was not great, that things between them were cool, cold even, that somehow whatever had made them marry each other was not strong enough to make a marriage work, whatever that means. Work was the great shield, the great defender, without work everything fell away, crumbled, they looked at each other in a sort of panic. Work was what stood between them, but it was also what held them together. Who are we without it? What can we possibly say to each other? No, he thought, desperately, it wasn't that bad, we had a wonderful time in Jamaica. And then he realized that Jamaica had been five years ago. And that for the first time ever he had thought of his marriage in the past tense.

We need to work at things, he thought. No one has a perfect marriage, you have to work at it. Work. There was that word again. And work at what? What did he want? What did she want? To spend as little time as possible with him, or so it seemed lately. He remembered with a sort of rueful amusement how once she had admired him, or had seemed to; she must have done, she thought he was worth marrying, and Isobel was not a woman to marry recklessly, she was not a woman to do anything recklessly. If she had married him, it must have been because – even on the most cynical of reckonings – because she thought she could not do better. Yet now her scorn for him lay between them like a prickly branch; he could no longer reach out to her without that now-familiar sense of humiliation rising up in his throat. He tried to recall the past, the days when it had been different. It must have been different once. But however hard he tried, however accurate the memories, of his wedding day, of their honeymoon, of countless other lost little moments since, something seemed to be missing; he could not place the mood, the feeling, it was like looking at someone else's life, someone else's home movies, someone else's photograph album, it seemed very nice, but he couldn't find the emotion in it, even though he wanted to. He dredged the memories, trying hard to recall the day, the week, before his wedding, trying to remember things he said, things she said. His inability to recall even the most trivial things troubled him, and he wished that he had kept a diary. Here I am, he thought, taking refuge in the past again, hiding in it, cowering from the present and the future. He felt his heart sink with fear and foreboding, though why he had no idea. My life is not so bad, he said to himself, I even got made a recorder, I didn't really expect that. But he knew in his heart, even though he could hardly admit it to himself, that he hated being a recorder, ever since that fateful day when he had sentenced Daniel Powers. Every time he sat up on that bench his heart tightened within him, and he felt as though the floor was falling away before his feet. I only applied to please Isobel, he thought bitterly, and all I've achieved is to add to my own burden of misery. Suddenly he thought again of Hannah Casey, and he felt his heart wrench with a strange sense of freedom. Strange that I should associate her with freedom, after all, she's only just got out of prison. But still the feeling persisted, and he found himself pinning all his hopes on the forthcoming trial, as though in some way the mere fact of her presence with him for two whole days would heal him, would make things fall into place.

He heard a car pull up outside the house, and his heart sank unaccountably. As her key turned in the lock fear flooded him, and he felt an impulse to run away, to turn off all the lights and be invisible, to hide in the darkness. Don't be absurd, he said to himself, grow up. But still he was holding his breath as she came up the stairs.

'Are you asleep, Mervyn?'

He was shocked to find that his heart was pounding. 'No, no. Waiting for you. How was your day?' God, he thought, can we find nothing else to ask each other?

She yawned. 'Like they all are.'

'No, I meant the lunch. Was it a success?'

She gave him a sharp look, and he felt a stab of

dislike for her, which he fought to suppress.

'Well, it was a lunch, you know. Seemed to go all right.' She went over to the wardrobe to hang up her jacket, and he felt strangely embarrassed.

'Fingers crossed, then,' he muttered, annoyed at the fawning tone he always seemed to acquire when he was with her.

She didn't answer, and he felt piqued. 'I'm going to sleep now,' he announced, trying to keep the irritation out of his tone. 'I take it you're going to look over your papers first?'

She turned suddenly and looked at him, and to his horror there appeared to be tears in her eyes. 'What is it, Isobel? What's happened?' he cried, bewildered and alarmed, his mind already racing through the possibilities. The lunch must have gone wrong, or perhaps Penningdale told her her chances were poor. But the sight of Isobel crying, something he sincerely could not recall ever having seen before, was so confusing that he could only sit up in shock, his whole body filled with a sense of disaster.

She was staring back at him, her eyes hot through a mist of tears.

'Do you love me?'

'What?' He was genuinely shocked. 'What? Of course I do!' He wondered why, when he really felt that he meant it, his words sounded so insincere.

She was still staring at him, but now her tears seemed closer to anger, and she looked at him with a sort of contempt.

'You don't, not really.'

'Do you love me?' He felt the question burst out of him, he could not contain himself. He felt himself to be on the brink of an enormous relief.

She was still looking at him, and he moved restlessly under her eyes. 'Isobel…'

'I don't know.'

'What?'

'I don't know.' She no longer seemed angry. Her tone was dull as she said, 'Oh, I don't know what any of it means any more, do you, Mervyn? I don't understand any of it.' She was moving towards the door, and in desperation he called out, 'Oh, Isobel, come back, we need to talk about this, please–'

'For God's sake, I don't mean anything by it, don't be so dramatic. Go to sleep.'

'I can't sleep now, I – come back, Isobel, please, I don't know what you mean, I...' His voice trailed away as he heard the door to her study close firmly. Anger welled up inside him, she could not do this, she had no right. She had to tell him what she meant, she could not say that about not knowing if she loved him and then retreat to her study as though nothing had happened. But she had, and even in the welter of his fury and his fear he knew that there was nothing to do. Very slowly, shaking a little, he turned out the light and lay for a long time, his confusion and his anguish beside him like companions in the consoling darkness.

Chapter Five – To Protect The Innocent

The sunlight filtered into the room and across his bed, gradually waking him from the light sleep into which he had fallen somewhere around three o'clock in the morning. He stirred a little, dreamily, but there was no need for realization to dawn. All through the night, all through his dreams, he had known what the morning would mean. He sat up suddenly, anticipation hammering at his heart. He felt as though he could not believe the day had finally arrived, that it was really, truly here. The last week had felt like a year. It had seemed to last so long that he had in some strange way come to feel that it really would last for ever, that Monday the ninth of March was not a real day, it was a fantasy, it would never arrive. But it had, and now it was here, and he would have to go down to the Crown Court in less than an hour from now and appear for the defence in the case of R. v Burns and Casey. His stomach lurched with excitement and nerves; he felt thrilled and appalled at the prospect before him.

The house was empty. Isobel had been in Newcastle for the past five days, on a family law case. She had not even come back for the weekend, only dropping in on Saturday afternoon to pick up some of her things, and as she had not rung him that morning, he had missed her, as he had chosen that moment to go to the supermarket. He had come back and seen that she had been in the house, and felt hurt and disturbed that she had not waited for him. But as the evening wore on he began to savour his solitude, and even worried a little that he was not more concerned. He knew that she was staying away not because of pressure of work, but because she was unhappy at home, unhappy with him, and he knew that he should do something about it, but he couldn't, it seemed beyond him. There seemed nothing to do but wait for whatever happened next, and this fatalism buoyed him through the loneliness and dread of a nervous Sunday.

Now that Monday was here at last he felt immediately better, he felt that he was back on dry land. He felt in control of things, masterful, and he vowed to himself that he would not let Hannah Casey get convicted, that he would take the fight to Marlowe and win it. I am a far better barrister than he is, he said to himself, as he buttoned his shirt with trembling hands.

**

Hannah knelt on the bathroom floor, hardly able to breathe. She wondered if she might be sick, and even wished she might, anything to end this terrible nervous churning in her stomach. She stood up, slowly, unsteadily, and gripped the basin with both hands. She tried to breathe slowly, in and out on a count of five, as a counsellor had once tried to show her in prison, and gradually she raised her head and looked at herself steadily in the mirror. Her skin was white and her eyes were wide with fright. I look terrible, she thought, I must be ill. Maybe I could get a doctor's note. But in her heart she knew she would have to go through with it, and that really she wanted to, she could not bear any more of this waiting.

She heard her father's heavy step on the landing, and the rasp of his breath. 'You all right in there, love? You having tummy trouble?'

'I'm fine,' she called, willing him to go away, the nausea coming back in a wave.

'There's some stuff in the kitchen, shall I get it for you?'

'I'll be all right, dad. It's just nerves.' She was desperate for him to go, to leave her alone, but some instinct of kind-heartedness meant that she could never reject him when he was in one of his pleasant moods. She knew that he richly deserved her contempt, her rejection, but it just would not come, and she did not force it. But she must, must keep him away from court. She had to go alone.

'I'm going to pop downstairs and iron myself a shirt,' he called. 'I want to look smart, don't want my little girl to be ashamed of me. You give me a shout if you need anything.'

She stared into the mirror, horrorstruck and dumbstruck, disorientated. She opened her mouth to protest, but she had no energy, she could not frame the words. A sense of inevitability swept over her; why had she thought that her not wanting something to happen meant it wouldn't? Things happened; sometimes they were things you wanted, sometimes – more often – they were things you didn't, but they happened, irrespective, and that was all there was to be said. She choked down the protests in her heart, resolutely.

'All right, dad.'

**

The morning was fine, with very bright early spring sunshine, and the air was crisp with a touch of warmth to it. Walkinshaw loved mornings like these, they seemed to clear his mind, and he felt almost as though he were in love with the day, as though it were one of those days upon which he would look back with nostalgia and a soft regret. He felt the newness of it all; the trial had not yet begun, no mistakes had been made, no unfortunate admissions, no false steps made at the leading of an insidious prosecutor. It was all there to be won or lost, clean, in front of him, like fresh snow. He knew this feeling of old, the strange, intangible excitement of the morning of a trial, and knew to distrust it, knew how easily it was tarnished. This time tomorrow things would feel very different, he knew that well. And first-day-of-a-trial excitement always had to be followed sooner or later by waiting-for-a-verdict excitement, which was not so much excitement as dread. Still, he could not help but feel thrilled, almost happy, as he parked in his usual place and went in through the familiar doors.

As he put his keys and phone in the metal detector tray, and heard the automatic doors close behind him, he was suddenly hit by the realization that this trial was different, this trial was not only Hannah's, but his as well. Her future was in his hands, or at least, the lawyer in him argued, partly so. There were variables he could not control - the prejudices that jury members might bring, the attitude of the judge, the tactics of the prosecution, and not least Hannah's own performance in the witness box – but, despite all that, ultimately, it was down to him. His conduct of this case was the only thing that stood between Hannah and a significant prison sentence. He might have expected to feel this as an intolerable burden, an unbearable pressure, but as he stood there in the court foyer it seemed to him to be a kind of privilege, a way of binding his life to hers even if they never met again. It seemed to him that an acquittal, if he could achieve it, would be a great and humble gift to offer her, which she could carry with her back out into the world. She could know that at the very least he had believed in her, had done his best for her.

'Mr. Walkinshaw!' Ratchett was wearing a slightly smarter suit than usual, and he seemed to have polished his shoes – not before time, thought Walkinshaw. 'The punter's here already with her dad, will you be ready to have a word in about ten minutes?' Even Ratchett seemed to be affected by the atmosphere; his usually booming voice was replaced by a hushed, cathedral whisper, which only served to intensify Walkinshaw's nerves.

'Yes, all right,' he murmured, abstractedly. 'I'll need a moment to have a word with Marlowe about the disclosure first, though. Can you tell them I'll be twenty minutes?'

'Right you are. There's no chance of him taking the plea today, I suppose?'

'No. Anyway, it's a CPS decision, and they're standing firm. I suppose they think they've enough to convict Burns, and there's a good chance they can get her as well.' He shuddered a little. 'If the evidence was weaker against Burns we might have got away with it. As it is, they'll say she must have known.' His heart was suddenly like lead; he felt as though he had only just appreciated all the difficulties, despite all the hours and hours he had spent on the case.

'Well, we'll have to say there's no must about it.' Ratchett gave his bullish grin, and Walkinshaw did his best to muster an answering smile. Perhaps Ratchett was not so bad after all, he must try to get on better with him.

Slowly he made his way to the robing room. He had a sense that it was going to be important today to pace himself, not to rush, not to do things more quickly than they needed to be done. He would have to go about things wisely, carefully.

'Mervyn, old chap, I'm prossing you. Any chance it'll crack? Got a manslaughter in Bradford next week, could do without this, to be perfectly frank with you.'

'We're not pleading to the being concerned. If you'll take possession I'm happy to have a word with her.'

Vernon Marlowe grimaced, screwing up his face fastidiously. He was a tiny, bird-like man, quick of gesture and quick of speech, with a fast, easily assumed bonhomie which Walkinshaw had learned to distrust.

'Ah, but Mervyn, how can I take possession? It makes no sense. Either she knew the stuff was in the house or she didn't. I can't take possession on that basis.'

I've known you take pleas to all sorts of things on far flimsier bases than that, thought Walkinshaw, but all he said was, 'Well, my instructions are she didn't. As far as we're concerned it's effective. Of course, I can't speak for Burns.'

Marlowe gave an elaborate sigh. 'No go there, I'm afraid. He's holding out too.'

'Dakers is for Burns, isn't he?'

'No, I hear he returned the brief. David Jennings is doing it.'

'Oh,' said Walkinshaw, surprised and relieved. 'I was led to believe,' he lowered his voice a little, 'I was led to believe that Burns would be willing to plead if you dropped it against Casey.'

'Dakers tell you that?'

'Yes.' The lie would do no real harm.

Marlowe gave a rather unpleasant chuckle. 'You boys love trying it on, don't you? Sorry, darling, either both of you plead or both of you stand trial. I'm not Father Christmas, you know. Our little friend Burnsy – as they call him - is no position to make demands, and he knows it. I've got more than enough to put him away.'

'But you've nothing much against my girl. Nothing solid.' Walkinshaw felt himself getting hot, and told himself sternly to calm down.

'She was in the house all the time, as I shall impress upon the jury. Is she deaf and blind, Mervyn? Is that your defence? Personally, I have little doubt that common sense will prevail. Excuse me.'

He flitted away down the corridor, leaving Walkinshaw standing baffled and furious. He had not really expected anything else, but somehow he felt angry with Marlowe, angry with the system, angry with the whole sordid business. He walked restlessly up and down the room, his feeling of well-being of only a few minutes ago completely shattered. He knew that he had a fight on his hands, and he had an unpleasant feeling that Marlowe was going to win it.

'Hello, Mervyn. You're my co-d, aren't you?' David Jennings came in the room, and began wearily to hang up his coat. 'What a load of bollocks, eh? What a load of total fucking bollocks.'

Walkinshaw, though he was familiar with Jennings and his blunt manner, was nevertheless a little taken aback.

'What do you mean?'

'All this pissing about. Of course they're fucking guilty. Can't you get yours to plead? I'm going to give mine the hard word. I should have been in chambers today, not like I haven't got enough to do. I shouldn't even be here, but bloody Dakers has to take a few days off, doesn't he? Some 'personal situation.'' Jennings made exaggerated apostrophe signs with his fingers. 'No notice or anything, like him, the cunt. The clerks are bloody pissed off, I can tell you.'

'What's Dakers' personal situation? Does anyone know?' asked Walkinshaw, intrigued, despite himself.

'Don't know. Don't fucking care. All I know is I drew the short straw and had to do this fish's nest.'

Walkinshaw grinned. Jennings' malapropisms were

legendary on circuit.

'Don't you mean mare's nest, David?'

'Whatever sort of nest it is. If you think I'm a happy camper, you're – you must be – well, you're bloody wrong. And to put the tin hat on things, that twat Marlowe is prossing us. Bloody fantastic.'

Jennings sat down heavily, his face crimson. His complexion was always a strange colour, and when he was out of the room there was sometimes speculation as to what could be causing its curious reddish-grey mottling. Added to this he had a heavy, pugnacious jaw and iron-grey hair. His face was framed by an incongruous pair of blue-rimmed spectacles, which he now took off and polished on the corner of his shirt. After a few seconds of vigorous rubbing he put them back on his face and blinked confusedly.

'I hate drugs cases, I really do.' He gave a heavy, self-pitying sigh, and, producing a greyish handkerchief, blew his nose loudly.

'I don't mind them,' Walkinshaw said, mildly. 'Better than fraud.'

Jennings grunted. 'I hate the bastards. Could do with some Crown briefs, be nice to be putting them away for a change, eh, wouldn't it? Be nice to be banging up the fucking little buggers for a change?' He leant across the table, puffing hard through an open mouth, and Walkinshaw got to his feet hastily.

'Back in a bit, David.'

'You off to see your girl?'

'Yes,' said Walkinshaw, feeling a sort of pleasurable embarrassment. 'But don't get your hopes up. It's going to be effective.'

Jennings' face went redder than ever. 'Why, for fuck's sake?' he burst out angrily. 'The little shits were well in on it. Come on, Mervyn, use your famous charm on her. You can talk her round.'

'Maybe I don't want to talk her round,' said Walkinshaw, smiling. 'I happen to think she was in the wrong place at the wrong time. I don't want to see her convicted of this.'

Jennings stared, then gave a discordant laugh. 'Nice one, mate. Wrong place at the wrong time, I like it. Can see that one going down well with old Rogers. Is she fit, then, this girl? Could at least do with something nice to look at if I have got to be stuck here 'til Wednesday. Trust you to get the girl, I get stuck with some twatty lad, fuck him. Can't wait to get out of this shithole.'

'Well, at least it's only listed for a couple of days,' said Walkinshaw, with a slight pang at his heart. 'See you later.'

'Are you not getting changed today, then?'

Walkinshaw looked down at himself in momentary bewilderment. He was still in his collar and tie.

'First time I've done that in years,' he murmured in embarrassment, 'forgotten.'

He got up and crossed to the mirror, untying his tie as he went, and then unfastening his collar. He looked around him for his bag, dark blue damask cotton, his initials embroidered in gold copperplate on the front. M. R. L. W. He loved it, loved the thick looping cord of the drawstring, loved the safe feeling that pulling it closed gave him. Maybe, too, he thought, I love a little the feeling of belonging that it gives me, the sense that I've been accepted into a still exclusive world. He reached into it and pulled out his wig tin. Oval shaped, black enamel, his name in gold Victorian slanting capitals. MERVYN R. L. WALKINSHAW ESQ.

The sight of his name gave him an odd unreal feeling. Is that really me? Surely that is the name of a man who knows what he's doing, a senior lawyer, an establishment figure, a man who not only plays by the rules but who plays a part in making them. That man isn't me, he thought, a little shaky again, as he opened it carefully and took out his wig, studs and collar. I am not that man. But the name on the wig tin looked back at him, uncompromisingly, until almost in irritation he pushed it back inside his bag.

**

Hannah sat, mute and pale, in a corner of the dark waiting room. She had been dreading crowds; frightened that the court would be packed with people who knew her, knew Danny, would crush round her with questions, and loud and cloying expressions of support. She hated that; the saccharine pity she received from the older women in her street. She recognized it as the outer shell of something much less palatable; the mob instinct, the lust for detail, for condemnation, and ultimately blood. She instinctively flinched away from the public forum in which so much of her life seemed to be played out; she longed for a privacy which life seemed determined to deny her. But she was lucky today; the lists were short, the waiting room next to empty, as she leant over her knees and tried to concentrate on something, anything, nothing. Burns had arrived, and came and sat near her, but not next to her. He seemed to understand by some sort of instinct that she wanted a ring of space around her today.

'Your dad not here?'

'In the canteen.'

'Oh.' She knew that he understood how she felt; there was no need to say any more. They sat, a few feet apart, but still together, and she felt his silent understanding and his sympathy, and was comforted by it.

**

Walkinshaw sat opposite her in the same small grey conference room that they had been in a week previously, but now the atmosphere was charged, real, the air seemed to be filled with electricity, and he felt that he could hardly speak, that he was close to tears.

'You know what's going to happen today?'

'Yes.'

He wondered if this was what falling in love meant; he felt vertiginous, terrified, but joyful; adrenaline seemed to be coursing through him. He felt as though he were on the brink of achieving a perfect understanding; that just outside his reach was something infinitely precious, a happiness of a magnitude he had not known existed.

'It's only police evidence, no Crown civilian witnesses. Shouldn't take long, should it, Mr. Walkinshaw? Then you'll be giving your evidence after lunch, if it all goes to plan.' Ratchett reached across the table and patted her elbow. 'Don't look so scared, Mr. Walkinshaw'll guide you through it. You'll be fine.'

She looked at Walkinshaw, questioningly. The whites of her eyes looked very white against her dark hazel irises, and were covered in a sheen of moisture, as though she had been crying. He felt his mind reeling away from him, and swallowed hard.

'Marlowe will have some tricky questions for you,' he forced himself to say, 'but if you just stick to your version of events he won't be able to do too much damage.'

'I might have to leave you two to it later, got a couple in at the nick this afternoon,' said Ratchett. 'There's a new young lad at the office, if he's not too busy I'll send him over to take notes. You'll be fine, love, you take it easy.'

There was silence for a moment or two. Walkinshaw looked at Hannah, wanting to meet her eyes. He felt anguished for her, he could almost feel her pain and her anxiety running through his own body. For a moment he was as frightened as though it were he that might go to prison. But with his fear he was conscious of a new resolution, a feeling of determination that surprised him. He was being given a chance, a chance to save her and himself, a chance to redeem everything. He felt that if he could win this trial a new life would begin. He must win it. Losing it was unthinkable.

'Penny for your thoughts!' said Ratchett. 'We're on in ten minutes, best get to it.'

He stood in the courtroom, next to Jennings, waiting the entrance of the judge. All his papers and files were ranged on the desk in front of him. At the other end of the desk, nearer the door, was Marlowe, his papers all neatly placed into ring-binder files, carefully annotated, relevant places marked with yellow post-it notes. Walkinshaw compared them to his messy bundles and felt discouraged, intimidated. His stomach was knotted with anxiety, and he felt that his courage was draining out of him, haemorrhaging away. The courtroom was a modern one which allowed in no natural light; the fluorescent lights overhead were disorientating; they made him feel as though it were night, not a quarter to eleven in the morning on a sunny day. He stared ahead of him at the enormous royal coat of arms over the judge's bench, and he felt faint with fear. He glanced over his shoulder at Hannah in the dock. She was hunched, rocking a little, her hands clasped in front of her face, but perhaps she sensed his glance, perhaps she felt something of all that he wanted that glance to convey, for she looked up at that moment and gave him a smile. He knew at that moment that he had to win, that he need not even try too hard, that it was all going to be all right. His heart was full with a sort of love, for her, for himself, for this life of his, for this amazing chance that life had given him.

The door from the judge's chambers suddenly opened, and he jumped with nerves. 'All stand!' shouted the usher, and the ten or so people in the court shambled wearily to their feet, then sat down again with relief the moment the judge did.

'Now, gentlemen.' Judge Pelham Rogers peered at them over his half-moon glasses. 'We have a trial, I understand. Anything we need to discuss before we empanel a jury?'

Walkinshaw looked at him, apprehension growing in his heart. He knew not to trust too much to Rogers' silky manner; due to the stiff sentences he habitually handed out he was known on circuit as 'Appeal 'im Pelham.' Not many of these appeals were successful, however; Rogers was too shrewd to make his sentences manifestly excessive, and the unfairnesses in his summings-ups of which so many defence barristers complained were comprised more of meaningful glances and gestures directed towards the jury box than any spoken words which could be recorded. Sarcasm was his favourite weapon, and he was known to reserve its use for defence barristers.

The jury panel shuffled in, reluctant and bewildered. Looking at them, Walkinshaw reflected, as he always did, that they seemed too ordinary to be true; they were all so uniformly normal that it seemed almost abnormal. They were mainly middle-aged; there were one or two younger ones who might have been students, others bore the unmistakeable stamp of the long-term unemployed. There was the mandatory severe and respectable-looking middle-aged woman. I hope we don't get her, thought Walkinshaw, she looks as though she'd want to hang all drug users. But who knows? There's no telling. I just have to do my best.

The jurors were sworn. Walkinshaw winced a little as some of them stumbled hopelessly through the oath, a couple of them having to repeat it. Rogers' jaw was already set in contempt, and his voice was crisp as he invited Marlowe to open the case. Walkinshaw leant back in his seat. He knew he needed to conserve his energy, and for a moment or two he concentrated on trying to relax his mind, trying to find the place within himself in which he could perform at his best. He was going to need to. He heard Marlowe, having at length gone through the names of all witnesses in the case, begin on the facts, and he sat up and took notice.

'Ladies and gentlemen, let me set out the facts of this case to you. Jonathan Burns and Hannah Casey appear before this court charged with the offence of being concerned in the supply of Class A drugs. The facts of the case are these. A man named Daniel Reynolds was arrested by the police as part of an undercover operation known as Operation Cleaver. This man, Reynolds, was living in a rented flat, a rented flat in...' He took a swift, covert glance at his notes. 'In Ransome Drive, which is on the Crosskeys Estate. Number ten, Ransome Drive. Also in residence at that address were the defendant Jonathan Burns, who is a friend and associate of Reynolds, and the defendant Hannah Casey, who was at the relevant time the- er- the girlfriend, or partner, of Daniel Reynolds. When the police searched the flat upon the arrest of Reynolds, they found a considerable quantity of diamorphine, or heroin, hidden in a large cupboard in one of the bedrooms. The bedroom, in fact, of Reynolds himself, and which he was wont to share' - Marlowe's voice was cold with disapproval - 'with the defendant Casey.

The heroin was valued by police officers expert in such matters as having a street value of in excess of five hundred and eighty pounds.' Walkinshaw shifted restlessly. What did he mean, in excess of? It had been valued at five hundred and eighty pounds exactly. He must make that point, although he knew it was really of no significance.

'Five hundred and eighty pounds.' Marlowe stopped and looked hard at the jury. 'Five hundred and eighty pounds worth of heroin, in individual wraps. By anyone's standards, a very large amount. When examined, the fingerprints of Jonathan Burns were found on several of these wraps. He was arrested and interviewed. At first he denied any knowledge of the heroin, but when confronted with the evidence of his fingerprints he asserted that he had handled them, as they were there for his and Reynolds's personal use.' His voice dripped with contempt, and he looked up sharply at the jury, as though to make sure that they understood his tone. They looked back at him, with blank, guilty faces, like a class of slow pupils at a quick-tempered teacher. 'I should make it clear that all three are or have been at some point addicted to heroin. The defendant Casey was then interviewed. She also denied any knowledge of the drugs, claiming that the cupboard and its contents were entirely the province of Reynolds, and that she had nothing to do with it. However, upon examination of the cupboard a partial fingerprint which matched that of Casey was found upon the handle.'

Walkinshaw raised his head sharply at this and looked straight at the jury, with a stare of defiant meaning. This is the best they have against her! A smudged fingerprint on a cupboard handle! He looked disdainfully at Marlowe, and then back at the jury. They looked back at him with expressions of confused boredom. A bald, overweight man at the back had already lost all interest and was busily engaged in picking his ear. One of the students in the front row looked at Walkinshaw with interest, though, and, he hoped, understanding. She was about twenty, about Hannah's age, thought Walkinshaw with a pang, and he looked at the girl with a sort of hope dawning in his heart.

'You may be wondering why the man Reynolds is not here to stand trial with the other two. The explanation is a simple one, members of the jury. Reynolds – or Powers, to use the name which he adopted at that time – pleaded guilty to all the charges he faced, including some unconnected to this matter, and was sentenced to a total of forty two months, which as you will know is three and a half years imprisonment.'

Walkinshaw sat, hot with horror and shock, his brain numb, unable to take it in. Marlowe's voice rolled on, but he did not hear a word. Reynolds – or Powers! How could it be? How could he not have known, how could he not have realized? He plunged furiously into his memory, trying to recall every detail he possibly could of the Powers case. He remembered that there had been two other people involved in the intent to supply charge, but no names had been given, and there had been no need for him to know. One of those two other people had been Hannah. And Ransome Drive! Why had that address not stirred his memory? Well, it was an address that cropped up fairly frequently on court papers. But still, how was this possible? And Hannah – he could not resist turning round to look at her again – Hannah had been his girlfriend, Hannah had slept with him in that fateful bedroom, with the cupboard full of heroin looking on. What did it all mean? And why did he care? Why did his heart hurt so much, thinking of it? What was Powers to him? What, for that matter, was Hannah to him? After tomorrow, whatever happened, he need never see her again. The thought wrenched his heart, and flooded him with a sense of abandonment. He breathed hard, and held on to the table in front of him. Powers! It couldn't be. Perhaps he had misheard. With hope in his heart he reached for the bundle of additional disclosure which he had been given that morning, and turned to the previous convictions of the co-accused, Daniel Reynolds. With his heart thumping in his chest, he turned to the first page. And there it was. Daniel James Reynolds. Alias names: Daniel James Powers. How could he have been so stupid? He should have known that a change of surname was more than likely, in fact, amongst a lot of his clients, it was more common than not. So what did this mean, for him, for Hannah? It means, he told himself fiercely, that you continue to do what you were going to do, that you go ahead and win this trial. And whatever happens after that happens.

He raised his head. Marlowe was calling his first witness.

DC Glover walked confidently into the witness box, with the air of a man who had done this countless times before. He took the oath glibly, fluently, then turned to the judge and said 'Detective Constable Michael Glover, 3209, Dursfield Police Station.'

Walkinshaw winced; he hated that habit of police officers, it always grated on him. Ordinary witnesses waited to be asked who they were. He looked at DC Glover carefully, trying to size him up. He was a stocky, shaven headed man in the late thirties, with an outward confidence, almost a cockiness in his manner. His small eyes, however, darted ceaselessly around the courtroom, and Walkinshaw thought he saw a sheen of sweat across his upper lip. He waited, biding his time as Marlowe ploughed through his routine questions, then launched into the reading of the police interviews.

'I shall read the part of Jonathan Burns,' announced Marlowe, grandly. 'Perhaps you would be so kind as to read your own part, officer?'

Walkinshaw had seen this done countless times, had even done it himself on the odd occasion that he had had to do a prosecution brief, but it never failed to strike him as utterly absurd and somehow shameful.

'Did you at any time handle the drugs?' Glover's delivery was wooden; he sounded artificial, even though he was reading his own words. You'll never make an actor, sonny, thought Walkinshaw, and smiled slightly. Glover seemed aware of this, and gave him a hard stare. There seemed already to be an enmity between them.

'It's like I fucking told you a thousand times.' Marlowe's voice hovered uncertainly between his own mellifluous tones and what presumably he imagined a drug user from the streets of Sheffield to sound like; the result should have been amusing, but was instead merely depressing, and somehow sordid, reflected Walkinshaw. Somehow it all seemed like a rather distasteful charade, and he felt an intense pity for Jonathan Burns, whose words, spoken in anger and frustration on a cold, dark night in a Sheffield police station, were now being read aloud, coldly and scornfully, to a room full of hostile strangers, by a man whom he did not know.

The little drama dragged on, pitifully. The jurors were plainly bored; Walkinshaw felt oppressed, and began to long for a coffee break. He shifted uncomfortably on the bench, nerves rising in him again. Then at last the two players were on to the second interview, that of Hannah Casey. Walkinshaw felt sick inside at the thought of Marlowe reading her words aloud; he felt his stomach tense with anger, and it was all he could do to just sit there as Marlowe and Glover floundered their way through the transcript together. There were places in the interview where Hannah had stammered, and cried a little; but Marlowe read her words with a defiant bravado, and Walkinshaw wanted to hit him.

At last it was over, and Jennings lumbered to his feet to cross-examine.

'Just a few quick questions, officer, on behalf of Burns.' Jennings waved a hand in the direction of the dock, with an air of embarrassment, almost of apology. You and I both know I've got to go through the motions, it seemed to say, don't hold it against me. 'When you informed him that you found his fingerprints on the wraps of heroin, he admitted handling them, didn't he?'

'He had to,' said Glover, smartly, to titters from one or two of the jury, quickly silenced by a stare from the bench.

'No,' said Jennings, nettled, 'what I mean is, he put his hands up behind his head and took it on the chin,' – Walkinshaw groaned inwardly – 'he took it on the neck – I mean he put his neck on the block –'

'I haven't an idea what you mean, I'm afraid, Mr. Jennings,' cut in Rogers sharply, 'and I'm sure the jury haven't either. What point exactly are you trying to make?'

'Your honour,' blundered Jennings, 'your honour, the point that I'm trying to make is that he did admit to handling the drugs.'

'Yes,' said Rogers, icily, 'after his fingerprints were found all over them.'

'Not all over them, your honour, not all over them, on ten of the wraps.'

Rogers shrugged expressively in the direction of the jury box. 'Go on, Mr. Jennings.'

'That's right, isn't it, officer?'

'That's right, yes.' Glover looked down pityingly at Jennings, who was now purple in the face and sweating heavily.

'But he said that he had handled them only because he was a heroin addict himself?'

'Yes.'

'And that his friend, Daniel Casey – Daniel Reynolds, I mean – had let him have them in return for work he'd done for him – for Reynolds, I mean?'

Rogers sighed heavily, and folded his arms. 'Mr. Jennings, why are you asking the officer all this? The jury has had the opportunity to hear everything that Mr. Burns said in interview. Why reiterate it?'

'Because... because, your honour, because.... I want to make the point that there've been a lot of fingers in the soup, too many cooks have spoiled the pie. What I mean is,' he added hastily, as Rogers' brow darkened in anger, 'that it wasn't my client who was the monkey, he was the organ grinder, I mean the other way round, he just did what he was told, he was an addict–'

'Mr. Jennings, you will have the opportunity to make such submissions in your closing speech. This, as you appear to be a novice in the courtroom, is not your closing speech. If you have no appropriate questions to ask the witness, then may I suggest you resume your seat.'

'One more question, your honour.' Jennings looked up apprehensively at Rogers, who gave the smallest of nods and then looked away in disgust.

'Daniel Reynolds has a lot of convictions for drugs offences, doesn't he?' said Jennings in a rush.

'He has a considerable number, yes.'

'Thank you, officer. No more questions.' The bench groaned as Jennings' weight dropped down heavily upon it. Walkinshaw looked at him sympathetically. 'Not too good,' he said in an undertone. Jennings' face was almost black with rage and humiliation. 'Fucking twat!' he hissed in fury, then looked around him in terror lest anyone might have heard.

Walkinshaw got to his feet, slowly, gravely. He looked hard at Glover, stern-faced. You might have had fun and games with Jennings, he meant the look to say, but I'm a different proposition. Gradually the smirk disappeared from Glover's face, and he shot a glance in the direction of the jury to reassure himself.

Walkinshaw waited a few seconds, to allow Glover's nerves to reassert themselves again. Then, as Glover shuffled from one foot to the other and ran a finger round the inside of his collar, he began.

'Detective Constable Glover. As a police officer, and vested by the state with powers far beyond those of ordinary citizens, you find yourself in a position of grave responsibility, do you not?'

Glover looked a little startled. 'Yes, I suppose. Yes.'

'And that responsibility carries with it a duty to protect the innocent which is as sacred as – more sacred than – your duty to convict the guilty?'

Glover stared hard, seeming to sense a trap. It was, however, a question to which there could be only one answer.

'Yes.'

Walkinshaw looked down at his papers for a moment. 'A little while ago, when you were answering questions from my learned friend,' he indicated Marlowe, 'you told us what you said when you arrested Miss Casey. Would you mind repeating that, please?

'The caution?'

'What you said.'

'I said,' Glover was uneasy now, 'I said 'you do not have to say anything, but it may harm your defence if you fail to mention when questioned anything you may rely upon in court. Anything you do say may be given in evidence.'

'And then you asked Miss Casey if she understood.'

'I don't know what you're getting at.'.

'Please answer the question.'

I did, yes.'

'So may I now ask you to have a look at page five of the interview. Can a copy be given to the witness, please.'

There was a brief and awkward pause while the usher fussed around with papers, and then brought a copy across to Glover, who stood there, irritated and perturbed.

'Where am I looking?'

'Page five, about ten lines down. You ask her 'Do you understand how serious this is?' and she replies, 'I don't know, I don't understand any of it.' The transcript then says 'unintelligible'. Is that because she was in tears at this point?'

'I can't remember.'

'You can't remember?'

'I interview a lot of people, some of them get upset.'

And do a lot of people say, 'I don't understand any of it?''

Glover stared at him sullenly. 'Yeah, some do.'

'And when Miss Casey said to you, 'I don't understand any of it,' what did you take that to mean?'

Glover shrugged slightly. 'That she was saying she didn't know how the drugs got there.'

'You didn't think she meant that she didn't understand the situation? After all, that was your question.'

'She had a solicitor.'

Rogers cut in, a weary voice from the bench. 'Mr. Walkinshaw, where are we going with all this? Your client denied everything in interview.'

'Your honour, I'm setting the scene, that's all.' He gave his blandest smile, and Rogers shrugged again, and looked ostentatiously at his watch, and then at the jury.

'So you took it that Miss Casey did understand the situation, despite the fact that she told you explicitly that she didn't, and despite the fact that she was visibly distressed?'

'She was all right. People do get upset, like I say.'

'Then, a couple of lines further down the page, Mr. Caldwell asks you to suspend the interview to give her a moment to compose herself. You refuse.'

'We were under time pressures, we'd only just started.'

'At this point in time, Miss Casey is only a suspect, isn't she?'

'She was under arrest.'

'She was not convicted of anything. Legally, she was innocent. Remind us again, officer, of what you said earlier regarding your duty to protect the innocent.'

Glover was silent, simmering with anger.

'What time was this interview conducted?' Walkinshaw looked up sharply at Glover, whose eyes flicked away.

'Twenty past twelve.'

'Twenty past noon, or twenty past midnight?'

'Twenty past midnight.'

'Thank you, officer. No further questions.'

'You did well with the copper,' said Ratchett, a little grudgingly, as they left court for the lunch adjournment.

'Bricks without straw,' said Walkinshaw, stretching.

His mind was already racing on to the afternoon that lay ahead, and all the potential pitfalls it contained.

'Did well, though. Unlike poor old Jennings, what a disaster. He must have broad shoulders.'

'We all have to take the heat sometimes. He was close to getting riled with me.'

He was suddenly struck with a sense of the futility of it all. What had he really achieved with Glover? Would the jury understand what he wanted them to understand, would they see Hannah as he saw her, as he wanted them to see her? Who knew? He felt a sort of exhaustion as he thought of all the factors that were beyond his control; the randomness of it all was terrifying. And yet he had to try to change that little part of it that he could change, for Hannah's sake, and for his own.

**

Hannah sat alone in the cafeteria, her mind racing through the morning and everything that had happened. Her heart was pounding; she felt dismayed and joyous, horrified and wildly excited. She felt that she would never be able to make sense of what was happening to her, never be able to understand it, but perhaps understanding it was not what mattered. It was happening, and nothing could take it away from her. A prison sentence seemed a small price to pay for the privilege of these moments in court with him, with him as her barrister, her shield against the world. She saw her father's heavy figure looming towards her, and she waited for the fear to come, but she felt nothing, a vague dislike perhaps, but nothing that could really disturb her. This must be love, she thought, and to think I lived through twenty years and never felt it, never understood it, however did I survive? Tears of happiness pricked her eyes. I will never forget this day, she vowed to herself, I will never forget this feeling, however long I live.

**

Walkinshaw felt he had to get out of the building, had to get right away and clear his head, try to make sense of it all, try to get himself into some sort of fit state for the afternoon. He went and sat on a bench just outside the court, facing the city square, watching people go by, and marveling at their unconcern. These people had no idea who he was, what he was, they did not even know that Hannah Casey existed. He pitied them for it. His thoughts turned again to the afternoon ahead. How would it go? He felt breathless, agonized. He would take Hannah through her examination in chief, but then he would have no choice but to abandon her to Marlowe's cross-examination, and he churned with apprehension at the thought. Still, he had a sort of faith in her. There was something at her very core which was untouchable, which even Marlowe would not be able to disturb. He felt that in some way it would be all right, it would all fall into place, even as his stomach growled with nervous indigestion. He took a few bites of his sandwich, but felt unable to face the rest of it, and threw it to the pigeons circling his feet. He felt a sort of sweetness around his heart as he looked at them, and he realized that he would look back on this day in the future with a sense of lost purity, of innocence gone. Nothing would ever be the same. He wished he could hold on to this day forever, this feeling, this excitement, this love, this not knowing what would happen. He had a sense of a sort of sacredness, and something of the solemnity he had felt when he had seen Hannah run across the road returned to him. He must preserve this feeling, it would protect him in the years to come.

Chapter Six – Domestic Bliss

Norman Tombs sat at his small wooden desk, idly tracing the ring made by a coffee cup with his forefinger. He had been at Caldwell's for a month now, and already he was accustomed to the routine, the occasional excitement which quickly yielded to boredom, a boredom which lasted for hours. He had learned, too, how to disguise inactivity, how to look busy when someone came into the room unexpectedly, how to read a piece of paper as slowly as possible. Of course, there was not really enough for him to do. Ratchett talked of training him to do police station attendance, but he had no real interest in that. He felt a great contempt for all of Caldwell's clients, and felt ashamed to be associated with them, to be seen to be helping them. He was a barrister. He had been called to the bar. He did not want to spend his days with prostitutes and drug addicts, with benefit cheats and paedophiles. He dreamed of the purity of academic civil law; it seemed to exist on a higher level, it shone above him, drawing him on. One day he would arrive, it would happen, and then he would be at smart, select little parties, a glass of champagne in his hand, telling amusing little anecdotes about his very brief time in a firm of criminal solicitors in Sheffield. So nice, he would say, so nice to be in a world where one's clients do not all have hepatitis, and there would be warm, amused laughter, he would be clapped on the back by a leading civil silk, and there would be girls, educated, classy girls, who would look invitingly at him, and indicate a willingness to go home with him. But at that point his imagination failed him, and he sat staring into space, lost to the world around him. These daydreams became more real, more layered, complicated even; he began to lose himself in them, so that when the telephone rang shrilly in his ear he thought for a moment that it must be Lucinda, Lord Wynne-Holt's daughter, who had given him such a meaning look that night of the organ recital at the Inner Temple church.

It was not Lucinda Wynne-Holt. It was John Ratchett. 'I'm down the nick in half an hour, son. Casey's effective at Crown, I need you to get down there and take a few notes. Nothing much happening at the office, is there?'

'Well...' Tombs hated going to the Crown court. He disliked the clients, he disliked the atmosphere, and he hated seeing the barristers, especially the ones from the chambers which had rejected him.

'You can leave Linda in charge. Anyway, Dennis'll be back from the Mags in an hour or so, he can hold the fort. Get moving, mate. I need to you do some Legal Aid forms with the punter before it starts again this afternoon.'

'Which one is Casey? The benefit fraud?'

'No, the one I told you about. Being concerned, pretty little thing, prostitute. Danny Reynolds's ex.'

'All right.' Tombs put the phone down and got up slowly, reluctantly. He had the beginnings of a headache, and all his grievances came back over him in a rush. 'Get moving, mate!' Who did he think he was talking to? My luck will change, I will make it change, he said to himself, cold with anger as he zipped up his anorak.

Ratchett was sitting waiting for him in the foyer. 'Here he is! Here he is, love, this is Norman, he'll be taking notes for me this afternoon, hopefully I'll be back tomorrow. He's got a couple of forms to do with you now, haven't you, Norman? Well, see you later, don't worry, it'll be fine. Be good.' And he was off through the doors, leaving Tombs alone with the girl.

He looked at her, his skin crawling with desire and disgust. She was beautiful, he decided, beautiful but corrupt, sinful, she did disgusting things, not just drugs, men, she slept with men for money. He stared at her, his pale eyes magnified behind his thick glasses, and she shifted a little, uncomfortably.

'Did you want to do these forms?'

She spoke to him like the others, she was rude, she was cruel, she had that off-hand manner. She was stepping away from him, moving back, moving as far away from him as she could, and fury welled up in him. Did she not know who she was? Did she not know what she was? She's a whore, he said to himself, she's a dirty whore, a common prostitute. He trembled, his whole mind sickened with the horror and the pleasure of it all. She does things to men for money. He felt as though a world was opening up before his eyes, a strange, frightening, exciting world, full of hidden sexual pleasures he had never known, had never known existed. His eyes gleamed and he felt the palms of his hands moisten.

'Yes.' He had trouble looking at her face; he stared instead at her breasts, her hips, her thighs, and wondered what it was she did, and how much it cost.

'Your full name.' The pen slipped in his clammy fingers; he could hardly form the letters.

'Hannah Marie Casey.'

'Your date of birth.' Still he could not look up at her.

'The twelfth of April, nineteen eighty eight.'

She was nearly twenty-one, younger than him, two years younger than him. And all those things that she knew, and had done.

'Do you work?'

'No.'

'In receipt of benefit?' She would be, he decided,

she was just the sort to live off the state, while she went on with her shameless, wanton behaviour.

'No. I just got out of prison. I live with my dad.' She wouldn't look at him, and he felt furious with her, felt an overwhelming desire to hurt her, to punish her, to make her take notice of him, to do something to her that would mean she never forgot him, ever.

'Sign your name here, on the back.' He handed her his pen, which she took with some reluctance. Perhaps she can't write her name, he thought with malicious pleasure, perhaps she will have to put an 'X'. But she could; she signed her name fluently, in a graceful looping hand, and handed the pen back to him, already rising to go. He could not let her.

'How much?' he muttered, almost inaudibly. He felt as though his whole body was on fire.

'What?' She stared at him, uncomprehending, and he felt he hated her.

'How much?'

'I said, I don't earn anything.'

'I mean, how much for what you do. Sex.' He felt that he was going to die. He stared at a dark blotch on the carpet, his eyes fixed on it, his whole body shaking.

She looked back at him, wide-eyed, astounded. Then, without a word, she turned and walked away.

He sat like a statue for a few minutes, his mind reeling with the horror of what he had done. What if she told someone? He was furious, ashamed, and, above all, humiliated. Turned down by a prostitute! No one was turned down by a prostitute. The court tannoy broke in on his thoughts. 'The Crown against Burns and Casey, Court Four. Court Number Four, Burns and Casey.' Automatically he got up, picked up his notebook, fumbled for his biro. He would have to go in there, sit in front of her, sit there taking notes of all the sordid details of her disgusting, drug-addled little life. They're disgusting, they're like animals, he said to himself, I don't know what came over me. It's stress.

He made his way to the top of the stairs. Mervyn Walkinshaw, in wig and gown, was already on his way to Court Four, and with him was her, that girl, Hannah, and as they got to the door of the court she turned to him, looked up into his face, and smiled.

**

She sat in the dock, staring blankly through the plastic screen, and abandoned herself to the unreality of it all. Beyond the screen she saw them, murmuring, coughing, talking softly to each other, a whole room, full of people that live in it, live in it day after day, only the people in here change, come and go, come in the front and leave through the back, in handcuffs, maybe shouting, swearing, crying, screaming, maybe silent and shaking, maybe about to die, but this room doesn't change, the people in it don't change, it stays the same for ever. It takes no notice. It takes no notice of me. She felt panic well up inside her for a moment, and with a great effort she choked it back down. She breathed hard, the fear still running like electricity through her, the contentment of an hour ago vanished, obliterated, forgotten, as meaningless and as hard to recall as a heatwave on a winter's day. It all seemed unreal, she seemed unreal, and she imagined herself dead, she imagined the room still there, still carrying on its business, the judge, the lawyers, the prison officers, all getting up in the morning, complaining, reading their papers, eating their lunches, standing around talking in low voices to each other, just as they were doing now, and the thought seared her with horror. Don't think like that, she told herself, you're not going to die. And if you did, you can't expect the world to stop; of course there will still be other people living their lives, the shops will still be open, there'll still be traffic in the street. But she could not shake off the terror of that thought, and she felt herself to be something utterly ephemeral, something that could barely be said to have existed at all.

'Your honour, I would like to call the defendant Hannah Casey.' She felt surprised, though she had been told that her evidence was next; for a wild moment her case, this trial of hers, seemed irrelevant, trivial, she felt a sort of desperate amusement at all the solemn faces, all the costumes, and an embarrassment that it was all because of her and Jonathan. She felt she wanted to say that it was all a mistake, that they shouldn't bother about it, she wasn't worth it, she didn't matter enough to go through all this. Again her head span with a feeling of meaninglessness as she made her way, in a sort of trance, to the witness box, and stood with the bible in her hand, her mind a blank. She looked at the jury members, sitting in their box not more than twenty feet away from her, but they seemed to be miles away, remote, and she felt a sort of wild anxiety at the idea that they would be able to hear her, to understand what she might say.

He was on his feet now, he was standing up to ask her questions, and she saw the concentration and the concern on his face and felt sorry for him, felt a sort of obscure love. She wanted to tell him not to worry, that whatever happened to her she would survive it or she would not, she would live or she would die, those were the rules, that was how it was. Still she felt a prickle of alarm at the tensity in his voice.

'In October last year, you were in a relationship with Daniel Reynolds?'

'Yes.' She was suddenly gripped with stage fright,

and felt anxious that she might be sick. The eyes of the jurors seemed to be boring into her. She felt her whole body flood with heat, and raised a hand to her mouth, shaking.

'And are you still in a relationship with him?'

Her mind was dead, she was going mad, she couldn't answer these questions, any of them, she had to go, this was terrible. She pressed her hand hard over her mouth, doubling over a little.

'Miss Casey!' She looked up and saw the judge's face, a little blurred, peering down at her. His expression appeared kindly and she wanted badly to believe that it was. 'Are you unwell?'

She felt that she was fighting for life, fighting for breath. 'I want,' tears were streaming down her face now, 'I want to start again.'

The judge sighed heavily and puffed out his cheeks. 'We can't 'start again', I'm afraid. However, I will rise for ten minutes to give you a chance to collect yourself.'

She looked up; she was vaguely aware of a mist of faces, a haze of voices. The lights overhead were unbearably bright. She saw Walkinshaw's face, concerned, turning and whispering something to the man sitting next to him, Burnsy's barrister, and she felt an intense curiosity to know what it was. She felt her fear recede a little, her heart seemed to slow down, and she raised her head and looked around her, simulating a boldness. She caught the eye of her father in the public gallery, and he gave her a pitying look, which angered her so that in her anger she forgot her fear for a moment. She drained her plastic cup of water and crushed it in her hands; she would show him.

It was the prosecution's turn now. As Walkinshaw sat down, reluctantly, she felt abandoned, terrified, wanted to beg him not to stop, to carry on with his questions for the rest of the day. But there was nothing more to ask.

The little man rose to his feet, with an air of importance. She was suddenly afraid that nerves would make her giggle; she bit the inside of her cheek, knowing that the thought, once planted in her mind, could very easily take control. Marlowe seemed to her an absurd figure, absurd and yet terrible. She felt a lurch of that terror; suddenly she imagined him as a figure of death, a character from a horror film. She felt his power, as direct as a knife thrust, from across the ten feet that separated them.

'You shared a bedroom with this man, this man Reynolds. Or Powers.'

'Yes.' She hated talking about it, everyone seemed to want to know about that shared bedroom. She blundered on. 'He was Powers then. He fell out with his stepdad, his stepdad got done for beating up his mum, so Danny went back to his real dad's name.'

Marlowe held up a hand; she found herself staring, fascinated, at his white, oddly long fingers. 'Please. We are not here to discuss your former paramour's complicated nomenclature and the history thereof, fascinating though it no doubt is. You shared a bedroom with him.'

'For two weeks.'

'For the two weeks preceding his arrest.'

'Yes.' Her mind felt numb again. Don't let the panic come back, don't let it. Keep it together. She hardly cared about the answers she was giving. She felt she would gladly have confessed to multiple murders if it would get her out of the witness box and away from this horrifying, terrifying little man.

'You knew that he kept drugs on the premises?'

'I knew there were some in the house.'

'Where did he keep these drugs? The ones you admit to having seen?'

She ignored the sarcasm. 'On the kitchen table, often. Wherever he was using them. Or in pockets and things. No particular place.'

'And the cabinet in the bedroom?'

'The what?'

Marlowe gave a heavy sigh, which said plainly, 'I am dealing with the sort of idiot who doesn't know what a cabinet is.' He shuffled his papers, then looked up sharply. 'The cabinet. The cupboard, if you will. What did you think that he kept in there?'

'I didn't know. It was always locked.'

'It was always locked. Did you not ask what was in this mysterious cupboard? Did not your feminine curiosity get the better of you?'

'No.'

'No? You must have wondered, surely, what was so secret that it had to kept under lock and key? Surely you must have wondered what your lover was keeping in that cupboard? Old love letters, perhaps? Or-'

She interrupted him, restively. 'I never really noticed the cupboard.'

'Really? Really? A moment ago you told us it was always locked. You must have noticed it if you noticed that.'

'I noticed it in that I knew it was there and I knew it was locked. But it never really made any impression on me. I had a lot on my mind then, I wasn't in the mood to start worrying about cupboards.'

'No,' said Marlowe drily. 'So, when you heard that a large quantity of drugs was found in this cupboard, you must have been utterly horrified, must you not?

'Sorry?'

'Well, here you are, living in domestic bliss with your lover and his friend –'

'It wasn't bliss. I never said it was bliss.'
'Living a peaceful life, shall we say – '
'It wasn't that, either.'
'You will please let me finish a question, Miss Casey. There you are, living with your lover and his friend, quite happy, thinking that everything was above board, that there were no nasty secrets, no skeletons in any cupboards, or drugs in any cupboards, if you'll excuse me,' he gave a quick smirk in the direction of the jury, 'and lo and behold! you find that all this time a serious offence has been in the process of being committed under your very nose! You must have been really shocked.'

'No.'

'No?' Marlowe betrayed his surprise at this answer momentarily, then quickly recovered his poise. 'Why not?'

She passed a hand over her forehead. She suddenly felt indescribably weary, and very old. 'Nothing Danny did surprised me. It wouldn't have surprised me if he'd killed someone.'

**

It was time to go home, nearly a quarter to five, late by court standards. Night was beginning to fall, the sky outside the robing room windows was streaked with pink as the sun set. The cleaners had already begun, and the faint familiar smell of disinfectant was in the air as he tied his tie, feeling close to tears, feeling an indescribable sort of anxious happiness. He had kept them talking afterwards, just for ten minutes, just to give Marlowe and Jennings a head start so that he wouldn't have to endure their chatter as he got changed. His head whirled with all the sensations of the day; he felt it would take him years to recall everything, to think about it, savour it, come to understand it properly. But there was something eating away at the back of his mind, something which he knew he would have to face. Should he have resigned the brief as soon as he knew that Powers was Hannah's boyfriend? Had he placed himself in a false position? He felt genuinely unsure. Of course, he had wanted to carry on with the trial. He had to carry on with the trial. He couldn't possibly abandon her now. And it was too late to say anything. No, he decided, press on and keep your mouth shut. If all else fails, I shall act as surprised as everyone else and say I genuinely had no idea, I can't be expected to remember every single case that comes before me. It's just one of those funny little coincidences, that's all. For all that, he was a little surprised that he was not more worried, he who was always so cautious, so careful. It doesn't matter, he told himself, it really doesn't matter. And he felt that it really didn't, it was really unimportant, except that in some way it made what he was doing for Hannah even sweeter, it gave him a pleasant sense of complicity with her, they were both rule-breakers, both kept secrets, both lived lives that might not bear scrutiny but that were real, vital, faceted.

He felt a sting of guilt as he realized that he had not thought about Isobel all day. The minute I get in I'll ring her, he said to himself, if she's not home before me. She must come home tonight, staying away yet again would be ridiculous. He felt a sort of foreboding, but dismissed it instantly. Today has been a good day, he thought, I was good, Hannah was good, Marlowe couldn't do a thing with her, not really. This has been a good day, not too many of those lately. Please God, let Isobel be in a good mood, let her have got over whatever has been making her so cold lately. He found himself wondering idly whether he had been happier without her, and then, horrified at himself, told himself firmly that of course he hadn't, that he had been lonely and miserable. Without this trial to distract him, he would have found it intolerable. He realized suddenly that that last thought was true, that he had been clinging on to the trial, using it as a sort of refuge, squeezing out of it every last moment of excitement and pleasure, and that without it – and it would finish tomorrow – he would be bereft. And, more than that, he would be forced to face his own life, his own problems. And it was problematic, he was not such an ostrich as to fail to see that. Things would have to put right between himself and Isobel, they couldn't go on as they had been. He felt almost a physical chill, a deep uneasiness, as he thought about it. Suddenly it all flooded to the forefront of his mind, and he felt desperate to sort it all out, to ease his mind, to be rid of it. He thought of the weekend, the whole weekend, that he had idled away, when he could have been demanding to speak to her, demanding to resolve things once and for all. How had he spent those days, drifting about in idle daydreams, while his marriage slid inexorably away from him? I've been an idiot, he thought, I should have faced up to this months ago.

As he drove up to the house, the empty drive gave him a shock of uneasiness, and of irritation. He glanced at the dashboard clock. Twenty past five. She might be still at chambers. Still, he had hoped to find her in, he was getting tired of these lonely, dark evenings. The air was harsh, and he found himself shivering as he fumbled for his key, suddenly struck by a strange loneliness. He hated this, coming home to an empty house, even though he had had to get used to it lately. He found himself feeling increasingly abandoned, increasingly anxious, in an empty house, and sometimes had to choke down feelings of panic. Sometimes the emptiness made him think of some sort of lurking danger, at other times it gave him uncomfortable thoughts of death; he would imagine his own death, and wonder if he was fated to die alone, or whether each hour spent alone was an hour taken off his life span, as though during those hours he did not really live at all.

He went into the hall, throwing down his bags and papers on the floor, and fumbled for the light switch. Isobel, who was fiercely economical, refused to allow him to leave any lights on in the morning for his return home, so each winter night he had to fumble around in the darkness for the switch. But tonight he couldn't seem to find it, and fear and anger welled up in him until he wanted to punch the wall. 'Where the fuck is it?' he said, loudly and uncharacteristically, groping along the side of the wall, and his voice frightened him in the darkness. He imagined someone hiding up the stairs, listening to him, and for a moment he shuddered in horror at the idea of a voice answering him, in cool, menacing tones, sliding down the staircase, a faceless, nameless figure, getting closer and closer, and he, frozen there, powerless to move, as the figure got closer.... and closer....

He breathed a sigh of relief. His fingers had finally found the switch, and light flooded the hall. He sat down on the floor for a moment, feeling unaccountably weak and again close to tears. He felt suddenly that he hated the house, that he had never had a moment's real happiness there, and that the house hated him, and was somehow taking its revenge on him. 'I hate you,' he muttered under his breath, looking up at the ceiling and breathing hard, and then he wondered what was the matter with him, why he was getting himself into a frenzy about nothing, about not being able to find a light switch. He looked up at the staircase in sudden fear. It seemed to be implacable, cold, terrifying, and he felt suddenly afraid, fearful that the house had heard what he had said, and would take its revenge, it would kill him in the night somehow, it wouldn't let him out alive. For God's sake, he said to himself furiously, stop this, you're going mad, this is insanity, houses don't kill people. He went into the kitchen, switching on all the lights as he went, and held his head under the cold tap for a second or two, and came up feeling a little calmer. I should eat something, he thought, maybe that's what's wrong with me. He started across the room towards the fridge, trying as he went to remember what there was in, and wondering whether to go out to eat, whether he would feel better getting away from the house from an hour or two.

It was then that he noticed the letter on the table.

For a moment he wondered stupidly who it could be from, then he realized it could only be Isobel. She must have been and gone, she must have come back here and then gone out again – but why? He felt in some confused way that he had to work out the answer to that before he read the letter. It was probably just a note explaining that she had to go out to chambers. But it wasn't a note. It was a letter. Why was she writing him a letter? He picked it up, feeling as though it was burning his fingers. Why was she writing him a letter? He stared at it blankly, looking at the scrawled 'Mervyn' on the envelope, as though somewhere in her handwriting was the key to the mystery. He knew instinctively that this was serious, he knew instinctively that it was the end of something, and his fear would not let him open that letter. His hands were shaking, and he realized with surprise that tears were rolling down his cheeks, and he made a half-hearted effort to wipe them away, but his hands were shaking so badly that he only managed to scratch his cheek quite hard with his cufflink. He must ring her. He must speak to her, then things would be all right, then he could make a difference. He fumbled his way over to the phone, and began to dial Isobel's number, but then, for reasons that he didn't know, began to dial Alexander Gregory's number instead.

The phone was picked up almost immediately. 'Mervyn. How are you holding up?'

'What?'

'How are you holding up, old chap? Would you like me to come over?'

This isn't real, he thought to himself. This is a dream, it must be. The floor seemed to be falling away from under his feet.

'It's Isobel...' he heard himself saying.

'I know, I know. Still, I did get the impression things haven't been great for a long time, it's probably all for the best, you know. They've been close for a long time, so I gather.'

He realized that unconsciously he had been trying to gauge the tone of Gregory's voice. Was he sympathetic, inquisitive, kindly, ghoulish? Was he to be trusted? So engaged was he in this that when the meaning of Gregory's words finally penetrated his mind he nearly fell with the shock.

'Who?' he said hoarsely. 'Who's been close?'

'You don't know?' Gregory sounded genuinely horrified. 'She should have told you. She really should. She said she was going to write...' His voice slid away into a mumble.

'You knew about this? She told you?'

'Mervyn, I'm an old man, the ladies sometimes trust me with their little secrets. But if she didn't tell you, or write you that letter, how do you know about this? I

142

mean, I thought as soon as you rang that you knew. Why...' Once again his voice trailed off in embarrassment, and Walkinshaw's mind, in its numbed state, took some pleasure in prolonging it. After a few seconds Gregory began again, in a wheedling tone, 'Well, what was I do? I'd made a promise, you see, I'd given my word, and –'

Something was eating away at his brain, there was something he had to ask, something he had to say. 'Who?'

'Oh, Mervyn, it shouldn't be me to tell you – '

'Who?'

A long pause, then Gregory said, with reluctance, 'The boy Dakers. But it really shouldn't be me-'

'Thanks.'

'What? Oh, don't thank me, I feel dreadful about it all, oh, don't thank me, it's a horrible duty. She really should have told you herself.'

'Where are they?'

'I really don't know, old chap. At his place, I imagine. Are you going to be all right, Mervyn? I feel so guilty, like this is my fault somehow, but I don't see what else I could have done, I did tell her it was foolish, I did tell her to take her time and not make any hasty decisions, but you know, I mean, what else could I have done, really? I mean, I'm your friend, and I'm her friend, and, well, it was an impossible position, and – '

'I have to go now.'

'Yes, of course, of course. Shall I pop round, just to see how you're getting on? In half an hour or so? I'll pop in, shall I?'

'No. Goodnight.'

He sat for what seemed to be hours, staring into space, looking stupidly straight ahead of him, glazed, staring

143

at a magnet on the fridge. 'When I count my blessings I always count you twice', it said, and he found himself racking his brains to think where it had come from. It had been a present from someone – Isobel's mother? – from some sort of holiday somewhere. He stared at it, unable to think, unable to feel. In years to come, whenever I think of tonight, I'll think of that magnet, he found himself thinking, I'll never forget it now. It really irked him that he couldn't remember where it had come from, and he wondered if he were going mad, if these were the first steps into some terrible decline.

He roused himself with an effort, and realized that he still had not read the letter. He went over to the table and picked it up, his heart pounding. Perhaps it was not what he thought, what Gregory had told him. Gregory was an old gossip, everyone knew that. An old gossip and an alcoholic, a miserable old alcoholic, who knows more about the state of my marriage than I do. He tore open the envelope, feeling suddenly sick, his hands shaking. It was typed, which gave him a little shock of coldness.

'This can't come as a surprise to you, Mervyn, it's been a sham for so long now that I think you will feel as I do, that it really is a blessed relief to come out in the open. Things haven't been right between us for so long now, and I think that we should acknowledge that, like adults, and not drag things out and make ourselves miserable in the process. The truth is that I have met someone else – it doesn't matter who – but it isn't because of that that I'm leaving you. I would have left you to be alone rather than be in our marriage, which has run its course, hasn't it, Mervyn, let's be honest for once? I know that deep down you feel as I do, however much you won't acknowledge it, you know that we don't make each other happy, if we ever did, really, though we had some good times in the early days.

Please don't try to call me, as this letter says absolutely everything that I have to say. I am sorry for any pain that I've caused you, but really I have no doubt that what I'm doing is right not just for myself but for you too.

Of course I want to be civilized about this, and I'm sure you do too. No doubt when the dust has settled we can make some arrangements. Isobel.'

He crumpled the letter up in his hand, shaking with anger. How could she be so cold, so unemotional? She wasn't real, this wasn't real, it was all some dream, some sort of nightmare. For a moment he felt that he wouldn't miss her, that she was right, and mixed in with his anguish he felt a sort of mounting freedom, that both exhilarated and frightened him. At least things have come to a head, he thought, at least there's an end to this limbo we've been living in. But then the realization that this was it, he was alone now, swept over him once more, and he put his hand to his mouth in a kind of horror.

At that moment the doorbell rang. It's her, she's thought better of it and come home, he thought, and he rushed to the door, almost frantic in his eagerness.

Chapter Seven – Upon Which You Are All Agreed

John Ratchett stood on the doorstep, sweating, holding out a notebook. Walkinshaw found himself observing it carefully, as though he had never seen a legal notebook before, and everything about it seemed vivid, the blue of the paper cover, the curled-up, dog-eared edges, the ragged curls of paper where sheets had been torn out roughly.

'How do, Mr. Walkinshaw? You look surprised to see me! You left this, I left it for you in the robing room, but blow me down if you didn't just waltz out without it. I said to Mick on security, he's only gone and left the notebook! He said, yes, he came out of here, head in the clouds as usual, in his own dream world. You'd forget your head if it wasn't screwed on, bless you.'

'Thank you,' said Walkinshaw mechanically, holding out his hand, but Ratchett still held the book, obstinately. 'Mind if I squeeze in for a minute? Only I'm dying for a cuppa, and we never did get a proper chat about today, did we? You were miles away in that conference, off in your little dream world again. I won't stop long, the wife'll be back soon, she's off at her evening class, should be back about eight, I'm supposed to be fending for myself dinner-wise, that's not much good, is it? Women, eh?'

'I've a lot to do,' said Walkinshaw feebly, feeling a sort of burning pain down his chest, and wondering if it could be his heart. I'm probably having a heart attack, I'm probably dying, and I'll die here, in front of him, his bloated, stupid face the last thing I see on this earth. He roused himself with what felt like a superhuman effort. 'Kind of you to drop this in, but –'

'No trouble.' Ratchett was in the hall now, taking off his coat. 'We only live ten minutes away, at Shelverton. Not like this, though, the wife'd die with envy if she saw this place. You want to have one of them sunken rockeries in the front, that's what I'd do with a house like this. Your front garden's doing nothing, if you don't mind me saying so.'

'I'm in the middle of things, not having a good day, actually.' Walkinshaw felt his voice break before he heard it. I will not cry in front of this man, I will die first.

His throat constricted and he felt the salty phlegm of tears forming in his mouth.

'You don't look too good,' said Ratchett, coming closer, and peering at him. 'I hope you're not getting this virus that's doing the rounds, Linda in the office had it, she was off for ten days, on antibiotics and everything, it got in her chest. They don't seem to have done the trick, though, she's still got a cough. Hers started with a sore throat. Have you got a sore throat?'

'No.' He was conscious of a strange, dull resignation, which he clung to as a respite from the pain which he knew was there, waiting for him to lose hold again.

'That's something. Where's that lovely wife of yours when you need some TLC, eh? Working round the clock, I expect? One of these power couples, aren't you? Someone was saying to me the other day it's a surprise you two haven't started a family, but I said I expect that's all to come, isn't it? You don't want to be leaving it too late, though, else before you know it you're into that UVF malarkey, that's no fun, I was reading about it.'

'IVF.' He was conscious of a desperate, overwhelming desire to laugh; Ratchett's slip suddenly seemed to him to be the funniest thing in the world, and he had to catch himself from slipping down into hysterical laughter. He managed at last to control himself, with something that sounded like a sob.

Ratchett chuckled a little himself, but looked annoyed. 'You're right. UVF's that lot in Northern Ireland. Is that where you're from?'

'No. I was born in Wexford, went to university in Dublin.' His head whirled with unreality, this was not real, this was some terrible nightmare, he would wake up soon. He felt tempted to laugh again and knew that he must not, that he would go mad if he let himself.

'You look all in,' said Ratchett. 'Tell you what, why don't I rustle us up some cheese on toast, then we can have a chat? Don't know about you, I hate eating on my own.'

'I have to go to the toilet,' said Walkinshaw desperately, in a rush, all his panic flooding over him again. He stood up, lurched with light-headedness, but somehow managed to reach the bathroom, where he knelt, his heart pounding, his whole body flooded with relief at being alone. Hot tears rolled down his face, he could not think, he could not feel anything, he was going to die and he almost wished he would. I've had enough of this, he thought, I've had enough of it all, just let me die now. He was faint with not eating, but the thought of food made him sick, the thought of sitting down with Ratchett at the kitchen table, that kitchen where the note had been, where Isobel had been, where Isobel would never be again, seemed to him to be the greatest horror he could imagine, and he stumbled to his feet, determined at all costs to get rid of Ratchett.

The kitchen was quiet as he entered. Ratchett stood, heavy with silent embarrassment, and immediately Walkinshaw's eyes went to the letter on the table. It had been moved. He had left it where it lay, near a candle, and now it was propped up against a stack of place mats, the flap of the envelope tucked in, self-consciously.

'Well, I've taken up enough of your time, Mr. Walkinshaw,' said Ratchett, purple with constraint. 'You did a great job today, see you tomorrow.' His eyes were hovering somewhere over Walkinshaw's shoulder.

'You read it, you read my letter,' he murmured. He knew he should feel angry, but he felt nothing, just a detachment, almost an amusement at Ratchett's discomfiture.

'I didn't, I didn't, what letter?' Ratchett blustered, and Walkinshaw looked at him with contempt.

'You know which letter-' he was beginning, when again the doorbell rang.

'I'll get it!' Ratchett almost shouted, rushing to the door, and Walkinshaw looked after him, rooted to the spot, overwhelmed again with a dreamlike feeling.

He heard Alexander Gregory's voice in the hall. 'Where's the old boy, then? I just popped round, see how he's doing, is he in the kitchen?'

'Yes, just come this way.' Then Ratchett added, in a stage whisper, 'You'll never guess what's happened, Alex. His wife's gone and left him. He's in a right state, poor bloke.'

'I know, I know,' said Gregory impatiently. 'That's why I'm here. I'm surprised he told you about it. What are you doing here, anyway?'

'I came to bring him my notebook for his closing speech tomorrow, he left it at court.' Ratchett's tone was injured. 'I thought I was doing him a favour. He looked funny from the minute he opened the door. Who's the other man, do you know?'

Walkinshaw closed his eyes, wishing he might

never have to open them again. He felt nothing now but a great and enveloping weariness against which there could be no resistance. He could still hear the two of them whispering in the hall, but he was too tired now to make the effort to listen. Let them talk about me, he thought, let them say what they like, all of them. In front of his closed eyes there flashed suddenly the image of Reggie Dakers' face, with its customary look of sarcastic amusement, and he felt a strange sort of pity for him. It must have been a strain, all that pretending, he thought, Isobel must have been so strung out with it all, and I never noticed. It all seemed pointless to him, all of it, even his own pain, and gradually his thoughts became swallowed up and dimmed in that great ache of exhaustion that seemed to be located underneath his eyes, or perhaps it wasn't his eyes, but behind his eyes, somewhere in his brain...

He was conscious of Gregory standing over him, with that concerned expression that everyone seemed to have today; he was getting tired of it. 'Poor old chap, how are you feeling?'

'Tired. Really tired. I need to be left alone, I really do.'

'You're better to have company at a time like this.' Ratchett was looming up; his face seemed vast, all-encompassing, and Walkinshaw began to wonder if he was feverish. 'You'll get through this, Mr. Walkinshaw. A similar thing happened to the wife's niece, Julie, well, I say a similar thing, what it was, she left her husband, the drink it was, you know, and anyway, she married again, they moved to Australia, had a couple of kids, and so, you see...'

'I think Mervyn wants a bit of peace and quiet now, Mr. Ratchett,' said Gregory, in his most authoritative tone, and Ratchett backed towards the door. He stopped with his hand on the door and murmured to Gregory,

'You know he's got to finish the trial tomorrow. Do you think –'

'It'll all be taken care of, I can promise you that. Please-'

'All right, I'll be off. Chin up, Mr. Walkinshaw. Though I really feel I should call you Mervyn, after all we've been through tonight, eh, mate? Well,' he added hastily, catching Gregory's eye, 'I'll make myself scarce. Night all.'

The door banged behind him, and at the sound Walkinshaw's nerves seemed to flame up again; he still felt exhausted, but desperately agitated as well. He suddenly remembered how afraid he had felt when he first came home, and something of that fear flooded through him again. He realized with surprise that his legs were shaking.

'Are you going to be all right, Mervyn? I genuinely feel awful about this. Will you be all right on your own tonight?'

Walkinshaw realized from the phrasing of this last question that Gregory was anxious to be off, and had come round only to salve his conscience. He raised his head and said, with some bitterness, 'Of course I'll be all right. Don't worry about me, you haven't so far.'

Gregory looked stricken, and Walkinshaw felt some compunction.

'I didn't mean that, I know it was awkward for you,' he said, his brain reeling with tiredness, 'I just don't know what I mean, I-'

'It's all right, old chap. I forgive you, under the circumstances.'

Walkinshaw, incredulous, felt his anger rise again. He opened his mouth to speak, but then noticed Gregory sneaking a surreptitious glance at his watch.

'Got to be somewhere?' he said, caustically.

'Well... no... not really, I can do it another night.

Dinner engagement, you know, but I can cancel, it's no big deal, if you'd like me to stay with you...'

'No, no.' Walkinshaw found himself speaking automatically, like an actor who has found his place in the script. 'No, I'll be fine. Honestly.'

'Well, if you're sure.' Gregory was already getting to his feet, in obvious relief. 'Did I leave my coat in the hall? You take care of yourself, Mervyn. If you want to come home after you've done your speech tomorrow, just call in, we can get someone to cover you after that.'

Tomorrow. It seemed impossible that there would ever be a tomorrow. This day was forever. The morning already seemed a year ago.

'I'll be fine,' he said again. He hoped wildly for a moment that Gregory would see that he wasn't fine, that he couldn't bear to be alone, and would cancel his plans and stay with him. But it was obvious Gregory wanted to be off, and his pride would not let him admit that he could not face the night alone, even as his stomach lurched in fear at the prospect.

'Good man.' Gregory was already in his coat and had opened the front door; the cold air seemed to strike Walkinshaw in the face like a personal insult. 'Better get going. You give me a call if you need anything.'

For the second time that night the door banged shut after a visitor, and once again the panic welled up inside him; he felt an urge to go after Gregory and beg him to stay, and then he remembered a time when Isobel had left and he had felt like that, wanted to run out in the street and beg her not to leave him. And Reggie Dakers had been waiting for her in the car outside. What is wrong with me? he asked himself. Why does everybody leave me? The loneliness was gaining intensity now, it was pressing on his heart, and he felt genuinely frightened, as though he were in the grip of some terrible illness. Numbly he made his way to his study, where he turned on the television automatically, and stared, as though hypnotized, at the garish screen.

As he slept carefully through that fitful night he thought that he was two people, that one of him was sitting beside his bed, watching the other one sleep; the night seemed interminable, and even as he dreamed he knew that there was a catastrophe waiting for him, that something terrible had happened. He woke suddenly at five o'clock, damp and breathless, woken by a feeling of humiliation, that seemed to have crawled from his stomach all the way to his brain and woken him. The previous evening seemed like a nightmare, an unbearable nightmare, and he was filled with horror that it was real; it seemed far too terrible to be real, it must be a bad dream. He sat up sharply, aware of a clammy nausea that seemed to be moving through his whole body; suddenly the idea of staying in bed seemed unbearable, and he got out of bed and went over to the window, staring out into the darkness, and wondering what he ought to feel, what people did feel at times like this. The street seemed almost beautiful; he looked out at the silence, feeling in some way that it was visible, and feeling that this was borrowed time, it was the night, nothing could happen to him until morning, all he had to do was hold onto it, and simply not allow the morning to come. But there were only three hours until he would have to get up, get into his clothes and face the day. Suddenly realisation hit him again; had all that really happened yesterday? It seemed like a bad play, farcical, it could not be real. It is real, he muttered to himself, she's gone, and I'm alone. All alone. He breathed hard to stop the fear rising up again, and all at once he felt a great anger towards Gregory, the thought

153

of that scene in the kitchen seemed an unendurable humiliation, and he felt, though he knew it to be unjust, that everything was Gregory's fault, Gregory had humiliated him, and he would never recover from that humiliation, nothing would ever wash it away, it was burned into him now, it was in his bones and his blood, he was a humiliated man. How long before everyone knows, he wondered, how long before I'm the main talking point on circuit? He remembered that tomorrow – today - he must meet Jennings and Marlowe, and that some point – please God, not today – he must surely meet Dakers again. He realised that he would need reserves of strength that he had never needed before if he was to face what lay before him. I must be strong enough, I must find a way to be strong enough. But as he went slowly back to bed and crawled under the covers, he felt as though his heart was going to break.

'Now then, old chap.' Ratchett was staring at him in undisguised fascination, his face arranged in what, presumably, thought Walkinshaw, was his idea of a sympathetic expression. He's like someone waiting for the next episode of a soap opera. Well, I won't give it to him.

'How did you sleep? You must be feeling a bit rough this morning. It all gets easier from here though, that's what they say.'

'Do they?' Walkinshaw was feeling more than a bit rough; he had not slept again after waking at five, and he felt unbearably tired and restless. His stomach was shuddering with nausea, and yet he felt empty and weak. Just one speech to make, he had said to himself on the drive to court, just one speech, ten minutes, fifteen at most, and then I can give myself up to my misery. I could be back home by lunchtime. Hold on to that thought.

'I've not said anything to anyone, you can rest assured. I know how to keep a secret. I was in the force for twenty years, you know, the things I've seen would make your hair curl. Last thing I ever do is blab people's secrets. Like I say, we're all entitled to a private life.' Ratchett's eyes were goggling with curiosity. 'Have you heard any more?' he burst out suddenly. 'Only people are saying...'

'What are people saying?'

'Well, you know what people are like, here especially, nothing to do but gossip, it's disgusting really. I just thought if you told me I could put them straight, you know, tell them not to spread rumours, and that –'

'Yes, it is true that Isobel has left me for Mr. Dakers. You can tell whomever you like.'

He walked off, leaving Ratchett open-mouthed, and felt a little stab of satisfaction. Perhaps that had been unfair of him, perhaps Ratchett was motivated by more than simple malice, but he was past caring, he was past caring about anything. He felt unreal as he walked up the stairs to the canteen, he felt that he would die of tiredness, of heartache. How was it possible to feel this bad and survive? He felt as though he would be dead by lunchtime, and yet he knew that he wouldn't, that somehow life would deny him even that. Your punishment is to have to carry on, he said to himself. You will always have to carry on.

He felt a sort of shock at seeing Hannah in the canteen, sitting by herself at a table near the window, seemingly absorbed in staring at an untouched cup of coffee in front of her. He wondered why he felt so astonished to see her; it was as though she had dropped out of another world into his, and for a moment his head swam in confusion. How beautiful she is, he thought, everything she does is graceful, and he felt a sort of warmth spreading inside him, in spite of everything. She did not look up, she did not seem to have seen him, and he felt her absorption, he felt her thoughts almost as though they were his own. He did not want to disturb her, she looked like a painting, she is like an angel, he thought, and smiled to himself at his foolishness. He wondered whether to turn and go out again quietly; he was conscious of a sudden shyness, a sense of intrusion, and as he stood there hesitating on the threshold she suddenly looked up at him.

'Hello,' she said, with a note of surprise in her voice. 'Are you all right?'

I must look terrible, he thought. He felt his eyes fill with tears; he choked them back in a panic, I can't cry in front of a lay client, it would be too humiliating for words. But for once he did not feel humiliated; instead he felt as though a doorway of hope was opening in his heart, he felt something that was almost like a sense of homecoming.

'Are you having a bad day?' She was looking at him with a new confidence; there was a strange sort of wisdom about her today, and he felt a kind of awe in her presence.

'Yes. A very bad day.' He found himself sitting opposite her at the little table; grey light filtering in through the tiny window bathed them both in a hazy glow. He felt absolved, redeemed; his heart seemed to sit more easily in his chest, even as his pulse hammered in his temples.

'What happened?' She had lost all interest in her coffee and had pushed it aside; she leant forward with her elbows on the table and looked straight at him. Once again he noticed the strange clearness of her eyes; the dark moistness of her irises, the whites so white they were almost blue. He held his breath for a moment.

'My wife left me last night.'

She still looked straight at him, impassive, solemn, and something in her reception of the news seemed to strengthen him, heal him. He felt a sort of balm around his heart, and he held his breath again, with a feeling, that he could not explain to himself, that these could be the most important moments of his life.

She was silent for a moment or two, and he found himself waiting, still breathless, for her words. At last, still holding his eyes, she said,

'She shouldn't have done that.'

He smiled a little, embarrassed. 'Why do you say that?'

She looked down at the table, a momentary sadness crossing her face. At last she said, 'Because... well, I wouldn't have left you.'

She stared down at the table again, colouring, and Walkinshaw leant back in his chair, wondering how it was possible to feel such happiness within hours of feeling such despair. He felt a sort of enchanted bewilderment; all the certainties of life were swirling about, changing in front of his eyes like the colours in a kaleidoscope. Is this what life really is? Have I been in some sort of dream all these years, from which I am only now beginning to wake?

'You wouldn't?' This is too good to be true, he thought, it must be a dream.

'No.' She had raised her head and was looking straight at him again; once again he felt his brain reel in a sort of delirious vertigo. 'No, I wouldn't.'

He sat there in silence, feeling as though he had just witnessed a miracle. The silence was warm, inviting, exciting; he was a little surprised that he felt no awkwardness at all.

'Why do you –' he was beginning, when the door swung open, and Marlowe came in, fussing a little to the clerk who trotted meekly behind him, and then stopped in his tracks as he saw the two of them, and Walkinshaw thought he saw a look of astonishment on his face, to be quickly replaced by his usual look of fastidious disapproval. He wondered what Marlowe thought, and for a moment defiantly hoped that he suspected him of a relationship with Hannah.

'Morning,' he said curtly, hoping that Marlowe would just quickly get himself a takeaway coffee and then go away again.

'Yes, morning,' said Marlowe, absently, still standing there, looking from one to the other, and Walkinshaw saw something indefinable in his expression and felt a faint chill, without knowing why.

'See you downstairs,' he said, meaninglessly, wanting to say something to break the moment, to end this uncomfortable sensation that he felt under Marlowe's gaze.

'Yes. Yes, of course.' Marlowe went over to the counter, with one last hostile glance at Hannah, who was still looking down at the table, oblivious. She has her own little inner world, thought Walkinshaw enviously, he's nothing to her. Then the thought that he might be something to her, that she had almost said as much to him, struck him again, and filled him with such wild joy that the baleful presence of the little man at the counter, who kept looking over his shoulder at them, was less than nothing to him.

She seemed to understand that further conversation was impossible until they were alone again, and smiled reassuringly at him as they sat in silence, waiting for Marlowe to get his coffee and leave. It's probably only been twenty seconds, thought Walkinshaw, but it feels like an hour. All he could think about was resuming his talk with Hannah, alone. The thought of what he might have said, of what she might have said, remaining unspoken simply because of an unlucky interruption tormented him. He looked at her again, wondering if his face conveyed his anxiety, his need for her, and was reassured by the clear, calm comprehension in her eyes.

Just then the court tannoy sprang into life. 'The Crown against Burns and Casey will now start in Court Number One. Burns and Casey to Court Number One.'

'Typical,' said Marlowe to his clerk, as he brushed past them. 'Still, probably better off without the dishwater they call coffee in this one-eyed little dump.'

He had hoped that his closing speech would be wonderful, exceptional, a tour de force, worthy of comparison with Marshall Hall at his most emotive, that it would be in some hidden way a message of love, that he would find a way of weaving into his words something which only she would understand and appreciate. But tiredness and strain got the better of him, and the best he could do, and did, fell a long way short, he felt, from the ideal. He spoke quietly but forcefully, looking directly at the jury as he always did, falling back on his years of experience to carry him through those terrifying moments when his brain clouded without warning and he felt as though he were tottering on the edge of a cliff. There were several points which Marlowe had made, in his silky closing speech, which needed to be refuted, and he did this with all the emphasis he could. At least he had the advantage of going after Jennings, who stumbled through his speech with a good deal of hesitation and repetition, clutching desperately at his bundle of papers as though it could save him. After that performance it was not difficult to come across as poised and calm, and when at last he sat down again it was a mingled feeling of relief and sadness. This trial, this precious trial, was drawing inexorably to a close, it could well all be over in an hour, and that thought smote his heart. He wished he could have gone on talking for ever, but the fatigue was still pressing away in his brain and behind his eyes, and he felt that he could hardly speak another word.

He knew he should pay attention to the summing-up, often the most crucial part of the trial, but he simply could not, and satisfied himself with the thought that Ratchett would be taking notes. Rogers' voice seemed to be very far away, and he realised with horror that he had come close to falling asleep. After that he sat forward, pressing his elbow hard into his hand to keep himself alert, but still he found himself unable to focus on a word that Rogers said, and he felt a great relief when at last the rasping voice fell silent, and the jury bailiffs were sworn.

'Do you swear to keep this jury in a safe and convenient place, and suffer none to speak to them, neither shall you speak to them yourselves concerning this trial held here today, unless it be to ask them if they are agreed upon a verdict?'

At the familiar form of words Walkinshaw's stomach lurched; the reality of the situation seemed to strike him afresh, as though he had never really thought before of all that was at stake. He had been so preoccupied with his part in the trial that he had not really imagined this part of it, the part that involved endless, dreadful waiting, a part over which he had no control. The very word 'verdict' seemed to strike terror into his heart, and he found himself glancing round at Hannah in the dock, almost as though to gain reassurance from her. Her head was bowed again, and he wished that she would look up, look them all in the eyes, and then they might believe in her as he did. The jurors, their faces glazed with boredom, shuffled out in the wake of the ushers, and he felt a strange fury with them as he watched them go. What right had they to sit in judgement on Hannah? What right had anybody? He felt that if they were to find her guilty he would not be able to control himself.

As he was gathering up his papers he felt a tap on his shoulder. 'You all right, mate?' Jennings' crimson face was inches away from his. 'I just heard – I just wondered – well, that Dakers has always been a tosspot, but this is fucking low for him, eh, fucking low even for him. What a fucking twatty thing to do, eh, what a twat. I tell you what, mate, I'm not even going to speak to him after this, if he speaks to me I'll tell him to fucking shove it. I will. I will.' He paused for dramatic effect, puffing heavily.

'Thank you,' said Walkinshaw faintly.

'No problem. No problem. That's what mates are for, I always say. Well, I'm in your corner, you can count on me. If you're lonely in the evenings, just give me a shout, we could have a curry together, we could watch a film. You just give me a shout.'

'That's really kind.' Walkinshaw actually felt that it was; he warmed a little to Jennings, even as he moved away slightly and began to fiddle with the string on his brief.

'No worries. Tell you what, your other half'll be back before you know it, once she finds out what a cunt he is. It'll be a case of fish that swim in the night, she'll not want to see him again 'til hell boils over. You mark my words.'

He sat in one of the tiny conference rooms, his heart thumping uncomfortably, his hands shaking, his mouth dry, a faint prickling sensation creeping up from his fingers, through his hands and up his wrists. No matter how he sat, or whether he sat or stood, his legs ached and felt restless. He kept on looking at his watch, feverishly, and drumming his fingers on the table. Then he would feel cramped again, and would get up suddenly, and pace about the tiny room, almost doubled up with nerves. He felt that this was torture, and yet simultaneously he felt an anguish that it would soon all be over. He felt an urge to savour his own pain. There's no feeling in the world like this one, he decided, the pain of it is exquisite. He half-wondered if he should go through to the robing room and chat to Jennings, but he knew that he couldn't, he couldn't talk to anyone. Every time there was a crackle over the tannoy his heart leapt again, and his whole body felt galvanised. He felt that the waiting was utterly unbearable, that it would kill him, but at the same time he felt that he could not bear hearing the verdict. If Hannah were found guilty – a sick heat flamed through him at the thought. It would be impossible to bear, he could not stand it. If she were acquitted – his heart rose at the thought – then, wonderful though that would be, it would be the end. There would be no reason at all for him to see her ever again. This strange bond between them, this mysterious understanding that seemed to have sprung up, miraculously, from nowhere – it would be gone, he would be left alone, that moment, those moments, those wonderful, transfiguring moments – would be only memories, left to him, like pennies in a pocket, he thought, old coins that I can get out and touch now and again, but with each touch becoming more and more worn down, faded, less decipherable. The thought of losing that sense of meaning terrified him; he felt that he must do something, but had no idea what, and still the white plastic clock obstinately informed him that it was only ten to twelve, and that he had been in his little self-imposed prison cell a paltry fifteen minutes.

'Burns and Casey, Court Number One. The case of Burns and Casey will now restart in Court Number One.' He jumped up, grabbed his wig and his papers, and hurried there, nearly sick with excitement. 'Verdict or a question, George?' he breathlessly asked the ancient usher, who was shuffling about the court in his rusty black, with infuriating slowness. Please God, let it be a verdict. No, no, I'm not ready for a verdict yet, a question, let it be a question.

'Verdict, Mr. Walkinshaw. Quite quick, weren't they? Forty two minutes, must have made their minds up before they went out, I should think. Bad news for you and Mr. Jennings.'

'There's no telling, George, you should know that after all these years.' He could hardly get the words out; it's like an execution, he thought, I can't stay here, I can't breathe this air, this place is killing me. He remembered all the verdicts, all the convictions, of his career; he remembered the screams, the tears, the threats of suicide, the wailing mothers, girlfriends, sisters, and the terrible sound of a human body being dragged forcibly down a stairwell, kicking and swearing, and then the thud of a heavy door, echoing around a silent courtroom before a blank-faced judge, who must betray no sign of having heard. He remembered it all, and he felt a terror he could not explain; I have seen and heard too much, he thought, too much to ever feel easy in my mind again.

Hannah was being ushered in now, with Burnsy close behind her. They were both very pale; they looked shocked, like survivors of some terrible accident. He heard the dock officer lock the door behind them; is it true, he wondered, that they only do that if it's a guilty verdict?

Ratchett was behind him now, turning his notebook over to find a fresh page, then writing laboriously in his unformed hand. 'Verdict. 12.18pm.' Walkinshaw felt the old rage rise up in him again; how could this man see so much and see so little? So much is vouchsafed to us, who work in these places, he thought, and yet so little is understood.

'All right, Mervyn? You look as though you're going to your doom, never mind those two.' Marlowe sat down with a flourish, spreading out his gown around him like a cape. 'I hope you're not getting – well, shall we say, over-involved?'

'What do you mean?' Walkinshaw felt a sudden danger; a vague sense of menace seemed to hang in the air between them.

'Nothing special. It's just another day, another punter, don't forget that. It's dangerous to forget that. But you know that, Mervyn, you've been around as long as I have.'

Marlowe turned away to put his head together with his clerk, leaving Walkinshaw trembling. What had he meant? What did he know? What did any of it mean? This can't be my life, he thought, suddenly I don't understand anything, I don't understand any of it. He remembered that those were Hannah's words in her police station interview, and his heart swelled with pain again. Just let me win this trial, just let me have this, and then whatever happens after that, well, I'll take my chances. Just let me win it.

'Are they ever fucking coming? What a bloody farce this is, eh? I reckon –' Jennings was interrupted by George, suddenly appearing through the door that led into the judge's rooms.

'All stand.'

This was it. This was the moment.

Rogers made his way precisely over to his seat on the bench. 'Gentlemen, we have a verdict. Bring the jury in, please.'

As they filed in, their customary air of boredom and resentment tempered a little by a new-found awareness of their importance, he felt that he hated them, he felt that they were a firing squad, that this was his own death scene, that he would never get out of this room alive.

'Would the foreman of the jury please stand.' To Walkinshaw's surprise it was the bald man who rose to his feet, the bald man who had not apparently paid the least attention to anything that anyone had said all through the trial.

'In the case of the defendants Jonathan Burns and Hannah Casey, have you reached a verdict upon which you are all agreed?'

'Yes.'

'In the case of Jonathan Burns, do you find the defendant guilty or not guilty?'

The bald man opened his mouth, stuck his chest out and said, in a loud, self-important voice, 'Guilty.'

'You find the defendant guilty, and that is the verdict of you all.'

This could not be happening, this was some sort of nightmare. If they thought Burns was guilty, then could possibly think Hannah was not? I've never known nerves like this in my life, he thought, for God's sake put me out of my misery.

'In the case of Hannah Casey, do you find the defendant guilty or not guilty?'

'Not guilty.'

He could not believe it. He must have wanted to hear those words so much that he had imagined them, he had dreamed it. He glanced back over his shoulder involuntarily to see what Ratchett had written. And there it was. Not Guilty. Relief and happiness flooded his heart, and he felt like crying.

Jennings put a hand on his shoulder, and he

remembered what he had to do. He stood up, exhausted and elated.

'Your honour, may my client be discharged?'

Chapter Eight – A Rare Opportunity

Norman Tombs sat on the bus, fastidiously leaning away from the woman next to him. She was sitting on the edge of his anorak, stupid woman. He hated getting the bus, especially when all the window seats were taken, and he had to perch like this, next to a total stranger. He hated it even more when the total stranger was a stupid fat woman, with a hearing aid, and endless shopping bags that she put next to her, so that he had to sit on the very edge of the seat, and hold on to the pole to stop himself sliding off when the bus went round a corner. He hated taking the bus, he had told them that, had even worked up the nerve to ask Linda for some petty cash for a taxi. 'D'you hear that, John? Lady Muck wants to take a taxi on his prison visit! Time enough for taxis when you're Lord Chief Justice, son. Here on planet Earth you can get the bus like any other mortal that's not learned to drive.' Lady Muck. Despite its almost risible lack of originality, it never failed to make him smart. The bus lurched suddenly, and his files and notebook suddenly slid off his lap and onto the grimy floor of the bus. He heard laughter behind him as he fumbled about on the floor, trying to reach his biro, which had rolled under the seat in front. As he groped for it his fingers closed over an enormous lump of still-moist chewing gum, and he recoiled, filled with revulsion, close to tears. The laughter behind him burst out again, and he thought he felt something flick against his hair, but he did not turn round. I will show them, my day will come. He muttered his mantra to himself for comfort, but he was beginning to believe in it less and less. Once failure had seemed impossible; now it seemed more likely than not. His confidence was ebbing away with every day that passed and nothing happened, nothing changed; he got up in the mornings, did his mother's breakfast and settled her in front of the TV, then walked into the office, sat there for eight hours, his chief occupation being to avoid having to talk to anyone, and then walked home again, did the tea and then sat in front of the television with Mum, and sometimes her friend Doreen, until bed time. My life could pass like this, he thought, and no one will intervene, no one will step in to stop it happening, to put things right. I will go on and on like this.

The bus was now shuddering into the depot, and he stood up, clutching his files and papers under one arm and the pole with his other hand, desperate to avoid losing his balance as the bus stopped. It was a ten minute walk to the prison, and there was another bus he could take that stopped directly outside it, but he could not face any more people, any more ridicule. He set off, marching up the street, his heart already heavy at the prospect before him. He hated prison visits, found them frightening, offensive, and the idea of doing one alone, without Ratchett, was terrifying. But Ratchett was covering the end of that trial at the Crown court, that prostitute. He had offered to do the prison visit if Tombs covered the trial, but Tombs had found even the idea of a prison visit less daunting than the idea of meeting her again. So here he was, alone, trudging along this rainy street with arms that already ached from the weight of the file, even after about thirty seconds.

He was ushered into the tiny room, grey, hot, with no windows, just a glass door leading out into a corridor, also windowless, and for a moment he lost his bearings entirely and panicked.

'If you have any problems with him, press the security buzzer on the wall,' one of the warders had said, and he had felt both alarmed and insulted. They never said that when Ratchett was there. What made them think he might have problems?

The door opened again sooner than he had wished, and the warder came in again, escorting a man who was handcuffed to the rear. Tombs felt a shudder of apprehension; he was sure the others he had seen with Ratchett hadn't been handcuffed.

'Won't you sit down, Mr...' Oh God, my mind has gone blank. 'Mr. Reynolds,' with a great effort he pulled the name out of his memory; hard to believe he had been memorizing it all the way over on the bus.

The man did not even look at him; he turned around, slowly, to the guard, and motioned for him to unlock the handcuffs; something about the gesture seemed regal, dominant. The guard, burly and imposing figure that he was, seemed somehow undignified as he fumbled at the key, and the task seemed servile, demeaning. Strange, thought Tombs, that a man in prison can make the man who unlocks his handcuffs seem like his servant, and he felt fear of this stranger crawl up his spine; he felt he wanted to run away from him, like a child, but at the same time he felt hypnotized, mesmerized, like a bird looking at a snake.

The prisoner sat down, slowly, and looked carefully at him. Tombs had been expecting a contemptuous look, but it was not quite that, it was a clever, quick, appraising glance, the glance of a man who has had learned to get the measure of people. Tombs felt hot and overwhelmed; he had barely spoken seven words, and already he felt utterly out of control.

'Where's John?' His voice was low, deep and attractive; it had a local edge, but it had something else to it, a note that Tombs felt was somehow familiar, but could not place.

'He couldn't come today. He had to cover a trial.'

Reynolds nodded, narrowing his eyes. 'Hannah's trial. How's it going?'

'I- I – well, I hope, I mean, I don't really know,' stammered Tombs. 'I think-'

'She'll get off.' Reynolds spoke slowly, thoughtfully, seemingly entirely unconscious of interrupting. 'It'll be another matter for dear little Burnsy.'

Tombs, who had been frantically shuffling through his papers in the hope of finding the link between this man and Hannah, had found the case summary, and light broke in. 'Of course, you're Powers. I mean-'

'Not any more. Not using that name again as long as I live. Which may well,' he looked hard at Tombs, again with narrowed eyes, and then smiled suddenly, 'be a very short time. When am I getting out of this place, then?'

'Well, we took Counsel's advice, as you know, and -'

'And he says I have a chance, not a great one, but a chance. I read it, you sent me a copy of it, remember?'

'Yes,' mumbled Tombs, flustered, 'but-'

'But you thought I'd never understand it. You want to stop taking things for granted, Mr. Tombs. Incidentally, that reminds me. You never introduced yourself. Not very professional, that. I might write and complain about you.'

He slowly raised one arm and rubbed the back of his head thoughtfully. Tombs saw a great pack of muscle move under his shirt, and he watched in fascinated terror. He felt paralyzed, unable to think for himself, and for a moment he wondered if this man had some sort of telepathic gift, if in some way he was controlling his mind. With an effort he sat up, straightened his papers, and said, 'I'm sorry. I'm Norman Tombs. How did you-'

'Know your name? You wrote it there on your notebook, like a good little boy. Your mummy will be pleased with you.'

'What do you mean, my mummy? What do you know – what do you know –' Tombs' hands were shaking; a little livid spot of red had formed in each of his pale cheeks.

'About your mummy? Nothing at all, Norman. I can call you Norman, can't I? Nothing at all. Except I get the feeling you still live with her, not that there's anything wrong with that, of course. And I also get the feeling you're not getting any.'

Tombs, crimson and furious, seized his papers in desperation. 'I think we should discuss your case, Mr. Reynolds, that's what I'm here for, after all. So, to recap, you were given three and a half years at Sheffield Crown court by-' He looked down at his papers and gasped. How had he missed it? This was extraordinary. He wanted to stop, but he heard his own voice continuing, as though he were in a trance. 'By Mr. Recorder Walkinshaw.'

He looked up, flustered and bewildered. He needed time, time to think about this, he mustn't say anything to anyone until he had thought it through, and worked out what to do for the best.

'What's the significance of that name, then?' Reynolds was watching him carefully, leaning in across the table, and he knew it was hopeless.

'Nothing. There is no significance, really.'

'You're going to tell me, Norman, or you're going to regret it. What's the significance of that name?'

'He was- he is- Hannah's barrister.' Tombs felt as though the words were being dragged out of him by some force he had no power to resist. He heard himself go on, 'I think he likes her – Hannah, I mean. They seem very close.' He went hot all over with horror at the impropriety of what he had just said. What was it about this man that seemed to destroy his better judgement? What could have possessed me to make me say that? But it is true, he tried to tell himself, I saw the way he looked at her, I mean, the way she looked at him... His thoughts tailed off in a fresh wave of horror. He had just made a baseless allegation against a senior professional to a dangerous convicted drug dealer. This was a nightmare. How had he let it happen?

'I didn't mean that, I really didn't, just a little joke, you know.' He tried to laugh, but the sound was so ghastly that he stopped immediately. 'Please just disregard it, Mr. Reynolds. I really didn't mean it. Put it right out of your mind.'

He hardly dared raise his eyes to look at Reynolds, who was leaning back in his chair, a pleasant smile of amusement on his face.

'Please don't worry about it, Norman. It's gone and forgotten. Why, it's as though I never heard a single word you said.'

**

The instant that she heard the words, 'Not Guilty', it seemed strange to Hannah that she could ever seriously have imagined any other verdict. It all felt so right, so natural, that the idea of having had any concern about a possible conviction seemed absurd. Of course it was all right, it was always going to be all right, she had known that ever since that first meeting with him down in the cells. She had worried, of course, but really out of a sense that she should be worried; deep in her heart she had always known that there was nothing really to be worried about. She had floated through the morning like one protected by a spell; she felt bound about by some sort of magical force, nothing could touch her.

Then she was free, the door was opened for her by the dock officer, who kept a watchful eye on Burns all the while, conscious that he might make a sudden bid for freedom, and go running headlong out of the courtroom, towards the doors, down the stairs, evading guards and policemen as he went, then out into the street, out into the fresh air; he might leap onto a passing bus, a passing train, he might disappear and never be seen again. Hannah put her hand to her forehead, suddenly dizzy; she was free and Burnsy was not. He had to go back now to that prison, to that place which he hated and which hated him, which made him cut his arms and talk about hanging himself, which gave his lips that bluish-white colour which she could see now, and made his eyes wide with fear. She felt a sort of guilt at her heart, and instead of leaving she slipped into the public gallery at the side of the court, feeling that she couldn't abandon him just yet. Besides, as she acknowledged to herself, leaning forward with her elbows on her knees, breathless, she had to say thank you to Mr. Walkinshaw.

'There's no application for an adjournment, your honour, we don't want a pre-sentence report,' said Jennings in a rush, already bundling his papers together, and glancing quickly at the clock above the door. Hannah noticed that at this Walkinshaw turned and looked at him with some surprise, and she felt a dread at her heart. 'After all, you've heard the facts of the case, we can proceed to sentence now, if your honour-'

'Yes, yes, quite.' Rogers was leaning back in his chair, puffing his cheeks out. 'Let's crack on with it, shall we, Mr. Jennings? I have a copy of his previous convictions, they don't make for pleasant reading, I'm afraid.'

Hannah glanced across at the jurors; the bald man

who had read out the verdicts was looking around at the others with a vindicated air, smiling.

'No, your honour. Well, they could be worse. This will be his first significant custodial sentence. It's true there's quite a volume of offending – I mean a quantity – I mean lots of them – offences, that is – but, as you'll see, your honour, nothing for violence, just theft, mainly, shop theft, he's a heroin addict, you see, and –'

Mr. Jennings, I may have my failings, but illiteracy is not one of them. I am perfectly capable of reading this young man's antecedent history and drawing my own conclusions from it. Have you anything else to add?'

'Well... well...' Jennings shuffled about with his papers hopelessly, 'just that he has had an unhappy life, your honour, an unhappy life –'

'And so, I imagine, have many of his victims, due to his offending behaviour. Unhappiness is not to be spread about like some infectious disease, Mr. Jennings.'

'No, your honour, he doesn't want to spread it about, he doesn't want to, but he has a lot of problems, and he finds being in prison very difficult, your honour, he served two months on remand, he found it extremely difficult. He has been categorized, your honour, he has been categorized...' Jennings paused, and rifled through his papers with increasing desperation, 'as a vulnerable prisoner, what is known in the prison service as a non-coper. He doesn't cope well with being in prison, you see, and – '

'I do see, Mr. Jennings, there is no need to labour the point.' Rogers shot a quick glance in the direction of the jury, as though seeking approbation, and leant forward wearily. 'You're asking me to spare your client a custodial sentence because he doesn't like it in prison. I'm afraid, Mr. Jennings, that that is rather the point of a prison sentence. Perhaps in future it will deter him from the sort of conduct which has brought him here today.'

'No, your honour, I – my client – my lay client – I – we... don't want to waste your honour's time, we don't want to bury our heads in the grass. My client has woken up and smelt the tea leaves, he knows that the writing is on the window. All that I ask, your honour, is that you keep the sentence as short as possible, in all the circumstances, bearing in mind that he has already served two months, that's the equivalent of a four month sentence, and that, as I've said, he wasn't a front runner in all this...' Jennings' voice trailed off, as though he were so accustomed to being interrupted that finishing a sentence was a novel challenge. 'So in all the circumstances, your honour, if you could keep the sentence as short as possible...'

'Yes, thank you, Mr. Jennings.' Rogers' head was already over his papers; he was making a few notes with a neat gold pen. Hannah felt a horror creeping over her; all her fear was back. She was conscious that she was gulping in air, and pressed her hands over her face, terrified. Surely someone would step in, surely someone would explain that it wasn't like that, that Burnsy wasn't like that? Surely his barrister hadn't really finished? There was so much else to say, and she almost opened her mouth to say it, but then sat back against her chair, overwhelmed with the anguish of her powerlessness. She looked at Walkinshaw, sitting ten yards away from her, and she felt as though it might as well have been a hundred miles, she felt the distance between them like a wound. She looked hard and urgently at him, hoping that he would sense it and turn around. Just as she was about to give up in despair he did, and met her eyes. 'He hasn't said enough,' she began to say, 'please –' but he frowned a little and shook his head, and she felt sick with shame and embarrassment.

'Jonathan Richard Burns, stand up.' Rogers was still looking down at his papers; Burns, a little confused, was pulled to his feet by the dock officer. 'You have been convicted after a trial of one count of being concerned in the supply of Class A drugs, in this instance diamorphine, or heroin. I have heard the evidence against you in this case, and I am satisfied that your involvement was such that the custody threshold is passed, and therefore to prison you must go. I take into account what Mr. Jennings has said on your behalf, which wasn't much, because, I fear, there is little to say. You are addicted to heroin. That is no excuse for this offence or for any other. Unless you take steps to put your life in order, the prison environment, for which you express such distaste, will become increasingly familiar to you. The least sentence I can pass in all the circumstances is one of thirty months imprisonment. The time you have spent in custody awaiting trial on this matter, which is, I believe, eight weeks, Mr. Marlowe? Yes, eight weeks and two days, fifty eight days, will count towards the time you will serve. Take him down.'

Hannah watched in incomprehension as Burns was led away, sobbing audibly. She tried to catch his eye, but his head was bowed as he covered his face with his one free hand, while the dock officer scrambled with the handcuffs. She noticed his hand, the scratches and scabs, the livid red patches across the raw knuckles, she saw the pallor of his face, the tears already matting his pale eyelashes, and she felt as though it was all impossible, that none of it was true. What are we all here for, she wondered, why are we born? He disappeared through the door at the back of the dock, and silence fell. Then a door banged, suddenly, violently, and someone shouted something, and her heart leapt into her mouth, she felt as though electricity were running through her. The judge was now giving some formulaic speech of thanks to the jury, but she could hear nothing of it, she could take nothing in. She was conscious of a great weariness, and a deep sense of grief.

She felt a hand on her shoulder. 'Told you it would be all right, love. There you are, you see, I'm always right. I get to take you back home with me, aren't I the lucky one? Are you coming, then? If we don't get the twelve forty bus we've to wait another hour.'

She flinched away from him, too overwhelmed for her usual caution. 'I need to wait and speak to my barrister, dad. You go, I'll see you later.'

'You don't need to thank him, he gets a pay cheque, that's thanks enough. Come on.' His face was kindling with anger; she looked with disgust at the reddish blotches beginning to form on his cheeks, and wondered idly, at the back of her mind, what he was getting angry about. But she was too exhausted to pay it any real attention; he was always angry about something.

'Dad, I really want to wait. Please.'

'Now you listen to me,' he was beginning, and she felt his fingers fasten around her wrist, 'you listen to me – oh, hello, Mr. Ratchett, how are you? You did a good job there for my Hannah, won't forget it.'

Hannah snatched her hand back from him with relief. Already she felt a strange sort of anti-climax dawning in her heart. It was good not to be in prison, but not so good to be outside. What did life hold now? Where could she go but back with her father? Was that so much better than going back to prison? Danny was inside, now Burnsy, and she was left, free, whatever that meant. And nothing to look forward to, ever, now that there were no more conferences, no more court dates, no nothing. Life was just an endless desert of pain and disappointment. She looked up and saw Walkinshaw sweep past her, talking to Jennings. 'If I were you I'd have sought an adjournment,' he was saying, and he didn't even look at her as he went by. Her father was still talking to Ratchett about something or other, something to do with a common assault he expected to be arrested for, and she felt suddenly overwhelmingly ashamed of him, overwhelmingly ashamed of herself. Why do I feel like this, now, she wondered, when perhaps today more than any other day I have a reason to feel happy? She thought again of Burns and his tears, and felt a little stab of guilt again. Why did life always give with one hand and take away with the other? She thought of Walkinshaw, and how she had waited to thank him, and now he was probably packing up his things to leave the building, and still she sat on here in the courtroom, stupidly, and he was probably going now, walking out of her life, she would never see him again. She wanted to speak to him, to thank him, but she felt so stupid, so sad, so confused, what could she say to him? She needed to thank him, wanted to, but at the same time she felt the gratitude she owed like an intolerable burden, a great and insurmountable barrier between them. She wished they could return to that strange moment only a couple of hours ago, when he had told her that his wife had left him, and she had been foolish enough, presumptuous enough to feel a thrill of excitement. He had probably only told her because she wasn't anybody, she didn't count, it was like telling a pet a secret, it wasn't real. Still, the thought of his leaving without a word forced her to her feet. She must say something to him before it was all finally over.

'Mr. Ratchett, I just wanted to say thank you to my

barrister.'

'Yeah, John, she's got this idea she owes him something.' Her father was smiling a little, but his eyes were still angry. 'You can pass a message on, can't you?'

'No, I must tell him myself, I mean-' She was desperate now, this was terrible. 'I wasn't expecting to get off, and...'

'Thanks for the vote of confidence, love. Well, I'll go and see if I can find him for you.' Ratchett was bundling up his files; she realized he was almost as anxious to get away from her father as she was. 'You take care of yourself, Mick. Drop in the office Tuesday.'

She followed Ratchett down the corridor, her heart thudding. She noticed with dismay that the palms of her hands were damp – what if he wanted to shake hands with her? - and tried to wipe them on the front of her coat, but her hands were shaking so much that she gave it up. Her tongue felt large and dry with nerves. This is it, she thought, this is my last chance, this is the last roll of the dice. She felt that something precious was within her grasp, but it would be so easy to miss it, so easy to spoil everything, and the fear of spoiling it gripped her so intensely that she stopped, resolved to make her excuses and run away.

At that moment the doors of one of the rooms swung open, and he appeared, already changed and in his coat, with his blue felt bag and briefcase, and she stood rooted to the spot. He stopped, with a look of mild enquiry, and smiled pleasantly at them. This is a mistake, an awful mistake, she thought, and she felt tears gathering in her throat.

'She wanted to say thank you, bless her, I told it was all part of the service, eh, the old dream team, takes a sharp one to get past us, eh, Mr. Walkinshaw? Anyway, she wanted me to find you, didn't you, pet?'

'Thank you,' she murmured, not daring to look at him, feeling as though she might choke. 'I really mean it.'

She looked up at him at last, and saw that he was still smiling, a little bemusedly. 'It was my pleasure. I'm very sorry about your friend, though. I'm afraid the fingerprints did for him.'

'That and Mr. Jennings, what a pillock,' said Ratchett, picking his ear. 'Bloody awful, even by his low standards.'

'I can't interrupt someone else's mitigation, no matter how weak it is, unfortunately.' Walkinshaw was still looking at her, and his tone was warm. 'I can imagine how frustrated you must have felt, though.'

'I'm so sorry about that.' The relief she felt was almost physical. 'I felt so bad for him, that's all.'

'Are you off already, then?' Ratchett's tone was injured. 'Only I thought we could pop out, get some lunch, we usually do, especially after a not guilty. The Wakefield's doing three for two on pie and chips lunchtimes, seems a waste to let that go begging. What do you say, love?'

She felt a kind of appalled excitement. This was all terrible, she should have left when she had the chance. 'I can't, I have to... my dad...' Something in her was desperate to be forced to go; she looked at Ratchett hopefully, anxious that her face was scarlet.

'Your dad'll be fine, love, you come and have your dinner with us. We deserve a celebration, don't we? What do you say, Mr. Walkinshaw?'

His hesitation was momentary, but she detected it. 'I should go home, really,' she was beginning, but he interrupted her.

'That's a very good idea. Just give me a minute to

put my bags in the car.'

**

Danny lay on his narrow bed, one arm flung behind his head, his eyes hooded, thinking. Today's visit had brought him a rare opportunity, he knew that, but he was puzzled by his inability to decide exactly what use to make of it. His instincts told him he must be careful, that it might well be a long game, and if he couldn't make up his mind what to do it would be better to wait until he could. A false step could ruin everything. He was aware of a strange and novel anxiety, the cause of which he could not identify, and a cold anger that seemed to burn, despite its coldness, in his stomach. He looked around him in contempt; he felt that he had never before noticed the sickly yellow of the peeling walls, or realized how oppressively low the ceiling was. He felt engulfed by a new weariness, almost a sadness, and instinctively he turned his face to the wall and closed his eyes. Time enough to look at that wall when he had to. For now he had to think, harder than he had ever thought before. There was too much at stake for him to lose his grip now. Mr. Recorder Walkinshaw. So that was who he was. He nearly laughed as he remembered his anger that November night, or rather how he had tried to be angry, but could find nothing in his heart to match the anger that he knew he should have felt. Instead he had felt a strange pity, and an echo of that pity stirred again in his heart. Life's a bitch, he thought, life's a bitch and then you die, what else can you do? He tried to conjure up a mental picture of the judge and Hannah together, tried hard, but for some reason his imagination, usually acute, could not reach it, and he frowned in frustration, disliking the fuzziness in his head where he had hoped to find a sharp picture, something real, something that would prove informative, valuable, give him a clue to something. He felt an urge to sift his memory, though for what he had no idea. Memory was invaluable in here, all the other seemed to live on it, clinging on to the past or the future, unable to live fully in the slow minutes of the prison days, weeks, years. He understood; he had always had a strange sense that time was different inside. It wasn't just that time went slowly because you hated being there, it was more than that, the very air had a different quality, the seconds passed in a different way, day felt like night and night like day. It was almost, he reflected, turning over again and staring hard at the ceiling, almost like slipping into eternity, almost like being dead. But he had always found a way of living within the present, alien though it was. Perhaps that's why I survive, he thought, perhaps that's why I'm still here, when some of the others leave via the mortuary with all their stuff in a black plastic bag, waiting to be collected by a grieving relative. And some of them don't have any grieving relative, their stuff's collected by a clerk from their solicitor's office. Oh, the shame. He grinned to himself, but he found his eyes wandering around the cell once more. There used to be a pipe running across the ceiling, back in the day, it was like a fucking invitation, but they took them all out. You could find a way, though, everyone found a way. One entrance and a thousand exits. Though I'd never hang myself, he thought, never, people think it's instant but it's not, you slowly choke to death, and by the time you realize it's too late, you can't do anything but wait to die, swinging there, choking. What an end. He'd known several who'd taken it. Like Tommy Lithgow from Edinburgh. Little Tommy, on this block for a week and a half, always laughing, a great big grin with missing teeth, and 'Marie' tattooed on his neck.

He'd had another tattoo, a great dragon that covered nearly all of his skinny chest, the tail running over his left shoulder. They'd laughed at him because it was an outline only. 'You couldn't take the pain, you fucking nonce.' He'd got all indignant, he was going back to get it coloured in on the Wednesday, but he'd got arrested on the Monday, the minute he got out of here he was going back to get it finished, etc. But he never did get it finished. Danny sat up, suddenly horrified by the thought of the unfinished dragon on Tommy's dead chest, the dragon dead too, never brought to life. It never had any fire coming out of its mouth, they had laughed at him for that too. He imagined Tommy lying in his grave with his dead dragon, and felt a cold terror in his heart.

**

They sat silently at a small table next to a dirty window through which the watery light streamed uncertainly. A slot machine against the wall sang loudly at intervals, and an elderly drunk with a scarlet, pitted face swore at it, waving his tankard. Walkinshaw felt unbearably tired; he felt as though he could never get up again. Somewhere in the back of his mind all the drama of the last forty eight hours kept playing itself out, endlessly, and he shrank from it in fear, the old feeling of unreality sweeping over him again. He looked at Ratchett, shovelling mushy peas into an open mouth, pausing only to wipe his forehead with his napkin, and wondered if he really had been there in his kitchen last night, reading Isobel's letter, whispering about him with Gregory in the hall. Surely it had all been some sort of dream? But then he realized that the house would be empty when he returned home at last, and he felt a kind of excited dread at the prospect. Everything seemed blurred, inside and outside his head; he felt that nothing made any sense, and that he hardly cared whether it did or not. He felt a strange new violence in his heart; he looked at Hannah and felt sick with desire. He felt a new anger with the idea that he should deny himself anything, especially now, as the threads of his life were unravelling before his eyes, everything was swirling about, meaninglessly, and nothing made any sense. He looked at Ratchett in anger; surely he could see that he ought to leave, that he wasn't wanted?

Ratchett put his knife and fork together, then screwed up his green paper napkin and put it alongside them, sighing with satisfaction. 'Not bad, that. I could just have a nap now, but no rest for the wicked, eh?'

Walkinshaw looked at him, almost puzzled. He was so tired now that he could hardly understand. Somehow he managed a smile. 'Yes, quite.'

There was a silence. Suddenly there was a crack of thunder overhead, and rain began to lash against the windows. Walkinshaw flinched, fear at his heart. His eyes met Hannah's, wide and anxious, but he could not find a smile. He felt detached from himself, filled with a calm desperation. In this sort of mood I could kill myself, he thought suddenly, or someone else. He shook his head, impatient, but still he could feel his heart banging insistently inside his chest, like someone locked in a dark room, he thought, desperately hammering to get out. I could go mad like this, maybe I am mad already, how would I know? I have to find a way of numbing this pain, I have to do something, I am not going home alone.

'We did all right, didn't we? I always thought you'd get off, you're far too pretty for prison, though I suppose I oughtn't to say that, should I, Mr. Walkinshaw? I say, she's far too pretty to be stuck in prison, isn't she?' Ratchett was embarking on his sponge pudding; he reached clumsily across the table for his jug of custard, waving an enormous spoon in the air as he did so. Walkinshaw's eye followed the spoon like one hypnotized; why have they given him such a big spoon, it's like a tablespoon, it makes no sense. I am dreaming this, either that or I really am mad. None of this is real, surely.

'She is very pretty,' he said, grimly, not looking at her. He could hardly recognize his own voice. The rain was still lashing against the window; he felt that the three of them were bound together, fenced off from the rest of the world. He felt that this moment would go on forever, it had to, there could be no future after this. He would sit at this table for the rest of his life, or perhaps for all eternity, listening to Ratchett, with tearless eyes and with a new and frantic longing crawling its way through every last inch of his veins.

'Oooh, d'you hear that, love, you've got an admirer!' Ratchett looked up from pouring his custard to wink at Hannah. He seems to have no sense at all of the strain in the atmosphere, thought Walkinshaw, well, he's the normal one, maybe it's me imagining things again. He turned his head to look at her; she was already looking at him, with a sort of anguished inquiry in her expression, and he felt a dryness spreading in his mouth and throat. He could not look away; at last she looked down in confusion and began to tear an empty sugar sachet into tiny pieces. Suddenly lightning flashed past the window; in the unnatural light the room seemed claustrophobic, eerie, and fear tore at his heart once more.

'Well, we can't go out in this rain, that's a fact. We might as well have another lager, eh, Mr. Walkinshaw? What do you say? Not like you're in any rush, is it? I must say this is nice, isn't it? Nice to relax, I was going to say at the end of the week, but it's only Tuesday!

Still, who cares, eh? It's a poor heart that never rejoices, I say.' Ratchett scraped his enormous spoon around the bowl, then picked up the custard jug and peered inside it, putting it back on the table with evident disappointment. 'We made short work of that custard, didn't we? I could have done with a bit more, to be perfectly honest with you.'

Hannah moved a little, leaning forward with her elbows on the table, and he found himself watching her carefully, as though in the slightest of her movements his destiny was written. He could think of nothing to say; he sat observing her mutely, as the rain beat down upon the flimsy roof, and small spurts of water began to appear in the corners of the room. Still they sat there; she began to twist her hands together, in a gesture that might have been nervous but seemed to be merely abstracted. At intervals she looked up at him through her eyelashes, uncertainly, and he returned her gaze, conscious of nothing but the everlasting ache in his heart, and the sound of the rain on the roof and on the pavement, falling all around them, but leaving them untouched.

At last it was over. He felt a trace of nostalgic regret for the afternoon, already lost, as he put his coat on, surprised at the steadiness of his hands. Ratchett was yawning as he fumbled for his umbrella. 'Half past three! Hardly seems worth going back to the office, does it? Well, a good time was had by all. Hope to see you again soon, Mr. Walkinshaw. Chin up.'

He watched him waddling along the dirty pavement, into a wet afternoon grown prematurely dark and old. He stared at the pub lights reflected in the puddles at his feet, and felt an urgent pull of memory, a need to conserve and recall everything. It all matters, he thought, everything matters, and how little of it I have understood. He felt that he could have stood there all night, like a statue, feeling nothing of the cold and the rain, but he knew that he could not, he knew that he would not have to, that it would not end that way. As she put her hand upon his arm he knew what it meant, and as he walked beside her through the darkening streets he knew that it was inevitable.

Chapter Nine – You Be Careful

Norman Tombs staggered up the steep narrow stairway, with both his arms full of files, and his briefcase balanced precariously under his chin. He stopped at the dirty green door that led into his shared office space; was it too much to ask that someone might have left the door open for him? Obviously it was. Somehow he contrived to open the door with his foot, and by twisting his body round against the doorframe he managed to slide into the room, only to catch the cuff of his anorak against the door handle. He stumbled, his files and briefcase falling to the floor with an angry thud, and one of the receptionists – the one who had laughed at him on the day of his interview, he would never forget her face – wandered past and unhooked him from the door, smiling slyly. As he straightened up, red faced, he dared to look at her for a moment, and felt something of that terrible, humiliating thrill he had felt at the court when he had had to see that prostitute. She was tall, taller than him, and pretty, though in a trashy, tarty way, as he kept telling himself; artificial yellow hair ran down her back and excited him with its wanton falseness. She had sex, he knew that, he had overheard her talking to the other girls in the typing pool, she had sex a lot, apparently, and with different boys, different men, but she wouldn't have sex with him, nobody would. This is terrible, he thought in desperation, my life is a nightmare, I'm a freak. For an instant he heard Daniel Reynolds' voice in his head again. 'I can tell you're not getting any.' What is wrong with me? It's mother's fault, I was too sheltered, all those Sundays at the chapel hearing about sin and judgement, no wonder I'm not normal. He almost wanted to die, then, as she handed him his notebook, and murmured, with a malicious softness, 'You want to be careful, you do,' then turned and walked slowly out of the room. He could feel her smiling to herself at him, even though he could not see her face.

Numbly he made his way over to the small desk in the corner of the room that was his, and opened one of the files on it, trying to read, but the words swam before his eyes. What is wrong with me? What have I done? He tried not to think about his terrible moment at the prison. Nothing was to be gained by fretting about it, it was done, there was no recalling it. It was probably forgotten already, Reynolds must have a lot on his mind, and he hadn't seemed all that interested. But Tombs knew in his heart that Reynolds had been interested, very interested, and his heart shrank in fear as he remembered those dark, hooded eyes, that low, commanding voice, that had seemed to follow him about all through last night, even when he put out his bedside lamp and lay cold and trembling in his clammy bed. 'I can call you Norman, can't I?' He had woken finally at five o'clock, after a dismal and restless night, and had got up hagridden with worry in the grey dawn, feeling that the most basic of the day's tasks were utterly beyond him. He had never loathed so much making his mother's breakfast and running her bath before in his life; never before had the task of putting her underwear on to wash so stung him with bitter resentment. He felt a new hatred growing in his heart; stronger, more aggressive, less tempered by affection and shared memory. He felt now that there was no part of his life that he could look back upon without this new hatred casting its dark light; every part of his childhood seemed now to have been cruel training for this bitter present, every suffocating day spent with his mother was another brick in his prison. He looked at his life squarely, and blamed it, found it guilty of causing the agonizing inadequacy he had to live with now. He felt tears coursing down his face; hastily he took off his glasses, fumbling in his pocket for yesterday's tissue.

'Now then, lad.' Ratchett loomed up towards him; in the crude fluorescent light, which only seemed to emphasize the darkness of the morning outside, he seemed grotesque, and Tombs closed his eyes for a moment with a shudder.

'You look a bit green about the gills, get yourself a coffee, sharpen up, mate. Don't forget to get those defence statements done, will you? They should have been in on Friday, best get 'em in today or the judge'll have our bollocks.'

'I wasn't sure what to put,' said Tombs unsteadily, blinking back his tears. 'I never heard back from Counsel.'

'Just put 'The defendant maintains his innocence of all charges and asks the Prosecution to prove their case at trial.' That'll do.'

'But –'

The door opened again, sharply. 'Phone for you, John. Daniel Reynolds.'

'Put it through to my room, Linda,' said Ratchett, his face assuming the expression Tombs had come to recognize contemptuously as his 'important client' look. 'I'll be straight through. Hope you didn't do anything to upset him yesterday, Norman, clients like him are worth five hundred of the usual scum. Dennis'll fucking kill us if we lose him.'

The door banged behind him, leaving Tombs at his desk, frozen with fear. He got up from his desk, desperate, and went to the door, hoping to hear something of Ratchett's side of the conversation. But he could hear nothing; Ratchett's room was too far away. He could feel the sweat breaking out on his forehead; at this very moment Reynolds must be telling

Ratchett what he had said. He must deny it, that was his only hope, denial. But he knew perfectly well that if it came down to his word or Reynolds', Ratchett and Caldwell would believe Reynolds every time. He had no idea why, but he knew that it was so. He felt a sting of hatred for Reynolds; what was his game? What did he gain from all this? Confused as he was, he knew that Reynolds was not a man to do anything for nothing; he must have some sort of plan in mind. Perhaps he wanted to make a complaint against Mr. Walkinshaw, perhaps he saw his way to making some sort of allegation of improper conduct. Tombs' brain went cold again as he thought of the dangerous information that he had left in Reynolds' hands. This was a nightmare, it was even worse than he had imagined. He could not stand it any more; hardly knowing what he was doing he started towards Ratchett's room. He had to know what was going on.

He stood, rigid with horror, on the threshold. Ratchett was still on the phone; he was leaning back in his chair, frowning, though his voice was strainedly pleasant. 'All right, mate. Yes, that's fine. Not a problem. You take care of yourself.'

Ratchett put the receiver down and looked hard at him in puzzlement. Tombs felt that his heart had turned to water, that he was going to faint. His head was swimming, but he had to get his question out.

'What – what did he want, then?'

Ratchett still looked at him, surprise and a new hostility battling across his face. 'Well,' he said at last, coldly, 'it seems he wants you.'

'What?'

'Are you deaf or something? He wants you to handle his case exclusively from now on. He said he thought he had a rapport with you. He always was a bit odd.'

'Me?'

'Yes. You. I'm surprised myself, I must say. Though they do this, villains like him, they get a taste for new blood every now and then. Steady on, lad, you're as white as the wall behind you. Still, good news he's staying put, I was afraid he was going to defect to bloody Anderson's, he did once before. Well, I'd better tell Linda to put your name on his file. Bizarre.'

He shuffled out of the room perplexedly, giving Tombs another hard glance as he did so. He paused in the doorway, and absentmindedly pulled a leaf from a dead pot plant standing on top of one of the filing cabinets. The tearing sound made Tombs jump; he looked almost with terror at Ratchett, standing there crushing the dead leaf to dust in his large, floury hand.

'One thing I will say to you, son,' he muttered, and Tombs found himself flinching back, horrified by the sudden ugliness in his face. 'You be careful.'

**

Night became day so imperceptibly that the first faint glow of light in the east of the sleeping city seemed like a dream, impossible somehow. The night seemed timeless, ordinary laws were suspended, obsolete, they had to yield to events that were so much greater than they were, so much more important. This night could not end like ordinary nights, the faint growl of traffic outside the window growing louder and more insistent as six o'clock became seven, and then half-past seven, and then there was no denying it at all, it was morning, it was tomorrow, the night was gone. But this night, surely, would obey its instincts, would draw itself about and around them like a veil, and hide their secrets.

He lay, wrapped in thought that was not really thought, but feeling, which, it seemed to him, had so filled his heart that there was no more room in it; now it was spreading through him, reaching up into his mind, his thoughts, everything now was feeling, he could no longer think without that fullness in his heart, which threatened to overflow entirely at any moment, flooding every cell of his body with an ecstatic pain. He felt himself to be a new, more realistic version of himself, a more faithful rendering; he was transfigured, real, alive, and all the dangers that his mind hazily saw opening up around him were nothing, nothing that could harm him, they existed only to serve as a contrast to the joy opening itself up inside his heart, only to show him how truly impervious he was to them.

The agony of a new happiness welled up inside him; he felt that each breath he took was a betrayal of this moment, a second nearer to the inevitable future that he dreaded. He raised his head from the pillow, hardly daring to look at the empty space, filled with a strange fear of it, of her absence. Already the memory of an hour past was redolent with pain; how could he ever hope to express it, but how could he ever bear not to, how could he bear to let it die, to let it fall into the fabric of the past? He had asked her to stay, he had begged to say that they could meet again, but already her eyes were lost to him, already she had become unknowable again. She had looked at him with a vague tenderness that cut him to the heart, but she was looking past him too, looking at something which he could never see, which he could never understand. He had watched her dress with an easy, unembarrassed practice; he felt that he was watching her disappear, that with every movement she was abandoning him, entirely and forever. He did not dare to ask her what the large red bruise was that throbbed inside her elbow, or how she had come by the still livid scars that ran across her forearms like little scarlet threads. He had felt a sort of anguish at her beauty; the rise of her thighs to her slim hips, her smooth flat stomach with its blurred tattoo, a pale blue butterfly surrounded by three stars. He had always thought that he hated tattoos on women, but he felt that he loved hers, and as she buttoned her jeans over it he had felt a stab of panic at the thought of never seeing it again. He closed his eyes again in a sudden pain. What is happening to me? Life is too wonderful and too fearful to be endured. He remembered her sharp fine shoulders, and the natural grace of her neck, as her dark blonde hair fell down her back, her beautiful long dark blonde hair, almost long enough to cover her breasts. What did it all mean? How could he ever hope to understand what had happened to him? He felt the familiar salt of tears rising in his throat, and he wished he could cry, he felt that he wanted to cry, for her and her beauty, and for himself, and for their love, so fragile, and yet so precious that he felt that he would die for it, he would die rather than live without it. Slowly he raised himself on one elbow, and looked out of the window into the sombre morning, awestruck, like a man who has seen a miracle.

**

Danny lay, silent, waiting for the shouting to die down, waiting until there was peace enough to think. The mist in his brain had cleared a little; he felt that he could make some sense of it all now, that at last he saw his way clear, or clearer. With the decision he had made came an obscure pain at his heart that he dimly recognised, but which he ignored resolutely; there was work to be done, there was survival to be fought for. Burnsy had arrived that night; he had seen him, just briefly, in canteen, and something in him had shuddered at what he saw, but he forced himself to ignore it, just as he forced himself to ignore the strange old prickle of emotion he had felt on deciding on his plan. Still he felt a sort of compunction at that blue-white, haunted face, the acne scars reddened with salt tears, the eyes swollen and blinded like those of a drowned man. They'll have to put him on Rule 43, he thought, he's a dead man going around looking like that. He remembered the cold night air – why was it always winter in his memory? – as they had stood together by the phone box on the corner, near the park, Burnsy with his hat pulled down over his red ears, alternately anxious and excitable. The memory of those nights cut at him sharply, and he wondered why; they were not friends, they were associates, both of them knew that. Still, Burnsy hadn't dared to grass on him in interview. That thought gave him a little thrill of satisfaction. He still had it, they were still scared of him. The time to worry was when that went, you could just lose it, you wake up one morning and it's gone, all the respect and the fear, and you're nobody, nothing, just some bastard that everyone hates because of all the shit you've done. I'm thirty next birthday, he thought, with a thrill of fear, thirty, none of this will last forever. Already he thought he had noticed a new tide of contempt rising around him in the faces of some of the others on the wing; there'll be those who think I've already had it, that I'm a spent force. Every year that passes, every month, every week, it gets just a little bit harder to maintain, it takes more effort to make less effect. I don't want to live much longer, he thought suddenly, struck by the idea of his death as though taken by surprise. He imagined his own funeral, and forced himself to smile, although that little thrill of fear still lay at his heart. Who would come? He closed his eyes, trying to imagine his father's face, and failing. It must be crimson now, crimson like blood, his eyes must be pale, liquid, swimming around like desperate fish in a shallow, slimy pond. He'll speak in that slow, stupid way, in a thick, lost voice, his tongue too big for his mouth, a mouth condemned to be always dry, always thirsty. He moved his head sharply, overcome by a sudden squeamishness at the thought. But that's what he'll be, that's what drunks are. Especially ones who've been on the street as long as he has. What would I say to him if he came in here now? If they said to me, 'Oh, Danny, we've got a nice surprise for you! Look who your new padmate is, why, it's only your dear old dad, what a touching scene. It must be eighteen years, aren't you going to say hello to your poor old dad, for old times' sake?' His imagination leapt so quickly at the picture that he found himself glancing anxiously around his cell, lest some hideous old alcoholic jumped out at him from somewhere, sentimental tears coursing down his raddled old face. Dad. From nowhere he found himself recalling the day they'd chosen the Mercedes together, or Dad had let him think they'd chosen it together. He could still remember the newness of it, the smell of the leather, the nearly unbearable excitement. He had looked up at Dad, almost sick with pleasure, and realised that Dad was excited too, that this was a big and important day, that he must never forget it. 'Epoch-making.' That had been Dad's word. 'This is an epoch-making day, Daniel. I always promised your mum we'd have a Mercedes one day. Well, one day is here. One day is today.' Danny closed his eyes, then opened them again sharply in panic. Leave the past alone, it doesn't help. You've always lived in the present, refused to look into the past or the future, it's helped you survive. Don't give in to temptation now. But he saw that car, couldn't stop seeing it, he would see it forever, even when I'm dead I'll not get away from that fucking stupid car, why the fuck did he ever buy it, fucking stupid show-off that he was. Stop swearing, he said to himself, swearing is loss of control, swear deliberately and calmly or not at all. Stop it. The car. He must stop thinking about it, must stop imagining it with blood all over the bonnet, that beautiful bonnet, there was probably no blood, there often isn't any blood. People don't always bleed, or if they do, the blood goes on the road, surely, not on the car? There wouldn't be time to bleed on the car itself. He had asked the policemen who came to the door at midnight if there had been blood, unable to bear the thought of the car being soiled, dirtied, violated. He could still see the look on the face on the older one, still see his ginger moustache, his expression of horror and disgust. He thinks I'm a monster, a heartless, ghoulish little monster. Well, he wasn't wrong, I suppose. Perhaps I was. Perhaps I still am. Why can I still see that copper's face when I've forgotten everything else, can't even remember the trial, not really? I remember Dad's face, grey, well, it'll be red now, years on the bottle does that to you. Poor old Dad. Away to prison he went, and the next day I got my first ever social worker. First of many. Danny raised himself with an effort; his breath felt tight in his chest, and for the first time in his life he felt something close to claustrophobia. This could be dangerous, he thought, calm yourself down, you stupid bastard, take control of yourself. Take control. Slowly he lay down again, pulling the thin grey pillow from under his head, and lying flat on his back, taking slow deep breaths. This doesn't really calm me down, he thought, with grim amusement, it just makes me feel I'm doing something to calm me down, I suppose that's better than nothing. Still, the pain lay quietly at his heart, he felt as though it were bruising him, maiming him, killing him slowly. He suddenly thought of Hannah; he felt as though he could hear her voice, always quiet, nearly whispering. Why did she never get angry with him? Why did she never shout? Recalling her now, she seemed pale and ghost-like, hardly real, and yet he was suddenly conscious that he loved her. And the things he had made her do. She had never seemed to mind, she had never seemed either not to want to do it, or to want to do it; she had accepted it, and that was all. He suddenly found himself wondering if she loved him, and whether, with a life like hers, she could ever really know herself. He had told her he wanted to marry her, and he had read the panic in her eyes, and understood it. Time would take care of that; he just needed to get out of this place, that was all. Thinking about the present was like a physical relief, like, he thought with irony, getting out of prison, the present was real, changeable, controllable, it was the past where nightmares lurked, where evil waited for him. Don't ever think about the past again, he warned himself, don't do it, there's danger and madness in it, there's the ruin of everything you want, everything you've worked for. Live in the present, the future if you must, but die to the past, let it die to you. He closed his eyes, making himself think of Hannah, her face, her eyes, her body, her voice, anything but the twisted chrome of that wonderful pristine badge, the oil and steam bleeding away into the wet tarmac, and the car, that beautiful, beautiful car, headfirst against a tree in its death throes.

**

Hannah made her way anxiously past the tiny box-like houses, wishing it were still dark, hoping desperately that her father might be out, might be asleep, might be dead even, anything, but not at home, not waiting for her. Yet she knew he was, she could feel it, she could feel the malignity of his presence radiating out from the house, so strongly that she stopped for a minute, uncertain whether to go home at all. Yet what else was there to do? Where else was there to go? She knew he would be angry, she knew that in going off without him she was storing up trouble for herself; she had known all through the afternoon and the evening that there would be a price to be paid. She had not dared to disobey him like this for a long time, not since Danny was around. But he had always protected her; his presence had always set a watch on her father's conduct. He had known, even in his rages, that there were lines that could not be crossed. But now she was defenceless, and she shuddered inside with fear, looking over her shoulder wistfully at the street behind her, the last traces of a vanishing freedom. Suddenly the fear overwhelmed her, caught her unawares, and she leant against the wall, breathless, wanting to cry, dizzy with the ache of it all, the uncertainty of everything, the endless search for something that could never be found. She was two doors away from home; whatever home meant. Presumably home meant this: years and years of this, until she was old, until she had not even looks to trade upon, until she had nothing at all but bitterness and anger. The only inheritance my father ever gave me, she thought, a little surprised at her own cynicism. All I ever got from him. And how disgusted Mr. Walkinshaw would be, how degraded he would feel if he knew. Her mind flinched away; she did not want to think about him, about what they had done. Already she felt a kind of disappointment. Of course, it was what he had wanted, and it had been an easy way to say thank you. At least he had enjoyed it. But she was conscious of a new emptiness, a growing void inside her; she had given all that she had to give, there was nothing left now, nothing more to be said or done.

What am I, she asked herself wearily, who am I? It was all too difficult, too confusing, and nothing made any sense. His house had been beautiful, overwhelming, embarrassing, and yet he was not happy; his unhappiness pervaded everything, it had even seemed to follow her home, so that she felt she could cry for him, and for everything of his that she could never understand. She was aware that his wife had gone, and that that meant something, though quite what it meant she could not fathom; he was hurt and distressed, she knew that, and he had wanted distracting from it all. That too she was familiar with, and could understand. But she was perturbed by the sense of desolation that she had felt in that spacious, silent house; what was wrong with him, what was wrong with them both? Why such a sense of tragedy? He had looked at her with such pain in his eyes that she had dressed and left hastily, running away from something inexplicable, something essential in herself that she dare not acknowledge. She was pursued with a feeling that something important had happened, something far more important than landing a wealthy client, though she could not explain it; she felt a kind of prophetic ache through her body as she leant, still, against the wall, trembling, a little nauseous, waiting to take the steps she knew she must take, sooner or later.

'I needn't ask where you've been.' There he was, and she waited for the old familiar disgust to flood through her as usual, the disgust and the fear. She felt the anger again, just like before, just like every time, burning through her stomach like acid, eating into her womb. She wondered how it was possible to feel such anger, such hatred, and survive, keep on talking, walking about, living.

'I stayed the night at Chelsea's. No curfew any

more, remember.' She stared at the floor, repulsed; she felt a new, cruel sense of violation running through her blood. This man had denied her everything, he had taken away her life, now he wanted to know about the only meaningful thing in her world, the only thing she could call her own. She would tell him nothing. She could not look at him, she would not look at him if it cost her her life.

'I can check that,' he said, coming closer to her, closer and closer, his face inches from hers. She backed against the wall, sickened. She tried for a moment to reconcile herself to it, to him, as she had sometimes managed to do before, in the past. But this time there could be no reconciliation. This time she knew what it was, what he was doing, that it was not love. She knew in her heart that there could be no resignation this time, no explaining it away, no peace to be gained by locking herself in the bathroom afterwards with a clean razor blade.

'Check then. Check all you like,' she muttered, trying to wrench herself past him, desperate. An image flashed into her mind suddenly, a picture from a book in the prison library; a fox gnawing off its own hind leg to escape from a trap. Horror flamed its way through her body; she was filled with a mute, unseeing fear, the fear of nightmares.

'You were with him, weren't you?' His face was in hers now, she felt his spittle on her face. 'You were with him, you whore. You little slut. How much did you get for it?'

She could not look up; she knew what his expression would be, she knew how he would be looking at her, and what he was going to do. Suddenly his hold on her changed, as she had known it would, and his breathing became heavy and laboured. She tried to raise her hands to her ears, in an instinctive attempt to block it out; that breathing, that terrible sound that would never leave her alone, that she had heard in her bedroom nearly every night, even at the old house, before mum died. That breathing. Every last inch of her body, her being, begged somebody, somewhere, to make it stop. But there was nobody to make it stop, and she knew that, knew that it would never stop, even as he dragged her bodily into the palely lit kitchen, and she heard, as though in another world, the door swing shut behind them.

**

Walkinshaw sat silent in the robing room, his eyes fixed on the bundle of papers on the desk in front of him, unable to take in a word, and just as unable to raise his eyes from them. He was conscious of a strange coldness in himself, an inability to connect with people, events, his own life. He wondered whether this was normal, whether it was understandable, given the turbulent events of the last few days. Three days ago my wife left me, less than twenty-four hours after that I slept with a lay client. In my own house. He felt a little muted pride at this, then felt hot with guilt, worrying that on some subconscious level he had slept with Hannah only to take some sort of revenge on Isobel. That would be unforgiveable. He wondered why it should be that he worried more about wronging Hannah, using her; surely it should be his wife he thought of first, irrespective of how she had treated him? He tried to conjure up images of Isobel in his mind, tried to piece together fragmented memories, impressions, moments, but they seemed tantalizingly out of reach; he could not grasp them, they seemed to flee from him, to hide in the shadows, away from the reach of memory. Yet last night she had come to him in his dreams, whispering to him, her eyes soft, softer than they ever were in life, and his heart had flooded with joy, he had reached out, drowsily, over the bedclothes, and clutched at an empty space, his heart pounding, his brain dry with the horror of loneliness. He felt then that she must be dead, somehow, she could not be alive, less than a quarter of an hour's drive away in Reggie Dakers' nice little city centre flat, one of those new developments. He has a sixth floor penthouse, one of those with a glass roof, and panoramic views of the city. Panoramic views of the city. He imagined Isobel and Dakers, sitting together, post-coital, in their half-a-million-pound panopticon, watching his anxious coupling with a young street prostitute, and his mind reeled; everything was too horrible to be endured. An image of Hannah flashed into his mind; standing on the embankment, leaning into cars, smiling, and suddenly it sickened him, suddenly he felt that it really was dirty, disgusting, and he felt a wave of relief that he had used a condom. You're the disgusting one, he told himself, you have the money, the status, the privileges, you can pick and choose, she can't. But still he saw Isobel's clear, lovely skin, her smile that showed perfect white teeth. He had always loved her teeth; his own were a little crooked, and he was self-conscious about them. But Isobel's were perfect, and her lips had opened over them perfectly, like something from an advertisement, and he shuddered inside with thwarted desire; what had gone wrong between them? It was his fault, it must have been. He had let her down somehow, he had not come up to her standards. It was not her fault, it could not be her fault, if she had been cold to him he must have deserved it. Suddenly he longed for his old life, coming home to her, that strange professional bond they had, the mild interest they took in each other's careers. He felt he would give anything to come home tonight and see her car in the drive again, see her profile, imperious, aloof, silhouetted against her study lamp as she worked into the night. She could ignore him all she wanted, she need never speak to him again, all he felt he wanted was to have her again, to feel she was still his wife, still his, however reluctantly. For a moment he wondered why she could not have kept Dakers as a lover; he felt for a wild moment that he would not have minded, not really. She must love him, he thought, a knife-like feeling at his heart, she must really love him, because he's not as senior as me, nor likely to be. Even people that like him – and there aren't many of them - admit he's of very average ability. And she was always so career-minded, had that strange ruthlessness at her core which frightened him a little sometimes. Yet she had sacrificed it for him. Not much of a sacrifice, perhaps, but a sacrifice nonetheless. You'd think she might have left me for a high court judge, if she was going to leave me at all, he thought, bitterly, and smiled a little, but still his heart ached with the harshness of it all, the cruelty that lay at the heart of everything. It was not her fault; if he had been hurt, damaged, it was because life was cruel, that was all. Sometimes you get hurt in life, because you can't cope with not being wanted by someone you want badly – and in his case – someone you've had but couldn't keep, couldn't make happy. It was not her fault, she had only one life, like all of us, and she wanted to live it to the full, with someone who made her happy. That was only fair. Perhaps he had made her happy, for a while, perhaps it's not meant to be forever, whatever the marriage service says, perhaps we are only meant to be with each other for a while, then things stale, and isn't it better to have the honesty to say so? Isobel was not one to live a lie, she was always honest, always blunt; it was something he had admired about her, loved even, her directness, her certainty, contrasting so painfully with his own hesitant approach to life. He thought suddenly of Hannah and her nervous self-effacement; perhaps we're two of a kind, he thought bitterly, perhaps I should marry her and install her in my nice five bedroom detached house, Isobel's old house, that would put the cat among the pigeons. Or invite even more scorn and derision. He imagined Isobel's face, he imagined her talking to Reggie about him. 'Well, this just proves what I've been saying about him, he lives in a fantasy world, he must be having a breakdown. Thank God I got out when I did.' And Gregory and the others, all of them. 'How much is that costing you, Mervyn? You don't always have to pay, you know.' His stomach crawled with shame; he felt as horrified as though it had really happened. He must see her again, he must end it, gently, whatever 'it' was; he must explain that he couldn't possibly have a relationship with her, it was impossible. He should have paid her, then it would have been clear, but somehow he couldn't, it would have been insulting, somehow. Though she probably would have taken it, she must be desperate for money. Perhaps he could give her some money this time, a nice large sum, something that she could start again with. But that wouldn't do; it would look like a blackmail payment; a man in his position couldn't start giving prostitutes large sums of money, it would look very strange if it ever came out. Perhaps a couple of hundred pounds; that would be a lot of money to her, and it would salve his conscience. He felt engulfed with misery; what had he done? How would it all end? It all seemed impossible, unbearable. He tried for a moment to recapture something of that feeling he had had after Hannah had left, staring out of the window into the pale morning; he had thought then that it was something wonderful, a revelation, a spiritual awakening, but was it really? Was it not more likely just the inevitable response of strained nerves to an intense physical experience? Everything was bleak, everything was confusing, and in vain he stared at the case summary in front of him, noticing grammatical errors in it automatically, at the back of his mind, even while he flinched away from the heavy ache at his heart.

'All right, Mervyn? We've all been thinking of you, you know, and....' Gregory's voice trailed away; Walkinshaw imagined his words suspended in the air, dangling, waiting for the next one to join them; God, he thought, I must be exhausted.

'I'm not doing so badly.' He looked at Gregory; the stiff, awkward grey hair pushed out of shape by his wig, the heavy purple cheeks, with their enlarged pores, like the skin of an orange, the oddly thin lips, always a little dry and cracked, his tongue occasionally darting across them like a lizard's. His stomach looked almost distended, pushing his shirt out of shape; a couple of buttons were in imminent danger of bursting open. Is this it, thought Walkinshaw, will this be me in fifteen years, because if it is, then let me die now.

'I'm not doing so badly,' he repeated, quickly, anxious lest Gregory should have read his glance, and stricken with a strange sort of guilt, a sense of disloyalty. 'I think maybe I'm in a sort of state of shock.' He laughed, nervously, but Gregory only looked solemn, and his laughter shuddered to a ragged halt. He felt suddenly desperate, anguished, and he looked at Gregory almost in panic. 'I might take a few days off,' he added, feverishly; he felt unable to bear even the briefest of silences.

'You should. You should. Very good idea. And I tell you something else you should do. You should come to my dinner party on Saturday as planned. I know you were going to come with – before – well, there'll be no embarrassing encounters, I can assure you of that. And you needn't worry about feeling awkward, there's another single coming, so no anxiety on that score. Cressida Jenkins. You remember her?'

'I don't think so.' He felt as though he were being suffocated; it seemed impossible to get enough breath into his lungs, and he clasped his hands together, in an uncharacteristic movement; vague memories of prayers in the school chapel stirred uneasily in his memory.

'You do. Well, you will when you see her. She did her pupillage up here, then went down to London, but now she's back up here, wanted to be nearer her parents. Lovely girl, really lovely girl, bright as well, got a Cambridge first. Margaret and I thought we could put you two together, it's just what you need to take you out of yourself, stop all that brooding, you're a bit prone to brooding over things, you know, and –'

'Oh, it's kind of you, it is, but I'm really not ready–'

'Not ready for what? A nice casual little dinner with some old friends who care about you? Would you rather stay in with your spaghetti bolognaise for one, eh, old chap? Come on, don't wallow, don't wallow. I'll lay a pound to a penny you're the last to leave.'

**

Hannah closed her bedroom door doubtfully; she wished it had a lock, but there was no use talking to her dad about that. Still, although she was alone in the house she felt somehow observed, under surveillance, so that as she opened her letter she unconsciously turned it to her chest, as though to hide it from prying eyes. She felt an unexpected rush of love, of pride, at the sight of that familiar handwriting; Danny's lovely handwriting, a legacy of his prep school days. It had always seemed wonderful and mysterious to watch him write; like hearing a very close friend, or a relative, even, speaking a foreign language fluently. She had felt a little in awe of him, it gave him membership of some hidden world, something beyond her reach, and she would wonder how he came to be here, with them, how he had come to be her boyfriend. He had dismissed it, laughing, though a little flattered; words were words, he used to say, it didn't matter how you wrote them. But he had told her, with pride, that his solicitors used to keep all his letters, saying they were too good to be thrown away. This letter had come via the solicitors; she had collected it from Ratchett that morning. Danny was far too canny to send his letters via the ordinary prison mail. She remembered how frightened she had been of his letters when they arrived in prison, how menacing they had seemed, how possessive. But now, after what her father had done, a letter from Danny seemed to be the most welcome thing in the world; at least she still had him, at least he hadn't broken up with her as soon as his release date got near, as some of them did. Of course he was brutal sometimes, but that was to be expected; at least he didn't let her dad get away with anything. And he knew the worst, and still he did not leave her. Of course, that didn't stop him using it against her when he was angry, or when he wanted something from her, or when he wanted to put her in her place. But he knew. That alone made him someone she was frightened to let go, even while something in her was frightened to keep him too. Something in her knew that he was inextricably bound up in her fate, her life, maybe even her death too; life with him had been terrible sometimes, wonderful sometimes; life without him was unimaginable. Or it had been, until she had met Mr. Walkinshaw. She did not dare to let herself think of him, or dare to imagine being with him again; she could not risk letting her guard down, even letting herself fall in love. She had felt that she was in love, that day, sitting in the pub, and later, in his house, in his bed, she had felt a happiness that she dared not trust, she must not trust. She must concentrate on what she knew, on what security she had. She had thought she had experienced everything; she had not thought it possible to hurt more that she already had done, over the twenty years of her life, but, looking at him, as she turned to leave in the early morning, she had felt a sudden access of pain that she had not imagined, like a chasm opening at her feet. She must not let herself think about what life could have been like if she were different, it was taking cruelty too far. She owed it to herself to concentrate on what she had; what she had was Danny, and her hand trembled a little as she laid the letter on her knee and began to read.

Dear Hannah,

Thanks for your letters – all two of them, all saying something and nothing. You're breaking my heart, babe, you know how what it's like in here, you should take pity on me, your poor incarcerated fiancé. Though not incarcerated for a whole lot longer, if things go my way. I met someone the other day – someone you might have met, the new clerk at Caldwell's – and I think I see my way to getting out of this shithole, and, what's more, making a bit of easy money. That is, if my information's correct. But you must be wondering what the fuck I'm on about. I'll tell you. The learned gentleman who presided over my sentencing hearing – or 'that cunt in Sheffield' as I like to call him – also undertook your defence. Bear with me, sweetheart, your part in this will become clear in a minute. Now I'm not sure whether I can do anything with this or not

– I had a look in the prison Archbold, but no luck. Never mind, it'll keep. It was the second bit of information I got that really interested me. Apparently – I'm putting this as delicately as I can to spare your blushes – it appears you made a bit of a conquest. Which doesn't surprise me – you always were popular with the older ones, do you remember? This is a bit of step up for you though, and I want you to take the opportunity. Make what you can of it – you know what to do, God, if anyone knows, it's you. Take pictures if you can – though only if you can without raising the alarm – I'll have to leave it to you. I know you don't like all this, but it's for us, you know that. And – cunt though he is – he must be an improvement on some of the blokes you've done it with, God knows. I'm relying on you, mind you don't mess it up. I need this to work, I'm getting out soon whatever, and I don't intend to live on fucking air when I do.

And tell your fucking dad from me that if he even fucking thinks about touching you while I'm in here I will take great pleasure in breaking every fucking bone in his fucking miserable little body. Tell him. Don't leave out the 'fucking's.

Well, write soon, darling, I want a progress report as soon as. Get on to him straight away, don't give him time to back out.

Love you lots and lots,
Your husband-to-be,
Danny xxxx

Chapter Ten – A Death

Walkinshaw stood in front of the fireplace in Alexander Gregory's drawing room, his head already swimming a little, a cold flutter in his chest. He wanted to sit down, but felt too anxious; he was preoccupied with the idea that Isobel would come after all, that she would walk in any moment with Reggie Dakers, and he felt an absurd impulse to hide. In his nervous haste to get the moment of arrival over and done with he had come rather too soon, and Gregory was still floundering about in his shirtsleeves, red-faced, sweating, and able to engage with only a surface politeness. Walkinshaw wondered if he sensed that there had been an argument just before his arrival; there was unquestionably some tension in the atmosphere, though he found it hard to say if it was his or theirs; it seemed to float about the room, unclaimed and menacing. The ever-present knot in his stomach tightened; he drained his glass of gin and tonic at a gulp, and grimaced slightly. He felt awkward and self-conscious; it was unlike him to commit the social sin of arriving too early, and he felt embarrassed, though simultaneously he felt a sort of dread of the others arriving, and felt a tightening in his throat as the doorbell rang.

There were raised voices in the hall, and the unmistakeable sound of a heavy body falling against a radiator. 'I heard it, Margaret! I'm going! Can't you keep that bloody dog under control? I nearly broke my bloody neck!' Not another couple heading for the divorce courts, I hope, thought Walkinshaw, and felt for a moment as though he might break out into inappropriate, excessive laughter; not that again.

There was Gregory's voice again, in strained cordiality this time. 'Why, come in, come in, come in, so lovely to see you both. Not a bit too early, no. Lovely to see you again, my dear.'

'Well, I thought I'd give her a lift, not out of my way at all.' A familiar voice. Walkinshaw's memory stalled for a moment, it was a voice he should know, he did know. Oh, bloody hell. This was not at all fair of Gregory. How was he supposed to get through an evening in the company of Vernon Marlowe? Panic began to course through him again; this was too much, he was not up to this, he would have to make his excuses and then –

Here they were, standing in front of him. He felt dizzy, unable to focus; he was conscious of Marlowe's ironic, quizzical gaze, and felt a desperate need to control himself, to make sure he did what was required, whatever the consequences later. There was a young woman with him; her perfume was Isobel's. That was why he felt so dizzy. He wanted to go out into the street, into the garden, or go upstairs and lock himself in the bathroom, anything but to have to take the hand of, and look into the eyes of, this woman who was wearing Isobel's perfume, who was wearing Isobel's black cashmere coat, and smiling at him in hopeful sympathy.

'This is Cressida, Cressida Jenkins. You may remember –'

'Oh, I'm sure Mr. Walkinshaw won't remember me. It's almost nine years since I left the north.' She was looking up into his face; he had to return her smile, or he would have seemed appallingly rude. He was surprised at her expression; her eyes and smile seemed rigid with exaggerated interest, her face almost mask-like. Does she do that with everyone, he wondered, or am I the lucky one? It's a little off-putting.

'You remember him, though, it seems.' Walkinshaw looked at Marlowe, surprised; there was something unpleasant, something unexpected, in his tone, and once more there came a flicker of that sense of danger which he had felt in the courtroom, waiting for Hannah's verdict.

'Oh, I couldn't forget Mr. Walkinshaw. We all had a bit of a crush on him back then.' She laughed gaily, and Walkinshaw felt a stab of pain through his temples. This was going to be awful.

'Mervyn and I crossed swords earlier this week, didn't we, Mervyn? A dreadfully tedious being concerned, it lasted all of a day and a half, and I felt like it would never end.' Marlowe was looking in his direction, but his eyes were not on his face; they were staring, apparently unfocused, a little over his left shoulder, and without knowing why Walkinshaw felt a little thrill of fear.

'Did you win?' Cressida Jenkins was turning her glass of white wine round and round in her fingers, leaving little clear trails in the condensation of the glass. Her nails were short, clean and varnished clear, very white at the tip, just like Isobel's, her fingers were long and lean, somehow intelligent-looking, he thought deliriously. All at once the image flashed into his head of Hannah's hands, with their chipped, glittery varnish, moving across his chest, gripping his back, and his brain felt hot; he felt that he was going to choke.

'You look a bit wobbly, Mervyn, let me get you a refill. Well, one got potted, but the other – Mervyn's – was the one that got away, I'm afraid. Still, I expect the little lady will be back for more, don't you?'

'Hard to say.' It seemed impossible to breathe; he stepped away from the fireplace a little, hoping to find some cooler air.

'I think our Mervyn made another of his famous conquests. I saw them with their heads together, up in the cafeteria, and, oh, the guilty look on our Mervyn's face! Did she give you a discount later? Oh, I really shouldn't, I shouldn't, should I, Cressida?'

Cressida tossed her head a little, looking confused and annoyed. 'So glad I don't do crime,' she said, rather petulantly, and Walkinshaw's mind reeled at her eerie echo of Isobel.

'Why so, dear lady?' Marlowe was peering at her with intense interest, standing just a little too close; does he hold a torch for the fair Cressida? Absurd, thought Walkinshaw, why, he's twenty years older than her and about four inches shorter.

'I couldn't cope with all those people you have to cope with. It must be so depressing. I had to deal with some gypsies last week, as part of some council mediation work I'm doing, I tell you, that was bad enough. I had to try to make sense in my speech whilst keeping my eye on my handbag the whole time!' She gave a laugh that was partly scornful, partly nervous; Walkinshaw winced for her, felt a strange sort of pain across his heart. This was the sort of talk he hated, and yet, unaccountably, he found himself feeling a little sorry for her. She looked up into his face, biting her lip, her face suddenly anxious. She is quite attractive, he decided; her eyes were clear and grey, though a little small. Not large and limpid, like Hannah's; Hannah's big, wounded eyes, that looked at the world with a gentle confusion that was somehow both exasperating and endearing. Cressida was still staring at him, crimson mounting in her pale cheeks. She fancies me, he thought, with a thrill of surprised pleasure. She really does. And if she finished her pupillage nine years ago, assuming she didn't do anything else first, she can only be about thirty four. He looked at her with renewed interest, and smiled encouragingly.

**

Danny paced round and round his cell, stopping at intervals uncertainly, then resuming his pacing, back and forth, up and down, though there was hardly space for more than one stride before he had to turn back again. He felt gripped with claustrophobia, and found his eyes straining at the tiny, obscured window in the corner, far too high to see out of, and even if you could there was nothing to see except another concrete wall. His knuckles began to ache; he realized that he had been clenching his hands tightly ever since – ever since the alarm had gone off and they had been on lockdown. He looked at his clock in a sudden fury – it was twenty to nine, it should be association, get me out of this cell. Something inside him crumpled in fear. What was going on? He was suffocated with the weight of presentiment; something had happened, and he knew dimly that it was associated with him. He thought perhaps he knew what it was, but he dared not name it, dared not give it a shape in his thoughts. He wouldn't be so stupid, it was all just talk. He was like that. Anyway, I gave him a fag yesterday, he seemed all right, he knew there were no hard feelings. He stopped again suddenly, his lungs seeming to contract inside him. Oh God. Stupid bastard. Stupid fucking bastard. It must be him. He knew it was him, the way the guard had looked at him when he'd asked what was up. 'You'll know soon enough, mate.'

In desperation he went over to the grille on the door and began banging it, kicking the door, shouting. He needed to make a real noise, the wing was loud enough anyway, but he persevered, picking up a plastic chair and throwing it, with as much force as he could muster in such a tiny space, against the iron door. He stood back, his chest heaving a little as though he were sobbing, though when he raised a hand to his face his eyes were dry.

Still no one came, only a voice from the next cell. 'Shut the fuck up, Reynolds, you cunt.' Fury and fear took possession of him; he took the chair by its metal legs and smashed it, over and over again, until there were ragged holes in the pale beige plastic, blood under his fingernails, and silence from the cell next door. Then he crumpled to the floor, astonished and aghast, his heart pounding, a strange sort of numbness spreading through his chest and arms.

The grille opened, and the blank-eyed, jowly face of one of the wing guards appeared. At the sight of him terror flooded through Danny; he got to his feet, trembling, pain spreading through his stomach, and conscious that at last tears were pouring down his face.

'You smashing the place up, lad?' The guard was a heavy Glaswegian, anonymous amongst the guards. He had almost nothing to distinguish himself from the others, no means of identification, except his impenetrable accent and his overwhelming body odour. He looked at Danny with a sort of impassive sympathy, which frightened him still more. He would have been reassured by anger, threats of punishment and withdrawal of privileges. This was far more menacing; he was almost struck dumb with foreboding.

'It's him, isn't it? Jonathan Burns,' he said, slowly, watching blood flood around the base of his thumbnail and trickle slowly down.

'Aye, lad.'

'Is he dead?'

'Aye, 'fraid so, poor wee fella. Was he a friend of yours, was he?'

'It was me got him put in here,' said Danny savagely, clenching his tongue between his teeth, pressing his fingers against his forehead, trying to stem the flood of tears. 'How did he do it?' Don't say he hanged himself, please, Burnsy, don't have hanged yourself. Please.

'Ach, it's nae a pleasant topic, you should be calming yoursel' down –'

'Tell me.'

The guard looked straight into his face through the grille, his eyes, despite his sympathetic demeanour, strangely inexpressive. A nightmarish panic struck at Danny's heart; the guard's dull, bloated face seemed to him to be something horrible, unnatural, terrifying. He had asked the question, but felt a sudden horror at the idea of hearing the answer; he had a sudden childish urge to put his hands over his ears.

'Poor wee fella choked himsel', you know the way, round and round wi' his collar. It's an awful shame.'

**

Walkinshaw sat back a little in his chair, pleasantly replete. He had imagined that he might be too nervous to eat, that he would struggle to get anything down his throat, but somehow despite himself he had managed to relax a little, and look upon the evening with something like enjoyment. I ought to do this more, really, he thought, surveying the table, the faces, already a little flushed, the conversations becoming louder and more animated. Some woman sitting a little way down from him, a woman he didn't know, spread her hands too widely in the course of some anecdote or other, and sent red wine spraying in an arc across the white tablecloth; it looks like blood, he thought suddenly, blood from an artery, and the fear pressed against his heart again for a moment. But the moment soon passed in a flurry of apologies and reassurances, and Cressida Jenkins turned to him again with a smile, and resumed her account of her recent trip to Argentina; relief flooded through him. He did not need to force a smile; he felt a genuine pleasure in her company, a sense of security, of restfulness. At the back of his mind he knew the conversation was a little banal, slightly forced; he knew that she was trying a little too hard to impress, but that was flattering, so he forgave her that, and leant back indulgently in his chair, laughing in the right places at her rather long stories. She was nice-looking, albeit in a bland, conventional sort of way, and when she gave that rather too wide smile her teeth were perfect, even, and he felt a prickle of pain for Isobel, but also a new desire for her; he felt a strange desire to kiss her, there and then, in front of all those people. She seemed to sense the warmth of his gaze; she became hot and flustered, and undid a button on her blouse with slightly shaking fingers. He thought suddenly of Hannah again; a sad tenderness rose in his heart, slightly fuddled with alcohol as he was. Poor girl, he thought, she is beautiful, what a pity she has to lead that dreadful life. But Cressida was talking to him again, leaning in close, turning her shoulder against the rest of them, and her eyes were bright with excitement and complicity. He closed his for a moment, overwhelmed; his pain seemed to be oddly numbed, and he wondered whether he had had more than he thought, whether he was drunk. He smiled into her face, conscious of a drowsy satisfied anticipation. He wondered for a moment if his contentment meant that he was shallow; three days ago I thought I was in love with a prostitute, now here I am. Back on shore. Back on dry land. I must stop calling her a prostitute, it's not nice. Hannah. I thought I was in love with Hannah, but now-

'You're miles away, Mervyn.' She blushed a little. 'You don't mind if I call you Mervyn?'

'Of course not.' Hannah never had; she had never called him anything.

'I hope I didn't upset you before, you know, what I said about crime. I do admire people who do it, especially those who really put their heart and soul into it the way you do. You must really care about people, and, well, that's really... well, admirable.'

'That's a very kind thing to say, but-'

'Oh, I really mean it. I'm not really what you call a people person, I'm better with the law, you know, I did a little crime once, but what do you say to them?' She gave a little troubled laugh. 'And yet Vernon says you even have coffee with them!'

'Just the once, I don't make a habit of it.' How had they come to be talking about Hannah? The idea of Cressida Jenkins even mentioning her, knowing she existed, gave him an odd little twist of unease. It was like a dream intruding upon reality, it was not meant to happen. He glanced over his shoulder nervously, almost as though he expected to see Hannah standing there, at the window, with that already familiar expression of gentle reproach upon her face.

'Was she very attractive, then?' Her teasing tone could not quite conceal the anxious tension in her voice.

'Who?' he parried, feeling that his guilt must be branded on his forehead for all to see.

'The girl, the one you had coffee with.'

'It was nothing, I don't why Vernon –' the Christian name seemed to choke him – 'I don't know why he made so much of it. I just happened upon her, and was giving her some last minute words of advice. Nothing more than that.'

'Was she attractive, though?' Would she never give up? For a wild moment Walkinshaw had the idea that she knew everything, and was playing with him, like a cat with a mouse. He could hardly meet her eyes, but when he did he saw nothing but anxious jealousy, and relaxed a little.

'Yes. Yes, she was, poor girl. It's a shame, but-'

'But what can you do?' she interrupted, eagerly. 'Once the drugs get hold of them, that's pretty much that, or so I've heard. It's a shame. A real shame.'

There was a solemn silence. Walkinshaw felt that everyone, noisy as the room was, must be able to hear the pounding of his heart. He looked at Cressida; her head was lowered, she was looking down at the table, the flirtatious mood of a few moments ago dampened, and he felt irritated with Hannah Casey; would she intrude everywhere? How could she spoil a moment between him and another woman - an appropriate, suitable woman – when she wasn't even there? He had made a mistake, an error of judgement, a very bad error of judgement, but he had been – still was – under enormous emotional strain, he still was. All of us have our moments of recklessness, we all do things that don't look like such good ideas in the cold light of day. That's the way life is. And I can't have hurt her, I can't have done her any real damage, it's what she does for a living, for God's sake. He shook his head impatiently, annoyed at finding himself thinking about her, here, on one of the first nights in such a long time that he was actually enjoying himself.

Cressida had raised her head and was watching him, a slight smile on her lips, and he felt warmth returning through his body; it was all he could do not to reach and take her hand.

'You look so wise and mysterious,' she said in a low voice, pulling close to him again, 'I almost wish I could be one of your attractive clients, and you could give me advice, alone, over a quiet cup of coffee.'

**

Hannah sat up in bed, her heart pounding, her whole body hot and shaking. It was a dream, it must have been a dream. But it wasn't, she was awake now, but still the banging went on and on. She sat there, paralysed, hardly daring to breathe, flooded with horror. They were under her window now, shouting. 'Police! Open up! Police!' She turned on the light and looked at the watch she kept beside her bed. Twenty to six. That was about right. It must be dad they've come for. In bewilderment she wondered how they could have known; she searched her memory for anything she might have said or done. Was it something she had said while giving evidence? She heard the voices again, and trembled with a fear that was instinctive, primal; she felt she would not open that door if it cost her life, she could not. Then all at once there was a great blow on the front door; she felt as though the house was shuddering, as though it would fall down, and in fear she sprang out of bed and ran halfway down the stairs, then stopped, petrified.

The door of her father's bedroom opened, and he emerged, bleary, still in the vest and tracksuit bottoms he had been wearing the previous night. She turned to him eagerly, but her voice died away as she saw the look on his face; it had a strange white tinge to it she had never seen before, and his lips were trembling as though he were about to cry.

'Dad –'

'Go back to your room,' he muttered, hardly looking at her, and she went, shaking so that she struggled with the light switch, and could hardly turn the light off again. She climbed back into bed, carefully, and lay, perfectly still, in the darkness, listening to the traffic rumbling by, watching the yellow lights of the cars tracing patterns of the artex of the ceiling, her mind blank with terror and disbelief. She heard her dad take the door off the chain, she heard footsteps and voices, one of which she recognized, and she felt a strange cold pain welling up around her heart, but still she did not move, could not move, she just lay there. I want to stay here, lie here forever like a dead person, I want to be dead, just let me die, I want to be dead. She thought she was only thinking it, but perhaps she was saying it aloud; she thought she heard her own voice in amongst all the noise and the endless banging, of doors and cupboards and drawers, and then she realized she did hear it, it was her voice she heard, shouting, shouting over and over again, incoherently, as her bedroom door burst open and DC Glover strode in, right over to her, the room flooding with light, harsh, frightening, searching light. His hand was over her face, on her arm; there were others behind him, they were swarming all up the stairs like flies, big blue flies, the ones you get in the summer. A big man she did not know was pulling the drawers out, one by one, and emptying them on the floor, and turning over the tangle of underwear with a large, gloved hand. She felt a strange sort of blackness in her mind; she reached out to stop him, to make him go away, that was all she wanted, to make him go away, but Glover still had her by the arms, he was whispering something in her ear that she could not quite understand, and she leant back against his shoulder, exhausted, hoarse. Then she was down in the kitchen, still in her pyjamas, and there was a cup of tea in front of her, though she had no memory of making it; surely she had not made it? He was still there, sitting next to her, he was calling her by her name, and asking her things, things that didn't seem to make any sense, but she had to answer, he was looking at her so insistently, and his voice seemed kind, he seemed to know it was not her fault, none of it was her fault. She took a gulp of the tea in front of her, it was far too sweet, but that didn't matter. Nothing seemed to matter; there was nothing in the world at all, nothing, except the taste of the strong sweet tea in her mouth and throat, and the firmness of Glover's knee against hers.

**

Norman Tombs hovered nervously in the doorway of Ratchett's office, rubbing his hands together, not quite daring to enter. Ratchett had had his door closed for twenty minutes, always a sign that he didn't want to be disturbed, and although he had now opened it, Tombs still hesitated to go in. There had developed a new strain between them since that visit to Reynolds; he felt oppressed by guilt, and sometimes was so overwhelmed by the urge to confess everything that he had to excuse himself for a moment, so sure was he that he was on the verge of blurting everything out. Once or twice he had made up his mind to do so, just to lift the terrible weight of it off his mind, but then he had decided that he would be sacked, and the thought of the ignominy was enough to make him decide to endure it for a little longer, and hold his tongue. Sometimes he felt a little more confident, and decided that he would have to be thicker-skinned about these things if he were to be a successful lawyer; after all, things of this kind happened to everyone now and then. Still, he had not slept soundly since; sometimes he wanted to tell anyone, even Mother. He had looked across at her the other night, as they sat together in front of the television, and wondered whether to; but her face in profile, illuminated by the flickering screen, was forbidding in its disappointed sullenness, and he had kept quiet, and taken his heavy heart up with him to bed again.

'Is that you, Norman? What are you dancing about

there for? Come on in, lad.' Ratchett seemed pleased about something, his manner was almost like his old one, and Tombs felt a little relieved. He entered the room with his usual caution; no matter how long I work here, he thought, I will always feel like an intruder.

'I'm off to the nick today, may be a long job, could be a good payer and all. Mick Casey's been picked up for those sex attacks down by the canal. They're doing the interviews this morning.'

'Mick Casey? Isn't that - ?'

'One of our regulars. Yeah. We've got a common assault file on him, but this'll be a Crown court job, if it gets that far.' Ratchett chuckled, scratching his nose. 'What a bastard he is, eh? Wonder what they've got on him. About to find out, I suppose.'

**

So he was really dead, then. Burnsy was dead. Danny knelt on his bed, unable to lie down, unable to rest, though it was now morning, and after a sleepless night tiredness was beginning to bore its way behind his eyes. The blood under his thumbnail was beginning to congeal into an ugly black, and the muscles of his arms and wrists were aching. He looked up at the lowering, dirty ceiling in desperate fury. He had to get out of this place, urgently, every night spent in this place was a fucking insult, one he wouldn't take any longer. He shivered a little; despite the cold night and lack of heating, he had taken his shirt off, unable to endure anything around his neck. He tried to picture Burnsy, but his memory was oddly clouded; the only image that he could conjure up with any clarity was that of only a few nights ago, when he had arrived straight from court, without any belongings, and had had to appear in canteen in prison issue clothes, his face raw with tears.

He closed his eyes to block it out, his mind flinching. It isn't my fault, he muttered, it's not me, it's this fucking system. Anyway, I didn't get him on the gear. He would have ended up in here whatever. He remembered suddenly that he had been only twenty, a thought that horrified him; so young, so young to die. It should have been me, he thought, I'm sick of it all, I wouldn't have minded. Except I'd never give them the satisfaction. If they want me dead, let them come and kill me. Just let them come and kill me. All at once he wanted Hannah; where was she, what was she doing now? Who was she doing? He remembered the letter he had written her, and felt ashamed of it, though he didn't know why; it was not such an awful thing to ask, she might enjoy it, and there'd be money in it for both of them, hopefully. Still, he found himself anxiously trying to recall what he had put, how he had phrased it – was he being too hard on her? He would write again, and say it was up to her, that he personally thought it was a good idea, but that he would leave it up to her to decide if she felt like it. That was a good compromise. He began to reach towards the drawer in his little table to find a sheet of paper, but lethargy overtook him, and his hand dropped to his side. Best not to write at all, probably, better to wait and phone her, the news about Burnsy would be better told over the phone than in a letter. He went cold inside at the thought of telling her; she would be distraught, she might even be upset enough to blame him, at least immediately, until she had time to calm down and put it in perspective. He must be prepared for that. People do cast about for someone to blame, they can't accept that shit just happens, it's the way life is. I used to look about for someone to blame, back in the day, it was all mum's fault. If only she'd not let them put me in that home, I would have been all right, I didn't need dad, not really. He lay down at last, stiffly, but he could not close his eyes; he felt a sense of suffocation around his throat, and for a moment he choked with panic. Oh God. He really is dead. He's dead, the stupid fucker. He didn't need to, I would have looked out for him, prison's not so bad, he'd have survived, at least for a while, he only gave it four nights, the silly little bugger. Oh God. And Hannah used to say he was her best friend. Fucking brilliant. She'll say it was my fault, that he wouldn't have been here if it wasn't for me. Well, that might be true. But Burnsy wouldn't have lasted anywhere, in or out, he was that type, but she won't understand that. As far as she'll be concerned, her friend is dead, I should have stopped it, and that will be that. At the thought of Hannah's grief he felt overwhelmed with a kind of grief himself, and a little spurt of anger; how could he do that to her, the fucking idiot? She'll be gutted. And once you're dead, you're dead; there's no undoing it. This thought suddenly terrified him; he felt he wanted to burst out of his cell, go and find Burnsy's corpse, and shake it back to life again, force him to come back. He could not have gone for good, really gone, never to say or do anything again. It was too horrible to be real. He couldn't be really dead, perhaps he was just in a coma, unconscious, maybe. That was all. People were in comas all the time, for all sorts of reasons; how would they know here at the prison, fucking lot of morons? He was probably just unconscious. Anyway, they had a duty of care, they should have been checking on him, it was part of their duty, they could be sued. They should have stopped it happening. All at once he was rigid with fury; hatred of the prison and everything about it surged through him. He looked down at the stiff, greying cotton of his bedclothes. How easy, how beautiful, to hold a lighter against it. It would be so much better if he had some accelerant, but still it would take. But it probably wouldn't spread, and he wanted to see it spread, on and on, avenging, purifying, until there was nothing, no one left. He would willingly die himself in a fire so magnificent, so free. Listen to yourself, he thought wearily, I'm not a pyromaniac, all the pyros I've known have been fucking nutters, don't let yourself go that way. But the image of the fire wouldn't leave his mind; as his eyes closed he saw it again, cracking, laughing as it went, burning all the corruption, all the disease, all the pain, everything, weak and strong, good and bad, and finally Burns himself, his pale corpse, with its purple and swollen throat, eaten up, eaten away to nothing, by the gentle flames that licked around him.

Chapter Eleven – Nobody At All

Walkinshaw sat in front of the gently flickering fire, his mind pleasantly blank, a restfulness, that did not preclude an edge of excitement, in his heart. Perhaps it was too late in the year for a fire, but somehow it had seemed right, appropriate, it took the edge off the coldness that seemed to have invaded the house of late, since Isobel left; he winced as he remembered how Hannah had shivered in the hall, on that strange evening, only a week ago. It could be a year, he thought, it seems ages ago, like another life. He felt a sudden, unexpected pang at his heart, but he fought it down; that time was over, it was in his interests and hers to forget it, to beat it down. It was hopeless, there was no future in it. He looked down at his hands, conscious of a sense of guilt that irritated him. I have not done anything wrong, he murmured to himself, I was a little selfish, perhaps, but not cruel, never cruel. And now, possibly, I have a future, there is someone who might mean something in my life, someone in whose life I might mean something. He thought of Isobel, with Dakers in that silly penthouse; well, two can play at that game. He hoped that gossip about himself and Cressida Jenkins might reach her ears somehow; he felt desperate for her to know, to feel humiliated, to flinch from the news, hoping that it wasn't true. Was she happy with Dakers? Did she regret it, now that it was done, now that she no longer had to sit in her little study, emerging with that familiar air of tired, dismissive resignation at the sound of his key in the lock? How did she greet Reggie when he came home? But perhaps it was Reggie who waited for her, perhaps she came home to him, calling out joyously as she deposited her bags, all haphazardly over the floor, and rushing upstairs to him. He realized, with a sudden lurch of dislocation, that he had been picturing them here, in his house, his and Isobel's house, but now they were in a sixth floor penthouse – or was it fifth? – so there would be no rushing upstairs. Perhaps Reggie went out onto the landing to wait for the lift. The idea struck him as comical, embarrassing; he felt a curious sort of awkwardness for them. Perhaps she missed him, a little, sometimes; perhaps she recalled those early days, the cohesion that they had had, the rightness of everything. It had all seemed like a sort of dream then, and it still did, but now the vagueness of it frightened him, and he clutched at his memories in a sort of panic, fearful of forgetting anything, of losing a clue to what had happened.

He roused himself with an effort; that unpleasant ache of tiredness still pressed away behind his eyes, despite a couple of good nights' sleep, and he felt disinclined to get out of his chair. I could almost sleep now, he murmured to himself, I could just fall asleep now, and then wake up into a new world, into a life where things made some sense, where I understood everything, saw it all clearly. He closed his eyes for a moment, but uneasiness still crawled under his skin, that uneasiness which he felt even through his sleep, in his dreams, and he opened his eyes again with a sigh. Peace was not to be found that way; he would have to wait for it, he would have to hold his breath, carefully, and pick his way through the hours, the days, the weeks that lay ahead, until at last the pain wore away, and let him take refuge in self-forgetfulness. He got to his feet suddenly, the calm of a few moments ago washed away with a new tide of anxiety; he walked over to the door, a little giddy, conscious of another wave of the old pain at his heart. There was nothing for it but to be brave, and let it pass. And think about Cressida. There was hope there, a real possibility. He must try to focus on that. He knew, somewhere, at the back of his mind, that if he had really fallen in love he would not need to tell himself to focus on it, but that was not really fair, he was fragile at the moment, he hardly knew what he felt, he seemed to have lost all capacity for recognizing his feelings. Besides, love is not always a thunderbolt, sometimes it grows, gradually, over time, indifference grows into attachment and attachment into love. She was coming tonight; his stomach crawled with a sort of shame, which surprised and alarmed him; why did he feel like this? Why did this horrible scrupulousness of his keep rearing its ugly head, spoiling his moments of satisfaction, of pleasure? He tried to identify moments of happiness in recent days; surely he had been happy at Gregory's party, sitting there with Cressida? He had felt calm, aware of a peaceful sense of belonging that had seemed to wash all around him, like a warm, comforting bath; well, I can have that feeling again, he told himself defiantly, I have friends, I have a place, there are people who like and respect me, and a very attractive and very eligible young woman is coming round to my house tonight. There is no reason why I should not hold on to that feeling, why it should not replace this awful anxiety that has chewed away at my stomach for the past I don't know how long. I just need to come home, that's all, I just need time, to get over Isobel, and to spend relaxing, with my own kind of people. That's all. He struggled to retain the sensation which had surrounded and buoyed him all the way home, through the dark streets in the taxi, and had made him feel like himself again. It was all so different to that strange incomprehension he had felt, here, in this very house, that dark, mysterious evening with Hannah Casey, when the world had seemed turned upon its axis, everything was upside down, and he had felt like a mystic, as though he was about to see and understand some great revelation. But she had floated away, like a dream, and he had gone about the business of the week, as usual, and as the days had gone on he had developed a reticence, a fear, a need for the comfort of familiarity, even a familiarity which his finer nature had come to despise. He leant back against the wall, his eyes closed; he must just wait for tonight, after that everything would fall into place, and he would understand it all again, and no longer be haunted by Hannah Casey's wide, wet eyes, and that pale blue butterfly, disappearing for ever as she dressed, with unhurried, patient attention, and went away into the darkness.

**

The chapel was brightly, even harshly, lit, smelling unpleasantly of wet plaster, and Danny could still hear the shouting and swearing from the wing adjoining it, dying down a little, then suddenly rising up again, reaching a ragged crescendo that seemed to shred his nerves. Still he sat there, awkwardly, feeling nothing of the peace he had hoped for, but still disinclined to get up and leave, conscious of a deep weariness pounding through his muscles. He was conscious that he was waiting for something, though he had no idea what it was; still he had an obscure hope that he would find something, that he would leave somehow richer for his visit. He hoped no one had seen him come; it would not be good for his reputation, but then again, there was no real need to worry, if anyone did start on him, well, it would be doing him a favour, really, he felt he would relish a good fight, was itching for one. He had a vague feeling that he ought to pray, but had no ideas, so he merely sat there, hunched a little, conscious only of the terrible weight of misery at his heart. He did not like closing his eyes, for when he did that terrible tear-stained face of Burnsy's seemed to appear in the darkness of his eyelids, reproachful, imploring, and so he opened them again, and stared at the dirty wood crucifix standing uncertainly in front of the small altar. He did not want to look at it, and yet he felt unable to tear his eyes away; it was just the size, just the colour, of the one in the children's home, in the chapel there. Perhaps they got them from the same place, perhaps there was somewhere that made cheap and nasty crucifixes for cheap and nasty places, places where it didn't really matter. He looked at the crudely carved face of the wooden Jesus. He doesn't look like God, he doesn't look wise or loving, he doesn't look as though he wanted to forgive anyone, thought Danny, with a sharp pain in his chest, he just looks bored. Bored and tired, like he can't be doing with any of us. Well, I guess he is bored, stuck in this fucking boring chapel all day, poor bloke. Suddenly he remembered the crucifix in his old school, mahogany, shining, beautiful. It matched the lectern, the one where you placed the book on the back of the eagle's wings, and he had imagined the eagle taking flight at any moment, just flying away, up and out of the stained glass window, with the school bible still on its back. He'd been only nine when he left, when he'd taken that uniform off one ordinary Friday teatime, and never put it on again. He felt tears pressing against his eyes, and screwed them up tightly. He wasn't going to cry any more. There was no need to cry. Things happened, that was all. Even God got executed, shows you what a screwed-up world it was. And if you don't do what you're told, if you're not a good boy, you go to hell. Well, put my name down now, like you do at the public schools, because I want to be first in the fucking queue. The tears were hard to hold back now; one rolled down his cheek, and he rubbed at it fiercely, until his skin was sore, conscious of a terrible oppression over his heart, so heavy he felt he could hardly breathe. I need some tablets, he thought, I need to get myself to the doctor, I can't go on like this. He felt that he hated the chapel, that he must get out, that its air was poisonous, fatal to him, yet his legs were slow and sluggish, and he could only stumble, wearily, to his feet. Like an old man, he thought, I'm like an old man, good for nothing. I'll never find the strength to make that phone call. I'll never do it, I can't do it. He looked again at the crucifix, aware of an unformed hope that in some miraculous way the wooden face would change, soften, acknowledge him somehow. But it can't, it won't, it will never change, it's dead. He got to his feet, blinded by tears; you're on your own now, Daniel, you're on your own, my son. It's no good looking for miracles, no good hoping for mercy; it's not for your kind. Slowly, painfully, he pulled open the stiff metal doors, unable to resist one last glance over his shoulder at the inexorable, motionless wooden eyes of the hanging Christ.

**

'It's – it's so lovely to be here with you – I mean – well, I'm so glad I met you at Alexander's the other night, I –'

'I know. I'm glad too.' Walkinshaw looked across at her, benevolently; she was leaning towards him, that expression of rather too intense attention on her face, but it was such a compliment, really, her nervousness was a compliment, even though it was beginning to make him nervous. There was an awkward pause, and in his haste to bridge it he reached rather too eagerly for his glass of red wine on the small table between them, his hands trembling a little, and drained it, waiting for the stimulating effect to work its way from his stomach, through his veins and into his brain. She was still looking at him, and he felt a little flutter of hope; this really could work, this could really mean something. I must just keep my head together, that's all.

'You – you must have been having a difficult time lately,' she ventured, her head over her glass, her eyes hovering somewhere over his shoulder, as Marlowe's had done, and he felt a spurt of irritation; just look me in the eyes, for God's sake. He was silent for a moment, trying to think of something appropriate to say, and she added, hastily, 'Oh, I don't mean to pry, don't think I'm prying, really, I just wondered – not wondered, I just felt that – '

'Shut up,' he said kindly, smiling at her, wondering at the back of his mind however she managed in court. No wonder she does civil, no advocacy skills required. 'I'm really all right. These things happen, you know, and –' His own voice trailed into silence; God, he thought, it's catching. He felt annoyed with himself; he didn't want to be trite, and yet what was there to say, how was he to express how he felt, properly, to her, without an embarrassing over-familiarity? He looked at her, hoping for signs of comprehension, but she was looking at him with that mildly irritating expression of hers, attentive and yet blank at the same time.

'Yes. Oh, I understand. My partner and I went our separate ways just before Christmas. He got offered a job in Cardiff, well, at first he wasn't going to take it, but, you know, I knew he wanted to, and it sort of put us under pressure, you know, the relationship and everything, and then – well, everything just sort of unravelled. It's a nightmare trying to sell the flat. Probably have to take another five grand off the asking price, it really has been awful.'

'I can imagine.' He felt a darkness gathering at his

heart; is this the onset of depression, he wondered, is that what's the matter with me? He felt that he must be visibly flinching from the misery of it all, the well of pain that seemed to keep pulling him down, no matter what he did.

'It was a very difficult time, yes, but, you know –' she laughed self-consciously, with a quick, shy glance at his face, 'you just have to do your best, don't you? And some good's come out of it, I've really settled in well at Ermine Chambers, it's a lovely, informal little set. And, of course, knowing Vernon has made the transition just that little bit easier.'

'I can imagine,' said Walkinshaw mechanically, then went hot with embarrassment, realizing that he had said exactly the same thing in reply to her last remark. But she didn't seem to notice, she was turning the wine glass round and round again, just as she had at the party. He looked hard at her, hoping to kindle some desire. She was there for the taking, even his natural reticence could not disguise that from him. He looked at her, trying to decide who she was, what she was really like, what else there might be to her. He had to do something, so far the evening seemed to be slipping away from him, slipping away from them both. She took a gulp of her wine, rather despairingly; at this rate she'll be oiled pretty quickly, he thought, with a slight smile, well, it could only improve matters, really.

'I told you about my trip to South America, didn't I?' She pushed her hair back from her forehead with almost a desperate air. 'So wonderful. I mean, such an insight into another culture.'

'You did, yes –'

'I've got some photos on my phone, I think. Shall I show you?'

'Oh, yes,' he said, with perhaps a shade too much enthusiasm, and she got up, tentatively, and came to sit beside him on the sofa. Her physical proximity gave him a strange and unexpected sense of longing; he found himself sitting closer to her than he had meant to, and stretching his arm out along the back of the sofa, his hand just inches away from her shoulder. It was dark now; the fire glowed in the grate, its light stuck him as primitive, threatening somehow, and he stretched out his hand for the light switch, but she stopped him, with a light laugh that seemed somehow unsettling.

'Oh no, Mervyn, we can see by the firelight. Anyway, there are some of me in a bikini that are probably better seen in a dim light!'

Oh, not that annoying laugh again, he thought, and to curtail it said quickly, 'No, no, I'm sure that isn't true.' He felt uncomfortably hot and breathless; please don't let this be another anxiety attack, not now, not here. He felt he wanted her to go, and yet that he would feel desolate if she did. He peered down at the tiny screen, staring blankly at the verdant forests and mountain paths of Colombia; what have they to do with me, he wondered vaguely; the isolated landscapes, even in miniature, gave him a strange sense of disorientation.

'Are there any of you?' he said at last, lightly, feeling that he could stand no more of it.

'Oh,' she turned to him, pleased and flattered, 'oh, I'm embarrassed now, let me see, well, this was our hotel.'

'Really? I mean, oh, that looks nice.'

'It was. Very comfortable, but still full of local colour. We didn't want to be somewhere anonymous, Westernized, you know. We wanted the proper experience. This is me with Pablo, our guide, he was very funny.'

'Excellent.' He wondered whether he should kiss her, put his hand inside her blouse, or on her knee; he felt a sudden impatience. Surely she doesn't really think I want to see endless photographs of the market in Bogota? That's not why she came, she wants it as much as I do, probably more. He put his hand on her shoulder; he felt a sort of agonized desire running up his arm, towards his heart, almost as though he had had an electric shock; I have to do this, he thought confusedly, I have to erase the memory of the other time, of her. This will heal me, this will put things right. She turned towards him, putting her phone to one side, as he noted with satisfaction, and he was filled with yearning again; she looked lovely, there in the firelight, with her eyes half-closed. The sound of the doorbell made him jump to his feet, almost panic-stricken; even Cressida looked surprised at the violence of his reaction.

'Who will that be? Are you expecting someone?' She could not quite keep the annoyance out of her tone.

'No, no, of course not, of course not.' He felt overwhelmed with a guilty agitation; who was it? No one came round at this time. Stupidly he went to the window, but it wasn't possible to see inside the porch. There was no car outside that he could see. 'Probably some sort of salesman or something.'

'At half past nine?'

'They do come late round here. Anyway,' as she opened her mouth, incredulously, 'I'll go and get rid of whoever it is. Back in a moment.'

He saw her before he had opened the door, before he was even close to it. It seemed to him that in some mystical way he saw her while he was still in the front room with Cressida, that he had seen her all the time, had never lost sight of her. As he drew near he saw her face, blurred and hardly recognizable through the frosted stained glass of the door, and he held his breath, transfixed, horrified, his heart thudding.

He did not want to open the door, he couldn't, he felt paralyzed, but he had to, she was raising her hand to ring the bell again, he couldn't let that happen. He struggled with the lock; the door seemed heavy, unnaturally heavy, as though it was determined to divide them, not to let her in. Some strange instinct urged him to keep the door on the chain; through the three inches or so he saw her face, wan, tearstained, smudges of mascara smeared across her cheeks, and he was a little alarmed despite himself.

'Can I come in? Please?' He was dumbfounded; never had his imagination conceived of this, that she would follow him here, lay siege to him in his own home. What a fool I was to bring her here, he thought, God, what have I done?

'No, Hannah, sorry, no, this isn't a good time, you see – '

He fumbled with the chain; it seemed cruel to leave her out there, somehow. The door swung open at last, and as he saw her properly something seemed to give way inside him; he felt that he would crumple to the floor, sobbing, begging her forgiveness.

'He's dead, he's dead, he killed himself,' she was saying, tears pouring down her face, and he felt a tide of relief; it wasn't about him after all, she wasn't going to blackmail him. It was just some problem of hers; that would make it easier to handle.

'Who has?'

'Jonathan, Jonathan, he killed himself.'

'Who's Jonathan?' His mind was a blur; he didn't know any Jonathan.

She looked up at him through her tears, astonished and stricken. 'Burns! From the trial. He's dead.' She bent over, with a loud sob, and he seized her arm, panic stricken.

'Shhh! Please! Don't make such a noise,' he said in

a low voice, urgently, filled with horror at the idea of Cressida emerging to find out what the matter was. 'That's a shame, a real shame, but you have to go. Go now, please.'

'You've got someone round. Sorry.' She straightened up, bravely, and looked at him, rubbing away her tears with the back of her hand. He could hardly speak; he felt an emptiness deep inside him, as though he were being hollowed out, drained. There was silence between them for a moment. She still stared at him, her mouth a little open, and he noticed for the first time the slight discolouration of her front teeth, and that there was a piercing hole on the right side of her upper lip that looked red and inflamed; he winced a little.

'Sorry I came,' she began again, pulling the cuffs of her jacket over her hands, 'only I thought – '

'Who is it, Mervyn?' Oh God, he could not let Cressida see her. Hardly knowing what he was doing he pushed Hannah back over the threshold, with a mumbled 'Sorry,' and closed the door firmly, breathing hard.

'Who was that?' Cressida was behind him now, mild concern on her face; he turned around slowly, trying to make his expression as natural as he could.

'Oh, it was no one. Nobody at all.'

Chapter Twelve - Bathwater

Norman Tombs moved restlessly in his chair, and glanced at his mother to see whether she really was watching the television, or whether she was absorbed in her knitting; perhaps he could change the channel, and watch something other than Coronation Street. He hated it; the dull, dirty street with its ugly houses, its ugly, ambitionless people, their harsh voices, which struck his ear with an unpleasant familiarity, raised in petty arguments and squabbles – all of it filled him with a dark desperation, so that he found himself unconsciously looking around the room as though for an escape. Mum didn't seem to like it either, at least she was vociferous in her criticisms, but still she never missed it, and so neither did he. He wondered why he didn't excuse himself, and go up to his room; but then Mum would take that as a slight, and be in a mood with him all evening, and he didn't feel up to dealing with that. He sighed, and shifted himself again in his chair, glancing at his watch; another twenty minutes to go.

'You're a puffing Billy tonight. What's the matter with you?'

'Nothing.' What a stupid thing to say, he thought, when every single thing was the matter, he couldn't think of anything that wasn't the matter. His whole life was the matter.

'Well, stop it. I can't hear with you making like the wind in the trees. Lord love the boy, huffing like a train!' She gave a mordant chuckle, and one of her shrewd glances at him, which always filled him with unease. He felt that in some way she knew it all, and was laughing to herself at him. But how could she? And anyway, there was nothing to know. In fact, there was no cause for embarrassment, if anything, it was a feather in his cap. He had been singled out by an important client. Not the sort of important client he had had in mind when he'd embarked on a legal career, but still; he had had to trim his expectations to make some semblance of fitting reality, and there was no denying that Daniel Reynolds was a big fish in the small pond of the local criminal fraternity. He shuddered a little at the recollection of that meeting at the prison; he felt that he would always shudder at it, that the horrifying thrill of it would never leave him. He could still hear that voice in his head, sometimes in his dreams, and that was the worst of all, he would wake up frightened, terrified even, but conscious of an unnameable excitement that was the most frightening thing of all. He was oppressed with dread, awake or asleep; surely he was not becoming homosexual? The thought was horrifying, and yet he could not shake it off; he brooded on it perpetually, until his brain ached with tiredness, but there was no relief even in that, still the thought kept returning, and returning, and each time he had to wrestle with it, try to conquer it, quieten it, until the next time. He had had to speak to Reynolds twice on the phone since the visit, and they had both been horrible, dreadful calls; his stammer had come back with a vengeance, and he thought he could hear contempt in the firm but curiously gentle voice on the other end of the line. As he had replaced the receiver, trembling, once again had come that agonising thrill, that crest of pleasure, and, assailed by fear and misery, he had quivered his way through the rest of that dragging afternoon, pretending to himself that home was something to look forward to, a sanctuary. Of course it was not; home was this, endless days of this. He remembered with a fresh wave of dread a phrase he had heard and thought disgusting, 'prison bent'. Perhaps, he thought, I am 'prison bent', after all, this is a kind of prison, I'd like to find anyone, of any walk of life, who'd change places with me. Daniel Reynolds certainly wouldn't, he'd think me the most pathetic creature on earth if he knew that I'd never even – he flinched away, unable to finish the sentence even in his thoughts; he felt a horrible, nauseous shame running through his veins, eating into his heart. He bit his lip, straightened up in his chair and tried to concentrate on the television, with a effort that seemed to him to be the highest form of courage; he felt he wanted to throw himself facedown upon the familiar worn beige carpet, sobbing, and never get up again. He felt he wanted to be a little boy again, too young to worry about all this, still with time on his side, time to do it all right and be normal, grow up the way you're meant to, well-adjusted. He looked at his mother in a sort of supplication; please, he wanted to say, please, I'm so miserable, so unhappy, please help me, let me be seven again, a bright, serious little boy, of whom great things are expected. Why, he can spell words his teachers can't! He remembered with a bitter tenderness this maternal boast, a little exaggerated, but he had been clever, and she had been proud of him, she had loved him. How had it come to this?

'It's the adverts. Stick the kettle on, Norman, there's a love.'

He got to his feet in automatic obedience, encouraged by the apparent conciliation in her tone. 'All right, mum.'

'And bring a few of those biscuits. The ones with the toffee in.'

'I will.'

'You're a good boy, Norman. A good boy. I wish it had all gone right for you. I do.'

'It's not so bad,' he stammered; the temptation to tell her everything was overwhelming, unbearable, and yet how could he? It was impossible, and all he could do was to go through into the cramped, familiar little kitchen, and turn on the tap, pick up the kettle, as he had done thousands of times before and would do thousands of times again. His head whirled for a moment; surely it was not possible to suffer this much, and in such a quiet, uneventful, meaningless sort of way. He could not even suffer dramatically; even his pain was mundane, boring, suffocating in its ordinariness.

'You should have been a barrister. You're clever enough. You were always going to be a barrister, even when you were little you wanted to be a barrister. I haven't ruled out writing to that Mr. whatever his name was, he wants setting straight.'

'No, mum –'

'Well, you should, then. You should stand up for yourself. Look out for yourself or nobody will, there's a lot of truth in that. You're like your dad in some ways, he was like that, never could fight his own battles.'

'It's not that easy.' He was indignant, but conscious too of the luxury of feeling allied with someone, of having someone in his corner, even if it was his often rather perfidious mother.

She tightened her mouth, dismissively. 'That's what he used to say. You remind me a lot of him sometimes. Not that he was clever like you, no, he was more good with his hands. But meek, just like you. Meek.'

'I'm doing all right. Mr. Caldwell says I might be considered for a training contract. There's a client who likes me, he's asked for me specially, and –' he paused for breath, trying to keep the fear out of his voice, 'and I've got him transferred to an open prison, at least I think I have, so –'

'Prisons! You, working with common criminals. It's a disgrace. Why, you were always so particular, even when you were little. I thought you being a lawyer meant you'd be mixing with nice people, making some nice friends. No, this won't do. I'm going to speak to that Mr. Winchester, or whatever it was, Walkington, I'm going to tell him straight he's made a mistake, I'll –'

'Oh, no, Mum, please, please –'

'Don't want your old mum interfering, is that it? Well, sometimes mother does know best, believe it or not. Still, if you really won't have it, I'll leave well alone. On one condition, though.'

'What's that?' He could hardly look at her; he felt smothered, entombed inside that little overheated room, and felt sweat break out on his forehead.

'That you speak to him yourself. Tell him straight.'

He felt the finality of the words like a sentence; they seemed oddly solemn, and he knew somewhere in his heart that he would, that he would have to, even though the thought horrified him, even though he felt that he would rather do anything, anything at all in the world.

'All right, mum. I'll have a talk with him.'

'Well, be sharp about it. Time and tide wait for no man. And don't forget those toffee biscuits.'

**

Hannah sat motionless in the dirty armchair, absently picking at a hole in the fabric, her knees drawn up to her chin. The room was silent, the house was silent, and this was both exciting and alarming; she kept glancing anxiously at the door, half in expectation that she would see her father's great bulk looming in the doorway. But she knew that she wouldn't; he was in prison now, he had been remanded, and here she was, alone. She had not known whether to be sorry or glad that Lisa had left, immediately, declaring she wouldn't stay another minute in the house of a fucking nonce, that she had known all along what a bastard he was. She had even tried to persuade Hannah to make a statement; as though there was any chance of that. Hannah had just stared at her, tired and blank, overwhelmed with a sense of meaninglessness, futility, the futility of putting something like that down on a piece of paper, sitting there telling some copper about it, while his cheap biro hovered nervously over the page. She knew what it would be like, knew those sweaty, harassed faces, full of false reassurance, false promises. 'Oh, we'll keep him away from you, oh yes, he'll have bail conditions, you see, never you fear, love.' But she knew in her heart that it wasn't fear of her father that made her reluctant, it was something else, far deeper in herself, too deep, it seemed, even for her ever to reach, but she knew for a certainty that she couldn't, even if she couldn't explain it. It was impossible, that was all. She looked at the clock, hanging on the wall, seeming to be suspended in time; for a moment she felt that it was standing still, that the tiny plastic hands would never move again, and it would be now for ever and ever. For Burnsy it was, she thought with a sudden horror, it was a never-ending now, the now of the moment he fastened his collar to the iron bedstead and began turning himself over and over again, like a fish, probably, like one of those fishes that flounder around desperately, trying to breathe in water, but there is no water, only air, and air's no good for fishes, it kills them. It had killed him too. There was no room for him, life just would not make room, and it wouldn't make room for her either. We're like aliens, she thought, this world isn't for us, and then she remembered that there was no 'us' anymore, and tears came into her eyes; she gripped the arm of the chair, a numbness spreading through her, until she felt that she would never move again, never think or speak again, just sit there, numb and cold, like the dead. Like him.

The sound of knocking at the door made her heart pound; for a wild moment she thought it must be Mr. Walkinshaw, come to say he was sorry he hadn't listened to her the other night. She thought about that and was surprised at that she had no sense of grievance, and felt that she would be glad of the opportunity to tell him so, to let him know that it was all right, that he was forgiven, for she felt that he would be feeling unhappy and guilty about it. But it can't be him, she told herself, he wouldn't come here. The thought that it could not be him suddenly depressed her, and she leant back a little in the chair; whoever it was could just go away again, she had no heart to speak to anyone, she would just pretend to be out. But the knocking went on, an insistent, official banging, that would brook no refusal. She recognised it automatically, without thinking – it was the police again. Her heart sank, but still she got to her feet slowly, tiredly, conscious of a pain in her temples. As she got to the door she saw a man's outline through the glass, his back towards the door, apparently speaking on his mobile phone, and was a little surprised that there was only one; usually they came in pairs, and she felt a little reassured. Perhaps she would not be so browbeaten this time. The man on the step turned towards her as she opened the door, and she recognised DC Glover with a sort of confused relief. He had been nice to her last time, perhaps if she explained it to him, just one more time, he would get the others to leave her alone. He was smiling at her now, pleasantly, and she felt that she almost liked him, despite that terrible night in the police station, that now seemed a lifetime ago.

'Can I come in for a minute?' His tone was mild, almost apologetic, and she found herself smiling back at him. He was in his shirtsleeves, despite the cold air, and she felt somehow comforted by this informality, as though they were friends.

'I can't – I can't give a statement, like I said, I just –'

He smiled again, kindly, taking a step towards her, over the threshold. 'It's not about that, Hannah. It's something else entirely. Something new. You'll want to hear what I've got to say.'

She shrank back, menaced; she felt completely unable to face the prospect of a new problem, a new decision to make, something else to worry about. She put a hand to her mouth, close to tears, and felt Glover's arm around her, his hand gripping her shoulder. His shoulders were broad, wide, not quite as muscular as Danny's, but still nice, exciting in a comforting way, and once again she leant against him, overwhelmed, wishing that nothing, nothing at all, would ever happen again, that she could just sleep, rest, let time pass away into nothingness.

'Don't worry, it's nothing you and I can't sort out between ourselves,' Glover was saying into her hair, 'we just need to have a little chat, you and me, as friends. Last thing I want to do is make life harder for you, I know how tough it is, eh? I know how hard you've had it.'

She looked up at him, puzzled, scenting danger, and suddenly frightened; she longed for Danny, an urgent physical longing that made her a little dizzy. All at once she was conscious of her loneliness; who did she have? She found herself looking into Glover's blunt, shrewd face, almost as though trying to find traces of something she could love in it. She knew she could not trust him, she knew he was her enemy, and yet she felt overwhelmed with a desire to pretend that he wasn't, even to pretend that he loved her. She broke away from him, ignoring the shameful reluctance in her heart as she did so.

'You'd better come in,' she said, conscious of a strangely adult tone in her voice, stepping back to let him pass, and then closing the front door. Funny, she thought, I'm already acting like this is my house, it's as though Dad was never here. Dad. Already his absence seemed permanent; his coming back seemed impossible. She was gripped all at once with a feeling that she would never see him again, that already she was lost to him, that this was not his house any more, nor was it hers; that the events of the past few days had somehow erased them both, destroyed everything. She felt a devastation at her heart; it was with a sort of relief that she went through into the kitchen, where Glover was filling the kettle with an easy, possessive assurance. At the sight of him she felt a little of that sense of comfort again, an easing of the pain. She sat at the table, trembling a little, suddenly self-conscious. He did not turn round, but went about the business of making the tea, calmly, with the ease of someone used to busying himself in other people's kitchens. Then he sat down, next to her, like before, his knees apart, stirring his tea; the sound of the spoon against the earthenware was restful, almost hypnotic, and she closed her eyes a little.

'Any idea why I'm here?' He leaned back in his chair, and turned to look at her, but she couldn't meet his eyes, filled with embarrassment. He was looking straight at her, intently, his face close to hers; she could smell his deodorant and the coffee on his breath. She made an effort to think, but could not; there was no point, anyway, he would tell her, it was inevitable. Everything was inevitable.

'No.'

'No? Really?' He was smiling a little, she could hear it in his voice, but still she couldn't look at him.

'You still want me to make a statement about my dad – '

'We've got enough on your dad to put him away for a while without your help,' he said briskly, with a return to his old manner, and her head swam; how long was a while? When would he be out? What had he done?

'Did dad – did he –'

'I don't think you need me to tell you what your dad's capable of, do you?' His hand was under her chin now, stroking her throat, and she put her hand up, intending to pull his away, but could not; slowly he turned her head round to face him.

'They all get you to do things you don't want to do, don't they, all of them?'

'Who?' Her voice was a whisper; she stared at him, mesmerised. His hand was now inside her top, rubbing her shoulder; she knew she should want him to stop, but somehow she didn't, she couldn't.

'Your dad, Danny, all of them. No one asks you what you want, do they? No one.'

'Danny –'

'Made you hide all that stuff for him. All that gold. At the back of a drawer, underneath your knickers, not very original, Hannah, not very original. But it doesn't matter. It really doesn't matter.'

'It was – I didn't –'

'I know. I know. But you know what magistrates are like, you know what juries are like. They don't understand how hard it is, what pressure you're under. They don't know what it's like to feel trapped, trapped so that you don't know where to turn. I do. I see what goes on. You're the real victim here, I know that.'

She closed her eyes again, trying to make her mind blank, completely blank, trying to feel nothing, trying and trying, but she couldn't. Still she was there, in that tiny kitchen, late morning sunlight streaming in shafts through the window, and the distant shouts of children in the street outside. They sounded far away, so far away that for a moment the sound frightened her, she felt as though she must be dying, that the world was slipping away from her. His mouth was on her neck now, his hand on her breast, and she arched away from him in muted pleasure, one hand gripping his back.

'What will happen – what will happen to me – about the jewellery –'

'I'll look after it all, don't worry, I'll take care of it. You see,' his eyes were already glazed, his lids heavy, and the large vein at the side of his neck was pulsing, 'you see, I know what a good girl you are. I know.'

She leant against him, overcome, her heart beating with a muffled intensity. For a moment she wondered what it would be like to be his girlfriend, to have him come at night, to have him love her, and she screwed her eyes shut tightly in pain, trembling. His hand was on the back of her neck now, warm, protective, and she pressed her cheek against the gentle abrasion of his; she felt that her whole being was shuddering in mute betrayal.

'You go upstairs now,' he murmured, 'you go and run yourself a bath. I'll be upstairs in ten minutes.'

She lay on her back, staring blindly at the ceiling, tears welling at the corners of her eyes and rolling down towards her ears; she hardly noticed them, absorbed in her loneliness, which seemed now to be the only thing in the world, the only reality she could understand. It seemed to be enormous, like a great grey cloud that enveloped her, that isolated her from the world, and suddenly she remembered that moment in the courtroom, just before her evidence, when she had imagined her own death, imagined the world continuing without her. Now she felt that it was, that she was not really alive, but she was not dead either, and she wished she were not afraid of dying, because it would be so much easier just to do it, just to go away, to wherever Burnsy was, to go away and never come back, because there was just too much pain here, too much to take. She had not felt quite so bad until he had left, she had even enjoyed it a little, but then he had gone, just left, and she had wanted to beg him to stay, felt so frightened of the empty, silent house that it took a great effort not to ask him to come back later, so that she had something to hold on to, someone to wait for. She felt a horror at the thought of his walking out, walking away, leaving her; she tried to tell herself that he was a copper, he was her enemy, and that she had lowered herself by having sex with him in the first place, but still the fear rose inside her, and it was all she could do to lie there, silently, as he went down the stairs and banged the door firmly behind him. She had found herself, to her shame, longing for some sign of tenderness from him, a promise, a look, but he had climbed off her quickly, and dressed with brutal efficiency; the sound of him buckling his belt, his back to her, had made her skin prickle with desire and shame, and she felt that she hated him for leaving her like this, for making her want him to stay. As he left he had turned to her, briefly, and kissed her forehead, saying 'Thanks, love,' and then he had reached inside his jacket and taken out two ten pound notes, and thrown them down on the bed. They were still there, fluttering a little with every slight movement she made, looking oddly fragile, and she looked at them, trying to muster up a contempt for them, but still she knew that they would be useful, that they were a godsend right now, with her benefit all gone to shit now that dad was inside. She would have to get herself to the social this week to sort it out, and she felt something inside her die at the thought, it was too much. And she knew that she should resent being paid, that it should make her angry; it was an insult, but it was a lifeline too, and she felt puzzled by that; why should paying her betoken a lack of respect? It was because she was something that could be bought, she knew that, and yet she never really understood it in that way; when Danny had lent her to his mates, and once or twice to men he owed money to, she had not seen it as being sold, just as helping him in a way she could. Likewise those horrible cold nights on the Embankment, when Danny's habit was at its worst and there was no money for anything, and she was sent out to earn money for the electric, money for food, until after a couple of weeks she couldn't do it any more, and Danny had taken pity on her and gone out and robbed that off-licence. She knew it was shameful, yet she could not really feel that it was; it was doing what she could, that was all. She had felt worse about Danny's other plan, the one in which she was bait, she'd stand there waiting for a punter while he and Burnsy lurked behind, just out of sight, waiting until a bloke in a car pulled up, then they'd come running up, feigning rage and disbelief, you fucking think my girlfriend's a fucking prostitute, what the fuck do you think you're doing? Danny would wave his knife about, and sometimes it worked, sometimes it didn't, it depended on how quick the man in the car was, whether he caught on in time and managed to push her away and drive off. If he didn't, he usually had to empty his wallet. Danny was scary in those days, worse than now, sweating like a horse on the coldest days, his eyes pinned to fuck. She'd been scared of him then, even though he was sweet sometimes when he was on the gear, he could be really romantic back then, she had really loved him, that must have been why she did it all. She suddenly remembered how he had said he wanted to marry her, and she smiled a little at the recollection; it was impossible to imagine, and yet, in a way, it would be nice. He was her fate, she knew that now, she felt it; she had allowed herself to imagine other things, other openings, another kind of life, that night at Mr. Walkinshaw's, but that was a fantasy, his behaviour the other night had shown her that, and she wasn't angry about it, she knew it was how it had to be, for everyone, and she fought down the pain that twisted inside her every time she said his name aloud in her thoughts, or let his face, with his kind grey eyes, rise up in his mind. She had to let it all go, now, there was nothing else to be done. She remembered the letter Danny had sent her – before Burnsy's suicide, before her dad's arrest, before everything, wanting her to seduce him – and it all seemed facile, foolishly optimistic. Poor old Danny had seriously overestimated her attractiveness, it seemed. There was not much chance of that, not after the other night. She wasn't angry, but when she thought about it hard a little edge of resentment began to grow, began to deepen in her mind. 'It was no one. Nobody at all.' He should have made sure I was down the path before he said that, so loud, all anxious not to lose his chance of getting laid that night, she thought, with a forced cynicism. He must have thought the glass was thicker than it was. All at once she longed to tell Burnsy about it, just as she had told him about it from the start, how she had a new barrister she really liked, and he had teased her about it, in his soft, quiet, vague way, so different to Danny's sharpness. She could tell Danny, she yearned to, she had to tell someone, but Danny would work it all out, he would be able to read her feelings, as he always could. She could put it in a letter; but somehow her heart sank at the prospect, it seemed to be an unbearable effort, and she had always hated writing. Danny was due to call that night; she found herself longing for his call with a desire that felt physical in its intensity. She wanted him to come out, she wanted him, now, in bed with her, it seemed unimaginable that she had ever been glad to see him go to prison, that she had wanted to him to leave her. But then she had imagined something new opening up around her, she had indulged herself in stupid dreams, fantasies, and she had been punished for it. It served her right. What had she been thinking? For a moment she regretted the impossibility of Danny's plan; she felt some desire for a kind of revenge upon the man who had opened a door in her world, allowing a little chink of light in, and then had slammed it shut again, leaving her in greater darkness than ever. And – she admitted to herself with shame – something in her hurt at the thought of never seeing him again, never going inside that big house again, never again feeling his hands on her skin. She moved a little, uneasily, conscious of Glover's smell on the bed, on her skin; her neck was a little sore from his great sucking kisses, and she put a hand up to it, half repulsed, half regretful. Danny must never know about this, he would never forgive her. She felt herself go hot with fear at the thought of his finding out; it was the one thing that he would not accept, would never overlook. She became anxious that he would detect it in her voice; he had always had a curious ability to divine her thoughts, and to tell when she had been with another man; he could even place it to the hour, sometimes. She rolled onto her side, exhausted, desolate; the street outside was silent, and she felt chilled with isolation, abandoned, cold. Another five hours until Danny was due to ring. How could she possibly live through five hours like this? She sat up, desperate, and then jumped out of bed, and went to the bathroom. She had not yet emptied the bath from before, from when Glover had made her have one before he'd have sex with her, and the sight of it, the cold, greyish, foaming water, made her feel she would be sick. Quickly she pulled open the cabinet and pulled out a packet of tablets. Temazepam, that would do, should help her to sleep the afternoon away. She put a couple in her mouth, shaking so that she nearly dropped them, and swallowed them with water from the tap; she felt as though as her throat was closing over, as though she would never get them down. Then, still shaking, she went back to her bedroom; she felt as though she would collapse with her anguish, that she couldn't survive it, and she lay down again, carefully, pulling the sheets over her head, praying softly under her breath for the tablets to get to work quickly.

'All right, darling?'

'Danny.' She felt she could only say his name, that one word, over and over, for the rest of her life.

'What's up, sweetheart? Heard about your dad.'

'Is he there? Have you seen him?'

Danny laughed, softly, and she gripped the phone tightly, her eyes closed, hot with longing for him.

'He's here, but I haven't seen him. He knows better than to get in my way. Though I'm told he has a pretty black eye. Hasn't he rung you?'

'No.' Her mind was still cloudy, and talking seemed to be an unbearable effort; all she wanted to do was to be with him, lying across his chest, while his fingers traced lazy patterns up and down her spine. She shivered a little.

'What have you been up to then, Hannah?' The use of her name brought her to herself a little; he did not often use it, and she tensed slightly.

'Nothing.'

'Nothing? You sound sleepy.'

'I had some downers. I'm so lonely,' her voice broke suddenly, 'I'm so lonely, I want you, I want you –'

'So what have you been doing, then?' She was a little shocked, taken aback; she'd kept him at arm's length for so long, ever since he went away, and she expected some reaction to her sudden warmth.

'Not much,' she murmured, feeling herself colouring, and knowing that in that strange way of his he would be able to tell.

'Who've you been shagging, then?'

'What?'

'You heard.'

'I haven't.'

'You have, you lying little bitch,' he said, but his tone was warm, with that soft undertone of arousal that she knew so well, and she felt herself moistening, pleasure mounting inside. 'You might as well tell me.'

'I can't.'

'Fuck it, tell me, Hannah.'

'That judge.' There, she had said it, and it couldn't be unsaid, it was said forever, now he knew. She held her breath, her brain burning, her heart beating in great thumps.

'You never.'

'I did.'

'You little whore. You clever little whore. God, you're making me hard. I fucking want you now. God. Oh, God. When I get out of this place I'm going to fuck you till you can't stand up.'

**

It was hard to think in canteen, it was hard to think anywhere in here, but it had to be done, he had to get it straight in his head. Danny stared straight ahead of him, his expression both alert and detached; in here you had to look like you were focused all the time, it didn't do to let your attention wander even for a moment. His mind was full of thoughts of Hannah, and the talk with her that he'd just had; he felt an odd sort of euphoria, as though he'd just fallen in love with her again, or as though he tasted freedom, real freedom, for the first time in years. Violent desire was throbbing through him, stronger and more potent than ever, so fierce that he felt it like a kind of madness, a disease. Something in her voice had moved him, aroused him; drowsy and disorientated as she was, the old connection was back, that old magnetic force, irreplaceable, unmistakeable, and he felt an urgency to get out of this place, to leave it behind him forever. It's funny, he thought, the nearer I get to my release date the more desperate I get, the more frantic I am to get out of here. Sometimes, at night, he fell prey to dark imaginings that they would somehow thwart him, prevent his release; that they would dream up ways in which he'd broken the rules, or decide that he was a danger to society, still, that he wasn't rehabilitated. Too fucking right I'm a danger to society, he thought, grimly, but still his mind kept returning to Hannah. He would have her again, soon, and it would all be all right, everything would make sense again. And she had done it with the judge. Perfect. It couldn't be better. All he had to do was make that phone call to Norman Tombs tomorrow, just to see how the land lay, and then sit back and wait. That was the hard part, the waiting. He closed his eyes for a moment, almost wanting to cry, almost able to taste her, feel her, feel himself inside her. But all that had to wait; before any of that could happen there was work to be done.

**

Norman Tombs replaced the receiver, carefully, trying not to let his hands shake, trying to make sense of the welter of feelings inside him. This was a lifeline, this was what could make it all work, all come together. And he had known it, he had guessed it, he had read that look, and he had been right. Perhaps I'm not so stupid after all, Mr. Walkinshaw should have thought about that. They all should have thought about that before they rejected him. But they had rejected him; and there was a new anger inside him, fighting with his elation. She turned me down, turned me down flat, he thought, bitterly, hardly able to believe it, and then gone off and done it with him, with a man who must be the best part of thirty years older than her, and me, for that matter. He burned with resentment and humiliation; he had been given a weapon with which he might be able to win the battle, but it was one that hurt him too, made him wince with self-loathing. He felt a sudden, overwhelming need for privacy; he hurried out of his office and walked quickly to the toilets, the only place in this horrible building where there was any privacy to be had, and that only sometimes. He stood in front of the mirror, not wanting to look at himself, but feeling his eyes drawn inexorably towards his own face. I'm ugly, he thought, I'll always be ugly, small, skinny, with little pale eyes and short sandy eyelashes, still with those acne scars that nothing will shift. I'm ugly, and nothing will help. Maybe I could get some new glasses, some trendy ones, these don't do me any favours. But fashionable glasses won't help, they might make things worse, just emphasise the awfulness of the face they lived upon, like wisteria growing up a tower block. No, it's me that's the problem, and these glasses suit me, if they're ugly, well, so be it. He looked into the cracked, smeared mirror; in its reflection he could see the dingy cubicles, their doors painted a murky green. One of the toilet seats was cracked, and none of the three doors locked properly; he had to resort to jamming his foot against the door, filled with nervous anxiety that someone would intrude. He had dared, once, to mention to Linda that the locks could be mended, but his request had been greeted with indignant incredulity at what she evidently saw as unreasonable fastidiousness. 'Well. Well. I've been here fifteen years, and that's the first time anyone's complained about that. The first time. I can't say it's high on my list of priorities, to be frank with you.' So he had mumbled an incoherent apology and sidled away, leaving her looking after him, affronted and contemptuous. These toilets said it all, he thought, these toilets just say it all about this place, dirty, unkempt, squalid, no pride in anything, no standards. I have to get out of this place, I have to. He remembered his mother's words. Look out for yourself or nobody will. Well, I will, he thought, trying to sound resolute in his own thoughts, I will, starting today. I can't spend my life here, it's unthinkable. But it won't change unless I make it change. And it will be daunting, but I have to do it. Mother is right. And what's more, she doesn't know what I have up my sleeve, she doesn't know that I have an ace to play. He felt a sort of coldness inside him at the idea of what he was going to do, but he was going to do it nevertheless, he had to do it. Mr. Walkinshaw himself had bent the rules, he had taken advantage of a situation, he would have no right to sit in judgement on someone else who chose to do the same. It was just a case of looking after yourself, of getting what you wanted, what you needed, without hurting anyone else. Mr. Walkinshaw would not be hurt by this; on the contrary, he and his chambers would benefit, as long as he was sensible about things, and there was no reason why he shouldn't be. He suddenly wished that he had had the courage to mention his plan to Danny, he felt that if only he could talk to him about it, he would be able to steel his nerve, to see it through. He suspected that Danny knew; he seemed to know, but then he seemed to know everything. 'I suppose there might be something in this for you, if you play your cards right,' he had said, in that soft way of his, and Tombs had been silent, unable to answer, feeling that his silence said more than any amount of words, any explanation. There was, as always, an undercurrent of menace. 'You see what a friend I am to you, Norman. Soon as I hear anything interesting, you're the first one I tell. That's friendship, that is.' He had gone a little cold at this; it seemed to remind him that he was out of his depth, dancing with the devil; at the back of his mind he remembered Ratchett's warning. 'You be careful.' Well, you don't get very far being careful, so far being careful had got him nowhere, or rather here, the last place on earth he felt he wanted to be, and if getting away meant cutting a few corners, well, he was more than ready to do it. He wondered nervously if anyone had overheard the conversation; he had been alone in the office, but that was no guarantee. 'It may interest you to know that a certain judicial personage has had carnal relations with my fiancée.' Danny had mentioned no names, and somehow this gave the knowledge an additional, illicit thrill; despite himself, he savoured the sense of being in league with Danny. Danny. He must stop calling him that. He was Reynolds. Reynolds. During his last phone call he had wanted to hint at his plan to Reynolds, had wanted his approval, but had not dared to, fearing that prison officers might be listening in on the call. Of course they wouldn't be, he told himself, it was legally privileged and they weren't allowed to, but then he was already learning that that sort of rule meant more in principle than in practice. He had already done well for Reynolds; a transfer to an open prison was on the cards, he should hear definitely in a week or two. He had no real doubt that Reynolds would get the transfer; it was hard to imagine anyone saying no to him, and he was clever, very clever; far cleverer than me, thought Tombs, with a clammy feeling down his spine. He knew that Reynolds would approve of his plan, but he also knew that he would know far better how to go about it, how to implement it with finesse. I will just stutter and stammer, he thought bitterly, I will make an idiot of myself, and he'll just laugh, confident that someone like me couldn't be taken seriously as a threat. He wondered for a moment whether he should put it in a letter, but no, that was ridiculous, crazy, he mustn't put anything in writing. His mind felt fuzzy and slow; was what he was doing an offence? If anyone should know it's me, he thought, bitterly, trying to recall the law on blackmail; surely it's an offence only if you demand money? Demanding money with menaces. Still, he felt uncomfortable about it, and resolved to look it up, then almost at once decided not to. I have to do this, he told himself, if I'm breaking the law, well, so be it, so it must be, but I must do this, and I will. As if to shore up his courage he took another look into the mirror, at his own pale, frightened face, and at the filthy ochre walls of the toilets behind him. This will be the rest of my life if I don't do this, so do it I will. He set his mouth, and turned to push open the sticky, creaking door. For an instant, as he did so, he seemed to see Daniel Reynolds' face for a moment, his eyes quizzical, his mouth curved in its habitual ironic smile.

Chapter Thirteen – These Things Happen

Walkinshaw slammed the door of his car shut, harder than he knew he should, feeling a mild sort of pleasure in it. God, I'm reckless, he thought, with a sour humour, what a rebel I am, slamming car doors. But then the thought of what he had really done, what it was and what it meant, rose up in his mind again, and he quickly gathered up his bag and papers, threw his coat over his arm and strode into the court entrance, like a man who feels he is being followed. Somewhere at the back of his mind a memory tugged at him; that day when he had arrived here, had gone through just the same movements, the same routine, that he had just done now - the day of Hannah's trial, that bright, fresh morning, when he had had an inexplicable sense of purity, of the freshness of everything. He had felt aware, he recalled, with a pang, that it was all there in front of him, to be spoiled, but at that one moment it all lay out in front of him, it was pristine, unsullied. He trembled at the recollection; well, it was all spoiled now. Hard to believe it was only three weeks ago, it felt like three months, or three years; but then again, sometimes, when he was trying to get to sleep at night, it felt like only a moment ago, and the emptiness and silence of the house shocked and frightened him all over again.

He got into the lift, automatically, hardly aware of what he was doing; usually he took the stairs. The full-length mirror inside gave him a little shock of unpleasantness and nerves, like meeting a rather alarming stranger. He looked at his face, though he didn't want to, and was surprised to recognise it; he felt sure that in some strange way he should have changed, at least aged, since that day. It was always going to be hard, he told himself, it was always going to be hard coming back here, I shouldn't have taken that time off, I should have got straight back in the saddle, as they say. The longer you leave it, the harder it gets, the more the anxiety gets hard-wired in, deeper and deeper into your brain, your blood, so that just the smell of the building, the sound, the echo, makes the sweat break out on the palms of your hands, your heart beat heavily, sickly. But it's not the building, he thought with an effort, it's not the building, it's what happened when I left it, when I went home to that lonely house, and it all fell apart, my life fell apart. Why wasn't I happy then? Why was I so troubled, so unhappy, when I had it all, or at least I thought I was? Perhaps I had a premonition, perhaps on some level I knew. And then there was that thing I had for Hannah, it all began here. For such a soulless building, it's seen a lot of emotion, a lot of heart, this place. It suddenly occurred to him that Isobel had probably met Reggie here, they had probably gone off to have coffees together, secretly, up in the canteen, the same canteen in which he had sat with Hannah, maybe at the very same table, in the very same chairs. The air seemed thick with ghosts; an odd idea flashed across his brain that they were all dead, somehow, all of them, Reggie and Isobel, Hannah and Cressida, and he was the only one alive, that everything was over, really, everything was post-apocalyptic. Oh God. A minute or two inside the building and already my hands are trembling. He closed his eyes for a second, suddenly panicking at the thought of the lift moving, wrenching him off the ground, and he took his hand away from the control buttons in fright. He became aware of a voice behind him, and his heart began to pound again, almost lurching inside his chest. It was getting closer, and he desperately looked about him for the button with which to close the doors, but his eyes seemed cloudy, watery, everything was swimming about in front of him, and anyway, it was no use, for here he was, Marlowe, in the lift beside him, pulling along his neat black trolley case behind him on its little wheels.

'Room for a little one? Good to see you the other week, Mervyn, at Alexander's. Going up to the second floor, I take it?'

The lift shuddered into action, and as it rose sharply Walkinshaw felt violently light-headed; Marlowe's head seemed enormous, his voice so loud that he felt it boring into his ears, into his brain. The lift seemed enormous and cramped both at once; he was desperate with claustrophobia, and yet it also seemed vast, like a great and nightmarish hall of mirrors. He realised that he must have staggered, for he stumbled awkwardly against Marlowe's trolley case, regaining his balance only with difficulty.

'Steady on, old fellow. You're not fond of lifts, I take it? You should have opted for the stairs. Still, lifts have their advantages, or so I'm told, if you're alone in one with the right young lady. I'm not speaking from experience, you understand. That's more in your line.'

'What do you mean?' It had stopped, the lift had stopped, the doors were opening, and he felt an ecstasy of relief.

'Little trysts with the ladies up on the third floor. We all know what you're like, Mervyn.'

'I have no idea what you're talking about. I wish you'd stop it, quite frankly. I've a busy morning ahead of me, and I want to concentrate on it.' He stopped, a little frightened of his own boldness, not quite daring to look at Marlowe, and fumbling awkwardly with the lock of the security door leading into the barristers' area. He began to feel hot; the door would not yield, and a great, nauseous anger began to well up inside him. He wanted to throw his papers, bag and coat, everything, down on the floor, and run outside, away from Marlowe, Isobel, Dakers, all of them, away from this ugly, sordid, evil building, which seemed only to manufacture pain.

'Allow me.' He had to stand aside as Marlowe smoothly opened the door, then manoeuvred his little case through it; he felt the anger well up inside him again, and forced it down. Why did he hate Marlowe so much? There was no real reason, and yet the tone of his voice, the look in his eyes, brought back the memory of that uncomfortable moment in the courtroom, waiting for Hannah's verdict; Marlowe had seemed to him then like something evil, a bird of ill omen, a presager of doom. He shook his head slightly, impatient, disturbed; how to reconcile all these thoughts and feelings, all this distress, all this restlessness, how to retrieve his old life, his old peace of mind? He felt that it had gone for ever, that there was no way of getting it back; that even if by some miracle it returned to him then he would have changed, outgrown it, it wouldn't fit him any more. There is no going back, no going back now, he said to himself, and felt slightly comforted, without really understanding why.

They were in the robing room now, and he set down his bags on the table; once again the force of memory pulsed through him; here he had sat, had moved about, talked to Jennings, and, in that strange lapse, forgotten to change his collar. He felt something of the whirling vertigo of that day again, something of the emotional pull of it, and he felt an alarming and inexplicable urge to recreate it, to make it all happen again, just the same way, like another showing of a play, a play he felt he needed to see again. If he only watched closely then maybe this time he would understand, he would notice something that had escaped him the first time, somehow he would find the key to it all. And perhaps he would understand his own role in it better this time, perhaps he would play his part to perfection, getting every line, every movement and inflection, exactly as it should be, so that he could be perfectly understood. But it wasn't a play, it was life, and there was no recalling the time, it had all changed, it had gone. He felt distraught, bereft, at the idea; all his life was just present and future, there could be no going back to the past. Any future happiness he was to have must be brought out of this, he must somehow find it, hidden in amongst all the wreckage that seemed suddenly to have littered his mind, his life.

Marlowe was over by the window, fussily arranging the studs in his collar; Walkinshaw looked at him, in his neat little black pinstriped suit, his gold-rimmed glasses, his small, glossy patent shoes, and tried to suppress the strange loneliness the sight gave him. Why could he not be like that, why could he not belong? He remembered that morning when he had seen Reggie Dakers, here, in this very room, and had had the same feeling; what is wrong with me? Why can't I take it all for granted? That had been about twenty minutes before he saw Hannah Casey for the first time, and despite himself he was conscious of a deep, tender poignancy in his heart; to attempt to dispel it he got to his feet briskly, trying to make himself think practically about the day ahead. There was that sentence, ought to be straightforward, and –

'So, how are you taking things, then, Mervyn?'

Marlowe was looking at him, directly, and he felt that thrill of fear again, and a coldness in his stomach. He fastened his collar in the mirror, slowly and carefully, making a conscious effort to keep his hands steady, and to make sure that when he did speak his voice was level.

'I'm all right,' he said at last, lamely, feeling an odd sort of nervousness, as though he were being examined on a topic about which he knew very little. 'I'm all right.' His voice sounded strained, awkward, and he began to turn back to the table, meaning to bundle together his papers and get out of there, get away.

'It must be difficult.'

'These things happen. And anyway,' he had his hand on the door, desperate, 'really, I don't feel like talking about it.'

'They say you ought to let your feelings out, you know. You suffer in silence, Mervyn. Or at least that's the impression you give.'

'What do you mean?' He felt genuinely menaced; he realised all at once that Marlowe hated him, and he felt a sort of shock, and a desire to get away from him, immediately, at all costs, but also a need to find out why, to face it.

Marlowe just smiled at him, coldly, and he felt a sort of wild fear rising up in him; he had to fight the urge to run away.

'If you've something to say, say it. I'm tired of all these riddles.'

'All I have to say is this. Stay away from Miss Jenkins.'

'What?' He was incredulous, breathless. 'What do you mean, stay away from her? I –'

He broke off, horrified. Marlowe's face was white, working as though he were about to cry, drawn in spiteful lines, like a malicious cartoon. It was like seeing a mask torn from a man's face, thought Walkinshaw, bewildered and frightened, or the skin torn away, the bone torn away, and what you see is the vindictive little soul underneath. His mouth was dry with fear; he could hardly speak. He must love her, he thought, he must love her, or want her, anyway. He felt a sort of pity dawn in his heart; how sad, how horrible, how grotesque everything was. He felt as though all his blood were draining away from him, as though he were trapped in some horrid dream; he gripped the handle of the door, tightly, to recall himself. He must do something, say something.

'Look, I'm sorry, Vernon, but I didn't – I didn't realise –' He could hardly get a sentence out; something about the baleful little man in front of him made him feel oddly in thrall, unable to move. 'I don't want to upset anyone,' he finished, feebly. He was uncomfortably conscious of a muscle twitching in his cheek.

'Yes, you don't want to upset anyone, do you?' Marlowe was in his face now, livid with a sudden fury; Walkinshaw found himself noticing the cracked, dry lines around his mouth, the cold watery blue of his eyes, and the thin veins branching across his temples; like tentacles, he thought, or a bare tree against a winter sky.

'You don't want to upset anyone, do you? You pathetic creature. Why do you think Isobel left you? Were you surprised? None of us were, I can tell you. We wondered why she stayed with you so long. Problems, were there? Oh, we all talked about you, she used to say she wanted a child, you see, she even told me about it once, yes, she did, but it didn't happen, did it, no, not while she was married to you? No, she used to worry it was her, she used to think it was her fault. Don't look so shocked. You look pathetic, but then you are pathetic, I was forgetting. Where was I? Oh yes, the Dakers baby. The baby she's going to have with Reggie Dakers. She had a three month scan yesterday, she was showing the pictures around chambers. I'm so pleased for her, and even more pleased I got to be the one to tell you, it's like Christmas, it really is, it makes up for everything. Such nice news, isn't it? Such good news, for such a lovely couple.'

He found himself outside on the steps, his head pounding, bending over a little as though to be sick, but nothing happened, only his breath would catch in his throat a little, and he had to cough, conscious of a stabbing pain in his chest as he did so. He found it hard to recall how he had got out of the robing room and down the stairs, he could only remember that Helena Gough had appeared from somewhere, and had, with unusual kindness, taken him outside, had even offered him one of her cigarettes. He thought perhaps he had been crying; he could taste a little salt in his mouth and his eyes were sore. Helena had given him a tissue from her bag; she had even volunteered to do his sentence for him. 'No problem for me whatsoever. It'll liven up what looks to be an otherwise mind-numbing morning. Just leave it with me. You go and take yourself home.' He raised his head, slowly, his mind cloudy; he felt that his whole body was still shuddering with shock, that he would never recover from it. He got to his feet, slowly, aware that his muscles were aching, as though he had been in a fight; his hands were so tightly clenched that it was almost painful to relax them. He could not let himself think about it all, he could not let himself think about Isobel and Dakers, but his mind kept pulling itself back to it, over and over again, and his mind went hot with horror, and with a terrible pain that frightened him in its violence, its intensity; he felt as though it would drive him mad, that there was no way back from this. He made his way down the street slowly, with an odd light feeling somewhere in his head, an odd feeling that he should not be here, that he ought to be at work;

it's like being off school when you're not really ill, he thought, or when there's been bad news and they let you go home. He remembered the day his uncle had come to school for him, to tell him his mother had died, and how he had stood there, outside the headmaster's office, alarmed and excited, and with this same strange lightness in his head, as though all the normal rules no longer applied, as though normal laws of physics had been suspended, and anything at all was possible, anything could happen. It all seemed bewildering, meaningless; he saw Marlowe's face again, malevolent, white with rage, and it seemed unconnected with him, unreal, dreamlike. But it was connected with him, that rage had been very real, and so had been his spite, his malice. There was danger here, real danger, but he felt far too stupid, far too confused to make any sense of it, to understand it. And still his mind kept pulling itself back to Isobel and Dakers, Dakers and Isobel. It could not be real, it could not be true. Marlowe just wanted to upset him, just wanted to see the pain and confusion on his face. It wasn't true. But something in him knew that it was true, that it was real, and the pain surged through him again, ignoring his attempts to hold it back. He must speak to Isobel about this, he must, even if it made things worse, he had to do something, he could not just hear this news and do nothing, say nothing, just go on living with this great hole in his heart. He found himself reaching inside his coat for his phone, then inside his jacket. It wasn't there, and its absence brought back a little of that dreamlike feeling, the unreality. I must have left it at court, he murmured to himself, almost aloud, I must have left it on the table in the robing room. His heart sank at the thought of going back inside, but he knew he must; he was not going to be cowed into hiding from Marlowe, he must stand his ground. He reached the doors of the court, and hesitated on the steps, reluctant; perhaps he could just send one of the security men up for it, then he wouldn't need to face anyone. It would be easier that way. Still he hesitated; it really would be better to go up himself, to show that he wasn't going to be intimidated, but he really couldn't face them. It wasn't cowardice, he told himself, just fatigue, terrible, soul-aching fatigue, and it was true, his tiredness seemed to be boring its way into his brain, so that he could hardly think, or speak, or move. He felt that he could hardly take a step forward, that he would stand on these steps forever, like a worried statue, frozen with exhausted indecision. Do something, for God's sake, he told himself, go in or go home, but don't just stand there, people will think you're an idiot. He pulled himself up, with an effort that felt intolerable, and was just about to step through the automatic doors, when they opened, as though by magic, he thought confusedly, as though by telepathy, and through them, his head thrown back, his coat over his arm, smiling confidently, came Reggie Dakers. He stopped short at the sight of Walkinshaw, the smile fading from his face, and another look came into his eyes. What was it? What is he thinking? I have to know, I have to know it all, he has to tell me, I have to know. He stared at Dakers, waiting for his anger to well up inside, waiting for it to come, needing it. Don't let the tears come, he told himself fiercely, don't cry, never cry in front of him, in front of them. Still he could not tear his eyes away, and Dakers too seemed paralysed, his eyes flickered a little, and suddenly Walkinshaw recognised it, he knew what he was reading in that face, he saw the fear, and felt a strange, primitive sort of courage flooding through him. Dakers lowered his head, quickly, and tried to move past him, with a muttered, 'Mervyn.'

'What did you say?'

'I said, I just said... would you let me past, please?'

'You said something. What was it?' He was angry now, there was no need to work himself up, no need to think hard about it, to try to force it. It was a pleasant feeling, he decided, it felt right, it felt good, there was a sort of luxury to it, to feeling himself so justified, so absolutely in the right. 'What did you say?'

Dakers was pale now; Walkinshaw looked hard at him, as though he had never seen him before. Is he handsomer than me, more attractive? He felt he had absolutely no idea, and never would have; in the midst of his anger his head swirled in bewilderment again. This is like a play, he thought, some sort of strange play, and I'm the aggrieved husband, the cuckold. I can get as angry as I like, and it'll all be acceptable, no one will blame me.

'Mervyn, please let's leave it alone, I'm sorry, really sorry, but things happen, you know, and I didn't take her away from you, you know, you can't take people, they come of their own free will, don't they? You understand.' Dakers raised his head at the end of his little speech, and Walkinshaw found himself noticing his pale, rather dry eyes; I wouldn't have thought they were very attractive, he thought, but then, who knows? It amused him a little to hear the tremble in Dakers' voice, the faint Northern inflections breaking through; what a fraud he is, what a fake, what a pathetic fake. And this was the man whom Isobel had chosen. Isobel had gone to bed with him, she had let him touch her, let him inside, and now his baby was growing within her, growing by the day, changing her body, changing everything, ruining and despoiling, and there was nothing he could do about it, it had happened, there was nothing he could do, and still that baby would be growing, bigger each morning than the night before, bigger all the time. He felt sick at the thought, horrified; he could not look at Dakers, he felt a sort of disgust deep inside himself, and a new and desperate anger, a sense of violation.

'You're disgusting', he muttered, hardly knowing what he was saying. 'You really are disgusting.'

Dakers looked genuinely aghast; his lips shook a little as he said, 'Oh, Mervyn, look, you don't know how sorry I am, you don't know –'

'I don't want to know, I don't care. Fuck off, and stay out of my way.'

He pushed past Dakers, leaving him there on the steps, and immediately regretted it; there was so much more he wanted to say, wanted to ask, needed to know. But there was no turning back now without losing face, and anyway Dakers was already off, making hurriedly for his car; he looked oddly chastened, diminished, and Walkinshaw's heart pounded with exultation; he felt an odd, poignant sense of victory. He needed to be alone, he needed to think about it all, to find his way through it. He ran up the stairs, still with that odd sense of lightness in his head. I don't care if Marlowe is up there still, he said to himself, I'm not afraid, I'm not afraid of any of them any more, they don't matter. He was almost surprised to discover that he really did feel it, that he really did feel that his fear had ebbed away, that he had looked at it squarely and found it to be nothing at all. He almost hoped that Marlowe would be there, while he was in this strange mood of reckless triumph; he felt that he wanted the opportunity to vanquish him, to show him how even his sharpest barbs could not even break his skin, would never draw his blood. Yes, he hoped Marlowe would be there, so that he could look in his little evil eyes and show him once and for all how ineffectual, how contemptible, he really was. He threw open the door of the robing room, a little breathless, and conscious of a presence inside it, a hostile presence. So he was there. All the better.

But the figure at the window, which turned round quickly as he came in, was not that of Vernon Marlowe. It was that of Norman Tombs. For an instant Walkinshaw could not quite place him; that party, the night of Powers' sentencing, seemed a lifetime ago, and he saw so many of them, pale, eager young men, boys almost, stumbling over their words in their eagerness to impress, to succeed, that Tombs' face had already faded in his memory, washed away by successive similar encounters in the intervening months. So he merely nodded curtly, irritated, and took his phone up quickly from the table, suddenly anxious to be home.

'Mr – Mr Walkinshaw, I –'

'Yes?'

'I – I – need to speak to you, well, I want to ask you – ask you –'

'What?' He realised that, in an uncanny echo of his only previous meeting with Tombs, he was taking an unnecessarily brusque tone, and softened it a little, trying to mask the odd distaste he felt. 'What did you want to ask me?'

'Well,' Tombs' face was a strange white colour; he looked ill, and Walkinshaw felt alarmed, disquieted; something was up. 'Well, you – you remember I applied for a pupillage – I applied – '

'I'm afraid the committee's decision is final. You're quite at liberty to apply again next year, though.' His hand was already on the door; the room seemed dirty, cramped, and he was desperate to get out of it, away from Tombs, who again seemed to fill him with a revulsion he could not explain.

'It's not that.' Tombs' voice was odd, strained; his pale eyes flickered into Walkinshaw's for a moment, then away again. He looked grey, wan, insubstantial; Walkinshaw found himself thinking of a moth, camouflaging itself against a tree's bark, and he felt an angry, fearful impatience rising up in him.

'What is it? I'm afraid I'm in a bit of a hurry.'

'You – you – '

'Really, Mr. Tombs – Norman – can we speed this up? I have to get going, perhaps you could write to me if it's really important.'

'You'll want to hear what I have to say.' Tombs' voice was a monotone; the line seemed rehearsed, stilted, but for some reason all the more menacing for that, and Walkinshaw felt a tightening in his stomach. 'You – you see, I know.'

'What do you know?' A great tide of fear and anger, deep, intense anger was flooding through him; he felt sick with it, yet simultaneously he felt conscious of a new strength, a new energy, and unconsciously he straightened himself up, and made himself look in Tombs' face.

Once again the pale eyes flinched away from his. 'About - about her. About Hannah Casey. And you.'

Walkinshaw breathed slowly, deeply, aware that he had been holding his breath. He felt a warm, false calmness spreading through him, and he knew it would save him, and held it tight. 'What is it you think you know?'

'That you – you – '

'That I what? Can't you say it? Are you too embarrassed?'

'That you were – that you were – unprofessional in your conduct.' The strange, sterile little voice jarred on his nerves unbearably; he felt hot with hatred, with a rebellious anger.

'I see. Jealous, are you?'

'No – no.' But he could see from the crimson circles on Tombs' white cheeks that he had touched a nerve, that there was something more to this, if only he could get to it.

'And how did you come by this information?'

'I – I can't say.'

'You can't say. So what is you want me to do?'

Tombs stirred uneasily, his eyes fixed on the floor. He began fiddling nervously with the cord of his anorak, and Walkinshaw found himself staring at his thin, chapped red hands, with their raw, awkward knuckles; boy's hands.

'I – well, I still want to go to the bar, and –'

'And you think you can blackmail me into giving you a pupillage, is that it?'

Tombs was silent; the line of his mouth was mutinous.

'You think you can blackmail me into giving you a pupillage. That's the funniest thing I've heard in a while. Listen to me, boy,' he stepped forward, consciously enjoying his controlled anger, 'listen to me, and you might learn something. Never,' Tombs was backing away from him now, chalk-white, trembling, until his back was against the wall; he seemed to be shaking, his face working, and Walkinshaw pressed towards him again, conscious of a new and enjoyable sense of power, of satisfaction, 'Never attempt anything like that ever again. Or, trust me, you'll never work in these courts at all, not even as a poxy clerk from a shitty firm like Caldwell's. You think I'm scared of you? Well, you do your worst. Go ahead. If you're all I've got to worry about, I don't think I'll be losing much sleep.'

Tombs' face was ashen; even his lips seemed white. He seemed to be struggling to speak.

'I'm sorry – I'm sorry – I – '

'You're sorry now? Sorry for what? Sorry for trying to blackmail me? Sorry for trying to take advantage of me to win a position that you couldn't on your own merits? Or just sorry you didn't get to shag her yourself? For what it's worth,' he stepped away from Tombs, suddenly, and began slowly to put on his coat, 'for what it's worth, the sex was amazing. I guess you'll just have to try and use your imagination.'

Tombs stood, defeated, shaking, his mouth like a red, wet gash against the shiny wetness of his face, his eyes still moving from side to side, desperately, like frantic insects. He opened his mouth, but said nothing; he seemed mute, petrified.

Walkinshaw turned towards the door, his head throbbing with a sudden rush of confidence, of excitement. As he reached it, he turned and looked hard at Tombs. 'A word of advice. If you do ever get to the Bar, whether honestly or by blackmailing your way there, you won't last long if you can't look anyone in the eye. And do something about that acne.'

**

Danny leant against the wall of the bus, pressing his shoulders into it; somehow that seemed to make it easier, though still his legs ached, and he could feel the beginnings of a nauseous headache spreading through his temples. It felt so strange, so unnatural, to travel like this, without being able to see anything, to have no idea at all where you were. He hated it, hated it so much that he had felt a dread when he had been told his application for a transfer was successful, simply because he hated these journeys, hated the anger they made him feel. He closed his eyes; that was supposed to help, but it was too late now, he was already feeling hot, sick, furious. He ought to be happy; after all, he told himself, you wanted this, you've got it. An open prison. Curious, in a way, that he'd never been in one before, but then it had always been violence in the old days. I'm getting old, going to a Cat D. In with all the nonces. Low risk. It'll be wonderful not to be locked in all day, able to come and go, wander round the gardens. There's a little farm and everything, a metal workshop. It sounded strange; he could not imagine it, and he became aware of a sort of fear in his heart, something he couldn't define. All at once he felt he wanted to go back to Blakemoor, back to what he knew, and, oddly, back to the place where Burnsy had died; he was conscious of a feeling that he was leaving him behind, that it was a betrayal, of sorts. But Burnsy wasn't there any more, he wasn't anywhere, unless he had gone to heaven. Or hell. Still, Danny felt this strange new sense of betrayal, of abandonment, growing inside him, and he found himself looking over his shoulder, looking back, though he could see nothing but the inside of the van, almost with a nostalgia for the place where Burnsy had breathed his last. He really is dead, he thought, bitterly, he really is dead, and now we're both gone. But I'm still here, I'm still alive, I'm not going anywhere. But he was conscious of a feeling of danger, as though he had left safety, predictability behind, and for a moment he regretted ever applying to transfer, he wanted to be back in his old cell, the one that he had hated so much. I don't belong anywhere, he thought, with a violent anger burning inside him again, I hated that place like fucking poison, but I don't feel safe anywhere else. I must be getting institutionalised. What the hell is the matter with me, I ought to be thrilled to be out of that place, that evil place that killed my friend, that nearly killed me. He felt tears trying to squeeze themselves out of his eyes; I'm so tired of fighting, he thought, I'm so tired of it all, tired of the struggle. He remembered a letter he had written, a letter to the judge who had sentenced him, not this last time, no, years ago now, when he had been young, brave, cavalier. He loved writing letters, especially the mock-remorse ones. Some of them were pretty good, though I say so myself, he thought, smiling a little, though he still wanted to cry. 'You put me in jail to break me. Well, you won, your jail broke me and I can't stop crying.' He hadn't meant it then, he'd just thought it was a good phrase, but, fucking hell, it's come true now. Perhaps I brought it on myself, he thought, perhaps I can see the future. This thought brought back his uneasiness; he felt he wanted to be free, to be at this new prison, the one with the rose garden and the swimming pool, but somehow it was not right, he shouldn't have put in for this transfer, it was all wrong somehow, in a way he couldn't put into words. Maybe it's because I know I don't deserve it, he told himself. Burnsy should have been in a prison like that, he might have been all right in there. He should have gone to this nice one, I should have stayed in Blakemoor, yes, it's a shithole, but I can handle that, Burnsy never could. I'm taking his place, I'm taking what he should have had. His stomach knotted in a sudden horror, and he pressed his head against the wall, his tongue clenched between his teeth to keep his urgent tears at bay.

**

Norman Tombs sat on at the desk in the robing room, staring into space, too stunned to think, only aware of a horror pounding through him, like a nightmare from which there would be no awakening. He was aware that his hands were shaking, that his mouth was working, and that he could taste salt in his mouth, but still he sat there, unable to rouse himself, even though he knew that at any moment someone might come in and find him there crying; yet more humiliation. He felt too weak to move, lifeless, paralysed. What had he done? It was all a disaster, all too horrible to be endured. Ever since I lost that pupillage it has been a nightmare, he thought, everything has been a living hell, and once again resentment surged up in him; if only they had seen sense, if only they had given me what was mine, what was due to me, none of this would be happening. But no, they had had rejected him, they had cast him out, and now look at the consequences. And Mr. Walkinshaw was at the heart of it all, he was the root of all the trouble. 'I hate him, I hate him, I hate him,' he said, aloud, in a sudden frenzy, and leapt to his feet, panic-stricken, as a voice behind him said, quietly, 'Who is it you hate so much?'

He looked into the cunning, cautious little eyes, fearful and yet conscious of a dawning hope. 'I just had – I just had an argument – a - a dispute, it –'

'With? Anyone I might know? Vernon Marlowe, by the way. I've seen you around here once or twice, with one of the local briefs, are you?'

'With Caldwell's.' His throat was dry; he could hardly get the words out.

'And your name is?'

'Norman. Tombs, that is. Norman Tombs.'

'Well, Norman, I rather think I may have overheard a little of your argument. I was working in one of those little rooms – just there – down the corridor, and, you know how it is, voices carry sometimes. You know what these modern buildings are like, the walls are paper-thin.'

'Sorry, I – sorry, I didn't realise – '

'Oh, don't worry. It sounded a good deal more interesting than the rather dull fraudulent trading case I was reading. Would I be mistaken in supposing that the other voice I heard was that of Mervyn Walkinshaw, learned in the law?'

Tombs froze, horrified, yet he heard his voice, as

though spellbound. 'Well, yes. Yes. That is – I just wanted to – to ask him about giving me a pupillage, and...'

'Have you applied for a pupillage?'

'Yes, at his chambers, and they turned me down, they turned me down, and I thought –' He stopped, aghast at the confession he had so nearly made.

'And you thought that a certain piece of information that you had stumbled upon might cause him to suggest to his colleagues that they ought to reconsider. But, my dear boy, you were a little too discreet for my liking. All I heard were the tantalizing words 'unprofessional in your conduct' – what a marvellously non-committal phrase, is it not – and the name of a young lady, which, strange to say, struck a chord in my memory. You know, you'd be doing yourself an enormous favour if you'd tell me the whole story, you really would.'

**

Walkinshaw lay on his bed, his hands clenched, his heart seeming to beat heavily and uncomfortably in his throat, his head throbbing. The little relief that his anger had afforded him had now ebbed away, and pain seemed to rage through him like an illness; he felt feverish, almost delirious, as though his life force was dwindling, as though he were floating, powerless, towards a kind of death. It was all over, and those words echoed inside his head with a peculiar resonance, a new clarity; it was as though he had not understood it fully until this moment. So it was all over, then, and finally; there could be no return from this. The three encounters of the day played through his mind, taunting him; he closed his eyes, wanting to sleep, but he seemed to hear Marlowe's voice in his head, harsh and frightening, seemed to feel the flecks of his spittle again, as he spat out his venom. 'You look pathetic, but then you are pathetic.' These words seemed to have made a strange impression on his mind; he tried to think about Isobel, about Dakers, but he could not; he could only feel it, like a great heavy weight lying across his chest, while his mind kept returning, over and over, to the enmity, the hatred, in Marlowe's voice, in his eyes. Was it possible that so much hatred could be engendered by a passion for Cressida Jenkins? It should be funny, he reflected, but it isn't. It isn't funny at all. What a day, he thought, what a day, when I get blackmailed for the first time in my life, and it isn't the first thing on my mind. Tombs seemed to him to be futile, ineffectual, his threats empty, and he almost regretted some of the things he had said; he felt he was turning into someone else, that he hardly knew himself, or of what he might be capable. It was a dark day I ever met that girl, he said to himself, bitterly, I wish I had never heard her name, and then he hated himself for not quite meaning it, for holding something back. I must never see her again, ever. That chapter of my life is closed. Like every other chapter, seemingly; he felt as though wherever he went, whatever he did, doors were slamming in his face; all he had left now was his work. And Cressida, who had sent him three text messages in the last two days, all, shamefully, left unanswered. For a moment he almost wished that Marlowe would take her off his hands; he had become conscious lately of a strange reticence, an embarrassment almost, that was oppressive, that gave him an inexplicable desire to run away, to hide. He had thought it must be guilt, the knowledge of that little lie told at his own front door, told purely to save his own chances with her. He kept telling himself that it had done no real harm, but still it tugged at him, until he felt disgusted with himself, and oddly – and quite unreasonably – resentful of her.

Marlowe was right, he thought suddenly, I am pathetic. I don't know what I want. All I seem able to do is to make myself unhappy, and everyone around me unhappy into the bargain. I am pathetic. He felt overwhelmed with fatigue, as though all he wanted was to lie there forever, for the rest of his life, and never get up again. When the phone rang it was all he could do to stumble to his feet and answer it; his head throbbed with tiredness.

'Mervyn?'

'Oh, Cressida. How are you? I'd meant to call you, actually, tonight, I was going to call you – '

'Well, you don't need to now, do you?'

He was perplexed, alarmed; her tone was cold, and he felt panic gathering inside him.

'No, no I suppose I don't. Do you fancy going out later this week?' His voice sounded high, false, and yet he pressed on; he had the sensation that he was falling, falling down and down, towards his death, and he swayed slightly where he stood, giddy. 'I'd say tonight, but I'm a little tired, I think I'll have an early night – '

'I'm not surprised you feel you want an early night. You must be exhausted.'

He was a little encouraged at this, but still her tone was oddly cold; he knew now that she was angry with him, and he felt suddenly that he couldn't bear it. 'Cressida, I am sorry, I was going to call you, really. I swear I was, only, well, things have been so difficult, and – '

'Yes. Difficult's one word for it.'

So that was it. Marlowe must have told her about the argument, and somehow got her to side with him. The bastard.

'Look, I don't know what Marlowe –' he could not utter his Christian name – 'I don't know what he told you, but he was very aggressive, very unpleasant, to be honest, I feel quite upset about it.' God, I sound feeble. 'What I mean is, it's an awkward situation, I had no idea about his – well, that he would take it to heart so –'

'Him take it to heart? What about me?' Her anger was breaking through now, her voice becoming shrill, raw, and he winced involuntarily. 'And you dare call him aggressive and unpleasant? All poor Vernon was doing was being a good friend to me. He happens to have some morals, some standards, unlike you, apparently.'

His head was spinning; this was too much, he could make no sense of it. 'What are you talking about? What am I supposed to have done?'

She sighed, sharply and unpleasantly, and he felt as though he hated her. 'I suppose I should give you a chance to deny or confirm it. That's only fair. Have you – have you – had an improper relationship with that – that girl you were telling me about, the one you had successfully defended the week we met at Alexander's party?'

So that was it. That terrible weariness descended upon him once more; he knew he should say no, that every survival instinct in him was begging him to say no, no, no, of course not, how could anyone think such a thing? But he didn't, he was silent, and he knew that every second that passed was condemning him, that there was no going back now.

'Well? What have you got to say for yourself?' God, he thought, she's just like Isobel.

'What do you want me to tell you?'

'The truth.'

'Really?'

'Yes, of course.' But her voice was beginning to break. She's frightened, he realised suddenly, she doesn't want it to be true, she doesn't want to lose me, and all at once that thought struck him as amusing, rather ironic.

'Well then, it's true. I did.'

'Oh. Oh. Well, I suppose – I suppose I should thank you for your honesty.' There was a moment's pause, and he found himself noticing how dusty his bedroom was; the cleaner hadn't been since Isobel left, he had better sort something out. She sounded on the verge of tears, and he felt a little guilty; he ought to feel something more than this, but how could he, when he was so tired?

'I'm sorry, Cressida. It was before I met you.'

'It's not that. It's not that. It's that it's so – so – disgusting. I hope I'm not a snob, I really do, but that – well – it's horrible. You could have caught something. You could have given it to me.'

'I can promise you I didn't catch anything. She's a really nice girl. Was, I mean,' he added hastily, as she took a deep breath of incredulity. 'It was only the once, I haven't seen her since. I promise I won't see her again.'

'Well. I shall need time to think about this, Mervyn. It's – well, perhaps you think me a prude, but, well – '

'No, no, I don't. I'm really ashamed of myself, if that helps. I know I haven't behaved well.' He was almost enjoying himself now; he rather liked himself in the role of sexual penitent, begging, but not quite begging, for forgiveness; it made a pleasant change from the image of himself that had been thrust upon him by the others throughout the day, and he found himself relishing it, and almost feeling a little excited. And furthermore he knew that it was really Cressida who was doing the begging, that it was she who had the most to lose, and this knowledge gave him a strange and luxurious sense of power; he was reminded oddly of his confrontation with Tombs, and hearing the defeat in his choking voice. He felt sorry for Cressida, suddenly, and added,

'I'd be really upset if you decided to end things. Really.' Do I sound sincere? Hard to tell.

'Would you?' She's desperate to believe me, he thought, well, let her. In a way I would be upset. Yes, yes, I would, she's very attractive, really. And I do like her.

'Of course I would. Is there any chance that you can forgive me?'

'Well, I – I still want to think about it, but –'

'Of course, that's understandable,' he murmured; he felt as though he were acting, and was rather surprised at how well he was doing, at how successfully he was playing his part. There was a lengthy pause; he knew that she wanted to forgive him then and there, but he couldn't allow that, she would be wanting to come round that night, and he badly needed to be alone. So he added, swiftly, 'You know why Marlowe told you, don't you?'

'No,' she said, a little too quickly, then, 'Well, because he's my friend, of course. He was in chambers with my dad, in Nottingham it was, I remember him coming round to the house when I was doing my A Levels – '

'It's nothing to do with that. He fancies you.'

'Oh, Mervyn, he doesn't, no.' She was silent for a moment. 'Do you really think so?'

'I know. He told me to stay away from you.'

'He didn't. He didn't. Did he?' She sounded half-flattered, half-disgusted, flustered, he thought, and smiled a little to himself.

'Yes. Yes, he did. So now you have a choice between us. I have a rival for your affections.' He tried to keep the ironic emphasis out of his voice; he had to sound as though he cared.

'Gosh, well, this has been a bit of a dramatic day. I can hardly believe it. Vernon,' she said, wonderingly, 'Vernon in love with me. I can't imagine.'

'A rose between two thorns. Which of us will you choose?'

'I can't – I can't – well, you, of course, Mervyn, though I'm supposed to be cross with you.' She gave a high, artificial laugh. 'I'll have to think it all over. What a day!'

Not by my standards of late, he wanted to say, but decided not to. 'What a day. What a day, indeed.'

'I'll call you, Mervyn. I'll ring you very soon.'

'All right. I'll look forward to it.'

Chapter Fourteen – An Uneasy Ghost

Norman Tombs sat on his bed in his little room, hunched, staring blindly at the grey net curtain that hung still, too still, at the little window. He could hardly think; he knew that he had been through some dramatic experience, something which he had no power to assess. Had it been good or bad? Had he behaved well? Or shamefully? And what did it all mean? His head was throbbing; he looked around his room almost frantically. It was hard to believe that it was the same little room that he had always slept in. It seemed to look back at him coldly, reproachfully, as though it knew, as though it could read his mind, and disapproved thoroughly of what it saw. What have I done? He had asked himself the question so many times that he was tired of it, and yet he knew that it still wanted answering, that something in him needed to be called to account. Was it so wrong? Of course, it was not nice, it was not really honourable, and he shouldn't have told Mr. Marlowe anything, that wasn't right, not really. But then Mr. Walkinshaw had had fair warning; if he chose to ignore it, that was his lookout. But Mr. Marlowe had been so kind, so sympathetic, he really seemed to understand what it was like, how hard it is. He sees my potential, he told himself, he really sees my potential. And the real possibility of a pupillage! Ermine Chambers would not have been his first choice a year ago, but after a few months at Caldwell's it seemed like the prospect of paradise. He felt a choking sensation in his chest; he hardly dared to trust it, it was too easy. It just shows, he thought, it just shows it's true, fortune favours the bold. I could have served out my days in Caldwell's, maybe one day, if I was lucky, getting offered a training contract, then years and years more in that filthy green office, until I turned into them, became one of them, stopped wanting anything more. But I wouldn't accept it, I knew that wasn't my fate, and now look, a very real prospect of something better, something more. Mr. Marlowe had told him to send his C.V. in; he had already printed one off, and laid it carefully on his chest of drawers, terrified lest it should get creased or crumpled, that something should somehow pollute it. He leaned back on the bed, overwhelmed, tears of what might have been joy at his eyes. It had been so easy, so much easier than he had dared to think. And Mr. Walkinshaw deserved whatever he got, for his rudeness, his arrogance, his insults. He had been given a fair chance. Now, whatever was to happen must happen; he could not say he had not been warned. Tombs raised himself on one elbow, suddenly, a cloud over his happiness; Daniel Reynolds. It was such a shame, a nuisance, that he had needed Reynolds' help in this, it would have been so much neater, so much cleaner, if he'd done it all on his own. Still, it could not be helped. He would just have to make it clear to Reynolds that there was to be no more of this hole in the corner stuff, that he was just another client, nothing more. Now I have a prospect of success, he thought, all at once a little hot with anxiety, I mustn't let myself be dragged down by anything, there must be no associations with criminal clients to drag me back down. My slate must be wiped clean before I start at Ermine Chambers. The lure of those magical syllables was too strong for him; he lay back again, lost to blissful daydreams, even as Daniel Reynolds hovered, menacing, like an uneasy ghost, at the edges of his memory.

**

Walkinshaw pulled into the car park, feeling a strange sense of unreality; surely it was not tomorrow already? It all seemed dreamlike, familiar and yet alien, and he felt that he should be afraid, angry, and yet he felt nothing, just a vague pleasure in his lack of feeling, in the nothingness of it all. At least the Ermine crowd would not be here today; Dakers and Marlowe were both down in London on an appeal, according to Alexander Gregory, who, prompted by Helena Gough, had come in to see him that morning, hot, flustered, and trying to hide his irritation behind a façade of kindly concern. Well, maybe that's a little unfair, maybe he is concerned, in a way, though what he's most concerned about is the image of chambers. 'You must remember, old chap, you're very senior now. I know it must be difficult, but just ignore them. Just ignore them. My old father used to say, 'The mills of God grind slowly, but they' – well, I can't remember exactly what else they do, but the point is, old boy, what I mean to say is, there's such a thing as dignity. Gravitas. Professionalism. I'm sure you were more sinned against than sinning, but nevertheless, we must show them that it takes more than a few barbed words to upset our apple cart, eh, old chap? I know you understand.' It was all so tiring; he had hardly been able to endure it; had mastered his boredom and irritation only with a considerable effort. The day had only begun, but so already felt himself exhausted, empty, and yet anxious for some sort of excitement; the prospect of another routine day in court seemed unbearable, and yet so did kicking his heels around the house. He knew it was only distraction that he wanted; he knew that he was trying to cushion himself from a blow that sooner or later he must feel, must take, but he felt obstinately that he wanted it to be later, that he had had enough pain for now. It was all so relentless, so unyielding; better to feel this not entirely unpleasant numbness, at least it gave him some respite from it all.

The security guard looked at him oddly as he came in; he felt an anger welling up inside him, and only nodded curtly in reply to his 'Good morning, Mr. Walkinshaw.' But the guard, a very tall, very thin and lugubrious man, whom Walkinshaw still thought of as young, though he must have been there for fifteen years, still looked at him, a little uncertainly, as though he expected an outburst of temper. 'You're very early, sir.'

'No, I'm not. If anything, I'm a little late.'

The guard pulled anxiously at the reddened skin of his knuckles, his muddy eyes peering into Walkinshaw's from beneath his peaked cap. 'Did they not tell you? They should have told you. Oh, dear, you've had a wasted trip.'

'For goodness' sake, get on with it,' said Walkinshaw irritably, then felt a little ashamed of himself, and tried to smile.

'His Honour Judge Cavendish's list is not before two thirty,' said the man, entirely unfazed, with that unruffled acceptance of barristers' anger outbursts that so many court staff seemed to acquire, and which was in itself, thought Walkinshaw, rather annoying.

'Bloody hell. Somebody could have told me.'

'Listing should have rung your chambers. If you like, sir, I can have a word with Karen about it, see if a message was sent.'

'Don't bother.' It was all inevitable, there was no point taking it any further. 'I suppose I'd better do some paperwork upstairs.'

'Yes, sir. Although –'

The guard's face, a little flushed, had assumed an expression at once stupid and knowing, and Walkinshaw felt a dislike and an unease growing in his mind; he shook his head a little impatiently. 'Although what?'

'Well, it's Miss Thornton, Miss Thornton, she's here for a family hearing, though it won't take long, won't take long at all, I spoke to Mr. Edwards, he's for the other side, and he reckoned it'd be straight on and off, because they've reached a modus vivendi or whatever it is, and they just need the judge to rubber stamp it, or whatever it is he does, you'd know better than me, wouldn't you. Mr. Walkinshaw?' He finished with an awkward, sycophantic chuckle, and a quick, hard, prurient glance into Walkinshaw's face.

'So you think I'd better stay away, is that it?' He tried to keep his tone light, level, sarcastic, tried to ignore the sensation that his heart was beating inside his throat.

'Well, it was just in the nature of a word to the wise, you know?' The guard had the grace to look a little uncomfortable at last, and turned away slightly, picking at the plastic surface of his desk with red and painful-looking fingernails.

Walkinshaw turned away abruptly; he realised that he longed to go up the stairs, to have the chance, the excitement, the risk of seeing her again. Would she be much changed? What would she say? What would he say? He felt as though every nerve, every muscle was burning, his bones seemed to ache with an agonized desire, but no, he had to go, had to turn back with a muttered 'Thanks,' and make his way clumsily through the heavy glass doors. As he stepped outside the wind seemed to strike him in the face like a blow.

He sat in his car, thinking; five whole hours until half-past two. Plenty of time to go home and then come out again. He could do a bit of tidying up, then read that aggravated burglary for next week; it would be a useful opportunity to get ahead of himself at last. But he didn't want to; he didn't feel ready to go back home, to unlock the door of that empty house and step inside, feeling, as he always did these days, that there was some alien presence inside, something malign waiting for him. No, he must find something to do. I could go and pick up my dry-cleaning, he murmured to himself, fumbling in his glove compartment for the ticket, and then smiled a little; that's hardly going to take five hours, unless there's a hell of a queue. His heart was as heavy as lead; he looked up at the obscured glass of the courtroom windows as he locked the car and made his way up the street, and the thought that Isobel was in there, could even be looking out at him at this very moment, seemed unbearably sad, too poignant to be endured. And the security guard, keeping them apart – had she told him to? Had she told him not to let her estranged husband inside, to warn him from entering? She might even have got the judge to put his list back until after lunch; she was well in with all that lot, old Cavendish had long had a senile little amour for her. No, no, that was absurd, she wouldn't do that. Anyway, they would have to meet sooner or later; there were plans to be made, all sorts of things to be arranged, sorted out. He felt weak and elated at the prospect; perhaps she would be sorry, perhaps it would all be a mistake, perhaps Marlowe's story was all a lie, a malicious lie and there was no baby, perhaps –

He stopped in his tracks, with a thrill of horror. On the pavement in front of him, staring vacantly into a shop window, was Hannah Casey.

She did not seem to have seen him; that was something. It was just a matter of walking past, quietly, gently, as long as she didn't turn round it would be all right. He just had to walk very quickly past, just a few strides, and then -

'Hello.' Oh God. This is what happens to me. If only my case hadn't been put back, if only Isobel hadn't been at court, I wouldn't be here, I wouldn't have to talk to her. He felt a sourness in his stomach; he did not want to look at her, and yet he felt a sort of wildness, a freedom, coursing through him.

'Hello. I'm afraid I have to go – '

'Yes. Yes. Of course.' She was already turning away from him, and for the second time that morning he felt ashamed of his abruptness. He did at least owe her an apology for that night when he had turned her away from his house.

'About the other night. I am sorry that I didn't have time to talk to you.' His tone was artificially bright, and he tried to soften it a little. 'I can understand what a shock it must have been when your friend –' what the hell was his name? – 'when your friend died.'

She said nothing, her face still turned away, and he felt relieved; this was going to be easier than he had feared.

'Well, goodbye, Hannah. Best of luck with everything.' She looks awful, he thought, momentarily pausing despite himself to look at her; is she on the drugs or something? She had dyed her hair a much lighter blonde than before, and the harsh, yellowy colour seemed to emphasise the premature darkening of the skin under her eyes, the faint acne marks pitted around her jawline, and the blackheads across her cheekbones. Christ, he thought to himself, did I really sleep with her? I must have been out of my mind. He looked at her clothes; she was wearing those horrible shapeless blue tracksuit bottoms that all the girls like her seemed to wear, and a worn looking grey top, could almost be prison garb, he thought to himself, it's such a shame. He felt assailed with a new and impenetrable sorrow; in that moment life seemed to him to be so unbearable that it seemed astonishing that happiness, however fleeting, could exist at all. She made a sudden, convulsive movement with her hand, and held it across her face; he realised in an instant she was crying, and stood transfixed with pity and embarrassment.

'It'll all be all right, I'm sure,' he said, ineptly, looking anxiously down the street; to his relief there were not many people about, and no one that he knew. 'These things are difficult at the time, but time's a great healer, you know, and puts things into perspective.'

'I can't live without him,' she mumbled, groping in her bag and coming out with a packet of tissues. 'It's all over for me. It is.'

'Can't live without whom?' His mind went in an instant to Daniel Powers, and he felt a disquieting chill of apprehension. 'Of course you can.'

'He was my best friend.' She was wailing now, her nose running as she fumbled to open out a tissue, and he felt a little disgust, but also a greater warmth; it really must be awful. But this was no good, standing out here in the street. What if Isobel were suddenly to walk past? He glanced over his shoulder, then back at her; she was looking straight at him now, and he felt himself wince a little, with a odd little twist of longing.

'You don't have to stay. I'll be all right. I'm off home now, anyway. I went to the social, but I needed my birth certificate, so I'm going home for it.'

God, he thought, is she angling for a lift? Still, something inside him prickled with a hidden excitement at the thought; he beat it down, fiercely. All this was over, and she had to know it.

'Well, as I say, all the very best for the future. I'm sure things will get better for you, in time.'

'No, they won't.' She was sullen now, staring over his shoulder, and he felt a violent impatience.

'Well, they won't with that attitude, will they?'

'What do you mean?' She was looking into his face now, startled.

'I mean as long as you see yourself as a victim all the time, pushed around and controlled by other people, you'll never build a life for yourself.' Her eyes widened; they were still beautiful, and for a moment his throat went dry, but he pressed on, a sort of desperation at his heart.

'You just wait for things to happen, don't you? It's no way to live, you know. You need to take control of your life, you really do.'

She was staring at him now; tears were pouring down her cheeks, but her face was perfectly still, so still that he felt almost frightened. He wanted to stop, his heart was pounding, and for a moment he wanted to reach out to her, he wanted her to put her arms around his neck, as she had once before, and his whole heart had shuddered, shivering with the cotton wool comfort of it. He thrust that memory from his mind, horrified, trembling with the effort of it. 'It's all very well crying for your friend, but the way he was living it was probably all for the best, let's be honest. Yes, life can deal us a bad hand, but it's up to us what we do with it. It really is. These last few months have been a nightmare for me, but I've had to keep working, I haven't just curled up in a ball and waited for someone to give me handouts. I've had to drag myself out of bed in the mornings to go and earn a living, to pay the mortgage. It's called taking responsibility for yourself, you should try it sometime.'

'I- you don't understand, you don't know –'

'No. People don't understand, do they? No one ever understands.' He heard his voice rising in an arc; passersby were looking at him, he had to stop this. But he felt himself being driven on, as though by a demon;

he had to say this to her, he had to make her hurt, he had to penetrate that awful sullen vagueness of hers. She was no longer crying; she was looking at the ground, her arms folded across her chest, her face impassive, even as her lips trembled.

'My dad's in prison, Danny's in prison – '

'And sweet little innocents both, aren't they? I'm sure they've done nothing to warrant such persecution!' What the hell are you doing? he asked himself furiously. This is insane, you have to calm down, she hasn't hurt you. But then, as though for the first time, a horrible thought came into his mind. How had Norman Tombs come to know that he had slept with her? After all, they were the only two people in the world who knew, and he had certainly told no one. He looked at her, slowly, and he saw fear spreading itself over her face, and he knew then that she had done it, she had betrayed him. 'You told him,' he said, slowly, numbly, and her eyes darkened, her cheeks became whiter still. He waited for the anger, the fear, but nothing came; he could only look at her, pain and longing spreading through his body, like a disease, he thought, like a fever. How easy it would be, how easy it had been, the struggle and the surrender, that surrender that had something of eternity about it, something that could never die, that would live, somewhere in some dark corner of his mind, until he breathed his last. He looked at her and felt that she was burned into his bones, written upon his soul, and that it all mattered and that none of it did, and that he could do nothing, nothing, but stare at her until some final oblivion came and had mercy upon them both.

'I had to tell him.' Her voice was a whisper, her eyes were on the ground. 'I had to tell him. You wouldn't understand.' There was no reproach, only sadness, as she raised her eyes and looked at him; he shook his head, gently, feeling, in some inexplicable way, that he did understand, and that that understanding would haunt him forever.

'You shouldn't have.'

'I know. I know.'

'I mean for your own sake.' He was oddly moved; strangely, her guilt seemed to have dispelled all his irritation and anger, and he felt ashamed of his earlier harshness. 'Hannah, you can't go on like this. You can't...' His voice trailed away, uselessly; still he could not stop staring at her, and he felt tears gathering in his own eyes. A rich, almost pleasant emotionality welled up inside him, a sort of funeral feeling, and he almost reached out to touch her face, to run his hand, comforting, across her poor yellowed hair. She raised her eyes to his again, suddenly, almost as though she expected to be kissed, and his heart smote him; this is your punishment, he told himself sternly, this is what comes of taking what was never yours to take. The seconds seemed to pass like hours; he felt that he had been standing there, looking at her, for as long as he could remember, everything else, all of it, seemed like a bad dream. All of them, Tombs, Marlowe, Dakers, Gregory, even Cressida – he did not like to think of them, he had the impression that they must be kept apart, that they would mar something infinitely precious to him if he let thoughts of them intrude. Hannah is not the only one touched with sordidness, he thought suddenly, she is not the only one who has engaged in the buying and selling of that which should never be bought or sold, but only given. If she has demeaned herself, so have I. He felt both ashamed of himself, but also deeply pitying; had ever a man made so many mistakes, had ever a man so lost himself in a labyrinth of confusion and pain? He must not kiss her, he would not, but he took her hands, as kindly as he was able, aware that his were trembling, and then turned, and walked away, quickly, bravely, without looking back, and with a heart that he felt would beat itself to death long before he ever got back to the court.

**

Danny sat on one of the freshly painted benches that bordered the vegetable patch, leaning back, his hands clasped behind his head, lost in thought. It felt strange, all of it, strange to be there, to be outside, and he wondered why his pulse quickened a little every time he looked at the sky, almost as though he was becoming afraid of it. He was conscious that he ought to be happy, or at least what other people would call happy, and that he would call peaceful, steady, in control. Things were not so bad. This place was easy, he was coming out before too long whether the appeal was successful or not, and Hannah seemed to love him again. And as an added bonus, her dad was inside, hopefully for quite a while. Yes, there was no real reason to feel bad, apart from Burnsy's death, and these things happened; if you let yourself get in a state about it every time you'd never stop crying. Anyway, he was better off out of it, he'd been a walking corpse, it would have happened somehow, sooner or later. No, there was no real reason to feel bad, but still he felt a nagging unease, a vulnerability, a new and alarming fearfulness. Somehow the new prison, with its white walls, pale pine doors, pale grey, one level brick façade frightened him; he felt it to be ill-omened, menacing. Even the minimal, discreet security made him strangely anxious; he felt, irrationally, that he had preferred the heavy locks, barbed wire and handcuffs in Blakemoor. The day was heavy, oppressive; he felt that he had waited all winter for it to be spring, and that now spring was here he hated that too; he had an obscure desire for it to be dark, to hide himself away. He looked at the vegetable patch with contempt; it seemed to him to be almost insulting. He had always hated physical work, and usually refused to do it on principle, despite spending hours of the day in the gym. This place, the table tennis table, the small and dismal pond, with a couple of dead carp in it, the garden, the chicken coop, all of it seemed to him to be a sort of expression of bureaucratic despair, some sort of attempt to create a false normality for people for whom life could never again be normal, who had had all normality taken away for ever. 'Society takes upon itself the right to inflict appalling punishments on the individual, but it also has the supreme vice of shallowness, and fails to realise what it has done.' He loved that quotation; he'd memorised the entire passage. But he couldn't take it quite as far as Wilde had. 'I claim on my side that if I realise what I have suffered, Society should realise what it has inflicted on me, and that there should be no bitterness or hate on either side.' No bitterness or hate. Something about that was comforting, and he closed his eyes for a moment, trying to imagine that he felt no bitterness or hate, trying to make himself feel love, feel loved. His mind went to Hannah again; did he love her? His thoughts of her were warm, loyal, nostalgic; was that love? What did love mean? For a moment he wondered if he had ever loved anyone, and the idea filled him with an anxious confusion; he had a sense that time was running out, that he had to access it now or not at all, that there was not much of anything left in this world for him. He had been bad; he was so used to thinking of himself as bad, evil, even, that he no longer addressed it consciously in his mind, and so now the idea gave him a strange, fresh shock. Am I really bad? Am I much worse than other people, really? His mind slid back over the past, all the people, names and faces, of twenty years in and out of institutions, homes, cells, prisons. Once again little Tommy Lithgow surfaced in his mind, but he hastily beat that memory down again. Someone had told him in canteen that the 'Marie' of Tommy's neck tattoo had been murdered in Glasgow, that she'd been raped and then beaten to death, half set alight and then thrown in a canal, and Danny, who usually heard these tales with impassive detachment, had felt curiously and passionately sickened, as though it were he who had been in love with her. He shifted his weight restlessly; the new bed was making his back ache all day, it was too soft. He felt suddenly that he too wanted to die, that he wouldn't fight it if it came; but then he knew that when it came to it he would, everyone did. Except Burnsy. He felt a new respect for him at that thought; perhaps the little bastard was braver than me, when it came down to it. He came into the world, took a look around, didn't like it and left. You can't say fairer than that. The clouds overhead were darkening, blotting out the light, so that the green grass began to look black, and he felt a chill over his heart. I have to get out of this place, he said to himself, struggling to maintain his usual calmness, and he got to his feet, a little stiffly, and walked back towards the small grey building, carefully, like a man who fears a chasm will open at his feet.

**

Hannah lay across her bed, her whole being absorbed in the composition of her letter. She hated writing them, and could never understand why Danny loved it, why he wrote letters even when there was no need to, to people he would see the next day. Still, this time she would make an exception, this time she had to write, and already she was burning with an impatience for him to read it, for its words to soften him, for him to understand. But it was difficult; she had wanted her thoughts, her feelings, to transmit themselves onto the page, she had thought that it was just a question of writing down what she wanted to say, but she quickly realised that there was more to it than that, that there was some obscure art to it that seemed to elude her. A couple of times she nearly gave up, but she wouldn't; it had to be done. She shivered at the prospect of posting it, recklessly, sending it to his home address; but that was more sensible, more discreet, surely, than sending it to his chambers, and, anyway, that address was written on her heart, she felt she deserved the luxury of writing it on a envelope, inside which would be a real letter, a letter from her. She wondered how he would take it, whether it would make him angry, or angrier; had he been angry with her, or just sad? Sadness was worse, infinitely worse; anger she was used to, deserved, but the thought that she could make him sad was unbearably painful. She wondered what the outcome would be, if she would ever see him again, if this letter would make him seek her out again, rekindle something inside him. But it seemed unlikely; there had been something unmistakeably valedictory in his eyes, his manner, as he had taken her hands; she knew in her heart that it was all in the past now, and that this letter was about restoring herself in his memory, not about securing any sort of future. It would be hard to have no reply, never to be certain even that it had ever reached him; but that was how things were. Shaking a little, clenching and unclenching her hands, she turned herself once more to the composition of those phrases, those subtle, gentle phrases that might, possibly, return to her his secret, elusive love.

Chapter Fifteen – Catch and Release

Walkinshaw looked across the table at Cressida, trying, as he had so many times before, to appraise her, to appraise himself, to work out how he felt, what he should do. As usual when with her his feelings seemed to alternate between a mild desire and a mild dislike, almost a disgust; but mild, always mild. He thought of Marlowe's contorted face with an inward shudder; now there was some real feeling that she had evoked. Why then could he feel nothing but indifference, a sort of gentleness that he felt he owed her, being twenty years older than her, and more senior, and a sort of flattered kindness arising out of her obvious desire for him? Everything about her was bland, predictable, she was like a composite of all the professional women he had known in his thirty years at the Bar; she had something of Isobel about her, too, without the bite, the sharpness; but give her time, he thought, there was a time when Isobel used to look at me just like that, with that softness in her eyes. A tired nostalgia gnawed at his heart; he felt he would give anything to have the past back again, to be out of this miserable, interminable present. He caught her eyes, and smiled self-consciously; she probably thinks I'm nervous, he thought; if only. He felt he wanted to love her, but had no idea how, and that thought was unbearably depressing.

'So you had a good day, then?' Why were their conversations always so banal? He realised that he always steered them away from the personal, away from anything too revealing; he had an odd but intense instinct to protect his own inner life from her.

'Well, yes. Yes. I suppose so. Though I had a sticky

moment when I thought I'd left my notes behind. I was running around like a headless chicken, well, you can imagine, you know what Judge Warwick is like, he'd have had no mercy. You can imagine how relieved I was when I found I'd left them in the ladies'.'

'Quite.'

'Do you know Roger Warwick? He was very nice to me afterwards, he said I had the makings of a fine family lawyer. Which was nice of him, I thought, especially as I got my sections and subsections all muddled in my final submissions.' She was growing a little pink with the wine; he looked at her, close to despair, and drained his own glass abruptly.

'A little, yes. Just to say hello to, you know.'

'I really like him. I know Vernon has a high opinion of him. Very able, Vernon says he is.'

'Does he?' I have to end this, he decided all at once, I really have to call it a day, it's not fair on her. But then the thought of his great lonely house intruded once more, and he flinched inside; why was everything so difficult, why did unhappiness lie at the heart of everything? Why is it so hard to do the right thing? All at once he thought again of Hannah, and the idea that he had seen her for the last time made him cold with horror; he felt he wanted to tear out of the fussy, over-heated little restaurant and drive straight over to that little house by the Embankment, where, presumably, she would be all alone, and then –

'Mervyn, are you all right? You're not listening.'

'I am.' He felt his heart was going to give way; he picked up his glass, though it was empty, and then put it down again, afraid that his hands were visibly shaking.

'What did I say, then?' He felt he could not look at her; he knew her face would have that trivial, roguish expression of which she seemed so fond.

'You were saying that Vernon thinks Roger Warwick is very able.' Oh God, the inanity of it all.

'No! You weren't listening! I'd moved on from that, I was saying that I've got another care proceeding next week, the work is definitely picking up. I'll be as busy as you at this rate.'

'I'm really pleased for you.' He made himself meet her eyes; she is not so bad, he thought, she's only young, really. And she is nice-looking, genuinely; Marlowe was not her only follower on circuit. That afternoon Jennings had said to him, 'Fair play to you, Mervyn, fair play, mate. Hooking up with a fit bird like her, that's the way to show them, eh, that's the way to fucking show them, good for you.' He had been surprised at the vehemence with which he had resented this; he had felt disturbed, almost violated. He was still perturbed by the violence of his reaction, which he could not understand.

'Thank you. I knew you would be.' She looked at him warmly, with such thinly-veiled invitation that for a moment his head swam.

'You'll do very well, I'm sure of that.' He looked down at the table, drumming his fingers a little, trying to make his mind a blank.

'Oh, Mervyn,' she had a little laugh in her voice that, as usual, worked his nerves, 'you sound so formal, please don't be. You don't need to be nervous. You're forgiven.' There was a note in her voice that warned him that he was not quite forgiven, that she wanted to talk about it, that it was still on her mind. So he avoided any reply, and only smiled carefully. She looked a little disappointed, and said, in a nettled tone, 'You really are, I mean it. I don't bear grudges. Once I put something behind me, that's it. I don't feel the need to keep revisiting it, that's no way to live your life. That's what I think, anyway.'

'Very wise.' He looked up and met her eyes, blandly. He knew he was annoying her, but he didn't seem to be able to stop; it was even mildly pleasurable.

'Wise. Well, that's more than can be said for you, you reckless thing,' she said, with an attempted lightness that rang a little false. 'You dark horse. I was very surprised.'

'Were you?'

'I was, rather. I can't imagine... I mean, I know you're a bit more liberal than me on these things, but – well – it does seem a bit of a radical thing to do. And dangerous. You must promise me never to do anything like that again.'

He was silent, a quiet anger dawning in his heart, and she pressed on.

'Of course, I understand, you've been under such a strain, I can't imagine how you must be feeling. With – with – your wife, and all that, and – and – well, it must be all be very confusing. And, of course, it's natural to want to, well, experiment.'

He raised his head at this. 'What do you mean, experiment?'

He wondered if she would heed the coldness in his tone, but she seemed oblivious. 'I mean... oh, you know what I mean. It's not – well, I know men get curious, well, I suppose we all do, we wonder, don't we, what it would be like to – well, you know, with someone like that. Well,' she was scarlet now, 'I mean, I don't, it's not my thing, but I wouldn't judge someone who did, you know, as a one-off, just to see what it was like.'

'Someone like what?'

'Someone like – well, her. But it was a stupid thing to do, Mervyn, you must see that, and –' She broke off, a kind of alarm breaking across her face.

He was silent for a moment. 'She's a human being,

just like you, you know, Cressida,' he said, much more gently than he had meant to; inside his anger still boiled its way inside his veins; he almost felt that he hated her.

'I know. Oh, I do know that.' She looked at him in apologetic fear. 'I know. I hope I haven't – I didn't mean - you're not angry with me, are you?'

'No. No. I understand why you said it.' But he would not meet her eyes, and she went on, in a voice high with anxiety, 'But you're so defensive of her, it makes me wonder, it makes me afraid...'

'It makes you wonder what?'

'If you... well, if you're perhaps, well, it's extraordinary, but –' she tried to laugh again, but it was little more than a panting breath of nerves, 'if you're perhaps a little in love with her?'

He could feel her fear of his answer intensely, as though it were his own; for a moment, despite his anger, he felt for her. But the words seemed to be drawn out of him as though he had no control over them at all. 'I don't know. I really don't know.'

**

Hannah sat in the little dark room overlooking the car park, vaguely aware that it was growing dark outside, though it was very hard to see anything out of the obscure little window, half-covered with a dirty blind. The tape recorder lay on the desk in front of her; she eyed it nervously, as though it might go off at any moment, like a bomb. She looked anxiously at Ratchett, sitting next to her, who crossed his legs awkwardly in his tight plastic chair, breathing heavily as he wrote in his notebook.

'Are they going to let me go tonight?'

The policewoman sitting opposite them raised her face, pale and wintry, from her papers and gave her a sour look at this; Hannah stared back, conscious of a bitter dislike.

'You'll just have to wait and see, won't you? Come on, back to your cell.'

'I've told you everything,' said Hannah, suddenly angry, 'I want to go home.'

'Don't we all, love.' Ratchett smiled at her blankly as she was bundled out; he doesn't connect with me at all, she thought in a sort of fury, I'm just one of them to him. He's just annoyed I've spoiled his evening in front of the telly. She was already desperate with regret; what a stupid, stupid thing to do, and to get caught. It had seemed as though it was going to be all right, she had really thought it would work. Now another court appearance, another shop theft on her record. And she had been so close, she was sure the guard hadn't seen her, and the doors had actually opened, she'd felt the air on her face, her heart quickening with relief, and then the familiar grasp of her arm, the rough voice in her ear. She realised that what she regretted most was not getting to keep it; it was only a small stereo, only thirty quid, and she'd only have got twenty for it. It seemed to her, illogical though she knew it to be, that you really ought to get to keep the stuff you stole, as a sort of compensation for all this hassle of getting arrested and locked up. It seemed hard to be punished and to be empty handed too; all this and nothing to show for it. She might have a night in here just for that, in this dirty horrible cell. She felt she might not mind it so much if it were not so brightly lit; it made everything seem unreal, overwhelming, her eyes were hurting after only ten minutes in there. She looked down at her tea in its polystyrene cup; it was undrinkable, it was a strange grey colour, a colour tea should never be. She wondered if DC Glover was there; she had thought she heard his voice, earlier, echoing down one of the corridors, but it was hard to tell. She had hoped, perversely, that he would be the interviewing officer, that she could sit opposite him and look at him again, revisit and make sense of that past encounter in some way, but presumably she was too trivial for the attention of a DC; I'll have to do something more serious next time, she thought to herself, with a bitterness that did not come naturally to her, that was a little forced. She remembered the tea that he had made her, and for a moment she could taste it again, hot and far too sweet, at the back of her throat, and she trembled inside, conscious of a strange ache in some part of her that she could not name. Perhaps it's my soul, she thought, maybe that's what hurts. She thought of banging on the cell door, demanding to speak to him; they might bring him down, a little flushed and anxious, but holding on to his authority, standing on his dignity, wondering what she could want to say. And of course she had nothing to say; it was over, and she couldn't really complain, his twenty pounds had lasted nearly five days. He had not done anything so very bad, although Danny would not see it that way; Danny would want to kill him, and her too, probably. She looked around her; in one of these cells Danny had scratched his name; was it this one? The walls were cream in daylight, if ever daylight was allowed in, but in this harsh florescence everything was a nightmarish yellow, and the scratched names danced in silver before her eyes, dazzling. A couple of names she knew; 'Daz Pearson' had been nearly obliterated with a fresh coat of paint, but she could just make it out. It must have been from a few years back, he'd been dead about eighteen months. He'd had septicaemia or something like that, then he got beaten up by some vigilantes and never came out of hospital. Danny had gone to his funeral, all done up in a black suit, and come home white-faced with his eyes all red, and in a wild temper. She could still remember that night, how she'd heard him crying in the bathroom, but when she asked him about it he'd turned on her, his jaw set, and thrown her against the wall. Then they were both crying. It seemed an eternity ago, and it seemed a mad thing to say, but they seemed to her now to be happy days; part of her longed for them. Then there was Jenny Watson's name; a huge, terrifying woman with a hoarse voice and tattoos like a man's; she'd been on the same wing as Hannah at Greenlands, and had smothered her with gruff affection. She couldn't see Danny's name; the thought that perhaps it had been painted over made her suddenly frightened; she could not bear the thought of its being obliterated, and she shuddered with a strange sort of premonitory sense; this will be his epitaph, she thought suddenly, with all his cleverness and his looks, what he'll leave behind is a name scratched on a cell wall, just like Daz Pearson. Her heart lurched at the thought; she realised that, without recognising it consciously, she had always felt that he could be more, that he was worth something, and the thought that it was impossible gave her a sweet sense of sadness, of loss. Mr. Walkinshaw did not need her; if he were to die, all sorts of important and worthwhile people would come to his funeral, he would have an obituary in the paper, and people would go on talking about him, better, cleverer people than her would remember him. Who would remember Danny? His world was dwindling to nothing, she felt this so clearly that it was as though she could see it happening before her eyes. He has only me, she said to herself, and she imagined sacrificing herself to him, going on in this life year after year just for him, so that he would not be alone, so that he would have someone with him to share his memories, to help him bear them. Mr. Walkinshaw was wrong, she could go on like this, and she would, it was inevitable, and she felt she no longer wanted to fight that inevitability. She would stay with him, if he wanted her, and that was how it was meant to be; it seemed strange to her that she had ever seen it differently, ever wanted anything else. She felt suddenly tired, anxious to get back to the house, though when she was there she felt she hated it; perhaps when Danny gets out we can start afresh, she thought, perhaps we can get another house somewhere else, somewhere nicer. Heavy footsteps went past the door; she thought immediately of Glover and her heart began to pound. What's the matter with me? she thought angrily, why should I want to see him again? It's stupid. The footsteps stopped and came back towards her door, she heard the rattle of heavy keys, and closed her eyes in mute gratitude.

She sat in the car beside Ratchett, watching the swirling lights of the darkening city; they seemed to rise and fall beneath her, she felt her eyes growing heavy, and a pleasant indifference settling inside her. It had been good of him to offer her a lift home; she regretted her harsh thoughts of him earlier, he was not so bad, really.

'Thanks for this, Mr. Ratchett, I really appreciate it.'

'Don't you worry, you've had a long day, and it's not far out of my way. Don't forget to take your stuff with you, love, it's on the back seat, under all my bits and bobs, I'm a messy so-and-so, aren't I?'

She clambered out of his car, overwhelmed with tiredness, and opened the back door.

'Here it is. Thank you.'

'That's all right, treasure. Goodnight.'

She looked down at the bag in her hand, and was suddenly gripped with an awful fear. 'Where's my letter?'

'What's that, love?'

'My letter. I had a letter in my bag,' her voice was rising in panic, 'I had a letter, and now it's not here. It's gone.'

Ratchett squinted over his shoulder at her with concerned stupidity. 'Oh dear. Are you sure you had it with you? Was it important?'

Her heart was beating with slow, painful thuds. 'Yes. Yes.'

'Oh dear. Well, I shall keep an eye out for it. And I'll ask at the station if I'm back there tonight. It'll turn up, love, don't you fret.'

Chapter Sixteen – All Her Bones Were Silver

Danny stood at the side of the road, hardly daring to breathe, unable to believe it. He had never imagined it was really possible, let alone that it would be so easy; he felt that he must be dreaming, that it could not be real. He had simply walked out, carefully, avoiding the pathways, holding his breath as he went, an excited fear mounting in him as he got nearer and nearer to the edge, nearer to the world outside. Something inside him wanted to be stopped; as he climbed over the fence he felt that his heart would give way. The silence was suffocating; there was nothing except the faint roar of traffic in the distance, and a dove calling in a nearby tree; the flat, green landscape seemed oddly sterile, barren, under the low grey sky, and for a moment he felt utterly terrified of everything, unable to comprehend the enormity of it all, and he nearly turned back, nearly climbed back over the fence and ran back to the little grey building, to the metalwork centre, the literacy suite, and the carefully camouflaged cameras. But he could not; he stood, transfixed with fear, frightened both of going on and of turning back, half wishing that someone would come and catch him, take him back, take it all out of his hands. But they wouldn't take him back, they would arrest him and have him charged with attempted escape, he would have to have another three court appearances, at the very least, and then get sent to prison again, only this time a Cat A; and he could forget about getting bail ever again in the future. This gave him a kind of nervous decisiveness; he would have to press on, already it was too late. You stupid bastard, he murmured to himself, only four months to go. Just four short months. But he knew four months was far too long, that he would never manage it; some impulse in himself that could not be reasoned down had urged him on, forced him over that fence, and he knew there was no fighting it, even as his mind reeled at the magnitude of the step he had taken. It seemed like fate, destiny; he had known the moment he had arrived at this place that he would not last here, that it was impossible. Already he felt a sort of regret for it; the privacy, the luxury of being able to have a bath, to leave his cell in the day. But somehow, in some mysterious, inexplicable way, all that was not for him, he could not live like that, even for four months; the place made him shiver, all of it. Even the guards alarmed him; their very civility gave him the feeling that he was in some nightmarish new world, where none of the old rules, the old certainties, applied; he felt a nebulous sense of menace, as though to go wrong, to misbehave, here would be in some inexplicable way much more serious, much more dangerous, than to do so back at Blakemoor. Perhaps it was a sense of obligation that unsettled him; perhaps he could not endure being treated well, feeling that he ought to be grateful, to like it there. But it was more than that; some looming sense of evil oppressed him, and he knew he had to go, even at the cost of another, longer sentence in the future; some devil of fatalism was driving him on. His hands were sweating, his skin prickled with a sense of danger; he felt as though a thousand pairs of invisible eyes were watching him, hidden; even the caw of the birds overhead made his heart shudder with dread. It had to be done. He turned, lowered his head and set off up the road, crushed with fear, and with a deep foreboding at his heart.

**

Hannah sat on the arm of the sofa in the front room, exhausted but unable to rest; her mind kept going back over the letter, reeling with horror at its loss. If only she had posted it before going in the shop! She had meant to, but something in her had kept putting it off, delaying the moment, though why she could not explain to herself; she did want him to get it, to read it. And now where was it? She had rung Mr. Ratchett that morning, hoping against hope that he would say it had been found at the police station, or that he had come across it on the back seat of his car. But she'd known even as she dialled the number that it wouldn't be, that it was lost for good. It was just her luck. She hardly knew what was more upsetting, the idea of someone else reading it, or the thought of the effort of writing it all over again. And what if somehow it fell into Danny's hands? That was hardly possible, surely, but still –

She trembled all over as the doorbell rang, with a sense that it must be Danny, and that he would read the guilt in her eyes. She got up hastily, trying to assume a normal expression as she went; she felt as though the whole sordid story must be written on her face.

She saw the dark figure through the glass, and recognized it at once; her heart lifted, a small hope dawning in her heart; perhaps she was not all alone after all, perhaps he did care. Why else would he have come back? She opened the door, struggling with the chain with shaking hands; in that moment she could almost have believed she loved him.

'DC Glover.' She smiled up at him, but his face was impassive, official, and she felt a coldness spreading through her. 'What is it?'

'I shouldn't be here, really,' he said, with a furtive glance over his shoulder, and she moved uncomfortably, suddenly oppressed with a sense of urgency, of danger. 'I shouldn't have come, but, well, I felt sorry for you, you see, and – '

'What's happened?' She was terrified now; she sought his eyes for reassurance, but they seemed to slide away from hers, unreachable. She held on to the doorframe; the wood seemed soft, flimsy, under her fingers.

'It's your dad.' There was a kindness in his voice that only served to increase her alarm; this is how they train them to break bad news, she thought, to tell them that someone's dead. She was already imagining how he might have died; had someone beaten him up in prison? That seemed the only possible way. She closed her eyes suddenly, trying for a moment to concentrate on the red patterns the veins of her eyelids made against the bright March sun; it could not be real, nothing was real anymore.

'What happened to him?' She opened her eyes, searching his face.

'Nothing's happened to him.' Glover gave a short, bitter laugh that somehow shocked her. 'Nothing happens to the likes of him. He's got bail, that's all. I thought it only right to give you a warning.'

She wondered, somewhere at the back of her mind, if she looked as white as she felt. It was incomprehensible; he could not, he would not, come back here, to this house. She felt sickened at the thought, disgusted and frightened; none of it seemed to make any sense.

'When?' A sharp pain was making itself felt in her stomach; she would have to sit down in a minute.

'This morning. He'll be out this afternoon. I am sorry, Hannah.' His voice was soft again, but she could not look at him, ashamed of the tears rolling silently down her face. 'I am sorry, but if you'd given us that statement like we asked you to, he couldn't have been bailed to this address. You're your own worst enemy sometimes.'

'When will he get here?' It didn't sound like her voice.

'Hard to say. Not before tonight. If he gives you any trouble – '

She nodded, unable to speak. He turned to go, but he couldn't, she mustn't let him. 'Please – '

'What?' His tone was short, but still sympathetic, still kindly, maybe there was a chance –

'Won't you – come in for a minute? I could – I could put the kettle on...' Her voice died in embarrassment; she knew what he was going to say; and flinched from it in advance, like an expected blow.

'No. No, I can't.' He was already out on the steps, stretching his shoulders back; he seemed to her in that moment almost magnificent, free, like an animal, and she felt a longing to join him out there, as though those few steps between them marked a huge, symbolic distance, a divide that could not be crossed. 'I'll see you around, Hannah. You look after yourself, and let me know if he gives you any bother.'

He was striding towards his car now; she raised her hand, timidly, as though to wave to him, but he didn't look back. She watched him, desolate, as he unlocked his car and drove away; she stood there for a few seconds after he had gone, as though waiting for something, but at last, with a mortal pain at her heart, she turned inside and slowly closed the door. As she did so she was struck with a sense that she was closing the door on her own life, that in some hidden way she was killing herself. This feeling was so intense that she went straight to the door again, and this time left it open for a few minutes; but the draught was so strong that soon, shivering a little, she closed it again, with a quick, quiet glance into the silent street outside, and drew the chain across.

**

Norman Tombs leaned back in his little chair, aware of an unpleasant cramp spreading across his shoulders. He looked up at the clock; ten to five. He knew he ought to wait until five, but there was nothing likely to happen in the next ten minutes; nothing had happened in the last three hours. He had spent the afternoon waiting for clients who never came. At first the enforced idleness had been pleasurable; after all, it was nicer to sit daydreaming, chair tilted back against the radiator, listening to the hum of traffic in the street below, and the snatches of conversations from the pavement, than it was to have to turn his mind to the tedious details of some extraordinarily boring common assault, and worse, to have to feign interest as yet another whey-faced lad in tracksuit and trainers, with spiky hair and an embarrassingly overbearing mother in tow mumbled inaudible answers to his half-hearted questions. But as the afternoon wore on he began to wish someone would turn up; it was surprisingly tiring doing absolutely nothing, and the silence of the office began to get on his nerves, fill him with an unpleasant but persistent sense of disquiet. If he left now no one could blame him, they all did it, and anyway, he wouldn't be here much longer, as long as he did enough to get a good reference that would suffice; he was not going to put himself out. He had fretted that Marlowe's promises were empty, idle, merely the tricks of a man who used words to get what he wanted from strangers for a living; he worried that all his fear and stress and striving would only serve to feather another man's nest, leaving him, as usual, empty-handed. But so far, he admitted to himself with inner exultation, it looked promising. He had been promised an informal interview at Ermine on Friday; the thought of it kept him awake at night, churning with excitement and dread. He would not tell Mum just yet; he felt sometimes that keeping the secret would kill him, but at the same time he knew that it would be so much better, so much more triumphant, if he waited until it was a certainty, until there was nothing left that could possibly go wrong. Besides, he had a sense that she would find a way of spoiling it for him; some muttered aside, or one of those hard, sardonic glances of hers which made him frightened of meeting her eyes. No, much as he wanted a confidant, he knew that this was a secret he must hug to his own chest for now. Ratchett seemed a little suspicious of his new demeanour; he was conscious of the need to hide a new arrogance, a resurfacing of his old contempt for them all, and an awareness that he must avoid becoming dangerously casual. After all, it was not in the bag just yet. This thought chilled him, and he moved restlessly in his chair, glancing up at the ceiling with an odd sense that it was getting lower, closer and closer to his head. All at once he got to his feet and took his anorak from the hook behind the door; it would be all right to go now. He went over to the window to draw the blinds across, and paused for a moment, looking down into the street below. He was not easily moved by beauty, but even he felt that it was almost pleasant in the first vitality of Spring, late afternoon sunshine streaming in; it seemed to illuminate everything, and for a moment his heart rose; everything would be all right, it would all work out, he would find the life he was meant to live. The telephone ringing on his desk jarred him; he was aware of an uneasy sense of premonition as he lifted the receiver.

'Hello? Is it for me?' He still found himself unable to call any of the office staff by name.

'It's me.' The voice on the other end rasped, as though in some sort of pain; Tombs could not quite recognize it, though he had a sense that he did know it, but was used to it speaking differently, calmly, that something terrible had happened, and for a moment he felt a rush of fear to his stomach, as though he had caught the desperation of this unknown caller; involuntarily he put a hand to his mouth, trembling a little.

'Who is this?' he said, with as much authority as he could muster. He wondered why his hands were suddenly so cold, so clammy; he could feel the receiver dampening under his grasp.

'It's me. Reynolds.'

'What do you want?' Tombs felt a strange sort of guilt at not having recognized his voice, a sense almost of having failed a test. What is the matter with me? he thought furiously. I shouldn't feel excited and bewildered like this, all this is behind me, I don't need him any more.

'I've run away.'

'What?' He was genuinely astonished; it did not seem possible to him, and for a moment he thought it must be some sort of joke, that he was being mocked in some way. 'What do you mean, you've run away? Where are you?'

'I'm – I can't say where I am. But I need your help.'

'My help?' This is a nightmare, he thought, like all those things I worried could happen, but couldn't really believe ever would. He's going to blackmail me, he's going to threaten to tell on me. His brain was hot; he felt feverish with horror.

'I can't help you. I can't. I can't.' His voice was rising; he glanced anxiously at the door, almost as though he expected to see Reynolds' shadow looming against the wall.

'I need it, Norman. I wouldn't ask you otherwise. I really need it. You won't get in any trouble. I just need you to leave some money for me, that's all. I only need fifty quid, you'll get a hundred back. Please, mate.'

Tombs hesitated, conscious that he was taking an odd pleasure in Reynolds' begging tone; and wondering what that meant, wondering why, despite his fear, he felt a impulse to prolong the conversation.

'I can't help you,' he said again, weakly. 'The best I can do is to advise you to hand yourself in.'

'Go to hell, then. No, sorry, I didn't mean that. Please. I'm desperate.'

'I shall have to tell Mr. Caldwell about this.' His voice sounded thin, high, pathetic, he thought, and suddenly he felt a fresh wave of panic. What was he doing? Standing here, at his desk, talking to a runaway prisoner, a violent junkie, whom he had somehow allowed to gain a strange ascendancy over him. It was disgusting. It was unacceptable. He became aware that he was gasping for breath; his head was whirling. 'I can't help you. I really can't.'

Reynolds was saying something; he could hear the low hum of his voice, growing fainter as he slowly lowered the phone to the desk; dare he do it? And then he had; he had replaced the receiver, and that soft, insistent voice was no more. His heart was thudding with dread; he almost ran down the stairs, terrified that he would hear the phone ringing again up in his little office.

**

Danny waited for a moment or two, wondering whether to call back. But it was no good, something in his heart told him that. He could put his loose change to better use than that. Fucking slimy little bastard, he might have known it would be a waste of time trying him. But he couldn't muster up much anger; it all seemed sad rather than anything else, all sad and useless, futile. He was exhausted with the walk; he hadn't realized how far it was, or how far it would be walking it. Still, he should be back in town by the evening. And then what? He wondered why he was not disconcerted by his lack of plans, by the formlessness of everything. It would fall right or it would not. He would get picked up sooner or later, and have to finish his existing sentence and serve another one for the escape. It would happen because it always happened. But today was special; he felt it in the air, time seemed to be hanging, suspended, as though today was not governed by the usual laws of space and time, as though normal rules did not apply. He stood for a moment, his back against the phone booth, and looked out across the rolling fields, hills and pylons, scattered farmsteads and brackish lakes, and felt something within him that he couldn't name; a sensation that something was breaking open inside him, rending and tearing, and that he was helpless before it. He felt he wanted to cry, but no tears came, and this somehow distressed him; he felt that it was a bad omen, that in some way tears might have saved him, might have purified things. The city lay just on his eyeline, dark and brooding, as though it were waiting for him, about to pounce, and he felt for a moment that he wanted to turn and run away from it, run and run as far away as he could, but he knew that he wouldn't, he knew that he would walk towards it, with the same cold, meaningless resolution with which a man steps towards his executioner. He shivered a little; it was getting cold, and he hadn't got his jacket with him. He had better go on, it was always better to go on; madness waited for those who turned back.

He stood for a moment by the gate, anguished, strangely nervous, a sort of awe gathering in his heart. This was meant to be, somehow, he felt that everything that had happened that day had been part of some mysterious, fatal plan, as though he had had nothing to do with it; and now he found himself, almost astonished, at Hannah's door, raising his hand to knock on it, conscious as he did so of what he felt were the last few moments of this pain, this lostness, in his heart, before she opened the door to him, and he saw her face, and then –

The door swung open suddenly, and in his confused, exhausted brain it seemed to him for a moment as though everything was false, unreal, this was some cruel dream. He knew he was staring, stupidly, and made an attempt to take hold of himself. He tried to look straight ahead, into his eyes, brave and bold, but still his head swam, and he felt as though he were drowning.

'I thought you were inside.'

'Likewise.' He could hardly look at him; he felt disgusted, appalled, shaken. Still he watched him carefully; even in extremes of tiredness, illness, injury, emotion, still you had to keep your guard up, your instincts alert. Years of prison training told him this, and yet he felt that for once he was utterly defeated; all he wanted was to sleep for years and years.

'They gave me bail.' His face was close to Danny's now, he could feel his breath. Profane. That was the word. He was profane, he violated things, he violated people. Profane. He took what was pure, what was beautiful, what was not his to take, and soiled it, destroyed it, rendered it useless. He found himself shaking a little; he wanted to close his eyes, but he could not. He felt that he had been standing out there on that step for hours; he felt he had no sense of time at all.

'They gave you bail.' He spoke slowly; he had trouble forming the words, like a drunk.

'Yeah. What are you doing here, anyway? Your release date isn't for months yet. You've fucking run off, haven't you? You stupid cunt.' His eyes gleamed with a sudden malicious amusement; Danny looked past him into the dim, shabby passageway, and realized with horror that there was no one else in the house.

'Where is she?' he said, cold with dread, and realized with a shock that he was shouting. 'What have you done?'

'She wasn't here when I got back.' Casey was backing into the hall, his face darkening with that old blustering fear Danny knew so well of old. 'She must have gone out somewhere. You fuck off out of my house or I'm ringing the police. I'm telling them you're here, then you'll be back inside for a nice long time. You fuck off.'

'What have you done with her?' Danny's mind was a whirl of jumbled images; bones in cellars, bloodied limbs wrapped in newspapers and hidden under flagstones, knives, blood, screaming faces; he fancied he could see Casey trying to scrub a blade clean under a sputtering kitchen tap, the florescent light above him flickering out its disapproval in a sinister Morse code.

'I haven't fucking done anything.'

'Where the hell is she?'

'How the fuck should I know? I just got here!' His face was black with fear and anger; he was backing away towards the kitchen, sweat beginning to darken the rims of his grey vest under his arms. 'Don't think you can come here and bully me, you fucking bastard. I've got a hotline, I can get a unit out straight away any time I like, 'cause of the vigilantes. Don't think you can fucking bully me.'

'What vigilantes?'

Casey's face was putty-like now, his lips pale and spongy. 'I won't talk about it to you. You fuck off or I'm calling them. I am.'

'You did those women, didn't you? The ones down by the canal. You did that. You did that, and she has to live with you.' He felt sick; suddenly he had a picture in his mind of Tommy's Marie, her half-burned body dragged from the canal in Glasgow, and he reeled with the horror of it all; how had he lived among all this and survived for so long?

'I won't discuss it with you. You fucking get out of my house, or I will call the police. I don't want to, I believe in minding my own business, but if you keep getting up in my fucking face – '

'Go on, then.'

'What?'

'You call them. Go on. I dare you.'

'You what?'

'You call them. Only you won't, because you're such a fucking coward. You won't.' He felt he hardly knew what he was saying, that he was speaking from some sort of script, some vague dream of a conversation, a confrontation, lurking at the edges of his mind; he was angry, though, really angry now, and he felt he couldn't go without doing something, punching him maybe, but doing something to him, just for Hannah. He had to.

Casey, blank-eyed now with terror, was reaching ineffectually for the phone against the wall; Danny noted with absent-minded disgust the dark grease stains on its cracked cream plastic. 'I will call them. I won't be threatened like this in my own home. I won't have it.'

He made a sudden lunge for the phone, his bulk

clumsy in his terror, and suddenly Danny was afraid, suddenly his fear was real, strong. He could not go back in there, not now, not yet, he could not let it happen, and as his fist crashed against Casey's jaw he felt a strange tide of relief, of calm. It would not happen, not yet.

**

Hannah knew that she couldn't stay there for long; it wouldn't even be possible to stay there for the night, not really, without any furniture and no heating. At least the water was still on, or it seemed to be; it had run out a dirty orange colour at first, but then it had come clear, gushing in sudden torrents. It was peaceful, somehow; she had half expected to be frightened, as she had the last time she had been inside the house, the day of her pre-trial conference. It seemed a very long time ago now, far longer than just a couple of months, and thinking back to it gave her a sense of deep tiredness; it all seemed exhausting. It was a small miracle that the house was still boarded up, still uninhabited; she wondered now what she would have done if there had been strangers living it, a family, perhaps. The randomness of it made her head swim; but no, it was all right, the house was still hers. Theirs. Hers and Danny's. It was still strange to see it so empty, but this time the strangeness was not alarming, just a little sad. She recalled the furniture, the table, chairs, the bed, cupboards, all the fixtures and fittings with the vaguest of recollections; none of it seemed important. It came and went, just as they did, but now she was back, and despite the echoing barrenness of everything she had a sense of homecoming. She could not go back and face him, not yet, that was too much to ask. She wondered a little whether she should make a statement against him after all, but something inside her crawled in horror at the thought, and she knew it was impossible. Besides, it would mean standing up in court, one day, and telling a room of people about it – it was out of the question, something that simply could never happen. Better to hide from him, now, hide from him for ever, and this house seemed strangely suited to hiding; its atmosphere was secretive, silent, protective. She sat on the floor in the kitchen, or what used to be the kitchen, for what she imagined was a long time, watching the sky outside the window turn a dusky pink, and then gradually a dark, heavy grey that presaged nightfall. All at once an uneasiness began to impress itself upon her heart; she felt suddenly and horribly lonely, and anxious in a way she couldn't define; for the first time in months she began to think of the things she shouldn't do, the things that were so beautiful, so comforting, and she even put her hands in her pockets to see how much cash she could scrape together, before she sat down again, horrified at herself, but still with that terrible new ache in her heart. All the pain of the last few months seemed to rise up in her all at once, and she nearly cried out with the anguish of it. Anything was better than feeling like this; and she had almost resolved to go out, back out on the street again, when she heard a sharp knocking sound at the back of the house, and sprang to her feet in a wild panic, boiling up with terror. She heard footsteps, inside the house now, and froze; she felt these must be the last moments of her life.

'It's you. Oh God. I was so scared.' She did not stop to wonder how he had come to be there, how he was not in prison, or why his shirt was streaked with ugly patches of brownish blood. Nothing mattered now, except that he was there, and she clung to him in desperation, thrilling with relief. Then she noticed that he was shaking all over, and that his face was white, and covered in a faint sheen of sweat; as she held him she felt his heart hammering wildly. 'What is it? What's happened?'

He threw his head back, with a high laugh that chilled her blood. 'I've gone and killed your dad, that's all. I've killed him. I've killed him.'

'You can't have done,' she said, stupidly, her brain numb. 'You can't have done.'

'I have. I killed him.'

She realized that her whole body was shaking in great violent bursts, and she felt almost interested by it; is that what happens when you go into shock? It was all like a dream, a dream in which things, people, are just as they are in real life, but different too, different in little ways that somehow make it all nightmarish, untrue.

'Is he dead?' She was horrified to feel a pulse of excitement at the words, a freedom throbbing through her.

'People usually are dead when you kill them.' His voice was strange, as she had never heard it before. He seemed to want to shout, but he was struggling to breathe at the same time; he leaned against the wall suddenly, biting his lip, his face working. 'It was one punch, Hannah. One. I hit him once. Just once, I swear it. I hit him and he went down, down, like that, and he must have hit his head on the table or something – and oh God, I'm going to get life for this. I'm going to get life.'

'Are you sure he's dead?' She was astonished at how calm she sounded; she went over to him and took his hand, gently. But for an odd floating feeling in her head she felt almost normal.

He looked at her, fear and love battling across his face. 'Yes. He wouldn't move. He wouldn't wake up.

There was blood coming out from his mouth and his nose. He wouldn't wake up, he just wouldn't.' His voice broke off in a hoarse sob. 'Oh God, I'm sorry, Hannah. I'm so sorry.'

She looked into his eyes; she felt that she had never loved him more, that she had never before understood him, and that now something in her did. It was suddenly beautiful, and she realized that she was smiling. 'It's all right. It's all right.' She was stroking his face; he was crying now into her shoulder, his tears wet against her neck, his breathing low, like a moan.

'I didn't mean to.'

'I know.' She wondered what this peace meant, and why she was not frightened; she heard a police siren wailing past the house in the street outside, and she caught her breath for a moment, but it went on past the house, gradually dying away into the distance.

'What am I going to do? I don't know why I ran out, I don't know what I was thinking. Now I've fucked it all up.'

She drew back from him a little; his swearing seemed to break the spell between them, and for a moment they stood there, silent, looking hard at each other, as though reading the truth in each other's faces.

'I got some gear,' he said, abruptly, his voice still shaking; he pulled away from her and crouched against the wall, his arms between his knees, trembling. She was silent, and he said again, almost angrily, 'I went out and scored, Hannah. I killed your dad, emptied his pockets, and then I went out and scored.'

Hannah stood perfectly still; she had the impression that if she moved Danny, the room, everything, would swirl away from her, never to return.

'How much?' she said at last; she felt as though each word was killing her.

'Ten wraps.'

'A hundred quid?'

'Seventy. I needed it. I need it now.' He looked up at her; she hardly dared meet his eyes, scared of what she might read there.

'Oh, Danny...'

'I have to.'

'But it's been ages. I'm not even on methadone any more. I was doing really well, and – you – '

'And I what?'

'And you – it's not the answer, is it?'

'What is the answer, Hannah? What is it?'

She was silent; the gentleness of his tone frightened her, filled her with a sense of fatality.

'I don't know,' she said at last. She felt an emptiness spreading up through her, and closed her eyes tightly for a moment; there was no relief to be had anywhere.

'There's no hope for us now. Nothing left.' He was not looking at her any more, he was not looking at anything; already his eyes were blank with longing, and she felt him slipping away from her. 'We're finished.'

She felt her nerves tighten, almost with pleasure, at this. 'We?'

At once his eyes were on her face, wide with pain, burning. 'You're not leaving me. You're not going.'

She felt herself shudder, somewhere in some unreachable part of herself, and she wanted to scream with the horror, with the inevitable horror of it, as she heard herself say, almost indifferently, 'No. No, I'm not going.'

He was already reaching inside his coat, and as she saw the yellowish-brown powder all the old desire rose up in her, and she squatted on the floor beside him, eagerly. He met her eyes, and smiled; that familiar smile that she had loved so much now seemed to belong to another time, another world. As she looked at him she felt her heart was bleeding; she reached out to him in a sudden rush of affection, throwing her arms around his neck. But already his mouth was set in lines of concentration. His hands were steady now, and reluctantly she turned her face away from his, and stared at the little pile of objects on the floor in front of them.

'You got a needle? Why? I don't want to inject. I don't inject, you know that.'

'You'll want to inject this, it's too good for toking, this is good stuff. Good, good stuff.' He was smiling at her now, his grin seemed to spread across his face, and she began to laugh, all at once, her arms around his neck, her face in his chest.

'Good stuff, is it? Is it the best?' They were both laughing now, and she wondered if this was happiness; she felt happy, she felt wonderful, suddenly, watching the liquid run up inside the syringe; there was a moment when Danny struggled with the almost-empty lighter, but then there was a flame, sudden and bright in the darkening room, and her heart had flamed up with it, she felt suffused with the wonderfulness of everything, and she had waited, waited, waited for it, but the waiting was no hardship at all, the waiting was beautiful, because it would end, she would get it, and the waiting was beautiful, yes, it was, really beautiful, all that anticipation was beautiful. There must be other words for it, but really everything was beautiful, Danny was beautiful, as he steadied his hands, the muscles in his arms swelling as he made a fist, and she loved him, she loved him more than anything else in the world, there was no room for anything else in the world but Danny, he was the world, and she kissed his neck again and again. Then there it was, it was ready, it was ready, it was now and now and now again, and again, and she could not contain herself, but she must, and soon it would contain her, soon it would make even the darkest places light, so light and bright that there was only peace and happiness, everything was beautiful, there was nothing to worry about at all. Perhaps she would think about other things again, perhaps there was another world, somewhere, of other people, people who did not matter, could not matter, because they were not her and Danny, perhaps those other faces rose before her eyes, perhaps, for a second or two, but seconds were valuable now, there weren't many of them left, no, they were precious, they were all that was real, all that there was now, and she grasped his hand, clutched at it, until the great tide carried her away, and at last her fingers relaxed, fell away, fell open, and she wanted to hold him, but there was no holding, there was no anything, and her tongue was made of velvet, all her bones were silver; she was on another shore now, another place, but still she held on, still she had to reach him, but the waves were stronger, the waves were fiercer, and they should have hurt her but they did not, nothing did, and at last her eyes closed, and she knew that it was coming now, and that the great hammer in her chest, the only thing that was keeping her awake, that was spoiling it, was beating away to nothing. Slowly. Slowly. Slowly the beats were dying away, each one now with a deep shudder, and she tried to hold him again, but she had no hands, she had no arms, but it was all right, it didn't matter, she could hold him still, hold him forever. It was all nothing now, everything was nothing, but that didn't matter either, because nothing was everything, and it was everywhere. And then all at once her head went back, over and back, and round, and the great hammer stopped at last, shivering into silence.

**

He knew as soon as he woke up that she was dead. Sunlight streamed in through the window, it was so bright he felt that he could hardly see her, that he would not be able to find her, but her hair was all over his knees, and her head lay light on his chest. He hardly noticed that he was crying; she was almost cold, but her lips were still warm, or his were, and he had an idea that his tears would bring her back to life, that she would open her eyes, now, or in a little while, she just needed time to come round. He tried to hold her hand, he tried to make her fingers close around his as they used to, but it was no use, and at last he lay on his back, the hot, implacable sunlight in his eyes, and gathered her body in his arms, crooning a little to himself, to her. He pushed her hair back from her face and whispered a little in her ear, struggling to speak through his sobs. Then he steadied himself enough to take the syringe again, to heat and stir and mix again; all this, for the last time and forever. He wanted to open her eyes, he wanted to look into her eyes again, but he did not dare, instead he kissed her eyelids, and tried to steady himself enough to find a vein and do it right; he could not get it wrong, he could not waste it. 'I'm coming, darling,' he murmured; he still felt that she could hear him, that she would reply, he looked into her still face and knew that she loved him, and he knew there was no more living to be done, not now. He bit his lip, slowly, and carefully pressed down on the top of the syringe. It seemed to take so long to empty, and tears started to his eyes again, but at last it was done, and he settled himself on his back on the floorboards, pulling her on top of him, arranging her head so that she would be comfortable, and kissed her forehead one last time, and waited.

Walkinshaw lay on his back, idly listening to the faint stir of traffic in the road outside. Cressida was downstairs in the kitchen; she had insisted on making breakfast, though he was not really hungry. It had been a good night, he had to admit to himself, and he smiled a little at the recollection; she was wonderful, really, and he had treated her so badly. He was glad now that he had run out of the restaurant after her the other night; it would have been awful, wrong, to have let her go. It had taken a lot of persuasion, but of course she had yielded at last, with a show of reluctance and perhaps quite a lot of relief, and he decided that he perhaps did love her, or could love her; it was too soon to know, of course, but there were distinct possibilities. He lay very still, savouring the peace of the day, the ease of her company; all this was very pleasant, very promising. And here she was, coming in with an air of nervous possession, a couple of his best cups in her hands. 'I couldn't find the others. I hope these are all right.'

'They could do with an airing.' He smiled at her; the coffee was a little weaker than he liked it, but it didn't matter. He patted the bed beside him, and she perched on it next to him a little shyly, turning towards him.

'I just put the radio on in the kitchen. Grim story on the local news.'

'Let me guess, they've cut legal aid again.'

'No, not as bad as that! Just some local sex offender got badly beaten up or something, it seems he'd just got out on bail, and then the police went and searched the area and found his daughter and her boyfriend both dead of an overdose in some derelict house or other. A squat, I imagine. The boyfriend just escaped from prison, so the police think he must have done it. At least they say they're not looking for anyone else. Oh, goodness, Mervyn, that coffee's gone everywhere. If you didn't like it, you should just have said!'

'She's dead.' He couldn't think. She was dead. Although it might be someone else, yes, surely it was someone else.

'What? Who's dead?' Cressida was staring at him, her face stupid in suspicion; his heart was beating fast now. It must be someone else.

'Did they give his name?'

'Who?'

'The man who was beaten up.' This was the last moment, then, the very last point at which there was something to hold on to.

'I can't remember the name. Irish sounding, Murphy or Cassidy, something like that. Why do you care so much? Did you know him or something?'

'Is she definitely dead? Really dead?'

'Who, the daughter? That's what they said. They said she was dead when they got there, but the boyfriend was still alive, apparently he died in the ambulance. Grim, isn't it? Just goes to prove what I've always said about drugs. Once you get involved with all that sort of thing, it really is end of story. I'll just go and see how the bacon's doing.'

**

He stood in front of the mirror, carefully adjusting his tie, which had an annoying tendency to stray off to the right; once again he tugged it back to the centre. But his suit was perfect, and he couldn't help smiling a little as he admired it; Gregory had been right, it was worth getting a really good handmade, even if it was just the one. He had winced a little at the bill, but it really was money worth spent, he had to admit it. He hadn't been sure about the pinstripe, he'd always avoided it, feeling that it was far too barristerish, but somehow it was perfect, just hit the right note. It was a shame for Gregory, really, but retirement was the only sensible option after that stroke, nothing worse than dragging on for years after you're past it. Still, he had been genuinely astonished when he was told he would be head of chambers; he had even had an idea that he would turn it down, but it looked so good after his name. Mervyn R L Walkinshaw, Head of Chambers. There was an idea of some new letters appearing after that name in due course, but he mustn't count his chickens, that would never do. And he was happy as he was; he would be able to say, in his little speech tonight, that he was really honoured to have been chosen as head of chambers, and mean it; he was honoured. 'It's a tribute to you, old boy, richly deserved,' Gregory had said, when he had gone to see him in the hospital, the left side of his face distressingly swollen, a small rivulet of tea running from the side of his drooping mouth. 'I know that business with the girl upset you. Ah, you think I don't notice these things. I know you've been through the mill, old chap, but here's to better things. For both of us. They say I'll be able to go home the day after tomorrow.' Poor old Gregory; he must make a point of calling in to see him this week, let him have some of the gossip. There wasn't a great deal; he had heard the week before that Isobel had given birth to a boy – eight pounds two ounces – but he hadn't wanted to ask the name, hadn't wanted to know any more. Her application for silk had gone by the board, of course, now there was a chance he would get it before she did.

It was time to go. He had invited Cressida to look in, but it didn't seem likely she would come; they had drifted apart steadily over the last six months. Whatever they had had not survived the death of Hannah Casey; frightened and repulsed by the intensity of his reaction, she had at last backed away from him. Lately he had missed her, had wanted to rekindle things, but she never answered her phone; there was some talk of her getting together with Marlowe, but he refused to believe that, it would be grotesque, ridiculous. He hoped she would come, though perhaps it was not appropriate, as she was at a rival chambers. She had her tenancy now, and Norman Tombs had his pupillage; Walkinshaw had seen him, once, following Marlowe around at the Crown court, and they had kept their distance. Still, it was probably only a matter of time before they gave the young man a minor Crown court brief, and he might end up in front of me; now wouldn't that be something? He had finally begun to feel comfortable on the bench; all his old inhibitions had gone, and lately he had found himself relishing the idea of a day up there, above it all; the best seat in the house. The other day he had sentenced a girl whose pale gold hair, slight build and timidity had made his heart pound for a moment; but she wasn't Hannah, when she had raised her head her face was quite different, and he had had a little shock. Still, he wanted to be kind to her, but he had to send her to prison, it was her second possession with intent to supply. He'd given the least sentence he could, twenty one months, and had watched her as she was taken down, hoping to meet her eyes, but she didn't look up. He had gone home that night lonely and confused, and the next day Ratchett had come up to him, his face burning with curiosity; he'd found a letter in his car, and fancy! it's addressed to you, Mr. Walkinshaw. He had taken it and stuffed it inside his jacket, but Ratchett had stared hard at his face, carefully. 'I think I know who left it, now I come to think of it. Poor girl, I can't get over it, such a sweet thing she was. A genuine tragedy. And to think, that dad of hers, if anyone was going to die it should have been him. You know what happened? DC Glover it was found him. He'd gone round there to give old Casey a gypsy's warning, tell him to stay away from the lass, like, and he finds him there with blood coming out his mouth and all sorts. So we've Glover to thank for saving a nonce's life. I said to him, you should have left him there, we'd all be better off. He's the laughing stock of the C.I.D., poor old Glover is. So what was she writing to you for, poor lass?' But Walkinshaw had hurried away, close to tears, and opened the letter in a cubicle in the toilets; he'd wanted to wait until he got home, but he couldn't, he had to read it. But it had been disappointing; it was just a few timid lines in unformed handwriting. 'Dear Mr. Walkinshaw, I am very greatful for all your help and for winning my trial for me. You are the best barrister I have ever met. I am hoping to find work in a shop soon, my cousin is going to help me. I hope you are well and wish you all the best for the future. Hannah Casey.' Still, he had kept the letter with him for days; he had meant to keep it for ever, for the rest of his life, but it had somehow got lost during the house move, though he had not given up hope that it would turn up in a box somewhere. One day he would have a proper look for it; it was somewhere around, perhaps mixed up in some of his papers.

A car horn sounded in the quiet street; he took one last look at himself in the mirror, then carefully put on his coat, a new, smart one with a velvet collar, picked up his wallet and keys and went out into the night, towards the waiting taxi.